UNDEAD ULTRA

BOOK 1 OF UNDEAD ULTRA

CAMILLE PICOTT

With deepest gratitude to my Zombie Recon Team, who helped me explore the trails and rails traversed by the characters in this book.

Lura Albee
Lori Barekman
Jordan Costello
Chris & Kylah Picott
Chris Urasaki

It is with much gratitude that I thank my writing partners and beta readers: M.G. Alves Jr., who's read more drafts than I can count; Arlene Ang, whose grammar and spelling expertise leave me humbled; Dinesh Pulandram, who isn't afraid to tell me when something sucks; Lan Chan, whose candidness helps me weave a better story; Chris Picott, who, despite being my husband, is possibly my harshest critic; and Mike Albee, who helps me understand my audience and the book world. All of your advice and feedback is invaluable and eternally appreciated.

I also want to thank the ultrarunners kind enough to share their stories with me: Lori Barekman, my running coach and physical therapist extraordinaire, who really did have to shave scar tissue off the bottom of her foot after running the Fat Dog 120; Karen Hanke, who really did survive the Bear 100 in a ten-hour snowstorm in nothing more than a pink running skirt; Skip Brand, who really did have his shoes duct-taped to his feet when he ran the Leadville 50; and Ted Neal, who shared the finer details of bonking.

Without all of you, this story would be devoid of the gritty details that make ultrarunning so fascinating.

I extend much gratitude and love to my running sisters: Lise Asimont, who talked me into running my very first race, a 10K around a mountain that scared the pants off me; and Jordan Costello, who gets up at the butt crack of dawn to run with me and endures countless texts and emails about ultrarunning and races.

To those of you in AA who shared your experiences with me: thanks. You know who you are.

FREE BOOK

Sign up and get an exclusive novella from the bestselling *Undead Ultra* apocalypse series!
Get your copy of *Foot Soldier* here:
subscribepage.com/footsoldier

1

DROPPING A DEUCE

THERE'S SOMETHING LIBERATING ABOUT A LONG RUN. I LOVE EVERYTHING about it: the salty dribble of sweat in my eyes; the smell of wet dirt on the trail in the morning; the burning in my calves as I plow uphill; the exhilaration of a stunning view after that uphill climb; the thrashing of my quads on the inevitable downhill; and the screaming ache in my biceps from pumping up and down for hours on end.

My soul finds peace in the mindless labor of the run and the untamed nature of the trail. Some call it the runner's high, some call it trail surfing. I call it joy. Bliss. Oblivion.

Unfortunately, all these fancy adjectives evade me this morning. I'm stalled only three miles into today's run. Standing on the single-track trail that circumnavigates Lake Sonoma in Northern California, I wait for my running buddy to drop a deuce in the woods.

"Hey, Kate." Frederico pokes his head out from behind a tree. His shoulder-length, curly gray hair is pulled back in its customary pony-tail. In his early sixties, he's been running and racing for over thirty years. "Can I borrow your socks?"

I make a face at him. "What's wrong with *your* socks?"

"I used them."

"*Both* of them?"

He wrinkles his nose. "I ate chili last night."

I narrow my eyes at him. "Mrs. Crowell's habanero chili?"

"Yeah." He doesn't even have the decency to look embarrassed for holding out on me. The little old lady who lives next door to Frederico is legendary for her chili.

Grumbling, I plop onto the ground and unlace my shoes. I hate running without socks. Knowing one won't be enough to mop up Mrs. Crowell's chili, I pull off both of them.

"You're washing these," I say, tossing them in Frederico's direction.

He gives me a wicked smile as he catches the socks. "Did I mention my washing machine is broken?"

"Fuck you." I half scowl, half grin at him. "Those are brand-new socks. The least you could have done was get some chili for me."

"I knew there wouldn't be enough socks for both of us, so I ate it all myself."

I chuck a rock at his head. He ducks back behind the tree. The rock bounces harmlessly into the brush.

I'd like to say this is the first time something like this has happened. I'd like to say I've never asked to borrow *his* socks. When you run for hours and hours out in the middle of nowhere, shit happens. Literally. And if you're lucky, you'll have a friend to help you out.

"All done." Frederico jogs back out to the trail. The front pouches on his hydration pack bulge with the soiled socks.

"Yick." I plug my nose. "You smell like shit."

He arches an eyebrow at me. "I'll have you know, little jackalope, that my shit doesn't stink. It smells like roses."

Jackalope is Frederico's nickname for me. It's a jackrabbit with antlers, an urban myth in North America.

"You wish," I reply with a roll of my eyes. "I'm running in front so I don't have to be downwind of you."

I break into an easy lope, skimming up the narrow, uneven trail. The thick tread of my trail shoes grip the damp earth and provide sure footing.

The morning is glorious, crisp with the smell of last night's heavy spring rain. Bars of sunlight break through the trees, ephemeral strands that dance with life. To my right, I glimpse the serene blue of Lake Sonoma. A hawk glides on invisible currents of air.

Frederico and I have twenty miles planned for today. I feel myself slipping into the joy of the run. My brain moves into a state of pleasant numbness, a special place where the ache in my heart subsides. Out here, running through the woods, I can almost pretend Kyle is home, waiting for me.

"Kate, I gotta go again."

Frederico's voice draws me up short, reality snapping back in around me. I turn around in time to see him dash behind another tree.

"All my other socks are in the car," I call, trying to keep the annoyance out of my voice. We haven't even done four miles yet. "I saw some poison oak a little ways back. Want me to get you some?"

"Fuck you, Jackalope," he calls back cheerfully.

I sigh, scuffing the tread of my running shoe irritably in the dirt. Through the dappled morning light, something red flashes in the corner of my eye.

I turn, peering through the trees. After a moment, I realize what it is I'm seeing: a dead pig.

Wild pigs are pretty common at Lake Sonoma. They wreak havoc in the parks with their rooting. What's not common is to find a dead one with its blood and entrails pooling on the forest floor.

"There's a dead pig over here," I call to Frederico. "It's stomach has been ripped out." Flies and maggots have already congregated on the animal's body. Poor thing.

"It's hunting season," Frederico calls back.

That's true. We've run into hunters out here on our runs, some with guns and some with bows. It can be creepy to come across armed men in camouflage in the middle of the woods, but so far all our encounters have been friendly.

"Poor bastard probably got shot but managed to get away," I agree.

"Mountain lion or coyote could have taken it down once it was wounded." Frederico trots out of the trees and takes a look at the dead pig. "Yeah, I'd say something with claws and teeth definitely got into that guy."

"God." I take a step back from him and plug my nose. "You starting to smell like portapotty."

He makes an apologetic face. "Oak leaves make shitty ass wipes." His expression morphs into one of earnest wheedling. "Can we go back to the car?"

I scowl in response.

"Pretty please?" he says.

"I really needed this run today," I mutter. When I run, I don't have to think about anything other than my next step, my next breath. Everything is better when I run and shut off my brain.

"Remember when I ran thirty-eight miles smelling my own shit at Western States?" Frederico asks.

I snort. Western States is a 100-mile footrace from Squaw Valley to Auburn. Kyle and I crewed for Frederico at that race, meeting him at the various aid stations with food and other running supplies. Some bad fish had given Frederico a serious case of runs. We ran out of extra shorts and socks by mile sixty-two. He was too tired by that point to care much about wiping. After that experience, he vowed never to run with a smelly ass again.

"I'll buy you breakfast," Frederico says, eyes plaintive. "Bread Box?"

I narrow my eyes at him. "I want breakfast at Bread Box, plus coffee and an apple fritter. And I want you to wash my socks."

"Deal." He holds out his hand, like we're supposed to shake on it. I give him a *look*. He chuckles. After a beat, I laugh, too. It feels good to laugh. Maybe this morning isn't a complete waste.

I take one last look at the dead pig. As I do, a vulture rustles through the trees and lands on the carcass, casting its beady gaze briefly on us before turning its full attention back to its feast. The bird pecks at a ropy length of intestine, its leathery, red head almost the same hue as the pig's blood.

I shiver and turn away, leading the way back up the trail.

FORTY MINUTES LATER, we trot back into the gravel parking lot. My white hatchback waits for us. It's covered with a permanent layer of dust because I'm always leaving it at trailheads.

"Do you have any extra shorts in the car?" Frederico asks.

"Yeah." I pop the trunk and rummage in my running gear box. "Here you go." I hand him a pair of fluorescent-pink running shorts. "These will complement your complexion."

He chuckles, amiably moving to the passenger side of the car to change.

I pull off my hydration pack, take a last sip from the water tube, then toss it into the trunk. As I close the hatch, I catch sight of my reflection in the glass.

God, I look like shit. My pink, moisture-wicking tee sits on thin shoulders. Short brown hair is pulled back in a tight French braid, revealing a lean face that borders on gaunt. My neck looks long and rubbery, like a turkey's. Lots of running and not enough eating. Food doesn't hold much interest these days, not without Kyle.

My gray roots are showing, making me look older than my thirty-nine years. I should get them dyed, but there just doesn't seem any point to it most days.

I make a mental note to eat two apple fritters at breakfast. Taking care of my hair might be a pain in the ass, but Frederico is paying for breakfast. Besides, eating isn't such a chore when I have company.

"There's another dead pig over there." Frederico gestures over the hood of my car.

I look across the gravel parking lot and catch sight of the pig carcass. Three vultures are having a field day with it.

"Some hunter out here is a bad shot," I mutter, plopping into the driver's seat.

"No kidding." Frederico, decked out in my pink running shorts, slides into the passenger seat. "We should let the park ranger know on the way out."

"Yeah." A creepy feeling crawls up my spine. I shake it off, turning my attention away from the dead animal and focusing on my friend instead. "Pink is totally your color, by the way."

He flips me the bird and gives me a mock scowl.

Grinning, I fire up the engine of the car. NPR blares out of the speakers as I pull onto the road.

"Rioting at the port of Portland, Oregon continues to escalate," the voice of the news reporter says. "Riots started just forty-eight hours ago when dock workers attacked peaceful protestors. Protestors are from Stop Hunger Now, an organization dedicated to ending world hunger. Members are protesting the port's union-mandated slow-down, which has caused hundreds of food containers to spoil. Thousands of tons of food have been left to rot in the containers during the slowdown—"

"Depressing." Frederico flips the channel, turning it to a classic rock station.

We stop at the ranger station. The light is on and the door is ajar, but no one's inside.

"Maybe the ranger went to grab a coffee or something," I offer.

Frederico shrugs. "Guess they'll hear about the dead pigs eventually. Can't say we didn't try."

"Guess so." I shake off the image of the gutted pigs, pressing the accelerator and exiting the park.

We drive back toward the town of Healdsburg with the windows rolled down, letting the morning spring air infuse the car. The rolling, tree-covered hills of Lake Sonoma disappear behind us. Vineyards take their place, the tips of green buds pushing out of the bare brown vines.

The thought of going home to an empty house makes my insides feel like a crushed can. I feel some relief as I detour toward the Plaza in downtown Healdsburg, where Bread Box diner is located.

The once-quaint farming town, nestled in the heart of Northern California wine country, has transformed over the years. The town I grew up in has morphed into a tourist destination with overpriced clothing stores, winery tasting rooms, and restaurants with menus that require a French-English dictionary. Even at this early hour on a Saturday morning, the sidewalks are already thronging with tourists.

Thankfully there are still a few places, like Bread Box, that cater to locals. Maybe I'll ditch the apple fritters and get scones instead with my breakfast. Bread Box makes *the* best cheddar cheese scones. They were Kyle's favorite. There was a time when he ate them every day for breakfast. That fad lasted until he started having trouble buttoning his pants. After that, the scones became a rare treat, though they were no less loved. Eating one will make me feel close to him. And I want to feel close to him.

"What the hell?" I slam on my brakes as a twenty-something in six-inch heels staggers off the sidewalk and nearly falls into my car.

2

DEAD DRUNK

"Watch where you're going!" Frederico shouts at the drunk girl.

She laughs uproariously, as if nearly walking into a moving car is worthy of a Comedy Central skit. Her pack of girlfriends laughs with her, hauling her back onto the sidewalk as they grin and wave at me. Every last one has on skin-tight clothing and ten pounds of makeup. They carry wine glasses and sport matching fluorescent-green wristbands, the sort you'd get at rock concert.

It's only nine in the morning and it's clear this pack of Barbies is already shit-faced. Did they start the day off with Bloody Marys and mimosas? Seriously, who greets the day and says, "Please pass the six-inch stilettos, I'm gonna get shit-faced today!" You'd think they'd at least wear sensible shoes for a long day of drinking calisthenics. But hey, if you're going to make an ass out of yourself, might as well look good, I suppose. That way *everyone* will notice you.

The drunk Barbie band roves off in search of the next tasting room. Hopefully they packed a few barf bags in those designer purses.

My car rolls farther into downtown. There are people everywhere, all of them carrying wine glasses and wearing fluorescent-green wristbands.

"Barrel Tasting weekend," I groan. I'd forgotten about that.

"Two weekends of drunken festivities." Frederico purses his lips.

People come from all over the world to sample wine out of the barrels of Healdsburg wineries. Our population of ten thousand will literally double with the influx of tourists.

I thought it was cool when I first moved to town twenty-five years ago. Now, as I nose my car through the streets, hoping to avoid hitting another drunk idiot, I just find it annoying.

I manage to snag a parking spot only a block away from Bread Box. Dressed in spandex compression pants, with sweat stains on my face and in my armpits, I look absolutely fabulous amidst the decked out stiletto tourists. I tug my visor down, avoiding eye contact with everyone. Frederico practically struts into their midst, my pink shorts ablaze.

Despite myself, I have to smile at the odd looks he gets. At least he doesn't smell like shit anymore. *That* would get attention.

We shoulder our way through the tourists and their wine glasses before finally arriving at Bread Box. The inside of the restaurant is like stepping through a time machine. Formica tables. Vinyl chairs. Chipped linoleum floor.

I love this place. While the rest of the Healdsburg Plaza has transformed over the years, Bread Box has remained unchanged. It's too dive-like to attract the fancy tourists that roll into town, which means it's mostly empty this morning. No French-English dictionary to eat here, thank you very much.

We order and take a seat next to a window that looks out on the Plaza. This was Kyle's favorite table, even if watching stupid drunk people wasn't his favorite pastime.

"I just signed up for an ultra," Frederico says, sipping his coffee.

Ultra is short for ultramarathon. An ultramarathon is any race longer than a marathon, or twenty-six point two miles.

"I hope you don't plan to eat Mrs. Crowell's chili the night before," I reply drily. He chuckles, a warm rich sound that eases the tension in my muscles. "Which one are you running?" I ask.

"Mount Tamalpais Fifty Miler." He cocks his head. "You should come. You haven't raced since you lost Kyle."

Part of me shrivels inside. I ran ultras all the time when Kyle was alive. He came to every race as my support crew. When I ran into an aid station, he'd be waiting with snacks, fresh socks, electrolyte tablets, a blister kit—whatever I needed to help me refuel and finish my race. His presence always kept me going, especially on the hard runs.

"I've raced since then," I say, trying to maintain a chipper exterior.

Frederico gives me a serious look. "You've signed up for races. You haven't actually run any of them since the accident."

"I don't like to start things I can't finish." I shrug. "My plantar fasciitis has been bothering me. You know that." It's true. Kind of. I've struggled with plantar fasciitis—an inflammation of the foot tissue—on and off for years.

"Kate, don't give me that. You're in the best shape of your life and we both know it."

I shift uncomfortably in my chair, studying my coffee. Without Kyle, I just don't have the desire to race. I have no one to run *to*.

"Race entry fees are too expensive," I say at last. "I need to save money to help Carter with school."

I'm full of shit and Frederico knows it, but he doesn't push me. I deal with the awkward silence by fishing my phone out of my purse and absently checking for texts or missed calls.

I'm not really expecting to find any messages, but to my surprise there are three missed calls, two voicemails, and two text messages from my son. He's twenty and attends college in a hippie town four hours north of Healdsburg. Frowning in surprise, I thumb through the texts.

Mom, where r u? the first message reads. The second one says, *Call me asap.*

"Huh," I murmur to myself.

"What?" Frederico asks.

"Carter texted me twice and tried to call three times."

Frederico raises an eyebrow. "It's barely nine o'clock in the morning. He must need money."

I chuckle at the joke. We both know Carter isn't the type of kid to ask for money. Rather, he's the sort of kid who would call to ask the best way to cook brown rice or how to make chicken stock from scratch. There's no telling what he's up to.

As Frederico smiles at my laughter, I know I'm off the hook for bullshitting him. I put the phone to my ear, expecting to hear my son's cheerful voice. Instead, his words come out in a harsh whisper.

"Mom? Mom, where are you?" There's an edge to his words that borders on fear. "Look, call me as soon as you get this message, okay? Wherever you are, I need you to find Frederico and get back to the house. God, I hope you're not on the trail today."

I blink in surprise, a lump of anxiety forming in my stomach. I'm always out on the trail on Saturday mornings. What's going on with my laid-back, quasi-hippie son? If I didn't know him better, I'd say he was playing some sort of fraternity hazing joke on me, but Carter would just as soon shave his legs as join a college fraternity.

"What's up?" Frederico asks, studying my face.

I shake my head. "I don't know."

I thumb to the next voice message. Carter's voice fills my ear. The edge is still there. If possible, it's been amplified.

"Me again, Mom. You're probably out on the trail. Hopefully with Frederico. Look, I need to you to drive home, lock everything, and barricade all the windows and doors. Fill up the bathtubs with water. I know this sounds weird, but please, trust me. Call me as soon as you can."

The lump in my stomach grows. I immediately call him back, chewing on my lower lip as the phone rings.

And rings. And rings some more, finally switching over to voicemail.

"Hey, sweetie," I say. "It's me. I'm with Frederico. Call me, please. You're scaring me."

"What's up?" Frederico asks.

I wordlessly hand the phone to him. Frederico listens to the messages, a crease forming between his brows.

"Think he's playing a joke on you?" He sets the phone down after listening to the messages.

"Maybe," I reply. "That's not really Carter's style, though."

"No, it's not." Frederico scratches his head. "Well, you can try him again after breakfast."

I nod, unable to dispel the unease lodged in my gut. I set the phone on the table so that I won't miss another call or text from Carter.

Our breakfast arrives. We dive into the meal. As I stuff a fork of hash browns into my mouth, I idly stare through the window out at the Plaza. It's a large grassy area with soaring, manicured trees, a gazebo, and a water fountain that doubles as a toddler swimming pool in the summer. This morning, it's thronging with tourists. I polish off my omelet and start in on the first of the apple fritters, watching the droves of wine lovers walk by outside.

A pack of metrosexual males staggers by in loafers, slacks, and pastel shirts. God, they are even more fucked up than the Barbie brigade we saw earlier. One of them has red wine smeared all over his button-down shirt. Another has red wine splashed over his face. All of them move with a shuffling gait. Maybe they started Barrel Tasting weekend with mimosas, Bloody Marys, *and* tequila shots. Maybe they're just hungover from a full night of partying. Whatever the case, they look like hell.

"This is better than reality TV," Frederico says around a mouthful of biscuit.

I nod, shoving a chunk of apple fritter into my mouth.

The metro with red wine all over his lavender shirt lunges at a pretty girl in tight pants. The neckline of her shirt practically plunges to her navel. The metro paws at her breasts, a loud moan passing between his lips.

"This is more like a bad porno," I reply, picking up the second apple fritter.

"Get away from me, you pervert," the girl shouts.

She tries to shove the man away. He's nearly twice her size and doesn't flinch under her pathetic force. He moans again, still pawing at her breast.

"A really bad porno," Frederico agrees, anger seeping into his voice. He shifts, and I know he's considering going out to help the girl.

The metro suddenly seizes the girl and buries his face in her neck. She screams. It's not a cry of disgust or violation; it's a piercing shriek of pain that jars me to the core.

Frederico jumps up, knees hitting the table. The plates and silverware bounce and rattle.

The girl twists in the man's grasp, her eyes wide like a desperate animal's. The man in lavender leans back, blood staining his mouth and raw flesh hanging from his lips. Blood gushes down the girl's throat, a river of it running between her breasts.

"What the fuck?" Frederico cries.

We both stare, paralyzed with shock and horror.

The girl is screaming, screaming, screaming. The metro in lavender leans back in, sinking his teeth into her jugular. Blood sprays, splattering all over the window—right by my face.

3

RED HATS

"Fuck!" I jump to my feet, knocking over my water glass. "Fuck!"

I gape, transfixed, as the pastel shirt club swarms the girl. They bear her to the ground, sinking their teeth into her flesh and eating her alive. I stumble back, bumping into Frederico.

"What the—" He stares as the metro horde devours the girl, mouth hanging open.

Behind us, our waitress screams. I turn in time to see her drop two orders of biscuits and gravy to the floor. The few other patrons in the diner are on their feet, all of us stupidly watching the horror movie unfolding in front of the restaurant.

A group of gray-haired men dressed in sensible sneakers—all with Barrel Tasting bracelets—stumble into the metro gore. One man sees the girl on the ground and tries to intervene. Seconds later, two members of the metro club pounce on him. One claws into the man's enormous gut, tearing through his shirt in a spurt of blood.

Two other men—restaurant patrons—race past us, bursting through the front door. They grab onto the closest of the metros, attempting to drag him off the girl. At the table next to us, a woman is on her cell phone, eyes wide.

"I need to report an attack," she says breathlessly into her phone. "There are drunk men mauling people in downtown Healdsburg!" Her voice goes up an octave as the body of the girl is abruptly hurled against the window.

Blood smears the glass in thick, gloppy rivulets as the body slides to the ground. Through the red gore, I see one of the restaurant patrons go down under a rush of pastel shirts. The mass smashes against the front door of the restaurant. One metro in pastel green-and-yellow stripes nearly tumbles inside, but he rights himself and launches back into the melee, blood dripping down his chin.

"We've got to get out of here," Frederico says. "Move!"

The remains of an apple fritter fall from my hand. I snag my purse and phone before retreating after him.

"What's going on?" I say, voice coming out in a squeak. "What—what's wrong with those men?"

"They're probably fucked up on some designer drug," Frederico replies. "We're not going to stick around to find out."

Drugs. That must be it. Those guys are on drugs. It wouldn't be first time wine tasters tried to amp up their experience with drugs.

Frederico and I hurry toward the swinging white door that leads into Bread Box's kitchen. Behind us, patrons are on their cell phones to the police, shouting about drunken attacks and murder.

We push through the swinging door into the kitchen. The two line cooks and dishwasher look up in surprise as we burst into the tiny space. The waitress, right behind us, launches into a frenetic retelling of events.

"Those men just started—started *chewing* on her!" she cries shrilly.

Carter's frantic message reforms in my head, taking a different shape. I stop dead. Has Carter seen attacks like we just witnessed? Is that why he called me this morning? Is he in danger?

I fumble the cell phone, awkwardly swiping at the screen.

"What are you doing?" Frederico snaps.

"I have to call Carter. What if—"

"Not now." The severity in Frederico's voice brings me up short. "Move, Kate. *Move.*"

My hand numbly shoves the phone into my purse. I nod, knowing he's right. Somewhere outside is the wail of police sirens.

We head to the back door, slipping into the alleyway behind Bread Box. It's devoid of people. In contrast to the chaos of the restaurant, it's quiet. I can't even hear the screaming from the street, although the wail of the police cars grows louder.

"Let's go," Frederico says. "If you see trouble, run like hell."

I nod. Side by side, we hurry north toward the street. We're nearly to the alleyway exit when a hunched form steps into view.

The figure is dressed all in purple with a bright-red hat. The hat is a small thing perched jauntily on the owner's head. A small red mesh veil hangs from the hat, covering the woman's forehead and part of one eye. The hat is almost the exact same color as the red staining her lips. It could be lipstick gone bad, but it could also be blood. The one visible eye is an eerie milky white.

"Holy shit." Frederick skids to a halt. "It's the Red Hat Society."

The Red Hat Society is a social organization for "mature women." I occasionally see groups of them roving downtown Healdsburg, shopping, wine tasting, and generally having a grand time. They always wear flamboyant purple dresses and bright-red hats.

The hunchbacked woman in purple suddenly multiplies. She is joined by at least a dozen more old ladies, all of them dressed in dramatic purple-and-red outfits. All have the same milky white eyes. Many have red smeared on their mouths.

"Do you think they're on drugs, too?" I hiss. My voice echoes off the walls of the alleyway. The red-and-purple pack swivel in our direction. As a unit, they lurch toward us.

"I don't know," Frederico whispers. "But something's not right. You know that plan we talked about?"

"The one where we run like hell?"

"Yeah. That one. Now would be the time to follow it."

He doesn't need to tell me twice. We turn and run south, heading for the opposite end of the alley. Our footfalls make crunching sounds on the loose chunks of asphalt. The Red Hat Society lumbers after us, many of them gnashing their teeth. Lucky for us, they don't move fast.

Just as we reach the other end of the alleyway, a middle-aged woman with a boob job runs screaming toward us.

"Help!" she screams. "Someone help me!"

A chunk is missing out of the shoulder of her designer dress. The skin beneath bears a large bite wound. The woman is wild-eyed. One foot is barefoot; the other limps along on a stiletto heel. Blood seeps down her shoulder.

"She's bitten," Frederico says, holding an arm out in front of me. "Steer wide."

I give him a sharp look. Neither of us has said the "z" word, but clearly I'm not the only one thinking it.

"Help me, please!" the woman howls. She paws at her face. "There's something wrong with my eyes. Please, help me!"

Her noise agitates the Red Hatters. One of them lets up a loud keen. The others snarl and growl, continuing their steady shuffle toward us.

"I'll call nine-one-one," I say, wanting to help the woman. I grope in my purse for the cell phone. "We'll get an ambulance over here."

"They attacked us in the tasting room," she whimpers, tears running down her face. "They—they *bit* us. They bit *me*." She makes that last part sound like the biggest insult.

Frederico and I hug the wall, moving in a semi-circle around the wounded woman toward the mouth of the alleyway. The pack of Red Hatters inches ever closer.

"I'd stay away from them," I tell the woman, indicating the purple-and-red women.

She nods, still sobbing.

We peer out of the alley. Police have set up a barricade on the corner, blocking access to Bread Box's street. A cluster of tourists gathers at the barrier, sipping wine as they gawk. Beyond them are more tourists, oblivious or unconcerned with the bloodshed.

My questing hand at last locates the cell phone. Just as I'm about to pull out the smooth rectangle, an ambulance screams into view, rolling past the barricade.

"There's an ambulance over here," I say, turning toward stiletto woman. "You can—"

A shriek interrupts me. I spin around and find the woman rushing toward me. Clinging to the hem of her dress is an old lady in a red fedora. Behind them come the rest of the Red Hat Society.

The woman stumbles under the weight of the old lady, dragging her across the pavement. One of her enormous silicone orbs slams into me. I stumble back, smacking into the wall.

"Help me!" the woman shouts again. Her eyes have a milky white film over them.

I am many things. A mother. A widow. A waitress. An ultrarunner. I'm not a trained badass who knows how to handle a situation like this. I scream like a girl and grapple with the woman, trying to twist away from her and the growling old lady latched onto her.

"Kate!"

Frederico plants one dirt-covered trail shoe on fedora lady's hip. He shoves. Hard. She staggers sideways, crashing into several of her red-and-purple brethren. They topple over in a tangle of red-and-purple. Half a dozen of them are still upright, but they're a good ten feet away and not moving fast.

Boob-job woman falls to her knees, clawing at her eyes. She screams and screams, the sound raising the hairs on the back of my neck.

"Holy fuck," I breathe, falling back against Frederico.

"Let's get out of here," he replies, grabbing my hand and pulling me backward.

"But the woman—" I gesture helplessly at the blond as the Red Hatters inexorably inch toward her.

"The police." Frederico jumps out of the alleyway, waving his arms in the direction of the cops. "Over here," he yells. "Someone needs help! There's been another attack!"

Two cops break away from the blockade and run toward us.

"Move back, sir," one of them shouts. The cop hits the corner of the alleyway at a dead run, nearly losing his balance when he draws up short at the sight of snarling, bloody old ladies and the hysterical boob-job woman.

The second cop is right on his heels. The both pull out billy clubs, stationing themselves between the Red Hatters and the panicked woman.

"Move back!" the first cop says again.

"Nothing else we can do here," Frederico says. "Come on."

He's right, of course. I wish I could say I was ex-military with a lifetime of survival skills under my belt. I wish I could say I had a black belt in badassery. But I'm nothing more than a widowed wait-ress with an obsession for running. People like me don't rescue desperate women with boob jobs from a pack of drugged-out Red Hatters.

I nod to my friend. Side by side, we break into a run, pelting away from the madness as fast as our feet will carry us.

4

DISCONNECTED

We head east, heading away from the violence.

Wine tasters are out in force, all of them armed with wine glasses and enthusiasm. With the sidewalks being so crowded, we're forced to alternate between jogging and fast walking as we weave through people.

Ahead of us is a group of college kids in tutus. They are a riot of color, ranging from Barney purple to CalTrans orange. Seriously, wine tasting really does take all kinds. One of the tutu-wearers rubs at a small wound on her arm.

"What a creep," I hear her say. "I can't believe he bit me."

Frederico and I exchange looks as we dodge through the tutu brigade.

"There's an ambulance just down the street," I say. "You could have that looked at."

A few of the kids turn. They take one look at our grimy running gear and dismiss us. A few of them even titter.

I open my mouth to say more, but Frederico grabs my arm and shakes his head at me. "We tried. We can't make them listen."

"But—"

"What are you going to say? Besides, we don't know what's going on."

This gives me pause. He's right. That metro gang could be high on yuppie designer drugs. Those Red Hatters could have been suffering from dementia and really bad lipstick jobs.

"We have to get to the car, Kate. You need to call Carter."

This snaps me out of my dilemma. "Okay," I say, glancing back at the tutu gang. They're laughing and sipping wine and generally having a grand time as they stroll away. "Okay, let's go."

We continue on, slowing to dodge through a crew of professional wine tasters. These are people who know they're going to get shit-faced, and dress for it. Sensible sneakers. Comfy clothes. Hats for shade. Smears of white sunscreen on their necks and noses. If there was a guidebook on how to attire oneself for wine tasting, these guys could be on the cover.

"Can you tell us how to get to Warrior Wines?" one of them calls to us as we hurry by.

"You don't want to go there," I call back. Warrior Wines is right on the Plaza. "Try Clandestine Cellars right outside of town—their zinfandel in the *best*!" I try to load my voice with enthusiasm, even though I've never had anything from Clandestine Cellars. I don't even know if they make zinfandel. But at least that will get those people away from the violence.

The professionals wave in thanks and cluster around a map, talking excitedly about zinfandel as they try to locate the winery. Maybe, just maybe, I saved their lives. Or maybe I'm a paranoid freak and just sent them on a wild goose chase for a wine that doesn't exist.

We reach my car without any further incident. Once inside, I lock the doors and check for messages. There's another text message from Carter.

Glad u r with Frederico, it reads. *Let me know when you get back to the house.*

I put the cell phone to my ear as I pull a U-turn and speed toward my house. To hell with California hands-free laws.

My son answers on the second ring. "Mom." There's relief and fear and tension all twined together in that single word.

"Carter! Are you okay, baby?" I ask. "What's going on?"

Silence. There're soft murmurings in the background, but nothing I can make out.

"Carter?"

"Yeah, I'm here. Are you back at the house yet?"

"On our way now. I'm with Uncle Rico. Baby, what's going on?"

"Mom, this is going to sound weird. I want you to get home before we talk more, okay?"

"Did you see people get attacked, sweetie?"

Another long silence. My stomach drops into my feet.

"Carter, did you—did you see people biting other people?" I brace myself. "People, um, eating other people?"

I'm not sure what I'm more afraid of—a skeptical laugh or a confirmation. I haven't been the sanest person since Kyle's accident two years ago. Carter watched me run fifty to eighty miles a week for most of his life; after his father died, he watched me ramp up workouts to anywhere between one hundred twenty and one hundred forty miles a week. He saw me break down into tears at the grocery store when I couldn't find my favorite chocolate chips. He even saw me chew out the mailman for not putting the mail in the box the "right way."

I'm ashamed I haven't been stronger for Carter. There's a desperate wildness always screaming inside me. I can usually keep it under control if I run myself ragged; otherwise I end up with mailman incidents and other embarrassing events. Before he moved away to Humboldt State University, Carter bought me two pairs of running shoes and ten boxes of electrolyte tablets.

"Take care of yourself while I'm gone, Mom," he'd said to me, all too aware of my fragile state of mind.

Fuck. My son is going to think I've completely lost it. "I'm putting you on speaker phone, sweetie."

"Uncle Rico?" Carter's voice projects out of the phone, which I hand to Frederico.

"I'm here, kiddo," Frederico replies, holding the phone in the air between us.

"Is my mom okay?"

"Yeah, kiddo. Your mom is fine. I got her to eat two apple fritters this morning."

I scowl at Frederico, annoyed they're talking about me like I'm not here. And eating those apple fritters had been *my* idea.

"You've got me and your mom a little scared, kiddo," Frederico says. "Tell us what's going on."

Carter's words come out in a rush. "Weird stuff has been happening this past week. There were reports of meth-head attacks around campus and in town. They said meth-heads were biting people. I didn't think much about it, but last night I went to a party and—and—"

A shriek goes up in the background, interrupting Carter. Jumbled shouting comes through my iPhone.

"Dude, we've gotta barricade the door!"

"Reed, grab the other end of the bed."

"Wait," I hear Carter say. "Jenna isn't back yet—"

"Carter!" I slam on my brakes and snatch the phone from Frederico. *"Carter!"*

More muffled shouting, then the distinct voice of Carter saying, "Oh, *shit*—"

"There're zombies everywhere, dude!"

Then a huge banging sound, like someone smashed the phone, and all is silent.

"Carter!" I lean toward the phone, as if proximity to an electronic gadget can take away what I just heard. *"Carter!"*

My breath comes in short, ragged breaths. Spots swim in front my vision. "Carter," I whisper.

"Kate, pull over." Frederico takes the phone from me. "Take a deep breath and pull over."

I jerk the car toward the curb, snatching the phone back from Frederico. I hit redial, heart pounding as I wait for Carter to answer.

The phone rings, and rings, and rings.

Another ambulance and two more police cars speed by us, sirens wailing.

Carter's voicemail picks up. "You've reached Carter. Leave a message and I'll call you back."

"Shit." I end the call and hit redial. Still nothing.

"Kate—"

I give Frederico a fierce look. He clamps his mouth shut. I turn back to my phone, tapping out several desperate text messages.

What is going on?

Are u okay?

Call me asap.

I lean my head back against the seat rest, heart pounding in my chest. A few tears leak out of my eyes.

"Kate?"

"They said the 'z' word." I swallow and force myself to look at my friend.

His face is pale. "Yeah," he says, nodding slowly. "Yeah, I heard that."

Zombie. The word buzzes in my head, hanging on the tip of my tongue, but it's too absurd to say out loud. There's no way those guys are zombies. Are they? No. They can't be. Zombies aren't real. There's another explanation. Right?

"Do you really think those metro guys outside Bread Box were on drugs?" I ask.

Frederico hesitates, then shakes his head. "Drugs can make a person do really fucked up things. I should know." He grimaces. "I may be twenty-five years sober, but you never forget the things drugs do to you."

"And what about those old ladies from the Red Hat Society?"

He shakes his head again. "I don't know of any drug that makes people bite other people. Those women definitely had blood on their mouths."

"The pigs at Lake Sonoma?" I ask. "Do you still think they were killed by mountain lions or coyotes?"

He meets my eyes. "In all our years running at the lake, we've never seen kills like those."

Reality crashes in around me. I feel it as profoundly as if chunks of cement are raining down.

God dammit. I'm going to say it. I'm just going to use the word.

"Zombies."

That single word hangs in the air between us.

Our eyes meet. I see my fear and dawning realization reflected back at me.

Carter.

"Fuck this." I slam my foot on the accelerator and nearly side swipe a limo as I pull back onto the road. The chauffer honks and flips me off.

"I'm going to Arcata," I tell Frederico, gripping the steering wheel with sweaty hands. "I'll drop you off."

He's silent as I make a hard left at an intersection, completely ignoring the stop sign. I drive another two blocks before he speaks.

"I'll go with you," he says.

"What? You don't have to—"

"When Carter went away to college, I promised him I'd look after you. I intend to keep my promise."

I scowl at him. "He just wanted you to make sure I didn't run myself to death. And apparently he wanted you to make sure I eat junk food."

"He wanted me to make sure you were eating, period."

I give him another dirty look, taking a corner a little too hard. The tires squeal and I smell burning rubber.

"I'm not going home to pack or change my clothes. Or take a shower." I say it like a threat, like it will make him think twice.

It doesn't, of course.

"Do I need to remind you that I rode in the car with you after you finished Bad Water?" he asks. "Do you have any idea how bad you smelled after forty hours of running? Your puny run this morning doesn't hold a candle to that."

I grimace. I *did* smell after that race. I had to endure jokes about my armpits for weeks.

Frederico sighs, shifting in his seat. A look of unease flits across his face. I jam my foot on the brake, pulling over in front of a row of condos.

"What is it?" I ask. "What aren't you telling me?"

"Aleisha," he says at last. "Dumbo Dan convinced her to move to Laytonville. She's tending bar in a dive, and he's changing oil at a lube and tire place." Frederic's expression grows stormy. Dumbo Dan is the not-so-flattering nickname for his daughter's boyfriend.

His insistence suddenly makes sense. Laytonville is on the way to Arcata.

"You want to stop in Laytonville and check on Aleisha," I say.

"I need to check on her," he says. "Make sure she's safe. I'd like to get her out of that place, but she'd never come with me. It won't take long. She'll probably slam the door in my face."

"She might hug you," I say, trying to be optimistic. The love he bears for his estranged daughter is painful to witness.

Frederico shrugs. "It doesn't matter. She's my daughter and I love her. I need to make sure she's safe."

"I get that." I give my friend's shoulder a quick squeeze, then pull back onto the road. "Let's go find our kids."

5

CAR TROUBLE

I PRESS THE ACCELERATOR TO THE FLOOR, SPEEDING UP HIGHWAY 101 northbound onramp to toward Arcata. I pull into the fast lane and lean on the gas pedal, careening past the tourist traffic.

"Do you want to call Aleisha first?" I ask. "And what about Brandon? Maybe you should call him, too."

"Brandon is deployed in Puerto Rico. There's no way for me to reach him. Aleisha . . ." He hesitates. "You know how things are between us. She usually won't answer my calls."

Frederico's daughter has never forgiven him for his years of alcohol and drug abuse. He doesn't talk about it much, but I never miss the pain in his eyes when he mentions her.

"I know you guys don't communicate much, but you should call anyway. Even if you just leave a message. You should warn her to stay home. She might not know about the zombies. Besides, my number will come up on the caller ID. Maybe she'll answer."

"Yeah, okay." Reluctantly, he dials her number. After a few rings, I hear the automated voicemail service answer.

"Hey, Aleisha," Frederico says. "It's Dad. Look, Kate and I are on our way north. Thought we'd swing by and say hi. Haven't seen you in a while. There're, um, I mean, uh, I don't know if you've been watching the news, but there have been . . . meth-head attacks up in your area. Stay inside if you can, okay? Carry one of Du—Dan's guns, okay?" He disconnects.

I glance at him in silent, open-mouthed disbelief.

He hunches his shoulders uncomfortably. "She's never listened to my advice. Why should she start now? At least if I tell her they're meth-head attacks, she'll believe me. She'll think I've gone over the edge if I use the 'z' word."

Zombies. God, I can't believe we're using that word to describe real life.

I flip on the radio and scroll through the news stations.

". . . strange reports of a viral mania sweeping through Portland," says an announcer. "A listener just sent me a YouTube video of a dog walker attacking an innocent woman on the street. He rips right through the shoulder of her shirt and bites hard enough to draw blood. You can see this disturbing video by googling Cannibal Dog Walker."

The station cuts to a commercial.

"Fuck." Frederico turns down the volume. "It really could be zombies."

"What do you think happened to Carter?" I ask softly, eyes focused on the road. "What about—"

"Don't think about it." Frederico cuts me off. "You have no control over it. All you can do now is get to Arcata."

I nod, flying around a corner at eighty-five miles an hour—and slam on the brakes.

"Shiiit!" My tires squeal against the pavement, sending up a gush of smoke.

Sprawled in front of us are three Hummer limousines. One has careened into the side of a bluff. The second one has smashed into the first. The third one has spun out and lost a tire.

When I see the three massive, obnoxious cars barricading the entire road, I know we're in trouble.

Hummer limos are a hot topic in the small town of Healdsburg. They ooze luxury and badass in one neat package and are all the rage for tourists when they go wine tasting.

Residents—myself included—hate them. No, hate is too mild a word. We *loathe* them. We write letters to the editor extolling their evils. They are agenda points at local city council meetings.

For starters, they're obnoxiously large. Around the Plaza, a Hummer limo can literally take up half a city block. Out in the countryside, they clog up the quaint one-lane vineyard roads and back up traffic for miles. Some wineries have gone so far as to ban them from their property.

So when I see the three wrecked Hummer limos completely blocking the road, I'm pissed off. These assholes are keeping me from my son.

Then I see the six bloody people with milky white eyes, each of them covered with bite marks and grotesque wounds. Based on their clothing, I'd say they were imported from San Francisco's financial district. Shiny shoes and Oxford shirts for the men, conservative pencil dresses and pumps for the women. They probably came up here on a team-building excursion.

As my car tires squeal against the asphalt, I see a terrified limo driver leap out from one of the vehicles. Three of the bloody finance people lumber after him. The other three, drawn to the noise of my car, come straight toward us.

"The hill, the hill!" Frederico shouts. "Get around them!"

The four-lane highway splits; the southbound lane to our left rises a good one hundred feet above us. To our right is a steep hill of dry grass that slopes down to a frontage road.

"The hill!" Frederico shouts again.

There's no way I can stop the car before hitting the people or the cars. Taking Frederico's advice, I swerve around the wrecked limos and head for the hillside slope. My little hatchback shoots off the freeway and goes airborne. I scream like a little girl.

"Brace yourself," Frederico roars, grabbing the oh-shit handle with one hand. "Hold on!"

I clench my hands around the steering wheel and press my feet against the floor.

The hatchback hits the ground with a tremendous *clunk*. It rattles every bone in my body. The airbags deploy in a rush of air, hitting me in the face with the force of a tornado. The car bounces, back end lifting higher than the front.

"Shit-shit-shit," I scream. My poor hatchback is about to go ass over teakettle down this bleak stretch of land.

But it doesn't flip. Instead, it bounces three more times. It settles, then stops. A hissing sound comes from the engine.

We sit in silence, absorbing the shock of the last thirty seconds. The airbags deflate, slowly revealing the scene before us.

The frontage road is empty and quiet. The dry grass surrounding my car is still and silent. In the distance, over the hum of the engine, I hear screaming.

"Try the accelerator," Frederico says.

I obey, tentatively pressing my foot against the pedal. I give a small shriek of surprise when the car lurches forward.

"Again," Frederico says.

I press the pedal, this time with more confidence. The car limps forward, rolling over the dips and bumps on the small stretch of grass. When it rolls onto the frontage road, I sigh in relief.

"I can't believe it still works," I say, marveling.

Frederico gives me a tight look. "We hit pretty hard when we landed. Let's stick to frontage roads for now." He glances back in the direction of the freeway. "Not sure one-oh-one is the safest route now anyway."

I follow his gaze. Several more cars have plowed into the Hummer obstacle course. There is more screaming. Oxford shirts and pencil skirts are piled on top of the poor limo driver.

I swallow, feeling sick. "Call the police," I say hoarsely. "Tell them about the wreck."

Frederic nods, woodenly complying with my request.

I head down the frontage road. We roll into Geyserville, a small town ten miles north of Healdsburg. The town sports one stop sign, a fire station, two restaurants, and a few tasting rooms. It's surrounded by gorgeous vineyards, and today, it's filled with tourists for Barrel Tasting.

I scan the tourists, looking for signs of trouble. At first, all I see is regular people strolling, talking, and laughing. A bit of tension eases out of my chest.

Then I spot a man in a linen suit with a big red stain on his arm. To the average person, it would look like a wine stain. But I see his staggering gait. The sun hits his face, illuminating eyes glazed with eerie whiteness. His nostrils flare, head tipping in the direction of the crosswalk and a group of wine tasters meandering between the white lines.

"That guy over there," I say, pointing. "I think he's—he's one of *them*."

"What are we going to do?" I ask.

Frederico looks at me. "What do you think we *can* do?"

"We—" I break off, really considering his question.

What *can* we do? Get out of the car and try to warn people away from the man in the linen suit? Who would listen to us?

We could tie the man up and call the police. For an instant, I have a crazed vision of us finding a jump rope and tying the man to a restaurant chair. I immediately dismiss the idea as impossible.

We could bash his head in with a crowbar. That's what heroes do in zombie movies, right? Except there's a big difference between real life and the movies. No way could I ever bash in someone's head, even if they are a zombie. Could I?

These thoughts flash through my head as I roll toward the crosswalk—and keep rolling, despite the fact I'm pressing my foot down on the brake pedal. I frantically pump my foot but nothing happens.

"My brakes! My brakes!" I stupidly flap a hand at Frederico, like that will solve anything. I roll down my window and shout at the tourists moseying through the crosswalk. "Get out of the way," I scream. "Move! My brakes are out!"

A few of the tourists hear me. They hurry out of the way, giving me wide-eyed stares. The rest of them continue their unhurried mince through the crosswalk, sipping on their wine glasses and wholly unaware that they're about to be run over.

The man in the linen suit chooses that moment to attack. He launches himself like a wildcat into the crosswalkers. Most of them scatter with confused and indignant yelps, but one poor middle-aged woman goes down under him. He wastes no time ripping her shirt open and taking a huge bite out of her breast. Shiny red blobs of flesh gleam in his mouth as he starts to eat.

Those nearest us go into full panic mode, myself included.

"Shit-shit-shit," I cry, yanking on the steering wheel, as if that will somehow slow the inexorable roll of the car.

Without warning, Frederico hoists his leg into the driver's side and slams down on the accelerator. My hatchback rockets forward, plowing right into Linen Suit and the woman he's eating.

Linen Suit is thrown onto my car. He latches onto the hood right below the windshield, snarling at us with bloody teeth. The woman is tossed through the air. She lands on the sidewalk, immediately surrounded by people. I careen through Geyserville's intersection without hitting anyone else.

Except that now I have a *thing* on top of my car.

Frederico shifts, retracting his foot. "Go!" he shouts, and I slam down on the pedal.

We zip down the tiny main street, carrying the zombie with us. I whip the steering wheel violently to the right. The man's legs slide to one side and dangle over the ground, but he doesn't let go.

A minute later, we're flying down a two-lane country road surrounded by vineyards. Geyserville is a dot in my rearview mirror.

Frantic, I turn on the windshield wipers and pound on my horn, hoping to startle Linen Suit and dislodge him. No such luck. His face is pointed in my direction, though it's impossible to tell if he's looking at me; his eyes roll oddly in his sockets, never settling on anything in particular. Can he even see? He gnashes his teeth together, clawing brainlessly at the window with one hand.

"That really is a zombie," Frederico says quietly, chilling calm in his voice.

To my horror, he rolls down the window and boosts himself out. He sits on the edge of the sill, one arm still inside the car gripping the oh-shit handle. In his other hand is the neon-blue Maglite I keep in the car, which he wields like a club. His curly gray hair flies in the wind.

"Frederico," I yell. "You crazy bastard, get back in here!"

He ignores me. I keep my foot on the gas, afraid that if I let up, Linen will find some semblance of balance.

The man shifts, saliva dripping out of his mouth. He tries to get onto his knees, one bloody hand slipping as he does. As soon as he loses his grip, I swerve again.

My plan works. Linen Suit tumbles off the hood of my car.

Unfortunately, so does Frederico. With a wild shout, he flies backward and lands between a row of grapes.

"No!"

I whip the steering wheel to the left, trying desperately to pull a U-turn. The car burns rubber as it spins. The left tires momentarily lift off the ground. The hatchback clunks loudly as it lands seconds later.

Linen Suit has regained his footing. His clothes are in tatters, as is most of the right side of his body. There is no way he should be conscious, let alone on his feet.

His milky white eyes roll in opposite directions, but his face is aimed in Frederico's direction like a hunting hound's. My friend grunts softly, struggling to his feet.

I don't think. I just act. Aiming the car at Linen Suit, I gun it.

My poor hatchback slams into the man. He is sucked underneath the tires. The car plows through three feet of vineyard, the thick stocks of the grapes denting the hood before falling prey to the grill.

I hear and sense something on the rear side sheering. The hatchback grinds to a halt, caught by the half a dozen vineyard trellises on the outskirts of Geyserville.

I throw open the door and leap out. Frederico is on his feet, bracing himself against a grapevine.

Linen Suit is still going. Both his legs are broken, but he's crawled out from under the car. Propped up onto his hands, he is dragging himself through the vineyard like a seal. He's heading straight toward Frederico.

I can't hide from the truth. This thing that used to be a man—it's not human anymore. No human could have survived what he's been through.

It's a zombie. As in, one of the undead. As in, a flesh-eating monster.

"You fucking undead asshole," I shout at him. "Stay the hell away from my friend!"

6

BROKEN SKULL

ADRENALINE SURGING THROUGH MY BODY, I SNATCH A LARGE ROCK LYING on the soft soil of the vineyard. I take several steps toward the zombie, arm raised high above my head.

Linen Suit hears my approach, his head turning in my direction. He growls, scenting the air.

Fear paralyzes me. I have the advantage, but what if I'm not fast enough? What if I go in for the kill, miss, and get eaten?

In a moment of girlish fear, I chuck the rock as hard as I can. My aim is off, but it does deliver a glancing blow to the chin, which pisses him off. He snarls, clawing his way toward me.

"Shit." This is not going well.

"The Maglite," Frederico calls. "It's over there."

His frantic gestures help me spot my neon-blue flashlight lying near the side of the road. Thank god I picked a bright color.

I rush to the Maglite and snatch it up, holding it in front of me like a bat. I advance on the zombie, palms coated in sweat.

"Circle around," Frederico says. "Come at it from behind."

Linen Suit whips his head back and forth, attention swiveling between me and Frederico. My breath rasps as the creature focuses his attention back on me, dragging himself in my direction.

Following Frederico's advice, I circle around the zombie. Still pushed up like a seal, he tries to follow my progress.

Squelching all reason, I dash in and swing the Maglite straight at his head. There's a sickening *thunk* as I connect with the skull.

"Again," Frederico shouts. "Hit it again, Kate!"

I grit my teeth, squashing the revulsion rising within. The zombie is wounded but still alive. I am not cut out for this shit. I can't even pick up the birds killed by my cat. I get my neighbor to do it in exchange for cookies.

Flinching, I swing the Maglite a second time. A shudder goes through me. The memory of beloved blue eyes momentarily blind me.

"Again!"

A third time.

"Again!"

A fourth time, and a fifth. I hit it over and over. The horrible sound of shattering bone blinds my eyes with tears.

Gentle hands close around my shoulders, pulling me back.

"You got it," Frederico says quietly in my ear. "It's over."

I blink away my tears, staring at the skull of the battered zombie, at the blood oozing from the big wound in the back of its skull.

The potent memory I've been fighting surges up and socks me in the gut.

"God." I stumble back, breaking out of Frederico's grasp. I fall against the hatchback and bury my face in my hands. My chest rises and falls in short, panicked breaths.

Kyle.

IT WAS three weeks before Carter's high school graduation. I dragged my son to the mall to pick out new clothes for the occasion. You'd think we'd undertaken some task of horrific proportions, like scraping gum off bleachers at the high school football stadium instead of shopping in an air-conditioned department store.

"I look like a yuppie." My eighteen-year-old son scowled at himself in the Macy's mirror. "A penguin yuppie." In Carter's world, yuppies were scions of the devil.

"You look handsome," I corrected, straightening the sleeves of the blue button-down shirt he wore. The color of the shirt set off his eyes, which were a perfect match to his father's. "What color of tie do you want?"

"A *tie*?" The anguish on his face was laughable, although I was careful *not* to laugh.

"We can skip the tie, but—"

"Yes," he said immediately. "I don't want to wear one of those things." He tugged at his shirt collar, as if wearing a tie was akin to having a constrictor around his throat.

"If you skip the tie, I want a trim."

Silence. His scowl shifted to me.

"I'm not getting rid of this." He drew a protective hand across his giant bushy beard.

"I wouldn't think of asking you to shed the lumberjack look," I replied with a straight face. "Not for graduation. I just want a trim. Two inches?"

"One," he countered.

"One-and-a-half."

"Fine." His shoulders slumped as he peered at me suspiciously. "One-and-a-half inches off my beard, and no tie?"

"No tie," I agreed.

My son was going to fit right in at Humboldt University, where he'd be moving in three months. I tried hard not to imagine a hippie girl with hairy armpits hanging on him.

God, let him find a girlfriend who uses deodorant, I thought.

Carter couldn't get out of the shopping mall fast enough. If I left things up to him, he'd never buy new clothes. It was up to me to remove ratty shirts and jeans from his dresser and replace them with new ones from Old Navy. Sometimes he even noticed.

Carter relaxed as soon as we got in the car and headed home. "I ordered some new malt," he said. "I want to try and make a stout." My son wanted to be a brewmaster and open his own brewery when he graduated from college. "The secret to stout beer is all in the grain you use," he continued. "I read all about it . . ."

He rattled on as I drove, telling me about his new beer yeast and the theory behind making a good stout beer. Which he wasn't even old enough to drink, but Carter never worried about little details like that.

"I'm researching different barleys," he said, keeping up his nonstop monologue. "Mixing malt and barley is key . . ."

I listened, enjoying the time with my son. I was almost disappointed when our riverfront bungalow came into view, knowing our one-on-one time was at an end.

At least my other favorite man—my husband—would be waiting for me. We had plans to make dinner together. Tri-tip with blue cheese butter and roasted vegetables—

"Dad? Dad!" Carter's voice jarred my train of thought.

My son threw open the car door and leaped out, even though I was still rolling up the driveway.

I slammed on the brakes, following Carter's sprint across our front yard. That's when I saw my husband.

Kyle lay face up on the cement walkway in front of our house. He wasn't moving. The hose was on, water spurting across his ankles.

"Kyle?" I yanked on the emergency brake and jumped out of the car, fumbling for the phone in my purse.

"He's not breathing!" Carter screamed. "Dad!"

He lifted Kyle's head, revealing the small pool of blood under my husband's skull. The certain knowledge of loss—of an awful, soul-crushing loss—made my feet and legs numb. I froze, mouth going dry as I stared in horror at the scene before me.

"Call nine-one-one!" Carter yelled.

The phone slipped from my fingers, cracking loudly against the cement walkway. I fell to my knees, snatching clumsily at it.

"My husband fell," I said breathlessly to the operator. "Please, send an ambulance. Please, please . . ."

Even as I said the words, I knew it was too late. Kyle was gone. His face was pale and flaccid, mouth hanging slightly ajar. His beautiful blue eyes stared sightlessly at the sky above him.

Carter placed both hands on Kyle's chest, pumping up and down. "One, two, three," he counted, choking on a sob. He bent over, tipping Kyle's head back and blowing air into his father's mouth.

I folded over into a ball, sobbing. I felt my world shatter delicately around me. Carter continued to administer CPR.

It didn't do any good. Kyle was gone.

A FLUKE. A stupid accident. Kyle slipped on wet pavement and cracked his head open. Just like that, he was gone. Stolen from me and Carter.

Sometimes, when I lie in bed at night, I imagine I hear the crack as the back of Kyle's skull connected with the cement. It's a dull sound. Distinct, but not very loud. Soft, but deadly and permanent.

In all my nightmares and morbid mental movies of his death, I am haunted by the sound of his skull connecting with the pavement. It's a deep, faint thud I've only imagined, and it's identical to what I just heard when I split this zombie's skull.

The sound often drives me into my running shoes and out onto the road, but it doesn't matter how far or how fast I run. I can't escape the fact that my husband, the love of my life and my best friend, is gone.

Did Kyle hear that dull, horrible noise before he died? Had he died instantly, like this zombie, or had he dwelled in unconsciousness while his life bled out of his head? Could Carter and I have saved him if we'd gotten home five minutes earlier? Ten minutes?

As I stare at the zombie's ruined head, all I can think of is Kyle. My dead husband's brown goatee and strong nose are superimposed on the face of the zombie with the bleeding skull. My hands shake. My chest is constricted, making it hard to breathe.

"Kate!" Frederico shouts in my ear, giving me a rough shake. "It's not Kyle. It's not Kyle!"

And just like that, the moment is over. Kyle's features melt away, replaced with the grotesque one of the zombie. Panic drains out of my chest, letting breath flood normally into my lungs. I sag, letting tears dry on my cheeks.

"I miss him," I whisper. "Every moment of every day. I miss him so goddamn much."

"I know." He squeezes my shoulder. "I know, Jackalope."

I press fingers to my temples, burying thoughts of Kyle. Grief and sorrow will not help me now.

Focus on something else. That's what I need to do.

I push off the car, frantically rooting around in the passenger seat until I find my phone. I nearly sag with relief when I see a missed text message from Carter.

I'm OK. Had 2 move furniture in front of door. Text when u can. Don't call. Can't talk. Need 2 stay quiet.

I press the phone against my chest, momentarily closing my eyes. Carter is okay. My son is still alive. Taking a steadying breath, I text back.

We've seen the zombies. Are you safe?

I purposely do not look at the mangled body lying a few feet away. Even if it was a monster, I don't like thinking about what I did to him.

I'm glad you've seen them, comes his reply. *Wasn't sure how 2 explain things.*

A strangled laugh escapes me.

Zombies aren't supposed to be real, I text back.

No kidding. Everyone said they were meth-heads. Then I saw 3 girls eating a guy at a party last night.

Frederico leans against the car beside me, glancing over my shoulder at the phone. In the aftershocks of my panic attack, I realized I'd forgotten all about my friend's catapult into the vineyard.

"I'm so sorry," I say, looking up from the phone. "I'm a complete shit. Are you okay? You flew at least fifty feet."

"I'm a tough bastard," he replies. "Don't worry about me. Carter okay?"

I study my friend, giving him a head-to-toe once-over.

"I'm fine, really," Frederico says. Other than a scrape on his elbow and dirt smudges on his face and legs, he appears unscathed. "I felt worse when I fell off that ledge in the Santa Barbara hundred."

I snort. Frederico had forgotten to change the batteries on his headlamp on that race. Instead of trying to tag along with another runner, he tried to forge ahead alone—and ended up plowing right off a ledge and twisting his ankle. The stunt had forced him into a DNF—a *Did Not Finish.*

The phone in my hand pings with another incoming text. Assured my friend is okay, I turn my attention back to the phone. I tilt the screen so Frederico can read it, too.

Zombies r attracted 2 noise, Carter writes. *That's why I can't talk. Think they're blind too. Hunt by sound. Cars aren't safe. They swarm cars.*

"That explains the white eyes," Frederico murmurs.

Are you safe? I text.

No response.

"He isn't answering my question," I say tersely.

"Let me talk to him." Frederico takes the phone from me.

Carter, he texts. Uncle Rico here. R u safe?

There's a long pause. I can just imagine Carter trying to figure out if Frederico is really the one sending the text, or if it's me pretending to be Frederico. Carter might try to protect me, but there's a good chance he'll be straight with Frederico. The two have always been close, even more so since Kyle died.

At last, his answer comes.

Safe for now. Can't leave my dorm room. Zombies in hallway. On campus 2. I can see them from the window.

A tremble goes through my chest, tears again springing to my eyes. Frederico rubs my back in wordless comfort.

Pull your shit together, I scold myself. Carter needs a strong mom, not an emotional basket case. He's already had to deal with that scenario one too many times in his life.

My phone pings with another text.

There are soldiers and CDC workers. Arrived this morning. Ordered everyone to stay inside. They arrest anyone they find outside. CDC people are in hazmat suits.

If the military and CDC are involved, things are worse than I imagined. I snatch the phone from Frederico, pulling up the Internet browser. A quick search of the news networks brings up disturbing headlines.

UNNAMED BIO THREAT DISCOVERED AT PORTLAND PORT

CDC QUARANTINE 500-MILE RADIUS AROUND PORTLAND

OREGON-CALIFORNIA BORDER CLOSED, CDC CHECKPOINTS AS FAR SOUTH AS EUREKA & REDDING

ALL US PORTS CLOSED PENDING CDC INSPECTION

ALL FLIGHTS GROUNDED IN PORTLAND AIRPORT

PORTLAND BIOTERRORISM ATTACK CAUSING OUTBREAKS
OF INSANITY AND CANNIBALISM

THE PHONE FALLS NUMBLY from my fingers. Despite my inner attempt to rally, all hope crumples up inside me. I slump over, wrapping my arms around my stomach. This shit is real. CDC quarantines and checkpoints. Bio threats. Port closures.

Zombies.

My son is out there, trapped. And I have no way to get to him.

Frederico picks up my phone, silently thumbing through the headlines. He lets me cry, administering more pats to my back. I sense him looking up and down the frontage road.

"This isn't over, Kate," he says. "Not by a long shot."

"What are you talking about?" I raise bitter eyes. "In case you didn't notice, my car is completely fucked. Even if I did have a car, there's the CDC quarantine and the fact that zombies swarm cars. Carter is barricaded in his dorm room with no one to help him. We're stuck here."

Frederico gives my back a final pat and pulls me upright. Looking me in the eye, he says, "Lace up, Kate. We're hoofing it."

I blink stupidly at him. "What?"

"Your car is totaled," he says. "With all the shit that's going down, maybe it's a blessing in disguise. You want to find your son? Then we run."

"You want to *run*? All the way to Arcata?"

He shrugs. "We scope out the situation as we go. If the roads look safe, we find a car to rent or buy. Or steal one, whatever. We can ditch it before we hit the CDC quarantine or if there are too many zombies. In the end, we'll need to be on foot to get into Arcata."

"But . . ." I work a quick calculation in my head. "That's at least two hundred miles."

Frederico takes my phone and pulls up a GPS app. After a moment, he says, "It's exactly two hundred and one point three miles from this very spot to Humboldt University."

"Two hundred and one *miles*?" I say, incredulous. "Neither of us has ever run that far before."

"How many miles did you log last week?"

"One hundred thirty-six," I reply instantly. I keep a running log and track my mileage and elevation work.

"I did one hundred and nine."

I think about this. For the average, non-crazy person, running two hundred or more miles would be impossible. At an ambitious walk, they may cover fifteen miles a day. Maybe twenty, if they're in great shape. But Frederico and I have both made a hobby of running ultra races. Insane long distances are our specialty.

My eyes dry. Something akin to hope blooms in my chest. If we only stop once or twice for catnaps—ultramarathons are run with little to no sleep—we can make good time. If we can find a car to use for a while, we can make really good time.

"Do you think we can make it in two days?"

Frederico, sensing my budding optimism, considers this. "Maybe, if we can knock out some distance in a car," he says at last. "If we make the majority of the trip on foot, three days is a safer estimate."

"But we'll be on the road," I say. "Road running is always faster than trail running, and we've both done one-hundred-mile trail runs in under twenty-four hours."

"I haven't done a sub-twenty-four in over five years, trail or road," he replies. "The farther we go, the harder it will be to hold a decent pace. There's no guarantee we'll even be able to stay on the road. If things get hairy, we may be bushwhacking."

"Seventy-two hours." I nod, letting this new reality sink in. I might not be cut out for zombie killing, but I *am* a long-distance runner. "Okay."

I pick up the phone and send one last message.

Sit tight, sweetie. Frederico and I are coming to get you. Be there as soon as we can.

Five seconds later, my phone rings. Carter's smiling face pops up on the screen, an odd juxtaposition to everything that's going on.

"Put that thing on silent," Frederico says.

I obey, then hit the speaker button. "I thought you said you couldn't talk on the phone," I say anxiously.

"You can't come here," Carter hisses. His words are barely above a whisper. "Cars are zombie magnets. I don't know how far south the outbreak has spread, but I've seen at least three cars get swarmed today."

"No problem," Frederico replies. "Your mom's car is totaled, and we're out in the middle of the vineyards without a taxi in sight. We're running to you."

Silence.

"You guys are crazy," Carter hisses. "You can't *run* here!"

"Your mom and I are indeed crazy, and we're coming to get you, kiddo. Deal with it." With that, Frederico hangs up.

It's my turn to snatch the phone.

Do u have enough snacks to hold u over until we get there? I text.

Don't come, he types back. *Not safe.*

We r coming. Do u have enough food?

Long pause. Then, *Yes, we have snacks.*

What about water?

Sink still works.

Good. See u soon baby. Love u.

Be careful Mom. Stay away from cars. Love you 2.

7

PREP

WHAT FOLLOWS IS A ROUTINE FREDERICO AND I HAVE DANCED FOR nearly two decades: prep for an ultra run. Even though this will be a very different type of run, the essentials are the same.

We pull my gear box out of the trunk. It's overflowing with running supplies. I never go anywhere without it. Especially these days, when I'm running almost every day. The amount of money I spend on running paraphernalia is barely short of embarrassing.

In silent symbiosis, we dive into the box. I pull out a headlamp and an extra set of batteries. Next come gloves, beanie, visor, and extra socks.

"You should swap out your hydration pack for this one." I pass Frederico my biggest spare pack, which has a two-liter water bladder. He nods in agreement, wordlessly dropping his pack into my trunk.

I have five different running packs in my car—not to mention a few waist packs—each for different types of runs. For what's in front of us, we both need packs with the maximum water and gear storage.

"Shit. I'm low on fuel." I scoop out three energy bars and one gel, passing them to Frederico. I follow this with a baggie of electrolyte tablets. These are all staples of the ultrarunner, except that I don't have nearly enough for what's ahead of us. "I was planning to go to the running store to restock."

I regret the fact that we didn't get to eat all the breakfast we ordered at Bread Box. A big meal would have been a good start to this insane junket.

"These won't get us two hundred miles," Frederico agrees, surveying our food supply.

"Maybe we can stock up in Cloverdale," I suggest. Cloverdale is a town ten miles north of us. "Maybe try to get a car there, too."

"Maybe," he replies.

Neither of us mentions the physical discomfort we'll endure if we can't adequately fuel our bodies. I try to eat two hundred to three hundred calories per hour when I run an ultra. I've distilled this down to a science over the years. My body can't digest more than this, and as long as I keep up a steady stream of fuel, I'm in good shape. Based on our meager supply of snacks, we have enough for three, maybe four hours.

"Fuck it," I say, breaking the silence and dropping the food into my pile of gear. "We'll have to figure out ways to refuel along the way." I won't let one little obstacle keep me from getting to my son.

"That's the jackalope we all know and love." Frederico grins at me. "If we let little obstacles keep us from racing, we'd never make it to the starting line."

"At least we have a blister kit." I pull out a little Ziploc filled with needles, Band-Aids, nail scissors, sterile wipes, and a tube of Neosporin.

"Don't forget to lube up." Frederico produces a stick of Body Glide and passes it to me.

To the normal person, this would look like a stick of deodorant. To an ultrarunner, it's the difference between finishing a race or DNFing. Body Glide is a lubricant for runners designed to protect the body from chafing on a long run.

I pull off my shoes and rub my feet with the stick, taking care to work it between my toes. I rub more along the base of my sports bra. These are the worst chafing areas for me. Then I pull on a clean pair of socks to replace the ones Frederico used to wipe his ass.

"Can I borrow these?" Frederico pulls out a pair of compression calf sleeves. They're fluorescent pink with orange polka dots.

"Be my guest."

I pass him the Body Glide. He goes around the side of the car to lubricate those parts of the male anatomy that need protection from chafing.

I set about filling our hydration packs from the water jugs I always keep in the trunk. Running out of water during a run is almost as bad as forgetting Body Glide.

Once the packs are filled, I consider my pants. I'm dressed in ankle-length, black compression pants. They're my preference for morning runs. They're warm and provide protection from various plants on the trail, but they can get downright uncomfortable on hot runs. They would not be my first choice for any race taking place in the heat of the day.

But compression gear improves oxygen flow and blood circulation, two things which will definitely be important on this run. And if there is indeed any "bushwhacking," as suggested by Frederico, I'll want to be in long pants. With a last glimpse at my extra pair of shorts, I decide not to change.

With the pants selection complete, I move on to my shoe collection.

Trail shoes. Road shoes. Trail-road combo shoes. Trail shoes with beefy soles for post-race recovery. Road shoes with a negative heel-toe drop. Old shoes encrusted with mud, which I use when running in storms; no reason to ruin more than one pair. Shoes I bought just because they were on sale and I liked the color scheme. Plus a few others that weren't on sale. Running shoes for every scenario, and then some.

After a few moments of thought, I pull out a trail-road combo pair with a thick, beefy sole. I won't be able to carry multiple ones with me, so I need to be prepared for as much variation as possible. The medium tread will work well enough on multi-surfaces, and the beefy sole will give my foot extra cushion on the long run.

After lacing them on, I load my pack, shoving as much as I can into the pockets. I scavenge a few maps out of the glovebox and stuff them into the compartment with the water bladder. There's a small pocket knife in my gear box, something I always carry when running trails that take me far from civilization.

I silently lament the loss of the things I don't have room for, like the extra batteries and shirt. The sunglasses, handheld knuckle lights, and the portable drinking straw that purifies water with UV light. There just isn't enough room for everything.

Headphones are a no-go, too. They could be suicide on a course infested with zombies. I sigh, tossing them back into my car. Running two hundred miles would be nicer with music or a podcast.

God, and what about my waterproof jacket? I just don't have enough room. Well, shit. I've done my fair share of training runs and races in storms. This may be another one if a spring rain decides to open up.

Frederico comes around the car, decked out in my fluorescent-pink shorts and matching compression sleeves with orange polka dots. If our situation wasn't so dire, I'd be doubled over in hysterics. As it is, all I feel is a sense of overwhelming relief that zombies are blind. Frederico is impossible to miss in those clothes.

He digs around in trunk, tossing handfuls of my gear into the backseat of the car.

"What are you doing?" I ask.

"Seeing what else you have in here. We could use a weapon or two." He pulls up the bottom of the trunk, revealing a spare tire, jack, and lug nut wrench.

"What do you think about this?" He hefts the lug nut wrench in one hand. "For crushing zombie skulls?"

"How are we going to carry it?"

He taps the wrench in his palm, considering. "Could we lash it to the back of a pack?"

"Maybe."

There's a zip cord meant for securing a jacket on the back of Frederico's pack. I take an extra shirt and wrap it around the wrench like a sling. After some fiddling, I get the wrench semi-secured to the zip cord.

"Not very stable," I say, rocking it back and forth. "But at least it won't swing free and hit you."

"Probably worth the nuisance if we get in a jam."

"We won't be able to get it out very fast if we need it."

"We could figure out a way to hang it from my waist, but I'd get bloody and bruised from it."

Another good point. I sigh. "I guess this is as good as it's going to get."

We stand there in contemplative silence. Nearby is the occasional hum of a car as it whizzes down the freeway. And in the far, far distance is a smaller, distinct sound: screaming.

"Do you hear that?" I ask softly.

He nods. "It's spreading."

I set my GPS watch to zero. For the next seventy-two hours, our lives will revolve around this watch as it tracks our time and miles.

My eyes meet Frederico's.

Our packs are full of water and supplies. We're laced into our shoes.

Time to run.

8

DON'T BE AN IDIOT

THERE'S A FAMOUS SAYING IN THE ULTRA WORLD, PENNED BY RUNNER-writer Scott Douglas: *In the first half of the race, don't be an idiot. In the second half of the race, don't be a wimp.*

This bit of wisdom has been hammered into me over my years of ultrarunning. It's guided me through dozens of races.

Even so, I find myself scowling when Frederico says, "We're doing nine-minute miles. Let's slow it to nine thirty." He catches my look and raises an eyebrow in silent challenge.

I swallow my frustration. He's right. We can't help Carter and Aleisha if we push too hard now and collapse at mile fifty.

I force my legs to slow and my breathing to ease. The act makes me feel like a wild horse in a cage. I want to bust free and run hard and fast. I want the world to blur by on either side, to pass in a rush and transport me to Arcata, to my son.

"Perfect," Frederico says. "If we can hold this pace for the next fifty miles, we'll be in good shape."

He's right, of course. We settle into a familiar rhythm, running side by side down the frontage road. We pass wineries, houses—some so old they look like they'll tip over in a stiff breeze—vineyards, and even a lonely church. I try not to think about how little food we have and how shitty we're going to feel when it runs out. Thank goodness the next town isn't far away.

Despite my worry about food, tension leaches out as we move

down the road. It always does when I run. There's an odd normalcy to me and Frederico running together. As I cruise along—my shoes landing lightly on the pavement and my breath feathering in and out of my lungs—I can almost imagine the world is still normal. That zombies aren't real, that my husband is still alive, and my son is safe in his dorm.

The road meanders northward, sometimes drifting closer to the freeway than I'd like. There's a chain-link fence separating us from the main highway. Will that be enough to protect us if we run into zombies?

"Do you think the news reports are right?" I ask. "Do you think this is a bioterrorism attack?"

"Don't know," Frederico replies. "It's not outrageous to think whatever it is—a virus, bacteria, whatever—came in on a cargo ship. It wouldn't be the first disease to get past customs."

I shiver. Nothing to do but put our heads down and keep running.

At mile three, we encounter our first car wreck. It's a single car crashed into a pine tree on the side of the road. Both driver and passenger side doors are open. A thin stream of steam hisses up from the engine.

At first I think the car has been abandoned, but then I see the pair of legs sticking out from behind the car. The legs are attached to a woman, who lies prone on the dirt while a man dips a hand into her stomach cavity and feasts on her entrails. I gag and look away as we run by.

The frontage road drifts away from the freeway. All is eerily silent and deserted. A lone cyclist passes us, bent low over his bike. He swings wide around us, looking at us with wide, panicked eyes before disappearing over a hill.

Two pit bulls bark as we run by their chain-link fence. Their shrill voices echo, crashing in my ears like cymbals.

"Is there a way to shush pit bulls, short of shooting them?" I ask.

"Maybe they'll pipe down when zombies show up to eat them," Frederico replies.

The dogs throw themselves at the fence as we pass, their snarls following us.

At mile six, we come upon a second car wreck. There are four cars in all. One engine still hums, the front wheels dangling into the drainage ditch on the side of the road.

There are five zombies, all of them clustered around the car with the purring engine. Glimpses of eerie, lifeless white eyes make my skin crawl.

I slow, worried my footsteps will draw their attention. Will that chain-link fence be enough to protect us? Can they climb?

"Keep moving," Frederico says. "Run on your toes."

I follow his instructions, rising up onto my toes. With less surface area to make contact with the road, my footsteps become softer, lighter.

The zombies don't turn toward us. They are fixated on the car. They claw and scratch at it, snarling and growling.

In the distance, a siren wails. The zombies hear it the same instant I do. All five of their heads turn, looking north toward the new sound.

Seconds later, an ambulance and two cop cars zip by, tearing southward. As a unit, the five zombies peel away from the car. They turn, breaking into a run, and follow the sirens.

One of them, a forty-something woman in blue jeans, smacks right into one of the other cars. She drops. An instant later, she's back on her feet. Snarling, she reaches out with her hands and feels her way around the car, then resumes her run down the freeway.

"Carter was right," Frederico says softly. "They are blind."

"And attracted to noise," I add, watching the zombie in blue jeans disappear down the road with the others. "I hope they don't have enhanced hearing."

Frederico's lips set in a grim line. "We'll be fine so long as there's something louder and more obnoxious to draw their attention."

"But if we're the only ones around, we're screwed," I reply.

The small town of Cloverdale comes into view at mile eight. It's a cute hamlet nestled on the northwestern side of Lake Sonoma. Frederico and I slow, stopping to survey the town from a distance. From where we stand, it looks peaceful.

"Maybe Cloverdale is safe enough for us to get a car," he says. "How much money do you have in your bank account?"

I hesitate. "I have Kyle's life insurance money." The idea of spending it opens an ache inside me. As if one more piece of Kyle is being taken away.

You're being stupid, I tell myself. *Kyle's gone.*

"There's a used car dealer on the south side end of Cloverdale," Frederico says.

"You sure we should go into the town?"

"No. But I do know this journey will be faster if we can knock out some miles with a car. I'm willing to run it, but faster is better."

I draw in a breath. "Okay. Let's get closer and have a look." I pause. "Maybe we should unhook your lug nut wrench?"

"Good idea."

Two minutes later, we're on our way again. Frederico, wielding the lug nut wrench in pink running shorts and polka-dot calf compression sleeves, looks like a vagabond nut job.

The frontage road, which has been running parallel to 101, climbs a small hill and meets up with the freeway off-ramp. We jog up the rise and cross onto the overpass. We drop into crouches at the top, staring out at the scene.

What stretches out before us is nothing short of suburban perfection. A Safeway shopping center dominates the scene, the parking lot flanked on either end by a gas station and McDonald's. There's a Boy Scout troop outside the McDonald's gathered around the outside of a big white van. A few cars roll in and out of the parking lot, most people going into the grocery store.

My gaze is drawn to the McDonald's. It's been at least a decade since I've set foot in a fast-food restaurant, but this one holds a potent memory for me.

I sat in the Cloverdale McDonald's bathroom stall, positioning the pregnancy strip between my legs. My bladder was about to burst. I clenched the muscles, holding back the urine.

I didn't want to fuck this up; the test kit cost twenty dollars. I couldn't afford to buy another one. Hell, I could hardly afford *this* one.

When the stick looked to be in the right position, I let out a trickle of pee, bending forward and intently watching the yellow stream. It successfully hit the end of the stick.

I relaxed, releasing a gentle stream of urine. I was careful not to let it gush out. The box said the urine needs to run over the tip for at least five seconds. I dragged it out for ten.

Nothing to do now but wait. Three to five minutes, according to the box.

I put the test strip on the toilet paper dispenser, rising to reposition my skirt. It was Kyle's favorite, a filmy blue-and-brown maxi I'd picked up at a thrift store. I wore it on our first date.

It seemed like the right thing to wear today. Like maybe my choice of clothing could influence the result of the pregnancy test. It was a stupid thought, but wearing it made me feel less afraid. I needed to feel less afraid. I needed—

My eyes jerked, gaze drawn to the white plastic stick balanced on the toilet paper dispenser.

A bright-pink plus sign blazed up at me.

I burst into tears, staring in horror.

I'm only nineteen, I thought. *I'm only nineteen.* The sentence repeated itself over and over in my head.

This was not how my life was supposed to go. I was supposed to transfer to UCLA, get a master's in psychology, and make a career for myself.

I hauled myself out of the bathroom stall, wiping my nose and forcing the tears away. I did my best to fix my makeup in the mirror. With puffy red eyes and smeared mascara, I looked like hell. Not even Kyle's favorite skirt could make me look any less a mess.

Screw it, I thought, glumly exiting the bathroom.

Kyle waited anxiously for me just outside, two uneaten Big Macs on a tray in front of him. We'd met six months ago in a speech and debate class at the local junior college. Since then, we'd barely left each other's side.

Kyle's eyes were wide with anxiety. He wore loose blue jeans and a plain blue T-shirt that matched his eyes. He was tall and lanky, with a kindness that ran down to his core. Even in my current state, my heart swelled at the sight of him.

His mouth opened to form a question, but no words came out. Silence hung between us as I stared at him with my swollen eyes. I saw the silent confirmation of my pregnancy hit him: a fleeting expression of terror passed over his face.

Then he closed his mouth, stood up, and wrapped me in a hug. I burst into tears all over again.

I sobbed uncontrollably, grateful that it was a Wednesday and the McDonald's was virtually deserted. Kyle rocked me, his arms never wavering in their grip. His embrace made the angles of the world seem less sharp. I clung to him, wrapping my arms around his neck. I wanted him to hold me forever.

I don't know how long we stood like that. At some point, Kyle peeled himself away. Despair filled me as space opened up between us. He was going to break up with me now. I just knew it. That's what the tears on his cheeks had to mean. He was going to break up with me. I cried harder.

When he dropped to one knee in front of me, I stared at him in complete confusion.

"Will you marry me, Kate?" he asked softly.

"Don't be an idiot," I said harshly, confusion and disbelief churning in my stomach. "You don't want to marry me." Did he?

"Yeah, I do," he replied. His blue-eyed gaze was steady. "I love you, Kate."

You don't get any more unromantic than that: knocked up and proposed to in a McDonald's, two uneaten Big Macs our only witnesses. I said yes to the tall, sweet, awkward boy I loved, even though every part of me was terrified.

GOD HOW I MISS HIM. I miss the good times, the bad times, and everything in between. I miss the sense of completeness we had when we were together. I spend too many days feeling like half my heart is missing. I'd give anything to argue with Kyle one last time or to cook his favorite dinner.

"What do you think?"

Frederico's voice pulls me back into the present. I carefully fold up my memories of Kyle and tuck them away. Now is not the time to be distracted.

I refocus on the scene below us, taking a long, hard look as I consider Frederico's question. "It looks safe," I say. Maybe, just maybe, the whole world hasn't gone to hell. Maybe it's just Healdsburg and

Portland. I dare to let myself hope. "I think we should go into Safeway and stock up on food."

"What do you think about trying to get a car?"

I shift, uncertain. "Let's focus on food first."

We jog down the overpass and into town. A minivan full of kids in pee wee football uniforms rolls by us. *Go Bulldogs!* is written in white paint across the van's side windows.

The woman behind wheel gives us a skeptical look before rolling onto the on-ramp. To her, we probably look like whack jobs on really good weed because who would run over an overpass wielding a lug nut wrench?

We jog up behind the McDonald's, wading through a margin of waist-high weeds as we circle around toward the parking lot. The drive-thru is empty, though I see a blond-haired teen spraying cleanser on the pick-up window ledge.

Two yards into the grass, a stomach curdling stench hits me. I draw to a halt, covering my nose and checking my shoes, wondering if I stepped on roadkill.

In the same instant, Frederico trips on something. He grunts in surprise, then lets out a surprised yelp.

"Kate, look out!"

9

BOY SCOUTS

A DREADLOCKED KID REARS UP FROM THE WEEDS LIKE AN ANIMAL, baring his teeth and snarling. His eyes are the now-familiar eerie, opaque white. His right arm hangs awkwardly, strands of sinew showing through the bloody gash in his shoulder. He's wearing a green shirt that says *Meat is Murder. Go Vegan.*

Oddly, the kid only rises to his knees before lunging. Frederico easily dodges aside, raising the wrench defensively but not attacking.

The zombie crashes to the ground, snarling. He struggles to crawl through the grass, fingers slipping in the damp earth. A closer look reveals a pair of legs twisted at odd angles.

"Something happened to him," I say, easing around the zombie. "His legs are broken."

"Good for us. Come on, let's get out of here."

I couldn't agree more.

We retreat, scanning the grass as we back away from the zombie. There's no one else around. The blond teen has disappeared from the drive-thru window. A battered forest-green Camry pulls around the corner of the drive-thru, the driver not even glancing in our direction.

The beast snaps his teeth, struggling to follow us. How did this poor kid end up here, anyway? From the looks of him, he's homeless. Northern California has its fair share of hippie-esque homeless and vagabonds.

"Kate, look what I found."

Frederico pulls a big frame backpack out of the grass. It's faded on the top and covered with dirt splatters. A dingy sleeping bag is rolled up and fastened to the top.

Poor kid. My eyes flick to the zombie, who's now a good twenty feet away from us. He really was homeless.

Frederico rummages through the backpack. He tosses me a granola bar, then takes a wrapper off a second one and starts to eat. I don't argue, scarfing down the bar in a few quick bites.

Frederico finds one last granola bar, which we squirrel away for later. He also finds a nice Swiss Army knife, which he slips into a pocket. A minute later, he pulls out a tie-dyed shirt that says *I Don't Eat Anything With Eyes*. Though part of me registers the humor in this, I can't find it in myself to laugh.

We leave the vegan zombie behind for good, jogging past the McDonald's and into the parking lot. Safeway is on the far side of the shopping center. I start compiling a mental list of the things we need to stock up on. Electrolyte powder, if we can find it. Some zip locks to put it in. Portable food. Energy bars would probably be the best, and maybe some—

A scream draws my attention. I freeze, head swiveling toward the sound. The Camry has pulled up beside the Boy Scouts and the white van. A woman—presumably a mother of one of the boys—screams hysterically. At her feet is a pile of McDonald's paper bags. Latched onto her right forearm are two Boy Scouts. Both of them have deep wounds on their shoulders and necks, blood covering their small bodies.

They snarl, digging their teeth into her flesh. The woman stumbles back. Blood spurts from her wounds onto her plain white T-shirt.

Frederico takes several steps forward, lips parting in a silent shout. The rest of the Boy Scouts shift, trampling the to-go bags as they converge on the woman. Growling and snarling, they bear her to the ground in a blur of green-and-khaki uniforms. She screams one more time, then goes silent.

Just like that, the poor woman is gone. It happens so fast that I can only stand there, paralyzed by the horror unfolding before me.

Then I see what had the kids distracted up until this point. I had assumed they were huddled around camping or biking gear, or something Scout-like. What I see instead is a pudgy Scout leader, his stomach ripped open. Viscous blood pools on the parking lot asphalt, pale ropes of shiny entrails trailing across it.

"We gotta get out of here," Frederico says, clamping one hand around my wrist. "Move, Kate."

We retreat, taking a dozen steps backward. Just as we turn, another scream splits across the parking lot.

I turn and see a chubby, brown-haired woman running out of the McDonald's—and coming straight for us.

"Call nine-one-one!" she shrieks. "The fry cook is attacking the cashier. Please, help!"

The commotion draws the attention of several Scouts. Blank white eyes turn in our direction as the woman nears us.

"Fuck," I whisper. I move toward the woman, thinking to quiet her, but Frederico yanks me aside.

"Shit's going sideways. We have to get the fuck out of here."

He hauls me toward a battered old Nissan parked about ten feet away. Right as we reach the car, five of the Scouts peel away from the group and start running toward us. Frederico swings the lug nut wrench, shattering the driver's side window.

"Inside!" he bellows, yanking open the door. He turns to the hysterical woman. "Come with us," he shouts to her.

I never know if she hears us.

I dive through the opening, scrambling over the emergency brake. Frederico leaps in next to me, tossing the lug nut wrench onto the floor. In his hand is the Swiss Army knife he lifted off the vegan zombie, the flat head screwdriver extended.

I look up to see if the woman is coming. As I do, three of the zombie Scouts barrel into her. Her shriek of, "The fry cook—!" is cut off as she's slammed to the ground. More screaming comes from farther away in the parking lot.

Two zombie Scouts smack into the side of the Nissan. Frederico unceremoniously jams the flat head Swiss Army screw driver into the ignition and turns it. The car hums to life.

Several more Scouts reach us, white eyes rolling in their sockets. They run straight into the back passenger door, hitting it so hard I'm pretty sure they dent it.

One boy lets out a high-pitched keen as he claws and scratches at the door. Several more surge across the parking lot after us. A few of them trip as they run. The falls don't stun or slow them down; they bound back to their feet, continuing their awful forward momentum.

Frederico throws the car into drive and slams on the accelerator. The tires squeal against the pavement.

He makes a hard left with the steering wheel. The little Nissan rockets out of the parking space. I grab my seat belt, trying to jam the buckle into place while simultaneously watching the Scouts.

The car hits the asphalt curb surrounding the parking lot. The right side of the car flies up; the left side makes an awful metallic sound. Frederico leans hard on the gas pedal. The back of the Nissan bucks as it rolls over the curb and we hit the street.

The pursuing Scouts crash into the car, this time running into the trunk. Frederico floors it. The car lurches forward, swerving to the left across the road.

"Dammit!" Frederico puts all his weight into the steering wheel, struggling to keep it from veering to the left. He curses, straining against the wheel as the car hums up the overpass.

Just as we reach the far side, the left wheel comes off. The car tilts wildly. The wheel bounces away. Sparks fly up as metal skids again asphalt. Seconds later, the poor Nissan screeches to a crooked halt.

"We gotta run." Frederico throws open the door and leaps out.

At least half of the Scouts have thundered after us. They crest the overpass, only about a hundred feet away.

I'm about to jump out after Frederico when something occurs to me. The car is still running, the Swiss Army knife standing sideways in the ignition.

I lean over, flip on the radio, and turn the volume to full blast. Then I catapult myself out of the car, hightailing it after Frederico.

"What the hell are you doing?" he shouts at me when I catch up. "Now is not the time for NPR!"

Sure enough, the honeyed voice of NPR's Weekend Edition host belts out of the car.

"Creating a diversion," I huff, sprinting along beside him, pumping my arms and legs as hard as I can.

I glance over my shoulder just long enough to confirm my suspicions: the zombie Scouts swarm the car like ants on a piece of cat food.

"Look," I say, slowing my stride. "They're not following us anymore."

Every zombie is in frantic mode, clawing and pushing one another in an attempt to get to the car. None of them so much as turns in our direction. Their focus is solely on the Nissan's blaring radio.

We hit the frontage road again and turn north, running side by side. To our left is a sharp slope angling down to the freeway; to our right is open grassland and vineyards.

"Everything will depend on how good their hearing is," Frederico says.

A shiver courses down my back, even though I'm drenched in sweat. "Guess we'll just have to see."

I take a long drink out of my pack. Adrenaline hammers at me. I keep looking over my shoulder, expecting to see at least one Scout coming after us.

None of them do. Only when we've put three-quarters of a mile between us and them do I begin to relax.

"You realize we are zero-for-two with cars?" Frederico says.

"Yeah. We only got a few granola bars for all our trouble. Though we got off better than some of the others."

I think of the two women we saw get attacked—the Scout mother with her McDonald's breakfast bags, and the chubby woman who saw the attack inside the fast-food restaurant.

"It wasn't a complete waste," Frederico says, giving me a clap on the shoulder.

His levity is forced. I can tell he's trying to lighten the mood, which I appreciate. "How do you figure?" I ask.

"You learned the easiest way to steal a car," he replies. "I bet they don't teach that to those Boy Scouts. You never know when that piece of information might come in handy. Screwdrivers are pretty easy to find."

I have to admit he has a point. If this is the end of the world, there's no telling how many cars we might have to steal between now and the grave.

"You sure know how to make lemonade out of lemons," I say.

"I'm a recovering alcoholic, kid. I'm a living lemon. I spend every day doing my best to make lemonade out of myself." He shrugs.

"Somedays I do better than others. You know that better than anyone."

———————

It was a Saturday night in late November. Carter, only four, curled in bed beside me as I read him a story.

When the doorbell rang, I didn't think much of it. I heard Kyle get up from the sofa in the living room and answer it.

I finished the book, kissed Carter good-night, and closed his bedroom door. Exiting the hallway, I was surprised to find Frederico on our living room couch. He and Kyle, having met in Alcoholics Anonymous, had been friends for several years. The two men had taken an instant liking to one another, a synchronicity that bloomed into a lifelong friendship.

Frederico's eyes, in a younger, less careworn face, were wild that night.

"She moved out," he said, voice tight. "She's been planning this for months. She waited until I went to my AA meeting, then called that jackass boyfriend of hers and moved out."

Neither Kyle nor I had to ask who *she* was. Aleisha, his daughter, had just turned eighteen. She was the only female of any importance in Frederico's life.

"What's the point of all this?" Frederico raged. He snatched a copy of an Alcoholics Anonymous book off our coffee table and waved it in the air. "What is the point of this if I can't earn her forgiveness?" He hurled the book across the room, chest heaving.

It smacked loudly against the wall before thunking to the floor. I suppressed a wince, knowing the sound would wake Carter.

"She said I would never be anything more than a stupid addict." His words were thin and strained. "I haven't touched alcohol in seven years, and it's still not enough. What do I have to do to prove myself to her?"

He crumpled over, crimping fists in hair that was more black than gray. "I want a drink," he whispered. "I need a drink." He lifted haunted, desperate eyes to Kyle.

"One drink will be too many. A hundred drinks will never be

enough," Kyle replied, voice gentle yet firm. "The pain will still be there when you sober up."

"Mommy?" Carter, drawn by the commotion, appeared in the hallway.

I intercepted him. "Come on, baby." I pulled him back into his room. "Uncle Rico is here to visit Daddy. Let's go read another story."

Fifteen minutes later, when I reemerged from Carter's bedroom, Kyle and Frederico were gone. Kyle didn't come back home until four in the morning.

"Uncle Rico is sleeping on the sofa," he said, sliding into bed beside me. "Hope that's okay."

"Of course," I replied sleepily. "Everything okay?"

"Yeah," Kyle replied, leaning over to give me a quick kiss on the cheek.

He didn't offer any details. I didn't ask for any, understanding the sacred privacy existing between AA members.

When I padded into the living room the next morning, I found Frederico fast asleep, curled around his Alcoholics Anonymous book. That was the first and last time I ever heard him say he wanted a drink.

———

I NEVER DID FIND out what they did that night, or what was said between them. What I do know is that Frederico made it through the crisis without drinking, and that's what mattered.

Over the years, he's learned to manage his daughter's rejection, though it's a pain he'll always carry. Like his sobriety, it's a razor's edge he's forever balancing on.

10

THE TRACKS

ONLY TWO SOUTHBOUND CARS PASS US AS WE RUN DOWN THE FRONTAGE road. Both whiz by us without slowing. I look for signs of distress and worry on the faces of the drivers, but they go by us so quickly it's impossible for me to tell.

We run another half mile before we're forced to slow. Two hundred yards in front of us, the road dead-ends at a two-way intersection.

At the intersection are two wrecked cars and a bunch of zombies. I count seven altogether. Five of them wander in small circles in the road; two others are stuck in cars, beating and scratching at the glass.

As soon as we spot the zombies, Frederico and I duck into a vineyard and hide between a row of vines. We dig the map out of my pack and spread it on the ground. While Frederico pores over the map, I pull out my phone and check for messages from Carter. Nothing. I tuck it back away, doing my best to ignore the fear chipping away at me.

Frederico runs his hand along the crinkled map. "We're right here." He taps the map.

"What's the best way north?" I lean over beside him. "I think we should stay off the freeway as much as possible."

"Agreed." Frederico frowns, studying the map. "We could try to maneuver these country black lines." He trails his fingers over the roads. "Risky, though. There's no straight shot. Worst-case scenario, we get lost. Best, we waste a lot of time constantly stopping to check the map so we don't get lost."

"What about the railroad?" I can see the tracks from here, running between the freeway and the frontage road. They run right through the two-way intersection and disappear into a tangle of trees and weeds beyond the zombies, heading in a north-bound direction.

"The tracks parallel one-oh-one for . . . looks like almost seventy-five miles. We can get all the way to Willits. A little farther, even. We'll have to get back onto one-oh-one after that, but there won't be as many people to worry about." The population of northern California gets pretty sparse. Some towns have populations of less than one hundred people.

"That's a good plan." Frederico traces the railroad with his finger. "It's a straight shot. We avoid civilization and the freeway for seventy-five miles. There's only one problem." He meets my eye. "We have to get through *them* to get to the railroad."

I don't have to ask who *them* is. Raising my chin, I peek through the vibrant grape leaves at the milling zombies.

"There're only seven of them," Frederico says. "Let's bust out a can of whoop ass and take care of them."

I'm not in the mood for his humor. "How about we just give them a wide berth?" I reply curtly.

Without giving him time to respond, I lead the way deeper into the vineyard. We cut through the vines, popping out three-quarters of a mile up the road from the zombies.

We crouch on the asphalt, watching the milling undead from afar. They continue to walk in mindless circles, periodically moaning or growling.

"We stay low and move fast," Frederico whispers to me. "Once we hit the vineyards on the other side of the road, head west until we hit the tracks."

I nod in agreement. In the movies, this would be the part where something goes terribly wrong and we end up with a horde of zombies on our heels.

In reality, when we zip across the two-lane road to the vineyard on the opposite side, nothing happens. The zombies remain near the wrecked cars, none of them so much as twitching at our passage.

"May the rest of our journey be so easy," Frederico says as we duck between the vines.

We cut through the vineyard. In a few minutes, we intercept the railroad tracks. I glance down at my watch and see that we've covered ten miles. Since we first ditched my ruined car.

Only one hundred ninety-one to go.

————

THE RAILS SIT on a manmade berm. The tracks have been abandoned and unused for who knows how long, a relic from a bygone era of logging and clear-cutting in northern California. They're rotting and choked with weeds.

In running, there are different types of terrain. Paved roads and wide fire trails are considered easy. Then there are hiking trails, single-track paths often littered with rocks, boulders, roots, plants, inclines, and declines. The more obstacles, the more technical a race path becomes—and the more mental and physical acuity required to navigate them.

As I canter along behind Frederico—the tracks being too narrow for us to run side by side—I quickly assess that these tracks are on par with technical trail runs. The wooden rail ties are rotted and uneven, making precarious footing. The spacing doesn't fit a natural gait.

At first I try to alter my stride so that I strike a tie each time I land. This forces me to shorten my stride to the point that my balance is off. I take myself back to my natural stride length. This forces my landings to alternate between the gravel of the berm and the rotting platforms of the ties. The gravel gives beneath my feet, requiring me to compensate and dig in a little harder on the push off. The ties are firmer but more uneven, often making me shift left or right to land on the smoothest piece of wood.

"Harder than it looks," Frederico grunts.

"Yeah."

I keep my eyes on the ground, avoiding the worst of the rotting planks and some of the sink holes in the berm. The importance of keeping your eyes on the path is a well-known fact among trail runners. Frederico once told me it's not *if* you fall as a trail runner, but *when* you fall. Let the eyes stray from the trail for even a second and a runner can end up eating dirt. I've done that very thing myself more times than I can count.

I start to notice the plants around mile twelve. Low, scraggly plants fill the abandoned tracks. Even though it's nearly noon, they are still saturated with rainwater from last night. With each stride, our legs and feet swoosh through the wet plants.

The legs of my compression pants are soaked. Water collects inside my shoes, saturating the outside and squishing on the inside with every step I take.

"Um, Frederico? Are your shoes filled with water?"

"Yeah."

Saturated feet are a runner's worst nightmare. Wet feet combined with the friction of running is a recipe for epic blisters.

"This is bad," I say. "It's too early for us to trash our feet."

"It's too early to get eaten alive," he replies. "We can always figure out a way to dry out our socks."

Can't argue with that. "I don't suppose you learned how to start a fire with old newspaper and a Corona bottle during your less respectable days?" I ask.

"Unfortunately, no. But we'll figure something out. You didn't think this was going to be easy, did you? Ultras aren't fun because they're easy."

He's right. The thrill of an ultra comes from doing something impossibly, excruciatingly hard. Of course, my son's life has never depended on the results of a race before.

"Remember, Jackalope. One mile at a time. We can do this."

By mile fourteen, I'm soaked from the bottom of my knees to the bottom of my feet. On top of the wet clothing are the cattails and burrs from the weeds. They catch in my pants, shoes, and socks. Some have wormed their way past the fabric. They rub at the skin of my legs and ankles.

"We should have put on some gaitors," Frederico calls back to me.

Gaitors are cloth coverings that fit over shoes and ankles. They keep debris out of shoes and socks. Now is not the time to dwell on the three pairs left behind in my hatchback.

"Better burrs than zombie teeth, I suppose," I grumble.

"Good point, Jackalope."

The railroad heads into a hilly area covered with oak trees. With the spring rains, the hillsides are bright green. There are still vine-yards, but they are few and farther between. The strip of land called home by the railroad is lined on either side by pasture fence.

"I think I like being inside the fence," I say, gesturing to the parallel lines of barbed wire.

"Yeah, so long as the zombies are on the other side and not in here with us," Frederico replies.

When I look down at my watch and see that we're at mile fifteen, I reluctantly admit it's time to eat. If we don't keep up a steady source of fuel, we'll bonk. Bonking is what happens when the body runs out of fuel during a run; it includes, but is not limited to, puking, extreme fatigue, cramping, and depression. Every runner strives to avoid bonking. I think longingly of the half-eaten breakfast left behind at the diner this morning.

Without slowing, I dig an energy bar out of my pack. Ripping it open, I hold out half to Frederico. He shakes his head.

"You eat it. I'm fine."

"Uh-uh," I say. "It's time to refuel."

"You go ahead," he says. "I can go a bit longer."

"Didn't we agree not to be idiots?" I push the bar back in his direction. "I can't make this run by myself. You need to eat. *I* need you to eat."

He grunts and takes the bar from me, shoving the whole thing inelegantly into his mouth.

Over the next mile, I parcel out the last two energy bars. Then I move onto the electrolyte tablets. Frederico takes the rations word-lessly, obediently consuming whatever I pass his way.

11

ONE TOUGH MAN

MILE SEVENTEEN.

"Do you remember when we first started running together?" I ask. "Kyle was ecstatic when he found out you were a runner."

"I remember." Frederico snorts. "He hated the fact that you ran alone. He had visions of you breaking your leg and rotting away on the trails."

"And getting eaten by a rabid mountain lion in the process." I laugh fondly at the memory, even though it had been a bone of contention in the early years of our marriage. I loved my time out on the trails, but Kyle always worried about me. We'd had our share of fights about my running, or at least we did until I started running with Frederico.

"There's something I've wanted to ask you since our first run together," I say.

He glances over at me with an amused expression. "And you decided now is the time to satisfy a lifelong curiosity?"

"Well . . . it's the apocalypse."

"True. Let's hear it."

"On that first day we ran together, you told me that you started running to stay sober."

"I did."

"Why running?"

"What do you mean?"

"Why did you pick running to help you stay sober?"

Frederico doesn't immediately reply. As we cover another half a mile in silence, I know he's mulling over his answer.

"If you'd asked me that question ten years ago, I'd have told you I was running away from myself," he says a last. "That's what I told my sponsor for years. It's partially true, but it's not the whole story. Alcoholics are notorious for lying, you know."

I stay quiet, waiting for him to continue.

"When I was ten, my dad took me for a hike in Yosemite. We got up at six in the morning to hike Half Dome, which is fourteen miles round trip. Part way up the trail, we paused to catch our breaths and drink some water.

"While we stood there, a runner passed us. 'What's your hurry?' my dad called after him. Without looking back, the runner said, 'Training for an ultramarathon. Doing two loops to Glacier Point and back today.'

"Dad and I stared after the man, dumbstruck. It's a good twenty miles round trip to Glacier Point and back. And that guy was going to do it *twice*. It sounded impossible. Insane, even.

"'Now that's one tough man,' Dad said.

"After that, we capped our water bottles and continued our hike. We never spoke about the ultrarunner again. But that moment stayed with me.

"When I decided to quit drinking, I knew I had to be tough. The only thing that sounded tougher than going sober was running to Glacier Point and back two times.

"When I finally admitted to myself that I needed to stop drinking, I took every bottle of alcohol I had in the house and threw them in the trash. Then I got in my car and drove all the way to Yosemite. Got there at three in the morning.

"I parked my car, drank four cans of Red Bull, and started to run."

"Ug." I grimace, trying to imagine running with six cans of Red Bull in my stomach. "What happened?"

"What you'd expect. I was wearing cheap tennis shoes from Walmart and jeans. The chafing from the jeans started around mile five. I made it about seven miles before the blisters on my feet got really bad. And I made it another three miles before I started throwing up. Some hikers found me and helped me back to my car. I had another four-pack of Red Bull in my trunk. I was famished, so I drank three, then threw up again.

"I had chafing all around my waist and thighs, so I took off my pants and drove away. I was starving, but I knew I couldn't walk into a store or restaurant in my underwear. I had to drive thirty miles to find a drive-thru. I scarfed down two burgers, two large sodas, and two orders of fries.

"I had a long time to think on the drive home. What I came to realize was that I wasn't as tough as I hoped or thought I was. I decided that come hell or high water, I was going to make myself tough. I bought three books on ultrarunning and signed up for the Marin Ultra Challenge. I threw myself into training. The race gave me something to focus on. Made it easier to ignore the booze. Been running ever since." He pauses. "Aleisha always says I traded one addiction for another. She wasn't wrong."

"They're not the same thing," I argue.

"I've always been a man of extremes," Frederico says. "Aleisha wants a father who's moderate in his daily practices. I wish I could be that for her. I've come to peace with the fact that I can't. But at least I can be sober."

The pain is there in his voice. She's the wound in his heart that will never heal.

Mile eighteen.

The uneven terrain of the rails blurs by beneath me. First there's the dark, rotted brown of the slots, then the grayish-black of the granite chunks between them. Brown-gray-brown-gray, dotted with invading plants in between.

"Kate." Frederico puts out an arm, halting me. "Do you hear that?"

I scan the countryside around us. It's quiet; no birds, no hum from the freeway—nothing.

And then I hear it: soft, distinct moans.

"Where's that coming from?" I whisper.

Frederico turns in a slow three-sixty. "Somewhere up ahead. We'd know if they were behind us, I think."

"What do we do?"

He shakes his head. "I don't know."

"Maybe we'll get lucky," I say. "Maybe they're on the other side of the pasture fence." I gesture to the barbed wire still bordering both sides of the tracks.

"Or maybe they're on the inside." Frederico grimaces.

"We can't go back," I say.

"I know. Let's just go slow. Can you get the lug nut wrench for me?"

I unfasten it from the back of his pack and hand it off. Then I find a sturdy oak branch on the ground for myself. I grasp it like a baseball bat.

"Ready," I say quietly.

Together, we advance down the tracks, creeping around a bend thick with oak trees. Poison oak wraps around the trunks, thick bunches of it spreading across the ground. Clusters of Spanish moss dangle from the branches.

The moaning grows louder. We freeze, listening.

"Just up ahead." Frederico's voice is barely a whisper.

Pressed shoulder-to-shoulder, we creep forward. The moaning makes my stomach knot. There are definitely zombies up ahead.

What are we doing? I think wildly. *Why are we walking straight toward zombies? Blind. They're blind. Don't freak out. So long as we're quiet they won't know we're here—*

Frederico's hand closes around my wrist, his grip like iron. I follow his gaze.

Bumping up against the barbed-wire fence are three zombies. Their white eyes roll sightlessly in their sockets. From their sturdy boots, shirts, wide-brimmed hats, and dark, tanned skin, I recognize them as vineyard workers. Barbs are caught in their clothing and skin. Drops of blood drip down their fingers.

Beyond them, out in the rows of grapes, are other workers. From the way they mill about in uneven circles, I surmise that they, too, have been turned. I count another six hats.

Nine zombies altogether. And only a barbed-wire fence separates us from them.

Okay, I tell myself. *Just move quietly. Don't make any noise to set them off.*

I give Frederico's hand a tug. He flicks his eyes in my direction and nods. We ease forward, stepping softly. The weeds whisper against our legs. The soft soles of our shoes are silent against the ground.

The zombies moan, shuffling against the fence. Another one drifts out of the vines, stumbling toward them.

One step, then another, and another. Frederico and I keep up a quiet, steady pace. My left hand aches from gripping the tree branch. As far as I can tell, the undead haven't realized our sounds are not part of nature.

Snap.

I cringe as a twig breaks under Frederico's foot. We freeze.

So do the zombies. The moaning ceases. They lift their noses, scenting the air like dogs. Their eyes roll in their heads, out of sync with the rest of their bodies.

Sweat beads along my forehead and drips off my nose. My palm, still gripping Frederico's, is slick. The air is unmoving and crisp, sunlight brilliant as it shines through the trees.

He gives my fingers a squeeze, ever so slightly tilting his chin north. He wants us to keep moving.

Holding my breath, I take several ginger steps. Frederico eases his foot off the broken branch and inches up the tracks with me.

The zombies moan, bumping against the barbed wire. For some reason, their movement makes me relax. There's nothing frantic or predatory in their postures. They no longer scent the air, no longer search for us—or at least, I don't *think* they're searching for us.

Thank goodness for blind zombies. It might be our one saving grace on this mad mission.

We turn a corner, the vineyard zombies disappearing from sight. Frederico's shoulders sag with relief. He drops my hand.

"That was a close one," he whispers. "We—" His sentence turns into a wild shout.

A zombie half stumbles, half crawls out of the poison oak. One mottled hand latches around Frederico's ankle. One yank, and he goes down.

12

SPIKES

THE ZOMBIE HAS SHAGGY GRAY-BLACK HAIR AND SKIN SEAMED FROM years of sun exposure. He's wearing a thick flannel shirt and blue jeans ripped at the knees. On his back is a large frame backpack filled with supplies. Half his face is missing, the blood-red muscles of his face exposed. Dried blood is matted in his hair and shirt. A stench that has nothing to do with being dead rolls off his body. Who knows how many months have passed since the poor man's last shower.

Another homeless vagabond. I hadn't considered the possibility of running into one—dead or alive—on the tracks. I now realize how stupid that was.

Frederico lands gracelessly, one shoulder hitting the steel of the track. He yelps in pain. The lug nut wrench flies from his hand, landing in a blackberry bush ten feet away. The zombie snarls, trying to haul Frederico toward the poison oak.

I scream, all my caution swept away in a burst of panic. Leaping forward with my oak branch, I swing with all my might at the zombie's head.

It connects. Instead of splitting the zombie's skull, the branch splinters in half.

Rotten. The fucking branch is rotten.

"Dammit!" I fling the branch aside. Why hadn't I tested the wood when I first picked it up?

"Kate, help!" Frederico braces his free foot against one rail, straining against the zombie as it tries to drag him into the poison oak.

I leap forward and deliver a kick to the zombie's head. It snarls and releases Frederico, taking a swipe at me. I scramble backward, trip on a rail, and fall on my ass.

Moving on all fours, the zombie scuttles toward me. I frantically look for something to defend myself—god forbid another rotten tree branch—and I spot a railroad spike sticking halfway out of a tie. Before I can reach for it, the zombie pounces. It lands on my stomach, teeth blindly snapping at my face.

His breath brings with it the rancid smell of death. I grab the creature around the throat, struggling to keep it from reaching me. A wordless shriek pours out of me as I grapple for the loose railroad stake with my free hand.

"Get off her!" Frederico looms over us, reclaimed lug nut wrench in hand. He swings it like a golf club. It connects with the zombie's ear.

Unfortunately, it doesn't puncture the skull. The creature snarls and spins toward Frederico, momentarily forgetting about me.

In that instant, I roll onto my side and wrap my fist around the stake.

"Come on, you dead slug!" Frederico yells, drawing the zombie up the tracks and away from me. "Come and get me!"

The zombie staggers to his feet, groping after Frederico.

Two strong yanks, and the spike slides free in my hand. I jump to my feet and take one, two, three steps—and slam the railroad stake into the back of the vagabond zombie's head.

Blood sprays me in the face. I yelp, spitting and wiping at my mouth. The zombie drops without a sound, landing in a boneless puddle at my feet.

I slump and lean over my knees, breathing hard. I spit a few more times, making sure my saliva is clear. Using the sleeve of my shirt, I do my best to wipe away the blood. It mingles with a few tears. My heart hammers in my chest.

"I'm not cut out for this," I mutter.

A hand squeezes my shoulder. I look up into Frederico's face.

"Do you think the sickness is transferred by contact with blood?" I display the stained sleeve of my shirt. A knot has formed in my stomach.

He hesitates, then shakes his head. "No way to know for sure, but you can't get AIDS from just touching blood. This could be the same." He shrugs. "There's a chance we're going to come into contact with a shitload of zombie blood between here and Arcata. Let's not worry about it until we have to."

I nod, some of the tension in my gut loosening.

"We have to move," he says. "The others may break through that fence at any moment."

My focus swivels outward. Around the corner from us, I can hear the vineyard zombies rattling the barbed-wire fence. One of them makes a terrible baying noise, sounding like a sick hunting dog. Others take up the cry, baying and rattling the fence.

The only things holding that pasture fence in place are metal pickets driven into the ground.

Heart still thudding, I straighten. I spare a single glance for the vagabond's backpack. It's too heavy and cumbersome for us to carry, and there's no time to scavenge. Nothing to do but turn north and run.

We don't look back. It's only a matter of time before the vineyard zombies break down the pasture fence, but we hope to be long gone by the time they do.

Mile nineteen.

The baying fades into the distance. No sign of the zombies behind us. I check my phone. Still no message from Carter.

"Quit looking at that thing," Frederico says. "Focus on our task."

He's right. I put the phone away and keep moving.

We hit an incline, the tracks snaking up a steep hill. We drop into a power hike. We know better than to run the hills with so many miles before us. Running hills in an ultra can kill a runner's race. Better to power hike and conserve energy for the long haul.

"I was scared," I say, huffing alongside Frederico. "When that zombie grabbed you. Really, really scared."

"Me, too, Jackalope."

"I—I don't think I'm cut out for zombie killing. I got lucky." I shake my head. "Luck isn't going to get us to Carter."

"I know."

My voice goes up an octave. "We almost died back there!"

Silence. Our rhythmic breathing fills the space between us.

I expect Frederico to call me Jackalope and tell me everything is going to be okay. I expect him to tell me we're going to get the hang of this zombie killing thing, even if he doesn't believe it himself.

He doesn't do any of those things.

"Do you remember the day Carter told you and Kyle he wanted to be a craft brewer?"

The question takes me aback. "What does that have to do with—"

"Do you remember that day?"

"Of course. He was fifteen. His friends rode their bikes downtown to get ice cream during the craft beer festival. He came back dazzled by the brewers with their big beards and long hair." Despite my current mood, I warm at the memory.

My son has always been on the granola side. The first girl he ever took on a date was a wannabe hippie girl who went braless and wore patchouli. He grew a lumberjack beard at age sixteen. He chose Humboldt State University, probably the most granola campus in the continental US.

"Do you remember Kyle's reaction to the I-wanna-be-a-craft-brewer proclamation?" Frederico asks.

That sobers me. A recovering alcoholic with a son who wants to make beer for a living?

"He had a hard time with it." Actually, he had called Frederico and gone to an AA meeting that night, though Carter never knew about it.

"After that meeting, he bought the Homebrewing for Dummies book. And helped Carter make his very first keg of beer."

"Then wouldn't let him drink any of it." I remember my angry adolescent son trying to take on his stubborn father. "Made him donate the entire keg to the Kiwanis Club for their annual fundraiser."

"They made quite a few kegs together, if I remember correctly."

"Three. And he never let Carter drink any of it. 'Not until you're twenty-one,' he'd say. There's one keg left in our garage. After Kyle died, Carter couldn't part with it."

Frederico halts. He stoops, bending down to stick his hand into a patch of weeds. When he straightens, there's a railroad spike in his hand.

He holds it out to me. "Take it."

I obey, hefting the chunk of rusted metal in my hand.

"I was with Kyle the night he had to come to grips with the fact that his son wanted to make alcohol. I'm going to tell you what I told him that night: you go the extra mile for your kids. You dig deep, get over yourself, and do whatever you have to do to support them. For Kyle, that meant helping Carter make beer. For you, that means sucking it up and learning how to bash the brains out of undead fuckers.

"Remember when you ran the Western States One Hundred and your shoe came off at the Rucky Chucky river crossing? It got swept downstream and we discovered you had accidentally left your spare shoes at home."

I nod. Forgetting my second pair of shoes had been a complete rookie move.

"You ran fifteen miles to the Highway Forty-Nine aid station with only one shoe," Frederico says. "Kyle spent that time bartering with the other crews to get you a replacement. Your foot looked like hell when you arrived. When I asked you how you ran all that way without a shoe, you told me that you just put your head down and focused on your goal. Remember that?"

"Yes," I whisper. Kyle had cracked jokes about me losing pieces of my mind on all the training runs I had done. Meanwhile, he had lovingly cleaned my foot and doused the cuts and abrasions with peroxide.

I recall the extreme focus and determination I'd summoned on that race. I'd wanted so badly to finish under twenty-four hours. The shoe fiasco had set me back, and the one-hundred-mile course ended up taking me twenty-seven hours to complete. But I had finished. I hadn't quit. I hadn't let the setback or the pain stop me.

"That's all you need to do here," Frederico says. "Put your head down and focus on your goal. Bashing in some zombie skulls should be a walk in the park for a woman who can trail run with only one shoe."

Again, I nod. I've done a lot of crazy things on races, but running fifteen miles without a shoe was definitely at the front of the nut job train.

"You've got the mettle for a post-apocalyptic world," Frederico says. "Stop thinking you're a helpless first-world woman who can't survive more than twelve seconds without her smartphone. Be the tough runner who endures utter hell to get a job done. That's who you need to be."

Frederico's words are like a slap of water in my face. They snap me out of my self-pity, reminding me that I'm capable and tough. My grip tightens on the railroad spike.

Maybe he's right. Maybe I am cut out for this world.

"Do you understand what I'm saying?" he asks.

"Yeah." I slide the spike into the front strap on my running pack. It fits snugly and is easy to pull out in a pinch. "Carter needs me. I have to put on my big-girl pants and get this done. No matter what."

I can feel my mental space shifting. I find the place that exists deep inside me—that place of impenetrable toughness that helps me endure long runs and prolonged physical pain.

Frederico, who's watching my face, sees the shift. "That's my girl." He pats my shoulder. "Kyle would be proud."

"He'd tell us we're batshit crazy," I reply, lips quirking. "Do you remember when he showed up at the American River Fifty dressed in that gorilla suit?"

Frederico laughs. "The Cal Trans orange gorilla suit? Yeah, that was grand. He thought a good laugh would get you to the end of that race."

"I got a PR in that race. Never ran a fifty miler in under ten hours again." PR stands for Personal Record. The pride of that day come back to me, along with memories of Kyle's beaming smile. "He kissed me with his gorilla mask and told me I was his bat-shit crazy woman and he loved me."

"He was proud of you, you know," Frederico says.

Yeah. Proud of his insane, ultrarunning wife. God, I miss Kyle so much. I could use a husband in a fluorescent-orange gorilla suit right now.

"Come on, Frederico," I say. "Let's find some more spikes."

There are some perks to running on an abandoned railroad. Within ten minutes, we are both armed with two spikes. They fit perfectly into the front straps on our running packs.

Without another word, we set out.

13

ULTRA DOG

Mile twenty.

The hills keep coming, one after another, undulating before us. We run down the declines and power hike up the inclines. Yellow, white, and purple wildflowers dot the countryside.

A hot spot has formed on the bottom of my big right toe and another on the inside of my left foot.

Blisters. Here they come.

Under normal circumstance, it would be time to stop and swap out for a dry pair of socks.

Today, there is nothing to do except run. The wet weeds continue to whack at my legs. My ankles and the tops of my shoes are covered with cattails and burrs.

Mile twenty-one.

I'm light-headed with hunger. I start to fantasize about food. Biscuits and gravy, turkey sandwich with avocado and bacon. Bacon. Bacon with tomatoes and lettuce on rye bread.

"What I wouldn't give for a Double-Double Animal Style from In-N-Out," Frederico says.

"I'll take a strawberry milk shake," I reply. "With a double order of fries."

Chili fries. Hell yeah. That would be good right now. Chili fries with pizza. And chicken wings with a double serving of buffalo bleu sauce on the side.

"Do you think we'll ever have a chance to eat at In-N-Out again?" I ask.

"Hard to say, Jackalope."

Mile twenty-two.

Something moves in the bushes. I don't hear any sound, just see a slight shivering of the undergrowth contrasting with the quiet, unmoving world around us. I fling out a hand, snagging the hem of Frederico's shirt. He gives me a questioning look, and I gesture toward the bushes.

We each pull out a railroad spike. Standing side by side, we scan the tall weeds. Again, I see that oh-so-delicate shiver of the undergrowth.

I tighten my grip on the weapon. Frederico drops into a crouch, raising his spike.

How many hobo zombies are out there? I wonder wildly. *Are we destined to have a run-in with every one of them between here and Arcata?*

Something whines, then barks.

I let out an audible breath.

A dog. It's just a dog.

The animal creeps forward, ears flat and tail tucked between its legs. It's a mixed mutt with long legs and short, brown-black fur.

"Come here, buddy." Frederico holds out a hand.

The dog whines again and slinks forward. It bypasses Frederico and comes to me, pressing a wet nose against my arm. I rub its head and neck. It leans against me, nearly knocking me over. I shift into a better position. Frederico joins me, both of us petting the animal.

My hand connects with a collar. It's a dirty, grimy orange.

"Her name is Stout," I say, reading the tags. "She's from Willits."

"Stout? As in, Guinness?" Frederico asks.

"I guess so. She's the color of a stout."

"She's a long way from home."

"Not a good sign." I pause, looking up at my friend. "The last beer Kyle and Carter made together was a stout."

"Maybe it's a sign."

"Maybe." I shrug, rising. "Come on, we have to keep moving." I give the dog one last pat.

When we break into a jog, Stout follows us. Frederico and I glance at each other without stopping.

"I wonder how long she can keep up with us?" I say. Dogs are fast runners, but they aren't cut out for long distance.

"Six, maybe ten miles at most," Frederico replies.

"She did come all the way from Willits. That's gotta be at least— what?—maybe forty miles or so from here?"

"Sounds about right. But who knows how long that journey took her?"

"Maybe we have an ultra dog on our hands."

"Ultra dog? I like that sound of that. What do you think, girl?" Frederico asks.

Stout wags her tail, ears pricking up as she paces along beside us. We have officially transitioned from a running duo to a running trio.

Mile twenty-three.

An old metal bridge comes into view, straddling the land that rises up on either side of the railroad tracks. The bridge is a hulking mass of trussed steel that's been painted a dark green. I recognize it. That bridge means we're about a mile away from the tiny hamlet of Hopland.

Frederico and I slow beneath the shade of the bridge, pausing to suck water from our near-empty hydration packs. Graffiti tags adorn the bottom of the bridge with garish color.

"We need to find water," Frederico says. "My pack is almost empty."

"Mine, too." I hesitate, then add, "We need fuel, too." As if either of us could forget how hungry we are. I've been dreading this time, even though I knew it would come.

"Water has to be the priority," Frederico says. "If we see an opportunity to get food, we can take it, but let's focus on water."

I shake my head. "We can't run two hundred miles on water."

He sighs and makes a face. "I know. I'm deluding myself because the idea of foraging for food scares the shit out of me."

The sound of a police car siren fills the air. We freeze, both of us automatically looking up at the bridge above us. The sirens draw closer, the wails growing louder.

Moments later, the sirens shut off. This is followed by the sound multiple car doors slamming.

"Police," I whisper. "They're just above us."

Frederico nods.

We remain where we are, crouched beneath the bridge. I hear the muffled voices of the police officers talking, but it's impossible to make out their words.

"Let's get closer," I whisper.

Frederico nods. With Stout by our side, we creep out from under the bridge. We manage to work ourselves to high ground. Luckily, a thick screen of oak trees growing beside the highway provides cover. The underbrush is thick and rough. There's poison oak, too. Nothing to be done about it. I lift my hands and elbows, doing my best to keep them above the poison oak. At least my legs are protected by long pants, but poor Frederico is bare from knee to thigh. Dozens of little cuts cover him.

Peering through the thick foliage, we see four Mendocino County police cars and eight cops. They've created a barricade with their squad cars at either end of the bridge.

"How long are we supposed to blockade the road?" one officer asks.

A dark-haired woman with the shoulders of a linebacker shrugs. "CDC said they'd have military reinforcements here in the next twelve hours."

"Shouldn't we be wearing, I don't know, biohazard suits or something?" another officer asks.

The woman shakes her head. "It's not airborne. They said it's transferred through bodily fluids. If someone contracts the disease, symptoms manifest at different rates. Some people show symptoms within hours, others not for a few days. Those are the only details they gave me. Here, we have these." She tosses a box of latex gloves onto the trunk of the nearest squad car. "We should all wear these when talking to civilians."

I tuck away these few pieces of information, mentally flipping through all the zombies we've encountered so far. Every single one of them bore some trace of a wound or bite mark. This makes sense, giving what the woman cop said about the disease being transferred through bodily fluids. This also means we don't have to worry about getting zombie blood on our skin.

"This disease must be pretty bad if they're shutting down roads and setting up CDC checkpoints," says the first officer. "Seems unlikely we have to worry about it this far south of Portland. We're going to have some pissed off people on our hands when we try to explain this."

"Here comes one now," the woman says, shading her eyes as a gray SUV hurtles down the road.

Frederico tugs on my arm. I nod, pulling back from the road. We retreat to the railroad tracks, which are conveniently tucked behind the oaks and shrubs.

"CDC is pushing their checkpoints farther south," I say quietly. "This isn't good."

"Being on foot is going to be an advantage," Frederico replies. "It'll be easier to evade the authorities."

I pause, staring north. I can just make out the outline of Hopland. The idea of going into another town isn't appealing after the cluster-fuck we encountered in Cloverdale.

"I don't suppose you're ready to take a chance with the river water?" I gesture to our right, where the Russian River babbles along. The water is clear and crystalline, but cluttered along the edges are discarded soda bottles and chip wrappers. "What do you think?"

Frederico grunts. "Too much irrigation nearby. I'd hate to screw up our digestive tract with bad water this early. Especially when there are alternatives."

He's right, of course. The river flows by dozens of vineyards and other farmland. Not to mention all the people who use the river for recreation. There's no telling what's in this water.

"Then we have to take our chances in Hopland?" I ask reluctantly.

"All we need to get to Arcata is food, water, and our feet," Frederico replies. "We're out of the first two. We have to stop in Hopland if we want to make it to the finish line."

The fear I experienced in Cloverdale resurfaces, making my chest tight. Stout, perhaps sensing my anxiety, leans against my leg. I reach down, scratching her between the ears.

"Okay," I say quietly, all my dread filling that single word. "Let's go."

14

HOPLAND

Frederico, Stout, and I lie on our stomachs in the weeds, surveying Hopland. The tiny town is home to less than one thousand people. It's known for a solar living center and ostrich burgers (the two not being related). From our current position on the abandoned railroad track, we have a clear view of the back of the solar center.

My parched tongue sticks to the roof of my mouth, an uncomfortable feeling. I suck futilely on my straw, getting a few measly drips of stale liquid. Hunger makes me light-headed.

"It looks quiet," Frederico says. "No signs of zombies. At least, not from here. We'll need to be careful."

I glance south, back in the direction of the police. Already, I can see the bright spots of cars stalled by the barricade.

"There's a gas station on the north end of town," I whisper. "That would probably be a good place to get water and food."

"The tracks run along the back of town. Let's just follow them in."

I scratch Stout between the ears. "What do you think, girl? Gas station?"

Stout flicks her floppy ears in my direction, tail thumping on the ground.

I pull out my phone. There's a message from Carter.

Still barricaded in room. Making spears out of chair legs.

My boy always was industrious. He got that from his father. Despite the situation, I can't help but feel parental pride.

In Hopland with Frederico, I reply. *Police barricade at Hopland bridge. CDC blocking all transit in and out. R soldiers coming 2 help u?*

Military placed everyone under house arrest, Carter replies. *Can't see what's going on.*

I recall that Carter's dorm window looks out at the back of another dorm building. He's stuck in his room with no way to see anything. Shit. I hate being so far away and unable to help.

Sit tight, sweetie, I reply. *Have to put phone away now. Text later. F and I are going to try and find food and water. Stay safe. Luv u.*

Luv u 2.

My chest tightens and tears momentarily sting my eyes. Carter might be twenty years old, but he's still my baby boy.

"What the fuck are all those soldiers doing in Arcata if they're not rescuing the kids?" I mutter, sliding the phone back into my pack.

"What?" Frederico turns to me, not quite catching my words.

"Nothing," I reply. No reason to dwell on something I can't change. "Carter is still barricaded in his dorm room."

"He's a smart kid. He'll be okay until we get there."

We skim down the tracks. Stout falls into step with us, tail wagging.

I spot a military jeep zipping by on the outskirts of town, speeding toward the barricade. Inside are four men in camouflage uniforms.

My attention strays as I follow their passage with my eyes. That's when my foot catches on a railroad tie.

I fly forward, knees striking another tie with an audible *thunk*. My wrists land in soft dirt and weeds. I lie there for a moment, stunned from the impact.

Stout pushes her nose against my cheek, whining. Frederico's shadow falls across us.

"Will it make you feel better if I tell you that was one of your more graceful falls?" he asks, holding out a hand to help me up.

"Not really." I grimace, taking his proffered hand and pulling myself up. Both knees throb. "Did you see that military jeep?"

"Yeah. Don't worry about that now." Frederico points to the wooden tie. "Look. You dented the wood."

Sure enough, two gashes mar the wood. The fact that it's rotted does not make me feel better. I lean over, picking splinters out of my knees.

"At least you're wearing long pants," he says.

I grunt, straightening and flexing my knees back and forth. Ouch. "Why couldn't I have tripped at mile one hundred ninety-nine?" I ask.

"Because this wouldn't be the run of your life if it was easy." Frederico gives my shoulder a squeeze. "Come on. We need to keep moving before more soldiers show up."

I force myself to move, even though the pain in my left knee feels like a knife. Hopefully it will shake itself out in a few miles. If it doesn't, it's going to be a major bitch in another fifty miles. Not to mention one hundred miles.

I don't even want to think about what it's going to feel like in another fifty miles, let alone another one hundred. Maybe I can snag a bottle of Ibuprofen at the gas station. At least some of the discomfort in my right knee is dissipating. One bad knee is better than two.

As we enter Hopland, Stout whines. She flattens her ears and tucks her tail between her legs. I half expect her to ditch us, but she doesn't.

We near the solar center, a fenceless facility sprinkled with yurts and large chunks of greenery. Between the parking lot and the tracks is about one hundred yards of open grassland. From here, the center looks quiet and deserted.

On quiet feet, we move deeper into the tiny town of Hopland. Stout slinks along beside us, nose raised to sniff the air. Thank goodness she doesn't bark.

The open land to our right is swallowed up, replaced by warehouses and some rundown buildings. To our left is the fenced lumberyard.

I spot a single bloody security guard behind the chain-link fence of the lumberyard. Fear grips my throat, making it difficult to breathe. Part of me wants to sprint, to get through the town. Another part of me wants to curl up into a tiny little ball.

Both options are stupid. Our best chance of staying alive is to move at a silent, sedate walk.

Beyond the warehouses, farmland opens up on our right. To our left are the backs of storefronts lining the main road through town. There's an odd quiet that sets my teeth on edge.

Between the buildings on our left are long alleyways, giving us glimpses into the town. A group of older men in Hawaiian print shirts bump into one another just outside a wrecked Mustang convertible. They look like tourists. There are two smashed wine glasses on the ground outside the car. I can't tell where the blood ends and the wine begins. A map of the Mendocino wine country blows across the tracks, bits of blood spattered on it.

What the fuck were we thinking? Why did we think it was a good idea to come into town? My parched mouth doesn't seem like a big deal anymore. Neither does our lack of food.

How the hell did the cops and the military patrol miss these guys? What else have they missed?

Frederico reaches out and squeezes my hand. I squeeze back. We don't speak or do anything that might draw attention to us. I indicate Stout with a flick of my fingers, still worried the animal will bark or whine. Frederico glances at her, then shrugs.

I ease both railroad spikes out of my pack, gripping them with sweaty hands. Frederico raises his lug nut wrench. We gingerly pick our way down the tracks. I step on the soft dirt between the ties in an effort to make as little noise as possible.

Stout seems to understand the need for quiet. She keeps her tail tucked between her legs and she pads along beside us.

Frederico waves his hand at me, drawing me to the edge of another alleyway. One hundred yards down the narrow street is Hopland's only gas station. It perches at the north end of town, a cracked yellowed sign proclaiming GAS. It has two pumps, a mini-mart—and another military jeep in its parking lot.

One soldier has his back to us as he fills the car with gas. Another walks out of the store with a bag in one hand, his other hand resting on his gun. There are two more in the jeep, both of them scanning the town. One of them shifts, head turning in our direction.

I hiss and leap behind a wall, Frederico right beside me. My heart pounds erratically in my chest.

Taking a gulp of air, I turn and run, putting as much distance between us and the soldiers as possible. Even though I know they're here to protect people and stop the spread of the outbreak, to me they're nothing but a potential obstacle between me and Carter. No way am I going to let those men catch me.

Frederico and Stout run along beside me. Stout's ears are pressed flat against her head. There are no sounds of pursuit, making me think—hope—the soldiers didn't see us.

A few minutes later, a big red-and-white *Ace Hardware* sign rises into the air. A chain-link fence encloses an outdoor storage area behind the store.

Just outside the fence are two teenage boys in red Ace Hardware vests. They're crouched on the ground, chewing on another person who once wore a red vest. Just beyond them, the chain-link gate hangs open.

Besides the two zombies and their victim, the back of the hardware store is deserted.

Frederico hoists his spike, giving me a *look*. I nod in understanding, lifting my own spike. We need to make our move here. This is the last store in Hopland, our last chance to find food and water. It's not a great choice, but it's all we have. If we don't get food and water now, who knows when we'll get another chance. Stout pricks up her ears, watching us.

Heart pounding, I creep up behind one of the feeding zombies.

This is for Carter, I tell myself. For my son, I can be strong. I *will* be strong.

I ignore the fact that I am about to put a railroad spike through the head of a teenage boy. Old world rules don't apply anymore. If I can't be strong, I'll never make it to my son.

Adrenaline roars in my ears. I pant for breath, the way I might after a hard sprint.

I come up behind the zombie and seize a handful of short dark hair. It snarls in surprise, rearing back. A chunk of skin dangles from his mouth.

I sense myself mentally shifting into the space I reserve for ultra races; the mental space that allows me to push onward, even when things are hard.

I ram the spike downward with all my might. I'm not a particularly strong woman, but I've got leverage on my side.

There's an instant of resistance as the spike connects with the skull; I feel the moment when the rusty iron shatters the bone and slides into the wet, squishy interior. The zombie teen drops to the ground in a motionless puddle, the chunk of skin still dangling out of his mouth.

I get my first glimpse of the person he'd been feeding on. It's a teenage girl, no more than sixteen or seventeen. Her stomach cavity has been ripped open, her insides shredded.

Beside me, Frederico drops his zombie, the railroad spike buried in the teen's temple. Blood sprays across his pink running shorts. He releases the dead zombie, moving toward the eviscerated girl.

"Can't leave her to rise," he says softly, then hammers the spike down into her skull.

My hands shake. I lift them, staring at the blood that flecks them. My empty stomach roils.

"You did it, Jackalope," Frederico says. "I knew you had it in you. Come on."

He steps over the bodies, heading through the gate. I follow with Stout at my side, adrenaline still hammering in my blood.

15

ACE HARDWARE

As we cross the threshold, a car horn blares. I freeze. Stout's ears go flat.

Seconds later, there's a crash—the sound of shattering glass, crumpling metal, squealing tires, and a loud boom that makes me think a vehicle ran into a building.

Frederico grabs my wrist, pulling me inside the fence. We're in an outdoor storage area covered with corrugated metal. Floor-to-ceiling pallet racks hold building supplies—bricks, lumber, sheetrock, and the like. Frederico leads us down an aisle lined with different sorts of bricks and pavers used in landscaping.

Stout's collar makes a soft tinkling noise as it shifts on her neck. In this deathly quiet area, it's like a gong going off.

Ahead of me, Frederico turns right around a corner. Paranoid Stout's collar may make more noise, I pause and wrap one hand against the jingling collar. With my other hand, I deftly unfasten the buckle. Taking care not to make any noise, I set the orange collar on the ground.

As I stand up, a zombie shuffles into sight. I swallow a shriek, stumbling back a few steps. I bump against a pallet and accidentally nudge a brick. It shifts, making a soft grating sound.

The zombie's head swivels, tracking the noise. It's a middle-aged woman with bangs teased halfway to heaven. She wears a red Ace Hardware vest. Her neck and one shoulder are gouged with blood and bite marks. Despite the obvious violence she's endured, not a hair on her head is out of place—a testament to the amount of hair spray applied.

The zombie moans and shuffles forward a few steps, reaching out toward the sound with her hands. I sidestep the grasping fingers and press myself against the bricks beside Stout. The dog slips her tail between her legs and cowers against the ground. I knot one fist in her brown-black fur.

Neither of us makes a sound.

The zombie stops just in front of us, sniffing the air. It's so close I can smell the ten pounds of hairspray holding up her bangs. My heart thuds erratically.

Her head rotates, white eyes rolling sporadically in her head. She inhales deeply, leaning toward us.

My left hand inches toward the stake in my running pack. I hold my breath, afraid even a small exhalation will draw her attention.

Fingers slick with sweat, I work them around the spike. Only twelve inches separate me from the sniffing zombie. Behind me is a pallet of bricks, which leaves me very little room to maneuver. When I draw the spike, I won't have the leverage I had last time.

The zombie snarls, lips peeling back from her teeth.

Fear shoots through my bloodstream like a rocket. My sweaty fingers fumble with the spike.

The zombie's neck muscles bunch as she prepares to strike.

I yank out the spike.

A single red brick drops into the aisle. It lands ten feet to my left, making an obnoxious clatter against the cement.

The teased-out zombie lurches toward the sound. A second brick drops farther down the aisle, drawing the zombie farther away. She gnashes her teeth, jerking toward the second brick.

Seeing the sudden opening, a surge of adrenaline shoots through me. Not giving myself time to think, I leap at the zombie's back. She turns, but my railroad spike is already punching through her skull. The rusty metal bores through the hard layer of bone before sliding into her brain.

The zombie collapses. I lean over my knees, breathing hard. After a moment, I pull the spike out of her bloodied, hair-sprayed head.

Only sheer willpower keeps me from throwing up. Now is not to time to indulge in revulsion.

Frederico looks down at me from the top of the pallet rack, giving me a grin I can't return. He gives me a thumbs-up, then gestures for me to follow him.

Stout rises, ears pricking up at the sight of our friend. We start down the aisle, scurrying away from the dead zombie.

A sudden, frantic gesture draws my eyes upward. Frederico mouths something to me, waving both arms at the end of the aisle. The look on his face says everything.

More zombies.

Beside me is partial pallet of cinder blocks. I scramble on top of it, squeezing between the cement rectangles and the rack above it. Stout hops up beside me, nostrils flaring. We lie side by side draped on top of the cinder blocks.

Five seconds ticks by. Ten.

Three zombies lumber into view. None of them have the red vests of Ace employees. They are—were—customers. They groan and emit soft, guttural sounds. Each has some sort of bite wound of varying degrees, one lady with half her calf chewed off. She crawls, her ruined leg dragging loudly against the floor.

As the zombies wobble down the aisle, I feel stupid for even worrying about blisters, thirst, and hunger. Those seem like small, stupid worries in the face of three monsters.

A spike of paranoia goes through me. What if the zombies have a supernatural sense of smell? What if they not only hunt by sound, but also by smell? Did teased zombie smell me only because I was close, or had she sniffed me out sooner?

I delicately nudge my nose into my armpit—and immediately pull it back out again.

Fuuuuck. I stink to high heaven.

One zombie—a fat man in a tight wifebeater—smacks right into our rack. He bounces off and rights himself, standing only a foot away from where Stout and I hide.

He tilts his head. At first I think he's sniffing, but then he shifts his body by ten degrees and takes another step. When he runs back into the pallet rack, he turns another ten degrees. This time, he finds a clear path.

He continues past us, letting out a soft moan as he does.

I let out a breath, relieved. It doesn't appear they hunt by smell. Thank god for small favors in the middle of an apocalypse.

From atop the pallet rack, Frederico hurls another brick. The first one strikes the fat zombie on the side of the head. Blood oozes out of his temple, and he drops to the ground.

The next brick misses its target, a white-haired woman with dirt-stained pants. She draws close to me and Stout, trips over the fat man, and falls to the ground.

She's close enough for me to touch. Climbing back to her feet, she tilts her face upward and snarls.

Frederico throws another brick. This time he aims down the aisle, drawing the old woman away from us. She follows the sound.

I don't know what Stout has been through, but it's clear that somewhere along the way she got an education about the creatures. The flick of her ears is the only response to the close proximity of the zombie.

Frederico throws three more bricks before, at last, felling the old zombie.

All that remains now is the zombie with the half-eaten leg. She drags herself down the aisle, somehow managing to miss running into the fat zombie.

A brick sails through the air and thunks into the back of her head. She goes still, the brick having crumpled the back of her skull.

I remain where I am for another thirty seconds. When no more zombies appear, I cautiously extricate myself from the pallet rack with Stout.

We make our way to the end of the aisle and find Frederico climbing down. I mouth a *thank you* at him. He nods, then motions for me to follow.

There's a bathroom ten feet in front of us, the door is closed.

I press one ear to the door, listening. Nothing. I cautiously ease the door open. The room is dark and empty.

I flip the switch, grateful to find electricity still working, and slip inside. Frederico and Stout follow me.

I head straight to the sink, pulling off my pack and unfastening the seal on my water bag.

Frederico stands over the toilet and turns his back to me. I politely look away while he takes a leak. This isn't the first time we've had to piss in front of each other.

I fill my bag, then stick my mouth under the faucet and take a long drink. Cool liquid splashes over my tongue, helping relieve the sticky, parched feeling. It does little to relieve the hunger gnawing inside me.

I take my turn on the toilet while Frederico fills his water bag. After relieving myself, I take a minute to assess my feet. I pull off my shoes and turn them upside down. A thin stream of water runs out. Shit.

In a race, I always have extra socks and shoes for situations just like this. No such luck now. I hadn't thought of wearing my water-proof shoes. I reserve them for rainy days, since they trap heat around the foot.

I gingerly peel off the socks, wincing at the sight of a giant blood blister that's already formed on the side of my right foot. That's not going to be pleasant in another fifty miles.

There are other blisters, most of them along the tops of my toes. When those get bigger, I'll start losing toenails. There's another large clear blister forming on the top of my left foot. The skin on both feet is whitish and wrinkled from the damp.

I wring out the socks and vigorously shake the shoes, doing my best to disgorge the water. I even stick my fists inside and press on the soles with the shoes upside down, trying to squeeze out as many droplets as I can.

What we need is a hair dryer. I consider trying to find one in the store but immediately dismiss the idea. A hair dryer, even if I could find one, would make too much noise.

Nothing to do but embrace the wet feet, the impending blisters, and move on.

Frederico spends a little time tending to his feet. Stout sticks her head in the toilet and laps eagerly at the water. Poor thing. How long has it been since her last drink? How long has she been on her own?

When the dog is done drinking, I crouch down next to Frederico. I hold my mouth very close to his ear.

"We need to find food," I whisper, voice barely audible.

"There should be snacks near the cash registers," he whispers back. "Candy, granola bars—something. Let's try that."

He gets to his feet. I don't bother asking about them; no doubt they're as trashed as mine are.

We stand in silence, staring at the bathroom door. Some part of me wishes we could stay here and hunker down, maybe wait out the shit storm. This tiny six-by-six gray room is the safest I've felt since we fled Healdsburg.

But there's no telling if there's an end in sight. If this is the end of the world, hiding in a hardware store bathroom won't solve anything. It certainly won't help Carter and Aleisha.

Steeling my nerve, I press my ear to the door and listen. Silence.

My hands are slick with sweat as I rest my fingers lightly on the door handle. I just need to push the handle down, but fear petrifies me.

Years ago, I ran Leadville, a one-hundred-mile trail race through the Colorado Rockies. I had the brilliant idea to ditch my jacket at the first aid station. I spent the next thirty miles getting strange looks from other runners. I thought I had mud on my ass or something.

Then I hit the summit at Hope Pass and it started to hail. It rained for the next seven hours nonstop.

"I feel like the idiot who shows up to race in Colorado without a jacket," I whisper, my hand still frozen on the bathroom door handle. "We're in the middle of the fucking zombie apocalypse with nothing more than running shoes and railroad spikes. We need Uzis, Frederico." I lean against the wall, staring up at the cheap panels on the ceiling.

"Do you remember how we dealt with the rain?" he asks.

"What?" I frown at him.

"At Leadville. Do you remember how we dealt with the rain?"

"You got me a garbage bag from one of the aid stations."

"Yep. And when the mud separated the sole from your shoes, Kyle and Carter taped them together with duct tape. Then you finished the race." He leans in, looking me in the eye. "We're finishers, Jackalope. We finish and survive. Even if all we have are running shoes and rusty railroad spikes, we'll figure it out."

I draw in a deep breath and nod. Yep. Survive. That's what we have to do. Survive so we can get to Carter and Aleisha.

"Besides," Frederico says, "you forgot about Luggy." He hefts the lug nut wrench.

I raise an eyebrow. "Luggy?"

"Yep. I've named him." He grins at me. Despite everything, I can't help my small return smile.

After that, there's nothing to do but suck it up and proceed with our plan.

16

STOREWIDE CLEARANCE

I PUSH DOWN ON THE HANDLE, OPEN THE DOOR OPEN JUST A CRACK AND wait, watching.

The storage area is quiet. There's nothing in my immediate range of sight. I give Frederico a thumbs-up, then ease out of the bathroom.

I pull out my spikes, holding one in each hand. Frederico wields his lug nut wrench. We creep past the pallet racks toward a pair of double swinging doors that lead into the store, each of them set with a small window.

Side by side, we peer through the windows. Stout sits between us, ears pricked forward.

Oh my god.

From the tiny windows in the door, we have a view down a wide store aisle. The shelves are filled with garden supplies—hoses, fertilizes, rubber boots, trowels, ceramic flowerpots, and pesticides. At the end of the aisle is an open space with a large fountain, plants and statuary arranged artfully around it.

And around the fountains are zombies. I try to count, but they keep shifting in their blind wandering. There're at least twelve. One zombie is a little boy in red shorts with a turtle on his T-shirt.

Strung just to the left of the fountain is a bright-red banner that says *Customer Appreciation Day, 50% Off Storewide.*

We've just stumbled into a zombie blowout sale. How's that for luck?

I think of the military jeep and police we saw earlier. They obviously didn't realize how bad things are in Hopland. How long since these people were turned?

"This is bad," Frederico whispers.

I chew my bottom lip. My body is running dangerously low on fuel. My stomach feels like it's been carved out with a spoon. If I don't get food soon, my energy is going to bottom out. I really don't want to go into the store, but we'll never get to Carter and Aleisha if we don't find food.

"The cash registers will be at the front," I reply, keeping my voice to a whisper. "What if we create a distraction and lure them to the back of the store?"

"That might work." He stares through the window for another thirty seconds. "What about getting some weapons?"

I frown. "Do they sell guns here?"

He shakes his head. "I was thinking hammers and screwdrivers. They're easy to carry and would be better than our spikes."

He's got a point. "Maybe we take a detour through the DIY aisle on the way to the cash registers?" I ask.

"We should try," he replies. "See those flower pots on the left side of the aisle?"

"Yeah."

"We're going to run out and pull them off the shelves. Make a shit-load of noise. Then run for it. Stick to the perimeter of the store and make our way toward the registers at the front. With any luck, the sound will draw most of them."

I roll this plan over in my head. "We may run into some between here and the registers."

He nods. "You gotta be ready to fight, Jackalope. Fight and get bloody."

He's right, of course.

Running shoes, railroad spikes, and flowerpots. Not much in the way of a zombie defense arsenal.

Stout sandwiches herself between us as we carefully open one of the swinging doors. Two-thirds of the way open, the hinges let out a loud whine. En masse, the zombies around the fountain freeze. A dozen heads turn in our direction.

Frederico and I exchange panicked looks, then charge forward.

We hook our hands into the terracotta pots and bring them crashing down. They shatter on the linoleum floor, reddish pottery shards flying in every direction.

I pull down one more stack of pots for good measure, then turn and flee. The zombies descend on the aisle in a chorus of growls and moans.

Frederico is by my side as I double back to the end of the aisle and turn right. Stout, who was too smart to follow us down the aisle, rejoins us as we skirt the perimeter of the store.

We haul ass, sprinting out of the garden section and into hardware. I scan the racks of crowbars, hammers, drills, socket wrenches —and there, just to my right, is a stack of screwdrivers.

Shoving the railroad spikes back into my pouch, I snatch up two screwdrivers, wielding one in each hand. Frederico grabs a hammer. The stop takes no more than thirty seconds, then we're off and running again.

A pudgy zombie in an argyle sweater shuffles into the aisle way, heading toward us. Though we aren't making much noise—especially not in comparison to the frenzy behind us in the garden department —the zombie is close enough to hear us coming. He bares his teeth and snarls, bloody hands grasping at the empty air in front of him.

Shit. I grit my teeth, raise my screwdriver, and break into a full sprint. Using that momentum, I drive my newly acquired weapon toward his eye. His chill, sticky hands close around my upper arms as I run into him, but I force myself to push in closer as I aim for his face. The squish of his eyeball and brains travels up the length of the screwdriver.

The hands immediately go limp, the argyle zombie dropping to the ground. I don't give myself time to think. Wrenching myself free, I yank out the screwdriver and keep going.

We hit the paint section and plunge down an aisle, heading toward the front of the store. Between us and the other end are a twenty-something man and woman in fashionable clothes. If not for the blood staining their clothing and a big bite wound in the woman's cheek, they'd have looked like catalogue models.

I hesitate, wondering if we should backtrack, but Frederico doesn't break his stride.

"You get the woman," he murmurs, sprinting past me.

I nod and pick up speed, using the same technique I used on the argyle sweater zombie. Raising the screwdriver, I aim it right at the woman's eyes. She snarls, sensing my approach, teeth snapping as she reaches out with her hands.

Those grasping fingers make my chest tighten with fear, but I ignore it. If I can run miles and miles at Leadville in muddy shoes held together by duct tape, I can deal with nasty zombie fingers.

I ram the screwdriver into her eye socket, brace my feet against the floor, then yank it back out. I shove the zombie away. She thumps to the ground—right next to her boyfriend, who Frederico has just dispatched with his hammer.

Stout zips past us, forging ahead. She skids to a halt at the end of the paint section, ears pricked forward. Seconds later, she tucks her tail between her legs and rushes back to us.

That is not a good sign.

We creep to the end of the paint aisle, pausing behind the paint-mixing booth. Ten feet beyond the booth are the cash registers.

"Fucking storewide clearance," Frederico whispers. "Dammit."

Beside the registers are six zombies, all of them facing away from us. On the floor are smears of blood and discarded merchandise: a broken cement rabbit statue; a box of nails; a brushed nickel faucet. The zombies are pressed up against the glass windows, staring at the road. From here, I can hear the nearby hum of a car engine. Apparently the car is more of a draw than the flowerpot commotion.

Between the zombies and the cash registers is a rack filled with food: granola bars, candy bars, trail mix, potato chips—every sort of junk food imaginable.

I feel like a treasure hunter standing before a chest of gold. My stomach practically leaps out of my body. If ever there was a time to cue heavenly music, now would be it. My mouth waters, and a wave a fatigue washes through me.

I *need* that food.

All we have to do is outsmart a pack of zombies to get it.

I look down at my hands. Blood is spattered all the way up to my elbows and across my shirt. Behind me lay several dead zombies.

Frederico has blood spattered on his face, a few drops freckling the end of his nose. Our eyes meet in silent agreement.

Time to get some fuel.

17

FUEL

Frederico and Stout guard my back as I slip into the paint booth.

In front of me sits the big automatic paint-mixing machine. There's already a can of paint inside it, probably put there before the zombies swept through the store.

I hit the red button that says *Mix*.

The machine immediately vibrates to life, filling the area with a low, steady rumble. The zombies pawing at the windows turn in half circles and rush the paint station with a collective howl.

The three of us dart out of the booth, ducking behind a rack of wallpaper.

As the zombies converge on the paint station, we skirt around them and dart toward the junk food, Stout at our heels.

My first instinct is to rip open a Cliff Bar. Even though my mouth is watering and my body is screaming for it, I force myself to wait. Making noise with a wrapper is too risky. Instead, I pick up the entire box. Then I grab a box of M&Ms and stack it on top. I'm just reaching for a carton of mixed nuts when I hear a squeal of tires.

The zombies around the paint machine turn, drawn to this new sound. The car engine rumbles loudly, though there's no sign of a vehicle. Two of the zombies break away from the paint machine, reaching out with their hands as they move back toward the glass windows.

"We gotta go," I say to Frederico, grabbing the carton of mixed nuts and throwing it on top of my stack. I hug the food to my chest with both arms. "Now."

Frederico nods, also balancing several cartons of food. We race toward the doors. I turn sideways, throwing my shoulder into the swinging glass door. I pause long enough to let Frederico and Stout barrel by me, then release it.

Other than a few cars in the parking lot, the area is deserted. A stroke of luck, thank god. We cut around the building, heading back to the railroad. As we draw near the back of the store, Stout barks.

It's a high-pitched squeaky bark, strangely feminine. It's the first sound she's made since joining us. Startled, I automatically draw to a halt, looking around in alarm.

Frederico also skids to a halt—but not fast enough. A zombie comes around the back corner. It's one of the old men in Hawaiian shirts we saw a few blocks back. What the hell drew him this way?

He and Frederico smash into each other. There's an explosion of candy bars. Snickers, Milky Way, and Reese's Peanut Butter Cups fly into the air. Frederico and the zombie go down in a tangle of arms and snapping teeth.

I drop my stash of food and raise my screwdriver. Frederico is on his back, arms locked around the zombie's neck as he struggles to keep the jaws from his throat. I pounce and puncture the zombie's skull with the tool.

Blood pours out in a viscous rush, splatting Frederico in the face. He shoves the zombie away and jumps to his feet. I scramble on my hands and knees, trying to scoop up Cliff Bars and shove them back into the cardboard tray.

"Forget the food!" Frederico grabs my arm, hauling me to my feet.

I squawk, momentarily forgetting the importance of being silent. "We need to eat—"

"They're coming!" Frederico hisses. His hand tightens on my arm and he again tugs me upright.

In the same instant, several zombies come around the corner of the hardware store—three more men in Hawaiian print shirts. Blood and wine stains mix on their clothing. Shit!

My free hand closes on two Cliff Bars. Then I give in to Frederico's pull and follow him in a dead run toward the railroad tracks. Stout streaks along beside us.

One Hawaiian-print zombie briefly turns in our direction. At that moment, the car we've been hearing rumbles into view.

It's the military jeep we saw at the gas station, and it's in bad shape. The paint along the passenger's side is scratched and dented. The door is missing. One tire is flat. The front hood is horribly crumpled. Smoke rises from the engine.

I recall the crash I heard earlier. Could it have been this jeep? Is that why it's in such bad shape?

I catch a glimpse of a bleeding, wild-haired soldier leaning into the steering wheel, as though the angle of his body can make the wounded car go faster. There's no sign of the other soldiers we saw with him earlier.

Behind the jeep is a good two dozen zombies. They move down the road at a shuffling run-walk. Every once in a while, one trips and falls. Immune to pain, he or she gets right back up and keeps going.

Had they been pursuing an undamaged car, they wouldn't have any hope of catching it. Pursuing a jeep with one flat tire is a different story. They gain ground on the car and the poor soldier inside. An eerie cacophony of sound rises from their ranks, a mix of moans, cries, and wordless growls.

The Hawaiian print zombies forget all about us and amble in the direction of the jeep.

Time slows. I see the jeep swerve as several zombies gain the open passenger side door. The monsters are knocked over. The vehicle bounces violently as it rolls over the bodies. The driver momentarily loses control, swerves, and hits the curb. There's a loud *bang* as one front tire explodes. The jeep leaps forward, skidding into the hardware parking lot.

The zombies immediately surround it. Two scramble onto the hood, clawing at the glass. Another clings to the open window on the driver's side.

The soldier inside screams in panic, but it's too late. One of the other zombies—a teenage girl that looks close in age to the driver—finds her way through the missing door on the passenger's side and sinks her teeth into the young man's shoulder.

The car skids, the metal of the tire rim making an awful screech against the pavement. The jeep shoots forward, moving with an

unbalanced gait, coming straight for the side of the hardware store
—and us.

"Run!" Frederico shouts.

I turn, breaking into an all-out sprint. Behind us is a tremendous
crash. The jeep plows into the corner of the Ace Hardware, not twenty
feet from where we'd been standing. Zombies close in, completely
blotting the car from view. The soldier's screams gain in pitch. Our
precious food supply is lost under building debris and zombie feet.
The poor soldier inside is lost, swarmed by the undead.

"Don't look," Frederico says, grabbing at my hand. "Keep
running."

I didn't even realize I'd drawn to a halt, mesmerized by the
unfolding horror. I break back into a run. We hit the tracks and push
north at a dead sprint.

18

WHEN THE WHEELS FALLS OFF

MILE THIRTY.

Hopland fades into the distance behind us, the tension of our narrow escape falling away. What remains of the experience is despair.

All that work, all that risk—and we don't have a single fucking scratch of food to show for it.

"Fuck, fuck, *fuck!*" The words come out in a half sob, half moan. I am so goddamn fucking *hungry*. Am I going to have to resort to eating my shoes? I'm ready for it.

"Water," Frederico says. "We got water, Jackalope. One out of two isn't bad."

I say nothing.

"You're bonking," Frederico says. "You can get through this."

I suck on my water straw, trying to satiate my desperate hunger with liquid.

I have nothing to be upset about. Nothing. I'm still alive, unlike that poor soldier. All the soldiers. Everyone in the hardware store. They're all dead. Bonking isn't anything to complain about.

This knowledge doesn't stop me from being pissed. My head throbs. My stomach cramps. My legs feel like blocks of lead. I'm considering the wisdom of eating the weeds cluttering the railroad tracks. I've heard dandelions are edible.

The hunger is wearing on Frederico, too. His shoulders hunch as he runs, chin nearly resting on his chest. His pace is sluggish, yet dogged.

It's not just the bonking that's wearing me down. My knee aches from the fall I took earlier on the tracks. Blisters are building up on my feet. A pressure on the side of my right foot is starting to throb. I need to lance the blister, but I'm afraid if I sit down, I'll never get up again.

Of the three of us, only Stout is in decent shape. She trots beside us, tongue hanging out and ears swiveling.

My foot catches on a railroad tie. I stumble and curse, managing to right myself before taking a face plant. I brace both hands against my knees, breathing hard.

I feel like complete shit. Worse than complete shit.

Frederico slows, turning to watch me. I stare at the weeds pushing through the soft earth at my feet.

Almost every part of me wants to collapse on the tracks and disappear into oblivion, to fade away from the physical pain and discomfort.

Almost every part.

This isn't the first time I've bonked. I wish I could say I'd been smart enough to avoid similar situations in the past, but the truth is that every runner makes stupid mistakes.

THE FIRST TIME I bonked had been at my first 100 kilometer—62 mile —race, the Miwok 100K. I miscalculated my nutrition needs, skipping snacks at two previous aid stations due to an upset stomach. The steep, single-track trails, combined with the heat, depleted all my reserves.

With only a measly thirteen miles to go, I staggered into the Randall Trailhead aid station, ready to quit. I was dizzy, my calves were cramping, and I'd been dry-heaving for the past two hours.

Kyle and Carter were there, waiting for me with all my gear. Carter, only five at the time, had been busy drawing pictures in the dirt with sticks.

"Hey, babe." Kyle greeted me with a hesitant kiss.

I thumped to the ground, feeling too shitty to comfort him with a return kiss.

I wish I could say our relationship had been all rainbows and roses, but in truth, the shotgun marriage and unexpected pregnancy had taken a toll on us. We were in the process of clawing our way out of a hellish hole. His being here was a huge step in the new direction our relationship was taking—and my current mood wasn't doing anything to heal the wounds between us.

Seeing the hurt on his face as I thumped to the ground, I reached out and grabbed his hand.

"Sorry, babe," I said, voice hoarse from the dry-heaving. "Love you. I just feel like complete shit right now."

His mouth relaxed into the kind smile I loved. He pressed his knuckles briefly to my cheek.

"Want me to refill your pack with water?" he asked.

I shook my head as another wave of nausea hit me. I scrambled into some nearby bushes, not wanting Carter to see me heave up bile. Kyle held out a peanut butter and jelly sandwich to me.

"You need to eat," he said. "Get something in your stomach."

I waved the food away. "I can't. I'm done, Kyle. I can't finish." I plopped back to the ground, feeling sorry for myself. "'The wheels fell off my bus,'" I said, quoting Frederico.

Carter, who up until this point hadn't paid any attention to me, perked up.

"Mommy," he said, "when the wheels fall off, just get out and walk! That's what Mrs. Robertson had us do when we went to the pumpkin patch."

It took several seconds for my foggy brain to follow his six-year-old logic. Then I remembered his school bus had blown a tire a mile away from the pumpkin patch a few months ago. Rather than make a group of squirrely kids wait on the bus while the tire was changed, Mrs. Robertson had marched them off the bus, broken them into pairs, and herded them on foot the rest of the way to the pumpkin patch.

When all was said and done, Carter had been more excited by the blown tire and the walk down the country road than the pumpkins. And here he was, months later, still talking about the adventure.

"He's got a good point," Kyle said, glancing at his watch. "You're still four hours under the cut-off time. You could power walk the last thirteen miles and still make it."

"I'm going to be dead last," I groused.

"Who cares?" Kyle replied. "What matters is not quitting when things get hard."

In that instant, the conversation switched from the fate of my race to the fate of our marriage.

When things had gone sideways between us, Kyle had been the most determined to hang on. It was his resolve to save us that gave me the strength to join him in the fight.

Now, looking up into his soft green eyes, I felt that same strength welling up inside me.

I could do this. Even if I had to crawl, I could do this.

"Fuck it," I said, pushing resolutely onto my feet. "I'm doing this. Give me that sandwich."

"Bye, Mommy," Carter said, glancing up from his dirt drawing. "See you at the finish line."

"See you at the finish line, baby boy."

Kyle and I exchanged looks. In that gaze was all that had happened between us. There was beauty, pain, ugliness, but most of all, there was hope.

Kyle kissed me on the cheek, handing me a second peanut butter and jelly sandwich. "For the road," he said. "See you at the finish line."

With that, I staggered off. It took me another three hours and twelve minutes to finish those last thirteen miles. I threw up both sandwiches along the way and spent my fair share of time dry-heaving. I couldn't go any faster than a power walk.

Despite all that, I finished. When I limped into view of the finish line, Kyle and Carter were waiting for me. Carter grabbed my hand. Fueled by his enthusiasm, I forced myself into a jog. Hand in hand with my son, I crossed the finish line. The accomplishment was so intense that I immediately burst into tears. Kyle folded me into a hug, covering me with kisses.

In the end, it wasn't about what my body could do. It was about what my mind could do. Kyle had helped me find the mental strength to finish something my body rebelled against. I couldn't run, but I could walk. Most importantly, I could finish.

DRAWING ON THAT MEMORY, I battle the despair and misery of the bonk. I think of my husband and find strength.

I can go on. I *will* go on.

Fuck pain. Fuck discomfort. Fuck bonking.

19

BONK

Mile thirty-three.

We walk.

The bonk still drags at us, but we continue to put one foot in front of the other. Our feet press into the soil and rocks, swishing through weeds. The rotting ties creak beneath our shoes.

My stomach feels like it's been scraped clean with a spoon. Everything hurts. Blisters throb. Knee aches. Skull feels like it's going to split in half.

Cattails and burrs speckle me from ankle to thigh. They scratch at me through the compression pants, some of them having wormed beneath the fabric. The dozens of small cuts on Frederico's legs have left tiny trails of blood all across his skin.

Still, we walk.

Stout never strays from our side. Her ears are on constant alert, swiveling at sounds we can't hear. I take heart in the fact that she'll sense a zombie before we will. She's only been with us for a few hours, but I already feel like she's family.

We pass vineyards, farm pastures, and open space with native oak trees. The railroad meanders back and forth with the natural curves of the land, always taking us north. The freeway moves in and out of sight.

The farther north we go, the more relieved I am to be on foot. We've passed so many wrecked cars I've lost count. Zombies wander the highway and nearby land. So far, we've been lucky that none have come near the railroad.

Still, I keep my eyes peeled, constantly scanning the land. The rest of my energy goes into propelling myself forward. One step after another, until I get to Arcata. And Carter.

If I don't collapse first.

Don't think like that, I berate myself.

"Tell me why you started running."

Frederico's strained voice jars me.

"What?" I ask stupidly, blinking through my haze of concentration.

"I told you why I started running," he replies. "You never told me why you started."

There's a rough edge to his voice that I recognize. I've only heard him like this a few times, all of them at tough ultra races.

Frederico's at his lowest. He needs me to help distract him from the pain of his fuel-deprived state.

I need someone to distract me from *my* fuel-deprived state.

Suck it up, I tell myself. *Frederico needs you.*

I take a long sip of water, then speak. "I started running to . . . to get away from Kyle." The truth sends a pang through me, even after all these years. "I told everyone it was because I was trying to lose post-pregnancy weight. I even told myself that. It was partially true, but Kyle and I were lost. We lost each other in parenthood, work, and school.

"I waited tables at night. Kyle went to school and worked part-time as an office manager for his parents. We hardly saw each other. When I went to work at night, he stayed up late, drinking. In the morning, when he didn't have to work or go to school, he'd be hungover and in no shape to spend time with me and Carter. I'd be angry that he was hungover, but too wimpy to speak up, so I'd put Carter in the stroller and go out running. Sometimes I couldn't stand being home with him. It didn't matter how hard or how fast I ran. Things didn't get better.

"At first, my runs with Carter were short. Kyle was depressed when we went out without him, so he started drinking during the day. My runs got longer. I'd go out for two, three, four hours at a time. The longer I was out, the more he'd drink. He started skipping school and work.

"I felt guilty for our situation. I was angry and resentful about everything. Parenthood had been a shock for us both, and I thought he needed the drinking to de-stress. I thought he regretted marrying me and having Carter. I thought he needed me to take care of him by buying him beer. How fucked up is that? I was so angry that he was drinking all the time, and I kept buying him beer because I thought I was taking care of him.

"One day, I ran twenty miles to my parents' house and didn't go home." I swallow, throat tight with the memory. Even after all this time, the memory of the pain is vivid and raw. "I stayed with my parents for six weeks, trying to sort out my feelings for Kyle. I had just about convinced myself our marriage had been a big mistake. And then . . ." Again, my throat tightens.

"And then?" Frederico prompts, huffing along beside me.

"Kyle came to my parents' house and told me he'd joined Alcoholics Anonymous and quit drinking. It was two in the morning. I'd gotten home from my shift in the restaurant, and he'd been waiting outside." I remember the way my stomach turned at the sight of him getting out of his car. "He said he loved me, he loved Carter, and he would do whatever he had to do to save our family and our marriage. He already had an AA sponsor. He'd been sober for sixteen days. He was . . . so earnest, so sincere. I . . . I decided that any man willing to work so hard to save our marriage was a man I wanted to meet halfway."

Tears prick the corner of my eyes at the memory. "Carter and I moved back home the next day. I started going to Al-Anon meetings. We got a marriage counselor. Things got better. Things got . . . good. Great, even."

I fall silent, letting out a long, shaky breath. I've never told anyone that story before. Retelling it now brings back all my shame—shame that I had been ready to give up on us, on our family. Shame that I had encouraged Kyle's addiction. Shame that I had run away from Kyle and our problems.

I feel like the dysfunctional, co-dependent, scared young woman all over again. I don't like that part of myself. No matter how far or how hard I run, I can't get away from her. It's the same part of me that went to pieces when Kyle died. There's a weakness inside myself I can't escape.

"In some ways, relationships aren't so different from ultrarunning," Frederico says. "Once you decide you're going to make it to the finish line, you will. Doesn't matter what hell you encounter on the way."

Is that the subconscious appeal of ultrarunning? Do I run to prove to myself that I was good enough for Kyle? Good enough for the man who loved me so completely? The man I almost walked away from? How many miles will it take before I proved to myself that I was worth loving?

I remember I'm supposed to be lifting my friend out of a bonk. A depressing story likely isn't helping him.

"Anyway, that's why I started running," I continue, trying to make my tone lighthearted. "You know how it goes. Before I knew it, I was signed up for my first fifty-kilometer race." Fifty kilometers is equivalent to thirty-one miles; they're considered the shortest ultramarathon distance. "I never looked back after that. Or stopped running."

20

IF I GET EATEN

I GLANCE AT HIM. "HOW ARE YOU FEELING?"

He grunts. "A little better." His face is pinched, the toll of the bonk still plain on his features.

I need to be strong for my friend and help him through this funk. How can I distract him and keep his mind off the pain? Depressing stories obviously isn't the way. If I hadn't been bonking myself, I'd never have told him that story.

I attempt to steer the conversation in a more lighthearted direction. "Let's play: If we get eaten by zombies in the next thirty minutes."

Frederico quirks an eyebrow at me; this is a good sign. "How do we play that?"

"I make a statement, like this: If I get eaten by a zombie in the next thirty minutes, I'll regret never getting to run the Hardrock One Hundred." Five times I'd entered the lottery for Hardrock—one of the most iconic one-hundred-mile races in the country—and had yet to have my name drawn. I grin at Frederico. "Now it's your turn."

"If I get eaten by a zombie in the next thirty minutes, I'll regret never getting to run the Copper Canyon Ultramarathon." He sighs, more of a thoughtful sigh than one of true regret. "I was saving money with the hopes of running that race for my seventieth birthday. With the world going sideways, I doubt I'll make seventy."

"Hell, with the way things are going, I doubt I'll make forty," I reply.

"Guess I don't have anything to complain about." He gives me a small smile. I smile back, relieved to see that some of the stress of the bonk is lifting from both of us.

"If I get eaten by a zombie in the next thirty minutes, I'll die knowing I finished Fat Dog," Frederico says. "Hardest race of my life."

Kyle and I had crewed for Frederico at the Fat Dog 120, a one-hundred-twenty-mile footrace also known as Mountain Madness. The combination of a wet trail and slanted terrain caused him to rip subdermal tissue in his right foot. That had happened around mile ninety-seven. When he'd limped into the Skyline mile ninety-nine aid station, I remember the set lines of his face. His expression told me he was going to finish the race come hell or high water.

"You're one tough son of a bitch," I tell Frederico.

"I paid for that race," Frederico replied, eyes crinkling in fond memory. Only an ultrarunner can look back on ripped foot tissue and intense pain with fondness. "Remember when I had to use a knife to shave the scar tissue off the bottom of my foot?"

"God, how could I forget that? I think you gave Kyle nightmares with that stunt." I laugh at the memory. "If I get eaten by a zombie in the next thirty minutes, I'll die knowing that I finished the Bear One Hundred Mile Endurance Run."

That gets a chuckle out of Frederico. Winter had come early to that September race, and I ran for over ten hours in a snowstorm. In a pink running skirt. That had been hell. Complete hell. A cold, freezing, wet, miserable hell. I'd even gotten frostbite on my legs.

But I'd finished. I'd come in dead last. Despite that—hell, maybe *because* of that—the Bear 100 is the single race I'm most proud of finishing.

"That was the only time I've seen Carter fret about you," Frederico says. "That boy is as calm as they come, but the snow had him on edge."

"Here's to being tough sons of bitches." I hold up one hand and we slap high fives.

"After all we've been through, what's two hundred miles to Arcata?" he says.

"Exactly." I grin.

The heaviness of the bonk is dissipating. Even the worst of the hunger has receded. Things really aren't all that bad.

This is how things go in ultras. They're an ebb and flow—a series of lows and highs strung together by gritty determination. A joke or kind remark can be as nourishing as food.

"If Stout gets eaten by a zombie in the next thirty minutes, she'll die with friends." I reach down to scratch the dog between the ears.

"That dog's too smart to get eaten," Frederico replies. "She'll survive both of us."

I laugh. "True. If I get eaten in the next thirty minutes, I can go to heaven saying I was a dog owner."

Frederico raises an eyebrow. "We've *owned*—and I use that term loosely—Stout for about two hours."

"Doesn't matter," I reply. "She's part of our pack now. That denotes ownership."

"I think we're part of her pack. That means *she* owns *us*."

We both look at the dog. As though aware she's the topic of conversation, Stout pricks her ears in our direction and wags her tail.

I feel more energy returning to me. Not wanting to lose the little momentum we've scraped together, I plow forward with our impromptu game.

"If I get eaten in the next thirty minutes, I'll die knowing what true love is," I say. Kyle's blue eyes flash in my mind. "I'm grateful to have had Kyle in my life."

"If I get eaten in the next thirty minutes, I'll die having experienced the many textures of sobriety," Frederico says. "I'm grateful I had the opportunity to give up drinking. Best and hardest thing that ever happened to me."

"Sounds like marriage," I reply.

"Yeah. It is, in a way." His voice softens. "If I get eaten by a zombie in the next thirty minutes, I'll regret not being able to make amends with Aleisha."

This makes me reflect on my life. "If I get eaten in the next thirty minutes by a zombie, I'll regret never going back to college. I always said I would, someday. Now I guess someday has come and gone."

"Why didn't you ever go back?"

"Kyle always encouraged me to, but I was making good money waiting tables. I couldn't imagine juggling Carter, a job, and college. So I never went. Seems stupid now."

"It's not too late," Frederico says. "If our country pulls out of this zombie apocalypse, you could go back to school."

I stop, planting my feet between two railroad ties. I turn to face my friend.

"Let's make a deal," I say. "If we survive the zombie apocalypse, I'll go back to college and get my degree, and you'll start calling Aleisha once a week, just to say hi. Even if she doesn't answer."

"What if . . ." He pauses, licking his lips. "What if Aleisha is . . . gone?"

I don't have to ask what he means. What if Carter is *gone* when we get to Arcata?

I shake my head. "We can't think like that. Our kids are going to be okay." I give my friend a *look*. "You *will* call your daughter once a week, and I *will* go back to college. When all this shit" —I make a vague gesture to the world at large— "is cleaned up and the world is right side up again. Deal?"

Frederico hesitates, then extends his hand. "Deal."

We shake. A shiver runs through me. There are no more excuses for me. If the world survives—if I survive—I'm going back to school. That's a pretty big if, but even so, I can't help feeling a little intimidated.

Stout lets out a small yip. As a unit, Frederico and I turn in her direction. She sniffs the air, nose pointed north.

Without thinking, I draw my screwdriver. Frederico pulls out his hammer. Both tools are covered in dry blood and bits of sticky matter I don't let myself think too hard about.

"Is it zombies, girl?" he asks.

Stout cocks her head at us, then trots away. We hesitate for a few seconds, then follow.

Several minutes pass before I realize we're jogging. I sense the moment when Frederico has the same realization. We look at each other and grin.

"Another bonk for the books," he says.

"Another bonk for the books," I agree.

We run for another five minutes, Stout leading the way. I glance down at my watch.

"Mile thirty-five," I say. "Only one hundred sixty-five miles to go."

We round a bend of oak trees—and there, in front of us, out here in the middle of nowhere, is a house.

21

BREAKING AND ENTERING

THE HOUSE SITS IN THE MIDDLE OF A LARGE PASTURE, PARTIALLY concealed by ancient, gorgeous oak trees. Stout stops and wags her tail at us, as if to say, *See guys? I knew where I was going.*

Frederico and I crouch behind a large patch of thistles, taking careful surveillance of the scene.

The old farm house has a deep front porch, peeling yellow paint, and second story dormer windows. To the right of the house are half dozen cars in various states of disrepair, all of them classics— two Mustangs, a Cadillac, and several cars with tail fins I can't name.

A few hours ago, my first instinct would have been to see if any of the cars was in working order. Now, between the military blockades and the zombie swarms, I want to avoid all cars like the plague.

There are two cows in the field to the left of the house—both of them dead. Four zombies—two teenage boys and two adults—feed on the animals. A family, before the outbreak got them. And if a family in the middle of bum-fucked Egypt got infected, is there any place that's safe?

"Do you think we can get inside?" I whisper. The property is surrounded by a pasture fence and topped with barbed wire.

Frederico gives me a *look.* "Do we *want* to get inside?"

"If we're quiet, we can avoid the zombies," I reply. "We really need food."

He sighs. "I know."

"Let's try the fence. We can dig under it."

There are natural dips and rises along the property. We find a small stream that has burrowed its way under the fence. We claw at the moist earth, slowly widening the opening.

As soon as Stout realizes what we're doing, she jumps between us. She paws at the earth, sending up great gouts of dirt. Frederico and I fall back, grinning at each other and letting her work. Within minutes, the opening is wide enough for us to crawl through.

Frederico goes first, dropping into the muddy hole and wriggling through. I peer through the fence, watching the zombies eat the poor cows. They give no sign of having heard us.

I follow Frederico, grimacing as I slide through the mud. Yuck. Cold and wet. It slicks the side of my face and the front of my shirt and pants.

Stout is the last one through. The three of us stay near the fence line, edging around the perimeter of the property.

One of the zombies is a little girl, no more than seven or eight. Her profile is outlined against the brilliant green of the surrounding grass as she dines on a cow's large intestine. The scene makes my stomach roil.

A long, low moan rolls across the pasture. I freeze, thinking we've been spotted. Frederico and Stout also halt, all three of us staring in fear at the zombies.

The sound rolls out a second time, and this time I recognize it for what it is: a moo.

One of the poor cows is still alive.

I look at Frederico. He shakes his head and continues on. There's nothing we can do for the poor animal without risking ourselves. Stout tucks her tail between her legs and slinks away.

We reach the porch of the farmhouse. There are signs of violence: blood pools by the front door and smears down the steps; an over-turned chair; a half-eaten finger on the floorboards. The gore makes my skin crawl, but now isn't the time to let my nerves get the better of me. With Frederico on my left and Stout on my right, we mount the stairs.

The old wood creaks underfoot. We freeze, automatically glancing at the zombies. One of them—the father—turns his head in our direction, chewing on a bright-red cow organ as he does. None of the others look up. The father chomps away, white-eyed gaze rolling in our direction.

The ten steps between us and the front door suddenly seem like ten miles. Eyeing the stairs and the battered wooden porch beyond, I see a field of land mines. One wrong step could alert the zombies to our presence.

"We go fast and keep our steps light," Frederico says. "Get inside and barricade the door."

"What if the door is locked?" I whisper back. Logic says it'll be open, since it appears the entire family is out in the pasture with the cows . . . but what if there's someone else? A survivor? An uncle, or a grandma? Someone—or something—inside?

Frederico pulls off his pack, removes his shirt, and wraps it around his fist.

"If the door is locked, I smash through the glass panel." He gestures to the small glass squares that fill the top half of the door, then winks and holds up his cloth-wrapped fist.

Holding up three fingers, I count down: three, two, one.

Tensing all my leg muscles, I bolt up the stairs and across the porch. I stay on my toes, keeping my steps as light as I can. Frederico does the same.

Despite that, the porch groans and creaks like an old man. Only Stout manages to whisper over the worn wood like a ghost.

We make enough noise to draw the attention of the zombies. The mother and teenagers lift bloody faces and turn in the direction of the house, but they don't leave their cow buffet. The father, however, rises to his feet, moans, and takes a few steps in our direction.

Fuck.

I grab the door handle, giving it a desperate wrench.

Double fuck. It's locked.

Frederico doubles back with his fist and rams it into the glass. In a decent display of prowess, he punches through a small pane on his first try.

As he extracts his cloth-covered fist, I dart forward and shove my hand through the opening. Some of the shards dig into my wrist as I fumble with the doorknob and turn the small lock embedded there. I try the knob—and the door swings open.

Stout, zipping past my legs, is the first one through the doorway.

Frederico and I barrel after her. It takes every ounce of self-preservation not to slam the door. I force myself to gingerly close it.

There's a dead bolt and a chain. I slide both of them into place, thankful neither had been in place before; they would have seriously complicated our breaking and entering. With only the doorknob being locked, it makes me suspect—hope—the house is deserted. During whatever violence had ensued when the family was turned, it would have been easy for the door to have swung shut on its own with only the bottom lock in place.

Still, it's never safe to assume.

"Sofa," Frederico whispers to me, moving across ancient, nasty shag carpet to a stained couch in the living room.

We each grab a side and move it in front of the door, then turn and scan our surroundings in silence. Nothing stirs.

With the living room cleared, we move on. Inch by inch, we make our way through the house. I'm armed with a screwdriver and railroad spike. Frederico has his lug nut wrench and hammer out.

We enter the family room. It's crammed with furniture and a large array of video game equipment. It smells like cat urine, a stench that makes my nose itch. A quick sweep of the room shows it to be empty.

Next comes the office and kitchen. Both empty. In the kitchen are three black trash bags filled with empty soda cans and beer bottles. My mouth waters at the sight of a can of kidney beans sitting on the Formica countertop, but I force myself to look away. We can eat when we're sure the house is empty.

We move up the stairs, Frederico in the lead. Blood spatters every stair. At first I try to step around it. After a few steps, I give up. I need to keep my eyes up and not worry about soiling the bottom of my shoes.

We find Stout in the upstairs hall, ears flat. She stares into what looks like the master bedroom.

Fuck. If Stout senses someone, it can't be good.

I mentally steel myself to the reality that I might have to kill another zombie. God, I hope it's not a kid zombie. Or a baby zombie. God, please no. Could I stab a zombie baby through the head to put it out of its misery? I don't know.

Nodding to one another, Frederico and I advance into the master bedroom, weapons raised.

The room is dark, the metal burgundy blinds lowered and closed. The bed is unmade, the comforter and sheets in a lumpy mess near the footboard. Goopy red stains mar the carpet.

The bathroom door is open. We pad forward, pausing every few steps to listen. I glimpse the edge of a toilet and yellowed, chipped linoleum.

Scratch-scratch-scratch.

The noise sends a jolt of adrenaline through my body. Heart pounding, I turn toward the sound.

There's something inside the walk-in closet. The door is shut, trapping whatever it is on the other side.

Scratch-scratch-scratch.

Frederico moves to one side of the door, knuckles white on his weapons. He gestures to the door with his chin. I nod, sliding the railroad spike back into my pack and only keeping the screwdriver out. With my free hand, I grip the doorknob. My breath comes out in ragged, frightened gasps.

Steeling myself, I yank open the door. Frederico takes half a step forward, wrench raised over his head.

A small, black-and-white cat zips out of the closet, tearing past us and out into the hall.

Straight into Stout.

Yowls of alarm fill the air, followed by frenetic barking.

22

PORTLAND MALADY

"FUCK!" FREDERICO DARTS INTO THE HALLWAY WITH ME ON HIS HEELS.

We arrive in time to see Stout and the cat streak downstairs. Barking rings like a cannon in my ears.

"Stout!" I hiss, barreling past Frederico and racing after the dog.

There's a humongous racket from the kitchen, followed by more barking and yowling. It takes me a second to register the sound.

The cans and bottles in the plastic garbage bags. They're spilling all over the kitchen. And from the sound of things, Stout and the cat are right in the middle of the mess.

"Stout!" I race into the kitchen, fisting my hand in the scruff of the crazed dog. She strains against me, woofing madly at the cat.

The terrified feline stumbles over several beer bottles in its haste to get away. It streaks out of the kitchen under a barrage of barking. I brace both feet against the linoleum, struggling to hang onto Stout.

Frederico strides into the kitchen, face dark. Without hesitation, he cuffs the dog on the side of the head.

I suck in a surprised breath. Stout whines and stumbles from the impact. She looks up at Frederico, ears going flat.

"Bad dog," Frederico tells her, his face a mask of fear and fury. *"Bad."*

Stout presses her belly against the floor, tucking her tail between her legs. She stares up at Frederico with pleading eyes.

He ignores her, stalking out of the kitchen. A few seconds later, I hear a door close.

"Locked the fucking cat in the bathroom," he says, returning to the kitchen. "You can let her up."

Slowly, gingerly, I peel my fingers from Stout's scruff. She slinks toward Frederico. He glares at her, then sighs, shoulders sagging.

"So much for keeping a low profile," he murmurs, gently petting the dog.

A dull bump sounds from the side of the house. A heartbeat later, there are moans, followed by more bumping.

I feel sick. Creeping forward, I lean across the Formica countertop. Peeking through the once-white drapes that cover the window over the sink, I have a clear view of the south side of the property.

The father and son zombies kick the house with their feet and claw at the siding. The mother and other son draw near, reaching out with their hands.

As I watch, the father zombie inches to the side, following the contour of the house and heading toward the back. I jerk away from the kitchen curtain, as though the creature might sense my presence.

"It's coming around the back," I hiss. "We have to block the other door."

We hurry toward to the back of the house, entering a room with a slanted floor that looks like it was once an outdoor porch. Somewhere along the line, it was converted into a laundry room.

I scan the narrow room, looking for something to block the door. If I wasn't worried about making a racket, we could just tip over the washing machine.

"Over here," Frederico hisses.

In a corner of the room is a six-foot cabinet made of cheap particleboard. He braces himself against one side. Understanding his intent, I position myself on the opposite.

"One," Frederico whispers. "Two. Three."

I heave. Thankfully, the cabinet isn't too heavy. Things rattle inside as we lift it a few inches off the floor and shift it away from the wall. We set it down, rest, then move it again.

We shift it two more times before a broom falls out and clatters to the floor. An answering moan sounds from outside. I wince.

"Fuck it," Frederico mutters. With a loud screech of particleboard against chipped linoleum, he slides the cabinet across the floor. The noise sends chills up my back.

"They already know we're here," he grumbles, wedging the cabinet in front of the door. "No use dicking around. Come on, let's eat and get the hell out of here before they figure out how to get inside."

Back in the kitchen, he dives into the refrigerator, pulling out everything edible. He piles up bread, cheese, apples, leftover pizza, and a six-pack of Coke. I rummage through the drawers, producing silverware and a can opener.

"Protein." Frederico plops down two packages of lunch meat.

Without another word, we gorge ourselves. I throw open the greasy lid of the pizza box and inhale three slices of what looks like meat lover's delight. Frederico piles lunch meat and cheese atop slices of bread, building a sandwich at least four inches high before shoving it into his mouth. With his free hand, he pops open a can of Coke, sucking down long draughts of the sugary liquid between bites of food.

I polish off the pizza and start in on an apple, simultaneously heading for the pantry.

"Carbs." I place several cans of black beans on the counter. More rummaging produces several cans of SpaghettiOs, chili, and corn. I make my way down the counter, methodically opening each can of food as I go. Frederico seizes a can of beans and starts shoveling it into his mouth. I inhale two cans of SpaghettiOs.

Stout wuffles softly. Still on her belly, she looks up at us with woeful eyes.

Without saying a word, Frederico upends a can of beef chili onto the floor in front of her. She pops up, tail springing to life, and eagerly laps up the chili. I dump another two cans onto the floor for her, figuring she must be at least as hungry as we are. Frederico finds a mixing bowl and fills it with water for her.

I spot a radio—a boom box that looks like it was transported from the eighties—sitting on the kitchen counter. It's covered in dust but otherwise looks intact.

I make sure the volume isn't too high, then flick on the radio and am rewarded with a classic rock tune. I tune into the AM bandwidth, turning the knob and scanning the stations until I find a news station.

". . . unknown malady has entered the United States through the port of Portland," says the radio host. "The CDC has erected a containment unit around ground zero. They are working 'round the clock to diagnose this unknown disease. All citizens with signs of infection are instructed to check in at CDC stations for immediate care.

"Though the CDC refuses to comment, there are rumors the illness is spread by bodily fluid. Initial symptoms are similar to the flu: fever, chills, and aches. If not treated within several hours, those infected begin to show signs of dementia. If left untreated, they will turn violent. In some cases, the infected have attacked and killed. There have been reports of over three hundred attacks and eighty-six fatalities linked to this unknown disease."

Frederico and I spend the next thirty minutes listening to the news while we eat and drink everything in sight. I'm so hungry I barely taste the food as it goes down. My body burns up the much-needed fuel; life and energy return to me, filling me from my toes to my head. We chew and swallow in silence, making minimal noise so as not to miss a word of the news report.

"Military checkpoints have increased. Every major road out of Oregon has a checkpoint. New checkpoints have been erected in neighboring states in the cities of Boise, Redding, Eureka, and Tacoma. No one is allowed past the checkpoints unless they submit to a mandatory blood test."

My mind boggles at the scope of the outbreak. Authorities are obviously trying to contain it, but it's not working.

"Portland is under martial law. Citizens are required to submit to mandatory blood tests. Mobile blood banks have been dispatched to draw the blood while police round up citizens. Anyone found dodging the mandatory testing is imprisoned immediately."

Frederico ventures into the freezer. He emerges with two gallons of ice cream. He passes the vanilla chocolate chip to me, prying the lid off a strawberry one in his hands. We sit together in silence, spooning huge mouthfuls of ice cream into our mouths.

"Flights in and out of Portland have been grounded. Military personal have been deployed to all ports in the United States. No signs of the Portland Malady have been detected at any of the other ports."

Portland Malady. Is that what they're calling it now? My mouth twists into a bitter grimace at the political sugarcoating.

Stout joins us, cocking her head and staring at us. With a shrug, Frederico spoons out some strawberry ice cream and plops it onto the floor. The dog chases it around the floor, tail wagging as she laps at the cold lump with her tongue.

"Joining us now is Charles Fitzpatrick, a member of the Portland longshoremen. He was a witness to the outbreak. Charles, tell us what you saw."

The longshoreman launches into a gory retelling of attacks he witnessed from a small bathroom window.

Frederico and I sit slumped onto the dirty kitchen floor, leaning against the cupboards. We're surrounded by the remains of our feast: empty cans, wrappers, and bags; dirty forks, knives, and spoons; crumbs, bread crust, and apple cores.

I pull out my cell phone. There's a single text from Carter, sent about an hour ago.

Fire somewhere in dorm. Going 2 make a run for it. Be in touch later. Love u.

Holy shit. My smile fades, mouth going dry as I read his words.

"What is it?" Frederico, seeing my expression, takes the phone from me. "Fuck," he breathes.

I take the phone back.

Are u ok? I type. *We r a few miles north of Hopland.*

I stare at the phone, waiting for a response.

The longshoreman drones on in the background. "There was so much blood . . ."

A minute ticks by. Two. Three.

Staring bleakly at my phone, I resolutely wall away my rising anguish. Panic and fear will not help Carter. Neither will staring at my phone.

There have been moments in my life where grief has crippled me. This isn't going to be one of them. Carter needs me. I'm not going to let him down.

Mouth tightening in determination, I slide the phone back into my pack. Then I lever myself to my feet and switch off the radio.

"Come on," I say to Frederico. "Let's take care of our feet and get the hell out of here."

23

VISITORS

GRIMACING, I PULL OFF MY SHOES AND SOCKS. MY BLISTERS ARE ridiculous. The outside of my left foot is filled with clear fluid, the blister about the size of a quarter. There's one on top of my foot, filled with blood, that looks like a kidney bean on steroids. Not to mention all the small blisters on, around, and between my toes.

"I'm going to lose this toenail." I prod the big toe on my right foot, wrinkling my nose at the large blister that's formed under the nail.

"Yeah, I got a few of those, too. Here." Frederico passes me the blister kit, a Ziploc bag filled with sterile wipes, a few needles, a mini pair of scissors, liquid Band-Aid, and moleskin.

We spend the next fifteen minutes cleaning, lancing, and bandaging blisters. We work in silence, sparing little comment for the blood, pus, nails, and dead skin we remove. My feet have been through worse; hell, I expect them to be fully trashed by the time we get to Arcata.

I'd love to take the time to de-sticker my shoes and pants, but there doesn't seem much point since we'll be heading right back out onto the railroad tracks.

After I tend to my feet, I pull out the stick of Body Glide and reapply the lubricant to my hot zones. I rub it all over my feet, along the inside of my waistband, and across my skin just under the elastic of my sports bra.

Frederico holds up his wet shoes. "These could use a good thirty minutes in the dryer."

"Yeah, if we want to draw the attention of every zombie within five miles." Even now, I can hear the zombie family scratching and groaning outside the back door. "What about a hair dryer?" I pull on my second and last pair of dry socks. "Maybe we could use it in the upstairs closet to blow-dry our shoes. It would muffle the noise."

"Good idea. Let's try to find some Ibuprofen while we're at it. My back is complaining."

"I could use some for my knee, too," I reply. It still aches, though the worst of the pain has receded. "What about weapons? This looks like the sort of house that would have a few guns around."

"Good point," Frederico says. "We'll look around before we leave."

We leave Stout sprawled on the kitchen floor, bleary-eyed as she enters a junk food coma.

After a few minutes of searching the upstairs bathroom, we find a bottle of Aleve and a hair dryer. We both throw back three Aleve. I then grab the comforter from the master bed and drag it into the closet, using it as additional insulation against sound.

"I'll fill our packs with water and search for weapons," Frederico whispers. "You dry the shoes. Then we're out of here."

I nod, pausing to look out the window. Downstairs, all four zombies cluster outside the back door. They bang and scratch at the door and windows.

Shivering, I retreat into the closet. I press the blanket against the door, flip on the hair dryer, and get to work on Frederico's shoes. After spending so long in silence, the blow-dryer sounds like a lion in my ears.

I've only gotten through Frederico's shoes when he throws open the door, eyes wild. I instantly shut off the hair dryer and leap to my feet.

"What is it?" I say, just as he says, "We have company."

Outside, I hear catcalls and shouts. Stout is barking.

"Come on, you dead fuck!" I hear a man yell. "Come and get me!"

"You want some of this, motherfucker?" another man yells. "You want some of this fresh meat?"

"There're four of them at the back of the house," Frederico whispers to me. "In a truck. They drove straight through the pasture fence and went for the zombies."

I crawl across the floor, heading for the window. Peeking over the sill, I spy four men. They look relatively normal—or as normal as guys waving blood-stained baseball bats can look. In jeans, T-shirts, and baseball caps, they look to be in their mid-twenties.

As I watch, one of them swings the bat and whacks the mother zombie in the kneecap.

"Take that, you dead fuck!"

The bone shatters, and the mother zombie falls to the ground. She lands beside her eldest son, whose hands and elbows have both been battered bloody. The father zombie and younger son are also down, both with bloody kneecaps and legs that look like they've been broken.

"Yeah! Take that, you dead fuck!" says another of the men. He swings his own bat, breaking the mother zombie's elbow.

My stomach turns. I'm no zombie fan—not by a long stretch—but there's something twisted and dark about the scene unfolding below us.

The zombie moans, digging her good hand into the dirt as she tries to drag herself forward. Beside her, the teen zombie lifts his head and bares his teeth. Unable to push up with his ruined arms, he propels himself forward with his legs. Stout's barking gains a fevered pitch.

"Shut up that fucking dog!"

One of the men pulls a handgun from the back of his jeans. Without hesitating, he fires into one of the kitchen windows. There's the sound of shattering glass, a yelp from Stout, then silence.

My blood goes cold.

Eyes wide with panic, Frederico shoves my pack into my hand, then proceeds to jam his feet into his shoes.

I stumble in my haste to pull on my still-wet shoes. Landing on the comforter, I yank them on, then scramble back up. My hands shake in their haste to strap on the pack. Dammit, I hadn't thought to put extra food in my pack while we were downstairs.

Wordlessly, Frederico grabs my sleeve and pulls me toward the stairs. The shouts and catcalls continue outside.

"Break her ribs!" one man shouts.

"Yeah, let's see how far she can get with broken ribs!" says another. *Sick fuckers*, I think.

As Frederico and I creep downstairs, my chest tightens with dread. Did that asshole kill Stout, or just injure her? If she's injured, how are we going to get her away from here? It's only a matter of time before those dickwads turn their attention to the house. If they'd shoot an innocent dog and torture zombies, I don't want to think about what they'd do to us.

Just as we reach the bottom stair—and as the raucous laughter outside reaches new heights—there's a soft whine. Stout limps into view.

I lunge past Frederico and throw my arms around our ultra dog. She licks my face, whining again. Blood runs down her right shoulder, but other than that, she's in one piece. It looks like she was only grazed by the bullet.

Frederico rubs Stout between the ears and gives her a gentle pat between the shoulder blades.

"Should we search for weapons?" I whisper.

"No time," he replies, voice soft. "We need to put distance between ourselves and those maniacs."

He leads me and Stout into the family room. It's on the north side of the house, opposite to where the men and the zombies are. He opens a window and pops out the screen, then deftly climbs out.

I hesitate, looking around for a chair or some other piece of furniture for Stout to climb onto. The dog surprises me by leaping out the open window after Frederico. She teeters and limps a few steps when she lands, but doesn't make a sound.

That's my girl, I think, scrambling after her. I land in dry dirt that looks like it was supposed to be a flower bed, even though now it's only home to weeds.

A chorus of cheers goes up from the other side of the house. I don't even want to think what they're cheering about.

"Door's barricaded," someone calls. "Let's break the window."

"Think someone's inside?" another voice shouts.

"If there is, we can make ourselves some more dead meat."

A shiver travels down my spine. I meet Frederico's eye and gesture north. Past the jumble of classic cars is an old vineyard that hasn't seen a tractor in years. It's unpruned, the gnarled vines growing in wild disarray and choked with weeds. It's close, and it'll provide good concealment.

Frederico nods in agreement. We break into a sprint, running as fast as we can. There's life and energy in my steps, now that my body has refueled. I might pay for gorging later, but I'd rather be overnourished than hungry.

Glass shatters behind us. A minute after that, the front door creaks open. I glance over my shoulder and see a man step onto the porch, the floorboards protesting loudly under his footsteps. He's wearing a plain navy shirt and a Giants baseball cap. He strolls onto the porch, swinging his bloody bat and looking around.

We are on open ground, only ten feet from the concealment of the car graveyard. There's the barest instant when the man's eyes meet mine. Fear makes my mouth go dry. I sprint for all I'm worth.

"Guys, I've found us some pussy!" he hollers. "Get the truck!"

Oh, shit. Shit-shit-*shit*.

Frederico and I streak through the cars and practically dive into the vineyard, hunching down into the waist-high weeds.

"We gotta hide," Frederico says. "We'll never outrun them. Come on."

He leads me deeper into the vineyards. Stout is at our side, keeping up despite her wound. An approaching truck engine roars in our ears.

Frederico and I run in a crouched position, moving as fast as we can while trying to stay below the wild, tangled vines. Untrellised and untended, the vines grow every which way and slap at our faces. As strong as the wine industry is, there are still neglected vineyards.

"Dead ahead," Frederico puffs. "We'll hide in that."

I hold up my arms to shield my face from the wild grapevines, trying to see ahead.

"All I see is a blackberry patch," I pant.

"That's right."

As we draw near, I'm struck by the immensity of the blackberry patch. Left untended, much like the grapevines, it's grown at least a hundred feet tall and twice as deep. It's surrounded by tufts of poison oak.

"Oh, fuck," I mutter. "Are you serious?"

"Dead serious."

The rows of grapes are too narrow for cars—or at least, that's what I assume. Until the big four-wheeler plows straight into the first row of vines behind us. Gnarled wood and budding green leaves spray into the air in front of them.

Have they seen us? They're heading straight for us, though with all the debris flying over the hood it's just as likely dumb luck is leading them in our direction.

Without warning, Stout veers away from us. Her shrill bark lights the air. I hiss for her to quiet, but she's too far away—running back in the direction of the truck.

I open my mouth to cry out after her, but Frederico grabs my hand.

"Move!" he snaps.

I obey, sprinting toward the wall of bristling brambles and poison oak.

Behind me, I hear the men hoot as they catch sight of Stout. The truck makes a sharp turn to the right, veering away on a new trajectory. Gunshots rip through the vineyard.

Instinctually I turn, Stout's name forming on my lips. Frederico ruthlessly yanks my arm, pulling me to the ground.

"There," he hisses, pushing me toward the poison oak. "Move."

Another gunshot. More barking. Tires spew soft earth as the engine is gunned. More barking.

Tears brim in my eyes as I crawl through the poison oak. The bright-green leaves part, revealing an oddly large animal trail that leads into the brambles. It's about two feet high and a foot-and-a-half wide. What sort of animal made this?

"Faster," Frederico snaps at my heels.

I tuck my chin to my chest and crawl as fast as I can, heedless of the brambles scratching at my head and arms. The spikes claw at my pack and clothing. I yank myself free and keep moving, pushing deeper into the berry patch. There are parts so low that I'm reduced to wriggling on my belly and pulling myself along on my elbows.

Another gunshot.

A high-pitched yelp.

A sob breaks from my throat.

I keep crawling.

In the distance, the men shout. They're too far away for me to make out their words. I strain my ears, hoping to hear Stout's bark. There's no more barking, only the indistinct chatter of the men. "You can stop now," Frederico whispers. "They can't see us." His eyes are wet with sadness.

I collapse, curling up in a tight ball. I bite the inside of my cheek to keep from screaming. Tears stream down my cheeks. Frederico squeezes my shoulder while I shake with soundless tears.

24

BONGING IN THE BRAMBLES

SHE'S GONE. THAT POOR DOG. SHOT DOWN FOR NO OTHER REASON THAN the fact she'd been alive and a group of assholes was looking for violent entertainment.

I squeeze my eyes, trying to squash the images that race through my brain. God, I hope Stout's kill had been clean. I hope she isn't alive and in pain. The thought makes me cry harder.

We'd only been together—what?—maybe ten miles? But that had been a long, long ten miles. In that ten miles, we'd braved a zombie-infested hardware store, plowed through a nasty bonk, and eaten enough food to put normal people into a coma. I'd bonded with that dog in those ten miles.

I'd experienced similar bonding in other ultra races. When I ran the Lake Sonoma 50 miler two years ago, I'd had the misfortune of running during a heat wave. My stomach had rebelled, and I'd started puking at mile nineteen. A nice woman—Kara had been her name—caught up to me as I heaved into the bushes. She stayed with me the rest of the course, buoying my spirits with her nonstop commentary on the beauty of ultra boys in spandex. I still credit her with my finish that day and, truth be told, I've never looked at men in spandex quite the same way. Kara and I have never spoken or seen each other since that day, but she still has a special place in my ultrarunning past.

My running life is filled with countless stories like that—bonds forged with fellow runners in the midst of grit and determination.

The only difference is that none of the runners has ever been shot and murdered.

Frederico smoothes hair back from my forehead, still holding me tight. He doesn't speak, just holds me and strokes my hair, giving me the time I need to grieve. He'd done the same thing for me and Carter when Kyle died. He'd been rock solid and steady in the face of our incoherent grief.

By the time my tears dry, my eyes are swollen and my nose is so stuffy I'm forced to breathe through my mouth. Small pinpricks of pain—residuals from my frantic scrabble through the brambles—cover my body.

I turn my head, looking back in the direction of the vineyard. The men are still out there. It sounds like they're arguing.

"One of the trunks from the grapevines got stuck in the undercarriage of their truck," Frederico whispers. "I think something got broken. They haven't been able to move the truck."

"Did they say anything about Stout?" I reply.

"No." He squeezes my shoulders. "Say good-bye to her, Jackalope. You need to get your head in the game if we're going to survive. Those men out there are pissed. They blame us for what happened to their truck."

I draw one last shuddering breath, closing my eyes. Summoning a mental picture of Stout's black-brown fur, I mentally say my good-bye.

So sorry, girl. Sorry you had to die for us.

"Okay?" Frederico asks.

I nod.

"Good." He gives my shoulders one last squeeze. "We need to move while they're distracted."

"You don't think they'll come in here after us, do you?"

"No, but they could shoot us through the brambles if they figure out where we are. Or light the briar on fire."

Bile rises in my throat at his words. "How are we going to get out of here?"

"Follow these animal paths."

I twist my head around, giving him my best skeptical look.

"Do you have a better idea?" he asks, raising his eyebrow.

A better idea than snaking around on my belly trying to find a way out of this massive blackberry bramble? I think for a moment, then wrinkle my nose in resignation. The only other option is go back the way we came, and death is the only thing in that direction. Danger, and poison oak.

As if in response, itching shivers along my arms. I ignore it. No doubt I got poison oak on me. I'm not going to make things worse by scratching at it. God, what I wouldn't do for a bottle of Tecnu and calamine lotion right now.

"You know what they say," Frederico whispers to me. "When you can't run, walk."

Despite myself, I smile. "And when you can't walk, crawl," I reply, quoting Dr. Martin Luther King, Jr. The ultrarunning community has adopted his sage advice.

Resigned, I flip onto my stomach and crawl deeper into the brambles. Sometimes the path is tall enough for me move on hands and knees, but most of the path is traversed on my belly. A few times, when the path dead-ends in what looks like an animal den, we have to backtrack.

"Did I ever tell you my bonging in the brambles story?" Frederico asks softly.

Bonging in the brambles? "No," I whisper back. "I'm pretty sure I would have remembered that. Shit, get ready for another belly crawl." I drop into the dirt. My elbows and hips are starting to get sore.

"It was something I did as a kid. My dad rented a little two-room cabin in Guerneville. It was right on the river. There was a big black-berry briar between our house and the neighbor's. I used to sneak into the briar with the neighbor's kids to get high. We called it bonging in the brambles. We thought we were so fucking clever, burrowing into that patch. We never considered the big pot plume we sent up with every bong hit. It was like a smoke signal. Needless to say, it didn't take long for Dad to figure out what we were up to."

"What did he do?" I ask.

Frederico snorts. "He confiscated all our weed but let us keep the bong. That night, he invited me to get high with him."

"*What?*" Having spent my adult life married to a recovering alco-holic, I'm unable to censor my horror.

"Dad spent most of his days high. When he found out I liked to smoke, he saw it as an opportunity to bond. It was one of the few things we had in common."

"You smoked weed with your *dad*?" I have to repeat this back to him out of incredulity, not because I have a hearing issue.

"Yeah. Of course, our bond went out the window when I went sober. By the time he died, we hadn't spoken in almost ten years. He thought sobriety was only two steps short of suicide. We never could relate to each other once we lost weed."

"God, Frederico. I'm so sorry."

"I've come to peace with it."

I don't know what to say to any of this. In my own mind, I compare my straight-laced family to the image of a dad smoking pot with his son. Frederico's experience is so beyond my own childhood, I can hardly grasp it.

We've been crawling around for nearly an hour when we hear the telltale sound of an engine firing to life. Cheers go up.

"They got their truck fixed," Frederico says grimly.

Minutes later, we hear the truck moving. As deep as we are in the blackberry briar, it's hard to discern a direction at first. After a good thirty seconds, it's clear they're driving in our direction.

"Come out, little kitties," one of the men calls out. "Come out and play!"

I flatten myself to the ground. As if that's going to protect me. We're so deep in this fucking blackberry patch, there's no way they can see us. Even so, the animal part of my brain requires stillness and silence.

The truck rumbles by, skirting the briar, then continues on. The heckler continues to shout taunts, daring us to show ourselves. From the sound of things, they're driving around the vineyard, trying to find our trail.

Frederico and I remain unmoving until the hum of the truck fades into the distance, then we continue our miserable crawl. Twenty minutes later, the truck returns. It roars past the briar patch, driving in the direction of the house. There's no more taunting, and they're moving fast enough to make me think they're not looking for us anymore.

"Hopefully this means they've turned their attention to other things," I murmur.

"Let's hope. Kate, do you hear that?"

"Hear what?"

"That."

I strain my ears. At first, my attention is on the fading rumble of the truck. It takes a few seconds for me to focus on a softer, closer sound. It's a low rustling of the briar patch.

"Animals?" I whisper.

"Yeah. Quite a few of them, from the sound of things."

We remain where we are. After another hard listen, I determine Frederico is right. There are animals nearby. It sounds like they're moving through the brambles and digging in the dirt. Then I hear a soft, distinct snort.

Frederico hears it, too. "Oh, shit," he breathes. "Pigs."

25

PIGS

DAMMIT. PIGS. DID WE ESCAPE FROM THE BASEBALL BAT MANIACS ONLY to face off against wild pigs?

I should have guessed from the size of the burrows we're following. They're much too large to have been made by rabbits and too small to have been made by deer. They are, however, just the right size for pigs.

Feral swine make their home all over this area. Farmers consider them pests and regularly hunt them. Frederico and I occasionally encounter them on our trail runs around Lake Sonoma.

They're notoriously bad-tempered, especially in the spring when they have babies. The general rule of thumb is to hide behind a tree and wait for them to pass. Frederico will occasionally clap his hands and make loud noises to startle them, but I prefer to lie low and give them space. Occasionally, feral pigs will attack and kill a hunter or unwary hiker. It happens often enough to give me a healthy dose of respect for the animals.

And now we're in their den. They're getting closer, snorting and rooting around in the brambles.

"We gotta move," I hiss to Frederico.

I wriggle forward as fast as I can, moving away from the pigs. As luck would have it, the path narrows to a tunnel too small for us to pass through.

"Back up," I hiss frantically. "Dead end."

He moves, body scraping against the dirt. I lever my elbows against the ground, pushing myself backward. Trying to see behind me is difficult; I constantly crane my neck, attempting to see even as I try to avoid the blackberry thorns.

"Over here." Frederico tugs on my ankle.

I follow the touch of his hand, backing into a small, round burrow. Frederico is backed up all the way into the brambles. I'm forced to spoon with him. He smells like a man who's run over thirty miles. Not that I smell any better.

"They're getting closer," I hiss.

"Just make yourself look nonthreatening," he replies.

"How am I supposed to do that?"

"Just—I don't know—don't make eye contact."

I curl into a tight ball, hiding my face behind my arms. As if that will save me if the pigs find us and decide they don't like us. With one eye, I peek out between my forearms.

A lone pig snuffles into view. He's russet brown with white stripes down his side. He noses the ground, scratching at it with his hoof and chewing on something; probably worms or insects. Pigs eat *everything*.

I barely dare to breathe as I watch the animal through my forearms. He's joined by another pig. They scratch at the ground and munch at low-hanging berries.

Over the next few minutes, another dozen or so appear, snorting and grunting as they forage for food. My tongue, dry with fear, welds itself to the roof of my mouth.

One gets close to me and sniffs. I clench both hands into fists, ready to attack. Frederico squeezes my shoulder in warning. I forcibly relax my hands, biting my bottom lip hard enough to draw blood.

The pig gets so close I feel his exhalations against my skin.

This is it. It's the zombie apocalypse and I'm going to meet my end by a sounder of pigs. They're going to trample us to death in this fucking blackberry briar.

The pig leans in close, closer—then snorts, lays his ears back, and abruptly retreats. He trots away, disappearing around a corner.

The rest of the animals cruise by without sparing us a second glance. Then, as quickly as they had come, they're gone. All the pigs, every last one of them. Snorting and rooting at the ground, they disappear in a snuffle of sound.

Frederico nudges me in the back with his elbow. "Good job," he says. "It was your BO that scared him off."

I let out ragged, hoarse whisper of a laugh. "Fuck you. It was *your* BO. I smell like a fucking daisy patch."

He chuckles lightly. I crawl out of our small burrow, peering down the way the pigs went. In their wake is a swath of churned soil.

"Frederico." I glance over my shoulder at him. "Our four-legged friends left a trail of breadcrumbs."

Thirty minutes later, after following the messy foraging of the sounder, we emerge into the sunlight. I flop onto my back, staring up at the blue sky and sucking in deep breaths.

"I am now officially claustrophobic," I say.

"I don't think I'll ever eat another blackberry again." Frederico sits back on his heels, surveying the land around us. "We're on the northern edge of the briar. I can barely see the roof of the house, which means those sickos won't be able to see us." He gives me a relieved grin.

"Good." I roll over and climb to my feet. I hold out my arms, surveying the dozens of cuts covering the skin. Frederico looks at his own arms.

"How long before the poison oak kicks in?" I'm not looking forward to itchy sores coupling with the cuts.

Frederico shrugs. "With all the time spent in the dirt, we may have gotten rid of most of the oil. Only time will tell."

I decide not to launch into a speech about my intense dislike of poison oak. It would serve no purpose right now.

"Daylight is burning, old man," I say. "Let's get going."

"Slave driver." He companionably gets to his feet.

We set off at a trot, heading north and skirting the old vineyard. To our left is open pasture land, a large swath cut by the truck when it drove through earlier. Luckily there is no sign of it now.

"That way." Frederico points. "I can see the pasture fence. We need to get off this property and back onto the tracks."

I nod, wordlessly veering toward the fence. We arch around the old vineyard.

A few vultures make lazy circles above the grapevines. I draw to a halt, my stomach knotting at the sight of them.

Stout.

Frederico stops beside me, following my gaze.

"Come on, Jackalope," he says gently. "We can't do anything for her now."

"We should bury her. Or at least, check and make sure she's really gone. What if they shot her and she's still alive? And in pain?" My throat tightens.

"She's gone, Kate. Make her death mean something."

I hesitate, then nod. I wipe at my eyes, determined not to break down again.

I feel like a complete shit. An ungrateful shit who turns her back on a friend.

But I do turn. Yielding to Frederico's gentle advice, I look away from the circling vultures.

"You know the worst thing about all this?" I gesture back in Stout's general direction.

"What?"

"Human beings were shitty even before the apocalypse."

26

REGRETS

IT DOESN'T TAKE US LONG TO FIND A BREACH IN THE PASTURE FENCE. A bit of eroded earth creates a gap just large enough for us to shimmy under.

It's nearly seven o'clock. The sun sinks in the sky, sending long fingers of shadows across the land. We've been on the move for nine hours, and we haven't even hit mile forty yet.

We lost at least two hours in the house and blackberry briar. Not to mention the time we wasted in Cloverdale trying to get a car, and the time in Hopland at Ace Hardware.

"It's going to be dark soon," I say, seeing the shadows thicken around us.

"Headlamps," Frederico says.

I nod. We rummage in our packs, pulling out the headlamps. They're stretchy bands of elastic designed to be worn around the head with a bright light mounted on the front. I slide mine on, snugging it down so that the lamp rests on my forehead. Frederico does the same. We click them on, sending out bright beams of light.

Then we're back on the tracks, the two of us running north. As the day darkens, we're forced to trade speed for caution, and our pace slows.

The tracks cross over a small, one-lane country road. Nailed to a tree is a wooden sign painted with the word *Strawberries*. Too bad it's too early in the season for there to be any fruit in the field.

"If I get eaten in the next thirty minutes, I'm going to regret never asking Marguerite out for coffee," Frederico says.

"Who's Marguerite?" I keep my eyes on the tracks as we jog along.

"A pretty redhead I see every Thursday night at my AA meeting."

"Have you ever talked to her?"

"All the time. Every week, actually. She always brings some sort of sweet to the meetings. The strawberry patch made me think of her. She made chocolate-covered strawberries last week."

"Did you eat any?"

"Three. Best goddamn things I've ever had."

"Did you tell her that?"

"Of course. I always tell her I like her food. It's an excuse to talk to her . . . I've been trying to work up the nerve to ask her out for two years."

I laugh sympathetically. "Why don't you just ask?"

"She's barely fifty. Too pretty for me. I know how I look. I'm a grizzled old man. I abused this body for more than half my life, and it shows."

"That's a stupid excuse. If she's too shallow to see past your exterior, she's not worth your time."

He grunts. "My idea of a great first date is a twenty-five-mile run around Lake Sonoma. I don't do dinners and movies. Too awkward. She deserves a man who will take her out. I'm just not that guy."

"You could have taken her to Lake Sonoma without asking her to run twenty-five miles, Frederico. Why didn't you ask her to go for a hike? Or a picnic? Better yet, how about a hike and a picnic?"

He's silent for a few minutes. "I never thought of that."

"You should have consulted me before the zombie apocalypse."

"Yeah, I guess so."

"You're an idiot, Frederico."

"Can't argue with that."

On we run, the land around us succumbing to darkness. Insects whir to life, filling the air with soft background noise—sounds that bring the illusion of a normal, pre-apocalyptic world.

At mile thirty-six, Frederico asks, "What will you regret, if we get eaten in the next thirty minutes?"

"I don't know," I reply, though my mind immediately flashes to my son. We run a few more minutes in silence, my mind churning. Finally, I find my voice.

"If I get eaten in the next thirty minutes . . . I'm going to regret being the person I became when Kyle died." I swallow against the lump in my throat. "I was a really shitty mom to Carter."

"Bullshit," Frederico replies, his vehemence catching me by surprise.

"I went into a dark place when Kyle died. I should have been strong for Carter. Instead, he had to be strong for me." The shame sits heavy on my shoulders. Even though Carter and I have a good relationship, I've never been able to shake free of the guilt. "I couldn't function after I lost Kyle. All I did was sleep and cry. You remember what a mess I was."

"You were grieving."

"I was so fucked up. I couldn't even drive Carter to school. He had to get up early and walk. He made a sandwich for me every morning and left it in the fridge so I'd have something to eat. I usually hid the sandwiches in the trash can. At night, he'd make microwave dinners for me and fret over me until I ate them."

"Your son is a good kid."

"Carter *is* good. He's always been good. I should have been there for him. I should have been the one making him sandwiches and microwave dinners. I almost missed his high school graduation."

Frederico nods. He's too kind to rehash that dismal day.

I STILL REMEMBER the low anger that simmered in me when my son pulled open the bedroom curtains, nearly blinding me after days and days in self-imposed darkness.

"Hey, Mom," he said, eyes alight with the same genuine kindness I'd always seen in his father's. "Graduation starts in an hour. I picked out your clothes. Just jump in the shower and we'll go, okay? Uncle Rico is here to drive us."

There in front of me stood my handsome son, dressed in the suit we purchased the day his father died. His face, framed by a neatly trimmed beard, was so earnest. Shaggy brown hair framed eyes as blue as his father's.

The suit looked perfect on him, the blue button-down shirt a perfect accent to his eyes. The sight of it made me want to vomit. That suit was the reason we weren't home when Kyle slipped and hit his head. It was the reason we hadn't been here to save him.

Sorrow felt like an anvil in my chest. I wanted to throw it at someone. I wanted to crush myself with it. I wanted the pain to stop.

"Just jump in the shower and we'll go, okay? Mom?" Carter hovered in the doorway, not trusting me to get my ass in gear. "Mom?"

It was his uncertainty that gave me the kick in the ass I needed. The anger and grief disappeared in an avalanche of shame.

I was a fucking wreck. I hadn't showered in days. I'd barely eaten in the past few weeks. I looked and smelled like hell. And my son didn't trust me to get my act together. He didn't trust me to be there for him, to witness this important rite of passage.

He'd already lost a father. He didn't need to lose his mother, too.

I got up. I showered. I put on makeup to conceal the dark circles under my eyes. I even managed a fancy twist with my hair. In an effort to get my light-headedness under control, I scarfed half a bag of Ghirardelli chocolate chips while applying mascara and eyeliner.

Carter beamed at me when I exited the bedroom in the red dress he'd picked out. I don't think he'd noticed I'd forgotten to brush my teeth.

Frederico had been too circumspect to tell me I looked like hell. Instead, he'd said, "You need to get back on the trail, Jackalope. The sunshine will do you some good."

───────

"CARTER HAD to take care of *me*," I say to Frederico. "It should have been the other way around. I was weak when I should have been strong." I shake my head. "Carter deserves better."

We run on, our feet light whispers against the rotting wood of the railroad. Our legs swish through the plants. That, coupled with our breathing, are the only sounds of our passage.

Mile thirty-seven.

"Maybe, if I can make it to Arcata—if I can get there in one piece without getting eaten—maybe Carter will know I'm strong," I say. "Maybe he'll know I can be there for him when the chips are down."

"If you make it to Arcata," Frederico says, "maybe you'll forgive yourself. Carter isn't the one holding resentments, Kate."

I have nothing to say to that.

Mile thirty-eight.

The city of Ukiah glimmers in the distance. It's the only thing that qualifies as a city in the next one hundred miles. The town is large enough to boast a Walmart, a Home Depot, and legalized marijuana.

"Fuck this." Frederico comes to an abrupt halt. "I'm not going out with regrets. Give me your phone."

"My phone?" I stare at him stupidly.

"I'm calling her."

"Who?"

"Aleisha."

I blink in surprise, then obediently dig out my phone. A quick glance shows me there's no text from Carter. Ignoring the tinge of worry that slithers through my belly, I pass the phone to Frederico.

"How the hell do you use this fucking thing?" He swipes at the phone.

I wrestle it back from him. "Here." I pull up the keypad, then pass it back.

Drawing a deep breath, Frederico dials. He looks like a wild man in my pink running shorts and polka-dot compression sleeves. Curls have come loose from his ponytail, framing his face in sweaty locks.

"Aleisha." His voice is low and tinged with intense emotion. "It's Dad. I want you to know . . . I want you to know I love you. I love you, and I'm sorry. Sorry for everything. I'm sure by now you've heard about all the crazy shit that's going down. I want you to know that I'm on my way to you. I'll be there soon. Stay safe."

A shudder goes through him as he disconnects. "No answer," he mutters, passing the phone back to me.

I stare at the phone, willing a text from Carter to appear. Nothing happens.

Just got 2 Ukiah, I type. *See u soon. Stay safe.*

When I look up, my eyes meet Frederico's. I see my own worry and anxiety reflected back at me. Without another word, we continue on.

27

ZOMBIE ROLLERS

THE TWO-LANE ROAD STRETCHES INTO A BONA FIDE FOUR-LANE FREEWAY as we near Ukiah. The railroad tracks run parallel to it. We switch off our headlamps and survey the scene before us.

At the south end of town, huge floodlights have been positioned on either side of the four-lane highway. They cast the dark road with blinding light. The faces of the soldiers are concealed by biohazard masks. We didn't see those on the soldiers in Hopland.

A large white tent has been raised on the west side of the road. A blue square with a white silhouette of a bird and the letters *CDC* is painted on one side.

"The CDC is here?" I whisper. "Shouldn't their efforts be focused in Portland?"

"Don't know," Frederico replies. "Maybe they've found something here worth studying."

Not good. A desperate need to find Carter tightens my chest.

I pull out my phone. Still no text. My battery is two-thirds of the way gone. Despite this, I pull up the browser and type *Ukiah CDC*.

A minute later, my phone brings up a list of headlines that make my stomach churn.

OUTBREAKS IN NORTHERN CALIFORNIA. MILITARY
DEPLOYED TO HALT SPREAD.

CDC BLOCKADE IN UKIAH AND EUREKA. MORE REPORTS OF
OUTBREAK IN HUMBOLDT UNIVERSITY.

RESIDENTS IN NORTHERN CALIFORNIA URGED TO STAY
INDOORS.

VIOLENT RESTAURANT ATTACK CONNECTED TO PORTLAND
LONGSHOREMAN VISITING FAMILY IN UKIAH.

OUTBREAK AT FRAT PARTY IN NORTHERN CALIFORNIA'S
HUMBOLDT UNIVERSITY. MILITARY DEPLOYED TO PROTECT
STUDENTS.

"Shit," Frederico breathes, reading over my shoulder.

I close the browser and dial Carter's number. It goes straight to voicemail. Tears of frustration well in my eyes.

"Kate." Frederico puts a hand on my shoulder. "Keep your head in the race. Don't fall apart on me now."

I swallow and close my eyes, trying to quell the panic and despair inside of me. *Carter!*

"Ultras are finished with the mind, not the body," Frederico says. "Keep your head in the race, Kate."

"Head in the race," I repeat, opening my eyes.

He's right. Panicking about Carter isn't going to save him, and it isn't going to help us reach him. If anything, it'll get us killed.

God, what I wouldn't give for a hug from Kyle right now. The feel of his arms around me would be a salve on my aching heart.

But Kyle's not here. Kyle is gone. All I have is myself, and Frederico.

It will have to be enough.

It *is* enough. I have water, food, and friendship. And a headlamp. I have everything I need to make it to Arcata, to Carter.

"I'm okay," I say, shaking myself. A familiar steel wells within me, solidifying my will. "Fuck self-pity."

There's a point in every ultra race where a runner has to decide to finish. There's always a reason to quit. Multiple reasons, usually. It takes a solid will to finish, to push through pain and doubt and excuses.

I seize that unflinching willpower, wrapping it around myself like a blanket. I *will* see this through. For Carter. For Kyle.

"Fuck self-pity," I repeat.

"Fuck self-pity, and fuck pain." Frederico grins and gives my shoulder one last squeeze.

"We have to sneak around the city," I say, my resolve solidifying into a plan. "If those soldiers see us, they won't let us pass."

"Yeah. Come on."

The tracks run directly into Ukiah. We step off, moving northeast through open grassland. We creep along, keeping one eye on the soldiers.

It's slowgoing. The moon is nothing more than a bare sliver, casting only the barest illumination for us to see by.

A quarter mile later, hidden behind industrial buildings and out of sight of the military barricade, we switch our lights back on. We cut around the city, going through fields, vineyards, and oak groves. Our progress is slow without a clear path for running, but we press doggedly forward. Neither of us suggests trying to get a car.

An eerie silence rests over the city—no hum of traffic, no distant voices. There's no sign of the chaos you'd expect from a city in the throes of a zombie outbreak. No screaming, no outward signs of panic or mayhem.

"What do you think's going on in there?" I whisper, glancing at the city.

Frederico shakes his head. "Nothing good, Kate."

"I think things are going to get worse the farther north we go."

"It could." He glances over at me. "One mile at a time, right?"

"One mile at a time," I echo.

Mile forty-five.

We leave Ukiah behind. Pausing only to check the map, we locate the tracks and continue on our way.

This far north, the population dwindles to almost nothing. I've driven this route enough times during the day to know there's an occasional house, but in the near-darkness, I don't see any of them now. Not even a telltale light in a bedroom window. With only the illumination from our headlamps to combat the darkness, it feels like running down a black tunnel.

Miles roll by. I run often enough and far enough that I've built up a good base over the years. My body can go a good fifty miles—especially with proper fuel and hydration—before it starts to feel the effects of the pounding.

When we hit mile fifty-five, I begin to feel early signs of wear and tear. There's a familiar fatigue in my legs, torso, and arms, though that's to be expected. With our last meal a good twenty-miles behind us, hunger is setting in again. I'm also getting low on water. The blisters on my feet are more uncomfortable than painful. I'll need to lance them again eventually, but for now, they're manageable. There are a few itchy spots on my arms from the poison oak, but again, the discomfort is manageable.

My biggest issue is the knee I injured when I fell outside of Hopland. I thought I was going to be able to shake it off, but the aching has returned. It wants to stiffen up on me. I do my best to push on and ignore the discomfort. Quitting isn't an option, and to be honest, I've run through much worse.

"How's your inventory?" I ask Frederico.

"My IT band," he replies, referring to the large ligament that runs along the outside of the thigh to the shin. "It always squawks at me on long runs." He glances at me. "How are you holding up?"

"Just the usual, but I'm okay. Knee is irritating me from the fall. We have to find food and water soon."

"I know. I'm not looking forward to that."

"I wish we had different packs." I think of the larger hydration packs I have back at home. They're made for long, self-supported runs. Because of their size and weight, I only use them for longer runs of thirty or forty miles, when I need to carry more gear, food, and water. "Of course, today would have been the day we suited up with smaller packs."

"I can't tell you how many times I've had that same thought in the last ten miles."

At mile sixty-one, we reach the outskirts of a town named Willits. It's a small town with barely five thousand people. We need to stop and forage for food. The knowledge makes my stomach queasy.

Something tickles the edge of my hearing. I put out an arm, halting Frederico.

"Do you hear that?" I whisper.

I tilt my head, straining my ears. After several seconds, I hear it again: low, wordless moans.

"Is it coming from the town?" I ask.

"I don't think so. It sounds closer. Maybe up ahead on the tracks?" He brandishes his tire iron.

I pull out my railroad spike and screwdriver, gripping one in each hand. Slowing to a walk, we carefully advance. Part of me feels like we should switch off our headlamps, but I know that's the scared, irrational part of my brain. With the zombies being blind, the headlamps will only give us an advantage.

Another two hundred yards, and we see them in the distance: three zombies standing to the side of the tracks. They walk in small, sightless circles, moaning softly. The light from our headlamps glosses them with the faintest illumination.

They look not unlike the homeless zombie we encountered outside of Cloverdale. All wear clothes that have seen better days. Each has a frame backpack and a sleeping bag.

They're young, perhaps in their early twenties. One wears a beanie over dreadlocks. Another has a big forked beard he's divided into two braids. The third wears a guitar slung in front of him.

They each have a ruddy, tanned face. They're the faces of homeless young men who spend their days exposed to the elements. There's a layer of grime on their skin and arms, more evidence that they spend their days without the common comforts of life.

The sight of the three men saddens me. What paths did they travel to end up here today?

"Kate," Frederico says, "we may not have to forage in Willits." He tilts his head toward the three zombies.

"You want to—what?" I whisper. "Roll the zombies?"

He shrugs. "I was thinking more along the line of spiking them and ransacking their packs."

I stare at him flatly. "You want to roll the zombies."

"You have to admit it has a nice ring: Zombie Rollers."

Despite myself, I laugh softly. "You're insane."

"You want to run two hundred miles to Arcata. *You're* insane."

"Fuuuuck." I tilt my head back, staring up at the spangling of stars. "We're both insane." I exhale sharply, then look my friend in the eye. "What the hell? I'm in."

I CROUCH on the right side of the railroad berm, weapons clutched in each hand. Frederico stands on the opposite side with his hammer and his lug nut wrench. The wind blows, carrying with it the chill scent of rot.

I nod, the beam from my headlamp bobbing up and down. At my signal, Frederico starts clacking his weapons together.

The three zombies instantly straighten, heads swiveling in our direction. They moan, arms outstretched as they walk toward us. I scan our surroundings, watching for other zombies. The grassland and oak trees around us are quiet, rippled by the nighttime breeze.

The first of the zombies—Dreadlocks—trips on a rock and goes down. He's back on his feet in seconds, a determined moan rising from his throat.

Guitar bumps into a tree, then quickly reorients and continues forward.

Forked Beard is in the lead. He's the most nimble-footed of the bunch, his booted feet practically gliding over the earth. He's the first to stumble into our barricade.

It's nothing more than a pile of sticks and branches we salvaged from the surrounding landscape. Three feet wide and one foot tall, it's just big enough to trip Forked Beard and send him sprawling.

That's my cue. I dart over the berm, weapons raised. Forked Beard rolls on his side as he hears me coming. My headlamp illuminates his yawning maw. His blind eyes shine like white marbles.

As I dart in, one hand closes around my ankle. I yelp in fear and ram the spike down as hard as I can. The hand goes slack as my rusted steel punctures his skull.

Breathing hard, I lean back on my heels and yank out the spike.

"Kate, look out!" Frederico's shout splits the air like an axe.

I look up just as Guitar trips on the barricade and goes down—right on top of me. I squeal, twisting around to get the screwdriver between me and the monster. The wooden guitar slams into my hip and grinds painfully against bone as the zombie lands on top of it.

Snarling, he lunges for me. I slam my hands against his throat, straining to keep his snapping teeth from my flesh. The screwdriver tumbles from my grasp.

Frederico darts forward, swinging the lug nut wrench like a base-ball bat. It connects with the zombie's skull, making a dull thud. The force, coupled with the slick surface of the guitar, throws the monster off balance. He slips sideways. Frederico swings a second time, delivering a solid thwack to the creature's skull.

I wriggle free and jump to my feet, turning to face the last of the zombies. Dreadlocks bumps against the barricade. Instead of tripping, he pauses and lets out a long, low moan.

He shuffles forward, straining against the barricade. Branches and sticks snap and tumble as he struggles to push through, but he doesn't trip.

Fuck this, I think.

I sprint straight at Dreadlocks, slamming both hands into his chest. He snarls at the impact and falls, landing hard on his backside.

Frederico barrels past me, vaulting over the pile of debris like an Olympic hurdler. He swings the wrench once, twice. Blood droplets sparkle like rubies in the light of his headlamp.

Dreadlocks drops, dead.

I lean over my knees, breathing hard. Adrenaline roars in my ears. A giddy, mad laugh rises in my throat.

Frederico gives me a crooked grin. My headlamp illuminates the blood flecks on his face. He steps toward me, raising one hand for a high five. I laugh again, slapping my palm against his.

"Zombie Rollers unite," I say.

"Zombie Rollers unite," he agrees, grin widening.

This is a single lighthearted moment in the middle of a day that's been fraught with fear and uncertainty. I decide to let myself enjoy it, even if it only lasts a few seconds.

28

PURPLE PASSION

The first order of business is getting the packs off the dead zombies.

"Grab his arm." Frederico motions to Guitar. "We need to roll him over."

"Hold on. I have an idea." I bend down and pat the pockets of Dreadlocks, searching. I come into contact with something long and smooth. I reach into the pocket, grimacing when I touch something sticky. It feels like dried gum or a half-eaten piece of candy. I reach farther in, smiling triumphantly when I find the prize.

"Check it out." I pull out a pocketknife, holding it up for Frederico to see. It's about six inches long with a rose mother-of-pearl inlay.

"Nice." He takes the knife and flips it open.

It only takes a few minutes to saw the packs off the bodies. We drag them a short distance away, then sit down to rifle through them.

A general aroma that has nothing to do with death hangs over the bags. It's the scent of unwashed clothing and flesh.

"Beef jerky." Frederico flashes me a grin as he rips open a package and passes me a few strips.

I greedily devour the jerky, relieved to have something in my stomach again.

I dig through the backpack of Forked Beard, pulling out several pairs of dirty underwear and stinky socks. Yick. I toss them away. Next comes a shirt. Then my hand touches crinkly plastic.

"Trail mix. Nice." I pull out the bag and rip it open, dumping some into my hand before passing it to Frederico.

Ten minutes later, we have a decent pile of water and food before us. We decant the water into our packs. Surprisingly, there's enough to just about top off both water bladders.

Most of the food is prepackaged stuff that goes well with traveling; nuts, dried fruit, granola bars, beef jerky, and crackers. We also unearth hard candies, Twizzlers, and a few candy bars. There's a half-eaten roast beef Subway sandwich with a suspicious aroma that comes out of Forked Beard's bag.

Frederico pulls off the stinky meat and tosses it aside, then slices the sandwich in half. Beggars can't be choosers. We eat in silence, polishing the sandwich off and moving into the packaged food. Within ten minutes, we've consumed almost everything. All that remains are hard candies and a few granola bars. Those we stash in our packs.

"What do you think?" I retrieve the stinky pair of socks that, at any other time in my life, I'd have discarded.

"What do I think about a stranger's dirty socks?" Frederico raises an eyebrow at me.

"They're dry." I tug off my shoes. "Which is more than I can say for mine."

"You didn't get a chance to blow-dry your shoes back at the house?"

"No. Ran out of time when those sick assholes showed up." A pang goes through me as I think of Stout. If we'd left the house sooner, she'd still be alive.

If the world wasn't filled with assholes, she'd still be alive.

With a sad sigh, I strip off my wet socks and inspect my feet. Frederico wordlessly passes me the blister kit. I angle the headlamp, studying the new blisters that have popped up between my toes. There's one under the middle toe on my right foot that has swollen to the size of a large blueberry. The toenail has started to pop off. The blister under my big right toe has nearly doubled in size, blood and clear pus oozing around the loose nail.

With a grimace, I grab the flagging edge of the loose nail and give it a firm tug. It comes free with a brief sting. I repeat the process on the middle toe.

"Two toe nails down," I say, tossing them to the ground. "Eight more to go." I wrap the injured toes with Band-Aids.

"With luck, you'll have a few left by the time we get to Arcata."

I laugh, using an alcohol pad to wipe down my skin. Then I pull out a needle and get to work lancing the blisters.

"This was the only part of ultrarunning Kyle couldn't stomach." I squeeze clear fluid out of the first blister. "We used to joke that it was a good thing he didn't have a foot fetish."

"Yeah, I remember." Frederico chuckles. "I think he actually turned green the first time he saw me rip off a toenail."

"I was on my own when it came to my blisters." I smile at the memory. "He didn't care if I puked or shit my pants, but he wouldn't come near me when I broke out the blister kit."

"You shit your pants?"

I pause, glancing up at my friend. "Only once. I never told you about it because it was disgusting. It was at the San Diego One Hundred. I thought it was a really good idea to eat spicy Indian food the night before the race." I look away, aiming my headlamp back at my feet. "I paid for that decision the entire one hundred miles. I went through three pairs of running shorts. Kyle and Carter thought it was hilarious. They made poop jokes all the way home."

Frederico bursts out laughing. I smile despite myself, keeping my attention on my feet.

Frederico, still chortling to himself, leaves me to my work. He goes about conducting a second search through the backpacks. He finds Skittles, M&Ms, and another pocketknife.

"Aren't you going to check your feet?" I apply some Neosporin to the lanced blisters.

"Nah. They feel okay," he replies. "I'll check them at our next stop. Whoa, look at this."

He holds up a small Ziploc. At first all I can see is a black lump inside. Frederico moves his headlamp, aiming the light and illuminating the contents. It's a small glass pipe and a dark green plug of marijuana.

"No wonder our friends couldn't escape the outbreak," I say.

Frederico sits down next to me, turning the Ziploc over in his hands. He's quiet, intent on the weed and pipe. The intensity in his gaze makes me nervous.

"Frederico?"

"Mmm?"

"What's up?"

"I was just thinking." He sighs. "When I first went sober, I used to fantasize about a time like this."

"A time like what?"

"The end of the world. An excuse to break my sobriety and go nuts."

My brow wrinkles with sympathy. "I understand."

"Of all the drugs I used, pot is the one I miss the most. This" — Frederico holds up the baggie— "was my favorite. It's called Purple Passion. See the little purple flowers?" He holds the bag out to me.

I take it, not wanting to leave temptation in his hands. Under the light of my lamp, I see the little purple flowers.

"I'd have the most fantastic hallucinations on that stuff." His voice goes soft around the edges, like he's recalling a long-lost friend. "I went to a Pearl Jam concert high on it once. Everyone around me sprouted angel wings. The ground fell away. The audience floated with the stars. Pearl Jam's music turned into ribbons of silk and flowed around us as we danced in the sky." Another nostalgic sigh. "That was a good high."

I close my fist around the Ziploc. "You're not thinking of getting high, are you?"

He raises his head to look at me. The bright light of the headlamp sinks his face into shadow.

"After the concert, I drove out to the beach with my friends. We took turns taking hits. Each time we took a puff, we held our breath and ran as far as we could across the sand before letting the smoke out. No one could run as I far as I could."

A fond smile pulls at his lips, showing a brief flash of white teeth. "At some point, everyone went home. I stayed at the beach alone, talking philosophy with a sand crab for hours. I lay on the shore, watching clouds turn into the Shanghai acrobats as the sun rose."

He raises his chin, eyes meeting mine. "I've told that Purple Passion story at least a hundred times. The part I've never told anyone is what happened when I finally sobered up and returned to the real world. I worked at a 98 Cents Store. Turns out I'd missed two days of work on my high. The manager fired me, of course."

"I loved that job; I could go into work stoned and no one ever complained or gave me shit. I pretended I didn't care when I got fired, but inside I was pissed at myself for fucking up a good gig." He looks down, headlamp shining on his shoes. "I was a fuck-up from a young age, Kate. If I took a hit of that stuff now" —he gestures to the Purple Passion concealed in my fist— "it would be the end of my world. If I'm going to die on this run, I'm going to die as the best person I can be, not the worst."

My grip on the Purple Passion relaxes. A moment later, I fling the Ziploc and its contents into the night. It soars through the air, momentarily captured in the beam of my headlamp, then disappears into the darkness.

"Thank you," Frederico says.

"I've got your back."

I reach over and give his hand a brief squeeze before returning to my feet. I apply liquid Band-Aid to the blisters and tug on the dry pair of socks. Then I pull out my phone, holding my breath as I swipe the phone and check for a message from Carter.

Nothing.

I swallow and shove the phone back into my pack, refusing to let myself dwell on possible reasons for my son's silence.

"You ready to get out of here?" I ask.

Frederico, who watched my silent exchange with my nonresponsive cell phone, nods. "Yeah." He rises, shaking out his arms and legs. "Yeah, I'm ready."

"We need to figure out our next move," I say.

I gesture to the tiny town about a mile away in front of us, illuminated by a scattering of streetlights. The tracks run straight into the center of town. No way do I want to go close to a town, not with zombies, soldiers, and CDC quarantines.

Frederico pulls out the map and spreads it out on the ground, weighting the corners with rocks. The two of us angle our heads, illuminating the map.

"It's going to be slow, going around in the dark," I say, studying the map and remembering the tedious trek around Ukiah.

Frederico shrugs. "We've both done our share of night running. We'll just have to move a bit slower and be cautious."

He pauses, peering at the map. "Look here." He points to a section on the map where the tracks veer away from Highway 101 and head in an easterly direction. "The tracks won't take us more than ten or fifteen miles past Willits. Once they head east, we're going to have to follow the highway."

I study the map, following the tracks with my finger. They split away from the 101 and run northeast for miles and miles, never circling back.

"Shit," I mutter. "You're right. We're going to have to use the highway."

"Come on." Frederico folds up the map and stashes it in his pack. "Let's get mov—"

There's a flicker of movement over Frederico's shoulder. I move instinctually, snatching the railroad spike out of my pack harness.

When the zombie steps out of the shrubbery, I fly into him, ramming the spike through his eye with brutal precision. His body crashes backward. I fall on top of him, grunting from the impact.

I stand up, brushing myself off and extracting the spike from the dead zombie's eye. When I turn around, I find Frederico staring at me.

"Damn," he says. "You've come a long way in less than twenty-four hours."

I look back at the dead zombie. The gashed eye socket yawns blackly. Frederico's right. Compared to my first few kills, this one was practically professional.

"I'm a mom on a mission." I clean the spike on the zombie's pant leg, then slide it back into my pack harness. "Don't fuck with me, and don't fuck with my friend."

29

TUNNEL

IT TAKES US A GOOD HOUR TO PICK OUR WAY AROUND WILLITS IN THE dark, even though we only travel about four miles. We're too far away from the main artery of town to see if there's any military presence, but I suspect we'd find a checkpoint at the very least. All the more reason to keep ourselves to the shadows of the open land.

Other than tripping on a rock and disturbing a dog chained to a doghouse, we make it without any major mishap. We reconnect with the railroad tracks at mile sixty-five.

"We've run over one hundred kilometers," I say. One hundred kilometers is a popular distance for ultra races, which is equivalent to 62 miles.

"Only one hundred thirty-five to go," Frederico replies.

I'm about to respond when I feel my phone vibrate. A shot of elation goes through me. I nearly drop the phone in my haste to fumble it out of my pack.

"It's Carter," I say, naked delight and relief in my voice.

Had 2 move 2 another room, his text says. *Everything OK. Where r u?*

What happened? I type back. I recognize my son's reticence to give me the whole truth. He's trying to protect me, like he did when Kyle died.

You don't have to protect me anymore, baby, I think.

A few seconds later, his answer comes.

Fire in room next door. Burned through wall. Everything OK now.

"What the fuck?" I mutter, ire rising in my voice. Fire? A hole burned in the wall of his dorm room?

"What's going on?" Frederico asks, tense as he watches my face.

"What the fuck are the soldiers doing on campus if they're not helping the students?" I snap.

Where r u now? I type.

Another dorm room. I'm safe. Where r u?

I grind my teeth, knowing I'm not going to get any more information from him.

Just passed Willits. Only 135 miles to go.

LOL. Only u and F can say that about 135 miles on foot.

A smile pulls at the corners of my mouth, dispelling some of my earlier anger. He must be relatively safe if he can joke.

Keep safe baby, I type. *See u soon.*

See you soon.

I pass the phone to Frederico, letting him read the exchange. I study my old friend as he scrolls through the conversation, seeing the telltale signs of weariness. His shoulders slump, eyes blinking a little too rapidly as he struggles to focus on the text. We need to stop and rest before he falls and breaks something.

"Our boy is smart and strong." Frederico passes the phone back to me.

"Takes after his dad." I glance at the phone. Shit. Battery is three-quarters of the way gone.

"Takes after his mom, too," Frederico replies.

I shrug. I might be able to run a long way, but I didn't have the strength when it really counted.

"It's three in the morning," I say. "We've been on our feet for seventeen hours. "Let's find a place for a catnap. Thirty minutes or so will give us some extra energy."

He nods. "We'll have to sleep in shifts. Let's find a place that offers some shelter."

We move at an easy lope down the tracks. Two miles later, we find it: an abandoned tunnel running through a mountain. The tracks lead inside, disappearing into complete blackness.

"Here," I say, drawing to a stop. "We rest here."

Either side of the tunnel opening has been spray-painted. On the left side is a purple-and-green, one-eyed dragon bursting from a blue egg. On the right side is a blue head of an old man with a giant nose and mustache.

We pick our way inside. I've done my fair share of running in the dark, but nothing has prepared me for the inside of a tunnel. Even on nighttime trail runs, there's ambient light from the moon and stars.

There's nothing inside the tunnel except unrelenting blackness. The light from our headlamps is swallowed, our circle of illumination shrinking inside the stone walls.

I crane my neck, trying to get a look at the walls and ceiling, but there isn't enough light. My headlamp illuminates nothing more than flecks of dust and more darkness.

I turn my attention back to the ground, focusing on the small patch of ground illuminated at my feet. We move at a walk. Forget running. I can barely see six inches in front of me.

The tunnel smells like wet dirt and stone. Somewhere around us, water drips. I keep my ears peeled for any telltale moans or groans. Inside this place, we're as blind as the zombies.

In front of me, Frederico thumps into something.

"Shit," he mutters.

"What?" I inch up behind him.

"It's just an old crate." He leans forward, headlamp shining on a battered wooden crate. It's intact, the lid held in place with great metal clips.

"There're more." I move past Frederico, hands feeling along the sides of three more crates. A rose is branded on top of the crates. The image tickles something in my memory, but I'm too tired to dwell on it. "What do you think is inside?"

He shrugs. "Who knows? Who cares?" He thumps the crates with his hand. "This is a good spot to sleep. If zombies do wander in here, it will be good to have something between us and them."

He unhooks his pack, tossing it to the ground to use as a pillow. "Give me thirty minutes," he says, lying down on the rocky ground. "Just thirty minutes, then you can sleep for thirty."

I nod, hopping onto one of the crates. Frederico is asleep within seconds, snoring softly. After a few minutes of consideration, I switch off my headlamp. No reason to waste the battery, especially when I can barely see anyway.

Complete blackness now surrounds me. I feel swallowed by unending nothingness.

Carter would like this. He wasn't into running, but he loved a good adventure. Skydiving, hang-gliding, zip-lining, hiking, rafting—he loved it all. I'm sure exploration of an abandoned tunnel would be at the top of his list. He'd love the graffiti art and the sheer unknown of it all.

Carter.

I pull out my phone again. To my surprise, there are two bars of reception.

Can u talk? I type.

I wait. No response comes.

I add, *We stopped 2 nap. I have first watch while F sleeps.*

Again, I wait.

Again, no response comes.

There aren't even little ellipses to indicate an incoming reply.

The battery icon turns red, indicating I only have ten percent battery life remaining.

Battery almost dead, I text. *When phone dies, will try 2 find another. Luv u. Stay safe. See u soon.*

"Where are you, baby?" I say softly. What had happened during the short time between our last conversation and now?

I close my eyes, willing myself not to give in to anxiety. I summon an image of my son's face. His tall, lanky body, so much like his father's at that age. His lumberjack beard, the cotton T-shirts with quirky slogans that he always wears.

I was a shitty mom those first few weeks after Kyle died. Here, in the middle of a fucking zombie apocalypse, I'm being given a second chance to be the mother I want to be. A mother who doesn't quit when things get hard. A mother who takes care of her son.

A mother who saves her son from monsters.

Please be safe, baby, I say silently. *Please be safe.*

30

GRANOLA BITCH

I LET FREDERICO SLEEP FOR AN EXTRA FIFTEEN MINUTES. WHEN I WAKE him, he glances at his watch and gives me a look that's half grateful, half reproachful. I just shrug and toss my pack onto the gravel.

The rocks poke me as I settle down, but they don't really bother me. In my years of ultrarunning, I've napped on roots, rocks, gravel, and boulders. I consider myself a master of the power nap and am asleep as soon as my head nestles onto the pack.

My eyes fly open when a hand presses over my mouth. I jerk, bolting upright and slapping the hand away. I don't know where I am, or how I got here, or why everything is so fucking black.

"Kate." Frederico's soft whisper brings reality crashing back into place.

I remember the zombies, the running, the railroad, and the tunnel. I relax, reaching out for his hand and grabbing it.

"What—"

His hand flies up, covering my mouth again. "Someone's here," he whispers. "Listen."

Rhythmic squeaking sounds in the distance. I strain my ears, trying to discern which direction it's coming from. The sound, coupled with the surrounding blackness, sparks panic in my belly. As the sound draws closer, the murmuring of voices materializes. People.

"We have to get out of here," I hiss. After our last run-in with the maniacs who killed Stout, I'm not eager to meet up with more strangers. "Can you tell which direction they're coming from?"

"South, I think. Does that look like a light to you?"

The sleep and the darkness have disoriented my sense of direction. For all I know, I could be facing the tunnel wall right now.

I turn my head left and right, looking for—for something. Anything. A wrinkle in this perfect darkness.

After several seconds, I see it: a single bobbing light off to my right. I have no idea if that's north or south. Whatever the case, we should be moving *away* from the light.

Which is easier said than done in the current situation. We don't dare switch on our headlamps and draw attention. Then again, without our headlamps, we can't see anything.

I reach out, turning in a half circle until my hands come in contact with the cool, damp wall of the cave.

"Do you see the light?" Frederico asks.

"Yeah." I grope blindly and find his arm. I grab it and press his hand against the tunnel. "We can guide ourselves along the wall."

"And hope we don't roll an ankle in the process," he replies grimly.

I nod in agreement, which is dumb since he can't see me. I shift onto my toes, walking carefully and trying to make as little noise as possible. Rocks and gravel shift beneath my feet. Every little noise sounds huge in my ears.

I sense, rather than see, Frederico behind me. The voices grow closer, more distinct.

Shit.

I pick up my pace, moving as fast as I dare. My foot connects with what feels like a large rock, causing a soft scuffing sound that may as well be a dynamite blast in my ears. Behind me, Frederico runs into something that sends a shower of pebbles pattering down.

The voices abruptly cease talking. They stop moving, and whatever squeaky thing they're moving goes silent. A flashlight beams cuts through the darkness.

I drop to the ground, trying to avoid the beam. Gravel bores into my knees and palms. I ignore the pain, scuttling along as quickly and quietly as possible. My palms and knees—especially my knees—are soon screaming with pain.

Thinking of Frederico in my running shorts, I inwardly wince; I have some protection from my compression pants, but Frederico's knees must be getting torn to bits.

Behind us, the flashlight continues to probe the darkness. After a few moments, I realize the beam is too small to catch us this far away. Maybe we can get out of here in one piece. Maybe—

"I know somebody's in here!" A new voice—a woman's voice— echoes down the tunnel. "You fuckers better not have touched Mr. Rosario's stuff."

Fuck. So much for a harmless nap in a tunnel. Fuck, fuck, fuck. Who are these people, anyway? What are they doing here and what do they want?

I keep moving. The sooner we get out, the better our chances of getting away.

Someone fires a gun, the shot echoing in my ears like a cannon. I bite down on a squeal and haul ass, crawling as fast as I can. Behind me, I hear Frederico scuttling along.

"All right, you fuckers," the woman shouts. "I was trying to be nice."

Shooting a gun is her version of nice? Holy fuck.

"Stop where you are and let us come to you. Otherwise—"

To emphasize her point, two more shots are fired, both of them flying over our heads and into the darkness.

Isn't this crazy bitch worried about zombies? If there are any nearby, that gunshot will draw them.

I frantically weigh my options. I can move faster on foot, but I'll be easier to shoot if I'm upright. If I keep crawling, there's a good chance she'll catch up with us.

Glancing over my shoulder, I see the flashlight beam growing brighter. She'll be able to see us soon.

I reach out a hand, fumbling for Frederico. My hand connects with his shoulder. I dig my nails into his shirt, asking a silent, desperate question. *What do we do?*

"Stop right there, assholes."

The flashlight beam glances off the top of Frederico's gray curls. I freeze, one hand still on his shoulder.

"Who are you?" the woman snaps. "Who do you work for?"

I turn my head, trying to see the owner of the voice. She's

concealed behind the bright beam of the flashlight. Based on the sounds of multiple feet crunching on gravel, I assume she's not alone.

"I asked you a question!" She fires the gun again.

"My name is Kate," I squeak, ears ringing from the gunshot. "I—I'm a waitress. This is my friend, Frederico. He's retired."

"Bullshit." The woman comes to a stop before us. "What would a waitress and a retired man be doing in Mr. Rosario's cave?"

"We're from Sonoma County," I reply, craning my neck around.

Now that she's closer, I can see the woman. She has long dreadlocks pulled back into a ponytail. She wears ripped jeans and a faded T-shirt that says, *What are you looking at, Dicknose?* Bits of light-brown armpit hair stick out from her cut-off sleeves. She looks like a bona fide Northern California granola hippie, except that hippies don't have a predilection for waving guns around and scaring the piss out of people.

"We're trying to get north," I continue, hoping to disarm her. "My son is a student at Humboldt University. My friend's daughter lives—"

"Why are you here in Mr. Rosario's tunnel?" She moves a few steps closer, leveling the gun at my chest.

Sweat breaks out along my chest and spine. My mouth goes dry. I swallow. I fixate on her hand, staring at the small rose tattoo on the inside of her wrist.

"We—ah—we're runners," I say. "Ultramarathoners. We're, um, running to Arcata. The roads were, uh, are, blocked, so we decided to follow the railroad tracks. See?" I twitch my shoulder, drawing attention to my hydration pack. "This is my running pack. We're runners. We didn't know this was Mr. Rosario's tunnel, I swear."

"You're ultra-what?" the woman asks.

"Ultramarathoners."

"What the fuck is that?"

"People who, uh, run races longer than marathons."

"Why the fuck would anyone want to do that? How far is a marathon, anyway? Twenty miles?"

"Twenty-six point two miles," Frederico says.

"And what the fuck does that have to do with the price of mayonnaise?" the woman asks, pressing the tip of the gun against my sternum.

"We, um, like to run long distances." I talk in a rush, balling my fists to stop myself from shoving the point of the gun away. "Like, twenty, thirty miles at a time. Sometimes more. We run all the time. When the zombie outbreak clogged the highway, we decided to run to Arcata."

"And where did you say you're running from?"

"Geyserville."

"Uh, huh. And when did you leave Geyserville?"

"About . . . ten o'clock this morning."

The woman's eyes bulge in surprise. Then she barks a laugh. "That is the most creative crock of shit I've ever heard. It's four in the morning. You're trying to tell me you've run, what—seventy miles? Seventy-five miles?—in less than twenty-four hours? Without getting eaten by the zombies?" She laughs again.

I swallow, resisting the urge to tell her Frederico and I have both completed several one-hundred-mile races in under twenty-four hours. And that we are in fact at mile seventy-three. And that we've become proficient—sort of—at killing zombies. Have I come all this way just to be shot to death by a granola psychopath?

"What, don't have anything to say to that?" The woman shoves the gun hard against my chest.

"It's the truth," Frederico says quietly. "We're ultrarunners, and we're running north to find our kids and rescue them from zombies."

"Listen, dicknose." The woman shifts her attention to Frederico. "I might look like a granola girl, but I've got shit going on between my ears." To my immense relief, she pulls the gun away from my chest. She uses the weapon to gesture in the vague direction of her brain. "No way in fucking hell the two of you ran all the way from Geyserville this morning. And if your kids live farther north, they're probably already dead."

Her words are like a kick in the gut. Frederico and I exchange desperate looks.

Aleisha and Carter are safe. They have to be.

"Squirrel, tie them up," the woman says, glancing over her shoulder. "We're taking these two back to base."

A ponytailed guy in a flannel shirt zip-ties our wrists and walks us down the tunnel at gunpoint. The woman, who I have mentally dubbed Granola Bitch, oversees two other men who load the crates onto a handcar. It's the handcar, I realize, that made the rhythmic squeaking noise we heard earlier.

The rose branded on top of the crates matches the tattoo on Granola Bitch's hand. What's inside those crates that has these whackos drawing guns on us?

Drugs, probably, I realize. Or maybe guns.

Maybe drugs *and* guns.

Considering the fact that we're in the heart of Mendocino County, one of the first places in California to legalize the personal cultivation of marijuana, I decide it must be drugs.

Holy fuck. One look at Frederico's face tells me he's coming to the same conclusion. We're prisoners of wacko drug dealers.

They march us out of the tunnel at gunpoint. The drugs, loaded onto the handcar, squeak along beside us. I half expect to see a zombie or two, drawn by all the commotion, but the woods are strangely quiet.

A mile down the tracks are two ATVs. The drugs are loaded onto them, as are Frederico and I.

I cast a searching glance at my friend. He gives a small shake of his head. Fear and despair tighten my chest.

Granola Bitch hops into the driver's seat. "Those two fucks try anything, shoot their asses," she says to Squirrel.

The ATVs roll off the tracks and into the underbrush, heading steadily uphill. As far as I can tell they aren't following a road, or even a path. Granola Bitch seems to know where she's going, though.

The landscape is a mix of oak and pine trees. Frederico and I bounce along atop one of the drug crates. Who the hell are these crazy assholes selling drugs to? Despair multiplies inside me. How are we going to get out of this? What in my life has prepared me for escaping psychotic drug dealers in the midst of a zombie apocalypse?

Nothing. Absolutely nothing. My life experiences consist of being a mother, a wife, a waitress, and an ultrarunner. Running shoes and electrolyte tablets won't get us out of this.

God. We are completely and totally fucked.

31

FUN RUN

DESPAIR SWELLS IN MY BELLY. HEAVY, THICK, SICKENING DESPONDENCY. It's a despair born of circumstances too heavy to bear.

I could just quit. I could jump off the ATV and make a run for it, force the Granola Bitch to shoot me and put me out of my misery. It would all be over.

The ATV hits a dip in the land. The vehicle lurches violently, nearly throwing me over the side. The physical jolt sends a bitch slap to my brain.

I mentally recoil, abruptly recognizing the dark spiral of my mind. It's the same dark path I took after Kyle died.

Don't go there, I tell myself fiercely. *Don't be weak.*

I reach deep inside myself, searching for my inner strength, the strength I draw on to help me finish ultra races. I am a woman who once raced fifteen miles with a missing shoe. A person who can do that isn't weak. Over and over, in ultra race after ultra race, I've proven I'm not weak.

Now it's just a matter of remembering I'm strong.

I push away all the periphery things that stand in my way; the sadness, the helplessness, the pain. I grab onto a razor's edge of focus, funneling my energy into one single, shining goal: to survive and get to Arcata.

Fuck the pain and fuck the sadness. If I don't mind them, they won't matter.

I feel my despair shucking away, sliding off my shoulders and puddling at my feet like a heavy blanket. I don't know what Granola Bitch has in store for us, but I'm ready for it. Glancing at Frederico, I see the same steely determination etched in his features. He gives me a nod, as if to say, *We got this.*

Mile seventy-nine.

The ATVs pop out on a small dirt road. Cresting one more hill, we arrive at a chain-link fence topped with barbed wire.

Inside the fences are at least two dozen zombies. They crowd up against the fence, drawn by the noise of the ATVs. They moan and gnash their teeth, rattling the fence.

"What the hell?" I murmur to Frederico, staring in horror.

He shakes his head in response, a frown on his lips.

Granola Bitch turns toward us, a sadistic light in her eyes. "Like our security system? We used to keep guard dogs, but Mr. Rosario realized the zombies require less overhead. We rounded these up from Willits. Fed our dogs to them." She grins, watching our expressions. "Now the undead keep our compound safe."

I swallow, trying not to let my unease show. Is Granola Bitch telling the truth, or just messing with us? What sort of sick fuck feeds dogs to zombies? And keeps zombies for pets?

Squirrel hops off the ATV as Granola Bitch pulls up to the fence. He keys a code into the security pad. A second later, the gate beeps and swings inward.

As we drive through, I get a better look at the zombie perimeter guard. They're inside a dog run that surrounds the compound. I guess technically it's a zombie run now.

We pass through the run—fenced off on either side of the entry gate—and head into an area of hard-packed dirt and giant, towering pine trees. Below the trees are small wooden cabins painted the color of dirt. They blend in with the landscape, which is probably the point if they're trying to avoid aerial detection.

I try to get a good look at everything. Three of the buildings are roughly the size of barns. They're probably used for storage or the manufacturing of drugs—maybe both. The rest of the buildings, all small, look like bunkhouses.

As the ATVs roll into the compound, people come out of the buildings. They look similar to Granola Bitch—dreadlocks, big beards, tie-dyed T-shirts, ripped jeans. A few of the women wear ankle-length skirts and loose, fluffy blouses. A number of the men wear dark, knitted caps. They all look to be in their twenties. If not for the guns they carry, I'd think we're in a hippie compound.

The people wave to Granola Bitch and the others, calling out greetings. Any of them could pass for the hobos Frederico and I encountered earlier. Perhaps this is how Mr. Rosario disperses his drugs across northern California; he takes on wayward young adults and turns them into drug mules.

"Found the goods," Granola Bitch calls, hopping off the ATV. "Tell Mr. Rosario we have prisoners."

Several people immediately descend on us. We're grabbed by the elbows and pulled off the ATV. A handful of other people grab the crates, carting them toward one of the big buildings. Most of them gather in a loose circle around the ATVs.

"Jeanie!" A chubby, middle-aged woman with tan skin comes out of a bunkhouse. The top of this particular bunkhouse is carved with a rose—the same symbol Granola Bitch has tattooed on her wrist, and the same symbol branded onto the drug crates.

The plump woman wears a tie-dyed sundress. A matching scarf covers her head and holds back graying, waist-length dread locks. She gives Granola Bitch a quick hug and a kiss on the cheek. "What did you bring me, Jeanie?" she asks.

Granola Bitch—Jeanie—waves the gun in our direction. The hippies holding us haul us forward.

My eyes flick back to the symbol carved on the house. Now that I've seen it, I spot it on the other buildings, too. Why does it look so familiar? I've seen it somewhere before, but where?

"I found the goods and brought them back, Mr. Rosario."

The fat woman beams. "I knew you would, Jeanie. Now we just need to sit tight and ride out this zombie bullshit." She pats Jeanie on the cheek, obvious affection in the gesture. "When the dust settles, people will still want their drugs. Hell, they'll probably want them more than ever. Mr. Rosario will be there for them."

Her eyes, which have been traveling over the crowd the whole time, land on us. Her smile instantly disappears. Eyes narrowing, she says, "Jeanie, who are these folks?"

"Mr. Rosario, we found these two in the tunnel with the goods."

Jeanie shoves the gun in my face. I flinch, and she laughs. "This bitch claims they ran all the way from Geyserville yesterday morning. Says it was just coincidence they were hanging around our goods."

"Really?" The chubby woman, who I can only deduce is Mr. Rosario, narrows her eyes at us. "Sounds unlikely."

"That's what I said, Mr. Rosario."

The woman moves forward. The hippies part to make room for her. She comes to stand before Frederico and me. We're pushed to our knees. Why does this woman go by "mister?"

"They kind of look like runners," she says after a long, silent assessment. "Doesn't account for them being with my goods, though. Well, you two?" My eyes jerk upward as I realize she's directly addressing us. "What do you have to say for yourselves?"

I open my mouth, but Frederico is quicker.

"Mr. Rosario," he begins, voice respectful and deferential, "I'm Frederico, and this is my friend Kate. We live just outside of Geyserville. Our kids live in Laytonville and Arcata. We're on our way to find them. We apologize for disturbing your goods. You have my word that we were only passing by."

"Uh-huh." Mr. Rosario crosses her arms under her substantial breasts, clearly not buying our story. "Jeanie says you ran all the way from Geyserville yesterday morning. That's not possible."

I swallow, mouth going dry. This is not going well.

Frederico keeps his voice level when he answers. "Kate and I are ultrarunners, Mr. Rosario. We run races longer than marathons. Both of us have run fifty- and one-hundred-mile races. We're, ah, the sort of weirdoes who get up Sunday morning and go for the thirty-mile fun run."

"A thirty-mile *fun run?*" Mr. Rosario's eyebrows nearly climb off her forehead. "You're either completely full of shit, or completely insane."

She flicks her fingers. Two hippies step forward, reaching out to rifle through our packs. They probably would have taken them off if our hands hadn't been zip-tied behind our backs.

A woman unzips the pockets near my breasts, pulling out precious food and tossing it to the ground. I curse myself for not eating it when I had the chance.

I watch my other few precious possessions fall to the ground: the railroad spike, screwdriver, gloves, spare shirt, the stick of Body Glide, headlamp, and my phone. I twitch, instinctively leaning toward the phone—my last link to Carter. Granola Bitch sees the motion and laughs at me.

"You expecting a call?" she asks.

"My son," I reply, voice chilly.

Granola Bitch rocks back on her heels. "Riiiight," she says, sarcasm thick in her voice.

I want to claw out her eyeballs.

Meanwhile, Frederico is undergoing the same treatment. Our blister pack is tossed aside, followed by his headlamp, food, hammer, and Luggy the lug nut wrench.

I watch the proceedings, heart sinking into my stomach. We're already running on bare essentials, much less than what we need for a run of this magnitude. By the time these assholes are done with us, we'll be lucky to have our underwear. Hell, we'll be lucky to be alive.

The man frisking Frederico pulls out the small pocketknife he'd lifted from the zombies outside Willits. I glance away, distracted by the contents of my pack scattered on the ground.

"Where the fuck did you get this?"

The hostility in the young man's voice jerks my head up.

He stands in front of Frederico, holding the knife between them. The mother-of-pearl inlaid handle flashes, and that's when I see it: the rose.

The *rose.*

The same rose that's on the crates, Granola Bitch's tattoo, and Mr. Rosario's house.

Oh, fuck. Fuck-fuck-fuck. How did we miss this?

A murmur of recognition and anger ripples through the crowd.

Frederico doesn't flinch. "I lifted it off a zombie corpse just south of Willits."

"This is Greg's knife." The young man turns toward Mr. Rosario, eyes bulging with grief and rage. "These fuckers did something to Greg. He never would have parted with this knife."

"Let me see it." Mr. Rosario holds out her hand.

The man drops it into her palm before turning a steely-eyed gaze back to Frederico.

My heart starts to pound, adrenaline pumping through me. We are so very, very fucked.

"This is Greg's," Mr. Rosario confirms. "Never went anywhere without it. Care to explain?" She levels a hard look at the two of us.

"The owner of this knife was a zombie when we came across him," Frederico says. "He heard us coming and attacked. We defended ourselves."

"You killed and robbed him," Granola Bitch says, a dangerous glint in her eye.

She's not completely wrong, but we can't let her know that.

"He was already dead," I reply, cold sweat breaking out over my body. "We didn't mean any disrespect. We were so hungry. After he attacked, we took the food he had on him. Just the food and the knife. That's all."

"So you say." Mr. Rosario narrows her eyes at us. "And yet Jeanie found you in the tunnel with our goods. Somehow I find it hard to believe this is all just a coincidence. I will give you one last chance to tell me the truth. Who do you work for, and who sent you?"

Frederico and I exchange anguished looks. What can we say to appease this pack of hippie whackjobs?

"Mr. Rosario," Frederico says, "I know our story sounds bizarre. I wish we had some other truth to share with you. But my friend and I are nothing more than two runners trying to get to Laytonville and Arcata. It was never our intent to disrespect one of your fallen or to trespass on your tunnel. Please, let us go."

It's an honest plea. It's the only plea we have. But I can see from the hardening lines around Mr. Rosario's mouth and eyes that it isn't enough.

"Runners, huh? That's the story you're sticking with?" Her dark eyes glitter. "Well, all right then. What's the phrase you used a few minutes ago? Fun run?" She hands Greg's knife to Granola Bitch. "You two are about to go on a little fun run, Rosario style. Jeanie, go get the jingle bells."

32

JINGLE BELLS

Frederico and I are dragged toward the zombies corralled in the dog run. The hippies flock around us, strangely subdued. A few of them murmur darkly in our direction.

Behind us comes a loud jingling. The zombies perk up at the sound of the bells. They groan, mashing themselves up against the fence.

My legs feel weak and my mouth goes dry. Are they going to throw us into the dog run with the zombies? Feed us to the monsters like they did their dogs? And what the hell is up with the jingle bells? If I believed in Santa Claus, I'd say he was behind us.

We draw to a collective halt just outside the compound gates. Mr. Rosario stands to our left, hands on her hips. There's a cold, unyielding gleam in her eyes. That look confirms my suspicion that I'm not going to like what comes next.

The crowd parts. Granola Bitch makes her way forward, grinning wickedly. Her hands carry two lengths of chain, the sort used to lock up a bike, only shorter. Large, shiny jingle bells are woven through the links on a thick silver wire. On one end of each chain is a small padlock.

My breath leaves me in the rush. My arm jerks as I instinctively reach for Frederico. The zip tie cuts painfully into my skin.

Don't be a wimp, I tell myself as Granola Bitch approaches.

Cold sweat bathes my body. My fingers tremble. I bite my lip to stop myself from begging. I will *not* beg.

Granola Bitch, still grinning, wraps the chain of bells snugly around my neck and clicks the padlock shut. She then does the same thing to Frederico. I swallow, feeling the chain move against my flesh. The bells jingle softly with the movement.

"You two claim to be runners?" Mr. Rosario says. "Let's see you run. We'll give you a sixty-second head start." She flicks her hands toward the gate.

A man in a flannel shirt and ripped jeans steps forward and keys in the code.

I swallow again, turning toward the gates as they open. I don't need to ask what Mr. Rosario intends.

I thought she was going to throw us into the dog run with the zombies, but that's not her plan. She's going to free us. With bells chained to our necks. And then let the zombies out after us.

"Will you cut our hands free?"

Frederico's voice brings my head around. His words are steady, devoid of the fear quavering in my belly.

"Please, free our hands," he says.

Mr. Rosario gazes at Frederico, head cocked, then shrugs. "Cut them loose," she says.

A woman steps forward with a box cutter and saws through our zip ties. I rub my wrists, turning once again to the open gates.

I lick my lips, eyes flicking to the people gathered around us. Time slows. I see an ankle-length blue skirt; a tie-dyed shirt; a dark blue headscarf. My heart pounds in my chest and thumps in my ear.

"The clocks starts now." Mr. Rosario glances down at the watch on her wrist. "You have sixty seconds."

Reality snaps in around me, making my ears ring.

Crazy drug queen doesn't have to tell me twice. I dash through the gates, adrenaline powering me into an all-out sprint. Frederico is right by my side. Our bells clang, loud as pots and pans in an earthquake. Behind us, a collective moan rises from the zombies.

I have no plan other than to run as far as I can, as fast as I can.

I give in to the pull of gravity, letting it pull me down the narrow dirt road. It's less of a road and more of a path forcibly forged by the ATVs. It's uneven and littered with a slippery layer of leaves, pine needles, and twigs. I keep my eyes on the ground, calculating each step as I fly down the path beside Frederico.

Tendrils of morning fog snake through the forest. The rising sun tinges the sky with pale yellow and gray, giving us just enough light to see.

I sidestep a slight divot that could roll my ankle. Next I extend my stride, flying over a thick clump of slippery leaves. A small stream cuts through the path; I splash through it without a second thought, not caring that my shoes and socks get soaked.

Each second brings dozens of minute details crashing through my brain. I absorb them with each stride, my mind and body merging to pick the safest and quickest trail.

Behind us, I hear it: the frenzied howl of the zombies as they're released. Their footsteps trample the ground as they come after us.

And our bells. Our fucking jingle bells are like a lighthouse in a storm, a beacon to the blind monsters on our heels. The chain rubs against my sweaty neck, promising nasty chafing in the near future. Where did that psychotic bitch even get bells?

"Keep heading downhill," I pant to Frederico. "We can lose them on the railroad tracks."

"We—" Frederico trips, sprawling forward and sliding roughly against the ground.

I bite back a yelp and rush to his side, grabbing his arm and hauling him up.

"We have to find a way to mute the bells," he says, scrambling back to his feet.

"Later," I reply. "We need to get a mile between us and those monsters."

"We're never going to get a mile between us as long as we have these fucking bells on." Panic makes his eyes round, the whites showing all the way around.

I grit my teeth, yanking on his arm and pulling him down the trail. We can't waste time arguing. Out of the corner of my eye, I see him digging at the collar. I ignore mine, focusing instead on the path.

The ATV trail ends fifty yards ahead of us. Just past it is crushed foliage, hinting at the diverse paths taken by the vehicles, none of them used with any frequency.

I crash straight into the foliage, keeping my steps aimed in a downhill direction. I may not recognize where we are, but I know we drove steadily uphill to get to the campground. Sooner or later—hopefully sooner—we'll hit the tracks.

A moan sounds behind me. I take my eyes off the trail for a bare second, glancing over my shoulder. Zombies plow down the open ATV trail, hands outstretched. Their white eyes almost seem to glow in the eerie, fog-lit morning.

Many of them trip, stumble, slide, or fall on the treacherous ground. A few of them stay down with a broken leg or ankle, but most get right back up and keep coming for us.

My foot catches on something. I grunt as I go down, bells abruptly muffled as I slam against the ground. Pain shoots up my right side.

Fuck. I know better than to take my eyes off the trail.

Frederico is there for me. He grabs my elbow, pulling me up. A slight jingling sounds underneath me. It takes a moment for me to realize the jingling isn't from me or Frederico. It's from a partially eaten body.

I squeak in surprise, leaping sideways away from the corpse. I have just enough time to take in a twenty-something woman in a tie-dyed sundress. She has a bell collar identical to ours. Her skull has been crushed, most of her brains eaten.

We aren't the first ones who've drawn Mr. Rosario's wrath since the start of the apocalypse.

"Look out!" Frederico hisses.

A zombie stomps through the underbrush, swiping at me. I stumble back, trying to keep my footing on the slope. Frederico picks up a large branch and swings it like a bat. It connects with the zombie's skull, spraying blood through the air. Droplets spatter Frederico's face.

He drops the branch and turns. Together, we keep running.

The forest thickens around us, dense foliage rising to tangle our legs. The good news is that it slows the zombies down; I hear them crashing and falling behind us. The bad news is that it slows us down, too.

Off to our left, I spot a fallen tree. I dart toward it.

"Where are you going?" Frederico pants. "They're gaining on us."

"I know." I circle around the tree trunk, positioning it between us and the zombies. Half a dozen of them bash though the undergrowth, searching for us. One of them impales herself on a pointed tree stump, mouth opening in a howl of frustration.

Extending my arms to either side of me, I shake myself violently. The bell collar jingles, echoing through the trees. The zombies pause, every head swiveling in our direction. The impaled zombie hisses.

Frederico, understanding my plan, joins me. He shakes his whole body, jingling the bells with all his might.

A high keening goes up from the zombies. They turn like a pack of hunting hounds and rush straight at us—and the fallen tree.

The first of them—a plain woman in jeans and a blood-soaked T-shirt—hits the giant log. She trips and goes down, chin connecting loudly with the trunk. Behind her, more zombies converge. They run straight into the trunk, falling atop one another in a blind dog pile.

Frederico and I don't wait to see what happens next. We turn and keep running.

33

DEAD END

We plow on through the forest. Breath burns in my lungs. My right arm throbs from the fall and my injured knee burns, but the pain is distant in comparison to the fear thrumming in my veins.

Behind us, moans and grunts escalate as more zombies get caught in the traffic jam we created. The bells overpower everything, jangling relentlessly around our necks.

Frederico puts out a hand, resting it briefly on my shoulder. "Stop for a minute," he rasps.

"We have to keep going."

"We have to deal with these fucking bells," he snaps.

His tone brings me up short. I skid to a halt, sliding in the leaves. Frederico jams his hand into the soft, damp earth and brings up a handful.

"Cover your bells with dirt," he says. "It will help mute the sound."

I immediately drop into a crouch, slathering dirt around the bells. Though the earth is wet, it's not saturated enough to stick as well as I'd like. After a moment's thought, I tear off my hydration pack and drop it to the ground.

"Wrap your shirt around the dirt and bells," I say.

Yanking up my shirt, I tuck it in around my neck. The chain was uncomfortable enough; the added padding of the shirt and the bulk of the soil makes me feel like someone is trying to slowly choke me to death. But the fabric does dull the ring of the bells. The clackers still rattle inside the metal balls, but they're not ringing like a Catholic Church tower anymore. We're going to make the zombies work a little harder for their meal.

Cool morning fog chills my bare stomach. We pull our packs back on. Fatigue pinches the corners of Frederico's mouth and eyes.

There's a crash somewhere behind us, followed by several moans. Exchanging a brief look, we set out again at a run.

I wish I could say Frederico and I were like wood sprites, gliding soundlessly through the underbrush. The clanging of our bells might be muted, but we still make a considerable amount noise as we thrash through the forest.

Branches and twigs snap beneath our shoes. Leaves crackle and bushes rustle as we barrel through them. In all honesty, we still make enough racket to wake the dead. Or in this case, bring the undead down on us.

The zombies follow us like hounds on the hunt. I glimpse one off to my right, moving at a trot down the slope. It's a middle-aged man in plain jeans and a polo shirt. He crashes into a tree, falls down, and gets right back up again.

"Should we try to hide?" I wheeze. "Climb a tree?"

"Too risky," Frederico replies. "If we get surrounded we'll have to fight our way free. I have more faith in my running skills than my fighting skills."

I can't argue with that.

"We have to get to the railroad," Frederico continues. "We can move faster and might be able to lose them there."

Gritting my teeth, I throw all my focus and energy into the forest before me. I am not going to die out here. I am *not*.

I jump over a branch, landing on a patch of leaves. My feet slide on the humus. Rather than fight the slide, I lean forward and push off. I barrel down the incline, riding the pull of gravity and relying on the tread of my shoes. I land lightly on my toes, barely touching the ground before pushing off again.

My quads burn and my chest heaves. I swing my left forearm, knocking aside low-hanging branches. A cluster of thistles springs up before me. I lift my arms, raising them above the bristles while my legs slice through them. Prickles snag at my clothing and cut at the skin beneath. Frederico curses softly under his breath as he tears through the thistles beside me.

We cut sideways, veering around a thick clump of pine trees. A zombie, only ten feet to our right, thunks into a boulder at a dead run. I hear the crunch of bone. The beast snarls, struggling to get to its knees, but it's clear he's broken one of his legs. We dash on, swerving around several more trees.

Snagging the straw on my pack, I take several quick drinks between gasps for air. I leap over a rock, crash through waist-high poison oak, and duck a low-hanging branch.

Another zombie comes through the trees to our right, holding out her arms as she runs. It's a thirty-something woman in a loose sundress.

I scoop up a rock as I run and lob it with all my might, aiming for the head. The throw falls short. Fuck. I throw like a girl.

Frederico lobs his own rock. It clocks the zombie right in the chest. The unexpected blow causes her to reel backward in surprise. Her foot catches on a fallen branch.

She goes down, impaling herself on a fallen tree limb. The wood pierces her through the chest, though of course she doesn't die. It does make it difficult for her to move, which pisses her off. As she struggles to right herself, she lets loose a high-pitched keen that raises all the hairs along my neck.

We speed away as answering keens fill the air around us. Most are behind us and on our flanks, but at least one is somewhere downhill of us.

"Shit," Frederico murmurs.

I bend down and pick up a thick branch. "We have to shut her up," I say. "She's going to bring the whole horde down on us."

The sundress zombie has managed to get onto all fours. She crawls in our direction, keening as she drags the branch with her.

Instead of running away, I run back uphill. The zombie, hearing my approach, manages a quick and eerie spider-like crawl with the branch hanging out of her body. She lets out another high-pitched keen, which is again echoed by her fellow undead.

I swing the branch with all my might. I might throw like a girl, but I have a decent swing. The wood crushes a hole in the side of her head. Blood sprays across my legs as her body smacks into me.

I fall backward, instinctively curling my neck to protect the back of my head. A rock digs painfully into my right ass cheek. The zombie woman lands heavily across my shins. Blood from her crushed skull drizzles onto my pants.

I bite back a scream, kicking and shoving at the zombie body. Frederico grabs her ponytail and hauls her off, then pulls me to my feet.

"That's a good branch. You should hang onto that," is all he says.

We keep running. My ass throbs from the fall; if it's not scraped, I'll definitely have a nasty bruise. At one point, Frederico pauses to scoop up his own branch.

We spot a few more zombies. Rather than confront them, we zigzag back and forth through the woods, doing our best to avoid them. None of them get close enough to send up that unnerving keen.

My eyes are in constant movement, flicking between the forest floor and the woods around us. I watch the ground to keep myself from eating trail; I watch the forest for the undead. An ache develops behind my eyes.

Then, without warning, the railroad tracks bloom before us. One second we're barreling through shrubs and dodging tree branches; the next, we burst through the undergrowth and find ourselves standing on the rotting wood of the tracks. Twenty feet to our right, two zombies stumble out of the woods.

I never thought I would be so happy to see these fucking tracks. Too bad the two zombies had to ruin the moment. Other than bits of leaves and twigs in their hair and clothing, they're miraculously unscathed by their trek through the forest.

Wordlessly, Frederico and I point ourselves north. We push hard, moving much faster now that we have a relatively clear path. Yes, there are still waist-high weeds and thistles to plow through, but even a rotting railroad is better than a forested hillside.

I glance back a few times. Though we managed to lose the bulk of the zombies to the natural obstacles in the forest, a dozen more have broken free of the forest. They follow the sound of our passage and the soft rattling of our bells. Several are badly wounded, dragging broken legs and awkwardly swinging broken arms. Any advantage is a good one at this point, even though there are plenty still on their feet. Maybe, just maybe, we can outrun them.

"Fucking tunnel," Frederico snarls.

I jerk my attention forward. One hundred yards ahead is the same tunnel that got us into this mess.

"We have to go through it," I reply. "It's our only chance to gain ground on these undead fuckers."

"I know," he replies tersely. "It just pisses me off."

The tunnel swallows us. The wild graffiti art that only a few hours ago had seemed artistic now appear sinister. The gaudy colors and larger-than-life images loom high up on the walls. I feel like they're trying to smother us.

Silently lamenting the loss of our headlamps, I run into the darkness. After a quarter of a mile, the tunnel takes a sharp turn, and I lose all sight of the entrance behind us. We also lose all ambient light.

"Shitballs," Frederico says. "I guess we're on level ground with those blind fuckers now."

"Let's feel our way along the wall." I keep my voice soft so it won't echo off the walls. Following my own advice, I step carefully off the track and grope for the wall. After a few seconds, my hands connect with the cool stone.

"At least if we're walking we're harder to hear," Frederico says. "That's something."

He's right. Now that we're forced to walk, the bells are—finally—silent. The only sounds are the soft crunch of our shoes on gravel and the rasp of our breathing. For the moment, I can't even hear the zombies. It's just me, Frederico, and—

A loud *thwack* sounds in front of me.

"Mother fucker."

"What happened?" I whisper.

"I hit my head on something. There's something in front of us . . . Kate, come here."

His hand, fumbling in the darkness, finds my elbow. I let him draw me forward, an icy shiver of dread making a pit in my stomach.

"Put your hands out," he says.

I obey. Where there should have been open tunnel, my hand connects with moist earth.

Oh, shit. My breath comes fast, rasping through my nose.

I move sideways, searching for an end to the mound of soil in front me. Frederico moves along beside me, presumably also feeling out the parameters of the cave-in.

I find what feels like a twisted chunk of track. Then more and more dirt.

My heart pounds.

When I hit the tunnel wall on the opposite side, I bite back a wail of despair. I stand my toes, feeling as high up as I can.

"It can't be," I whisper. There must be a way over the cave-in. There *must* be.

Frederico and I bump into each other. My forehead connects painfully with his elbow. A sob catches in my throat as the truth of our situation settles on my shoulders.

"Goddamn motherfucking asshole." Frederico swears a lot when he's stressed. "It's a goddamn dead end. Fuck!"

34

THE NEXT RIGHT THING

KYLE WAS SIXTY-EIGHT DAYS SOBER. We sat together on the couch. Pink Floyd's *The Wall* played in the background. It was one of Kyle's favorite albums. Carter, nearly four years old, had long ago fallen asleep. Kyle and I didn't speak. We just sat there, holding hands. Our relationship had only recently emerged from a near-fatal collision; we were doing our damnedest to patch things up. Sometimes that just meant sitting together. Just *being* together.

"I want a drink," Kyle said, breaking the silence. "Really bad." He turned his gaze to me, eyes wide and desperate with the longing that coursed through him.

I stared back at him, anxiety knotting my belly. I squashed the instinct to cajole and comfort him, to kiss him and tell him everything would be okay. To rush to the store and buy him a six-pack. The words of my Al-Anon sponsor rang in my ears.

"You have to DETACH, Kate," she'd said. "That stands for Don't Even Think About Changing Him. Worry on changing yourself."

With this advice looming over me like an avenging angel, I bit my lip and kept my mouth shut. I gripped his hand, determined to meet my husband halfway on this painful journey we were on. That meant staying silent and DETACHed, letting him work through his anguish as I worked through mine.

"My sponsor says I have to concentrate on doing the next right thing," he said at last. "I guess for right now, that means sitting here and not drinking." When he looked at me, the wildness in his eyes took on a new edge—a determined edge.

I saw in his face a rising will to resist. To survive.

In that moment, my love for him surged. It was a white ribbon of joy flowing through me.

We could survive. We *would* survive. We just had to do the next right thing—together.

———

"SON OF A BITCH." Frederico's string of virulence continues. "Cocksucking, no-good, assfuckers. Dammit all to hell and back."

His fear and frustration fade to the background as I focus on the feeling expanding in my chest. I don't know if I believe in ghosts or guardian angels or anything like that, but in that moment, I swear I feel Kyle's presence with me. It fills me with a comforting warmth.

"Cocksuckers," Frederico snarls. "Of all the fucked up bad luck—"

In a distance, a growl ripples through the tunnel. I squeeze Frederico's arm, silencing him.

The next right thing. That had been the mantra to save ourselves and our marriage, and it had worked. Why couldn't it save me and Frederico from zombies?

I draw a steadying breath, summoning the determination and focus of that time so long ago. I'm going to need it if we're going to survive the next ten minutes.

Right now, only one imperative thing must happen.

"We have to get back around that corner," I whisper in his ear. "If they pen us in back here where we can't see, we're dead. Our only chance of fighting free is to get someplace where we can see. Come on."

I tug on his arm, urging him back along the tunnel. After a few steps, he grunts in acceptance. One hand on the wall to guide me forward, I move quickly, staying light on the balls of my feet.

Within minutes, we're back at the bend in the tunnel. Something in me loosens at the sight of the exit. It's little more than a fist-sized white smudge, but it sheds enough light to cast our world into shades of gray. Since my eyes have already adjusted, I can see.

"Look for spikes," I say. This is our next right thing: arming ourselves. "Or rocks." I heft a large one and pass it to Frederico.

I continue forward, scanning the ground. Ten feet later, I find a railroad spike sticking halfway out of the ground. It comes free after a few tugs. A few seconds later, I find a fist-sized rock for my other hand. Frederico finds his own railroad spike.

Another growl ripples down the tunnel. I stare into the darkness, scanning for zombies.

Silhouetted against the light, something in the distance moves. I can't tell how many there are.

Frederico gives me a tight-lipped nod, gesturing toward the entrance. We pick our way forward. Now that we can see, we move back onto the railroad. Using the wooden cross ties as stepping stones, we're able to move quietly. The bells are thankfully silent, muted by the dirt and our shirts.

In another two hundred yards, the zombies become clear. There are six of them bunched together, steadily making their way in our direction. More follow behind them, though I can't get a clear count.

Now that they can't hear us, they move at a slower pace, occasionally moaning or grunting.

I chew on my lower lip, trying to figure out our next move—our next right thing.

We've been lucky so far with our zombie encounters, but we're a long way from being proficient killers. I'm not stupid enough to think we can take out an entire pack. Maybe if we had machine guns, but all we have between us is two rocks and two railroad spikes. Direct confrontation is not our best bet.

So if we can't confront them, what can we do? What is the right thing to do in this moment with a pack of dead zombies shambling in our direction?

"Get ready," Frederico breathes in my ear. "I'll take the three on the right."

The answer comes to me in a startling moment of clarity. "I have a better idea," I whisper.

Without another word, I turn around and lob my rock into the darkness—away from the zombies, and away from the tunnel entrance. It clatters loudly, pinging once off the metal tracks.

The zombies let out a collective moan. They pick up their pace, three of them breaking into a jog. They trip, fall, get up, and trip again. They never stop moving forward.

I take Frederico's rock and lob that down the tunnel, too. Then I flatten myself against the wall, gripping the spike in my right hand. I wave my free hand at Frederico, motioning for him to do the same. He frowns but follows my lead.

The first of the zombies jog past us. It's a teenage boy in a Lakers basketball jersey. His knees are badly skinned from falling, the bone of his right shin gleaming a dull, reddish white. He trips, hits the ground, and clambers right back up. He makes it look seamless—like it's completely normal to run blind.

The boy zombie continues straight past us, chasing the sound of the thrown rock.

Frederico looks at me, understanding dawning in his eyes. He chucks his railroad spike down the tunnel.

The noise excites the zombies. Three more of them hurry past us, arms stretched forth.

Two of them are on the tracks, but the third one crunches along on the gravel beside the rails. It's a slim, middle-aged woman in stretch pants and a tunic with red and yellow flowers. The left half of her face has been chewed off and she's missing several fingers.

She passes within inches of me, her stench filling my nose and turning my stomach. I press myself as hard as I can against the tunnel wall, thankful for my too-skinny frame.

She pauses in front of me, head cocked and listening. I barely dare to breathe, afraid to make any sound that will draw her attention. My fist tightens on my spike—the last weapon we have.

Can she smell me? I weigh the stench of her rot against the stench of my running stink. She definitely smells worse, and more potent. That has to count for something, right?

The zombie bares her teeth and snarls, lifting her nose and scenting. She's pointed forward, all her attention down the tunnel—not to her immediate right, where Frederico and I are hiding. My heart beats so fiercely I worry she'll hear it.

Several of the zombies moan as they bump into the wall at the turn in the tunnel. They scratch at the wall, growling as they feel their way around the curve.

The skinny zombie moans and continues on, leaving us behind. I sag in relief.

The rest of the zombies move past us, unaware of our presence. I count eleven altogether.

Frederico and I stay where we are even after they've all passed. In this moment, the next right thing is to let them get to the cave-in before we make our move.

A keen of frustration echoes down the tunnel, along with the sound of crumbling dirt and bouncing rocks.

"Okay," I whisper to Frederico. "Let's move."

35

RIVER CROSSING

WE STEP CAREFULLY BACK ONTO THE TRACKS. MY SHIRT, STILL TUCKED around the bells on my neck, is saturated with sweat and mud. We move lightly down the track, whispering along on the wooden ties. The tunnel mouth grows larger with every step. Behind us, the zombies continue to scrabble away at the cave-in.

We emerge into the sunlight. I blink as my eyes adjust, sending a silent *thank you* to my late husband for getting us out of that tunnel.

But we aren't out of the woods yet, literally or figuratively. Another five zombies are coming down the tracks in our direction. Frederico gestures, pointing east into the trees. I follow his lead.

Our legs swish through waist-high weeds. I glance back and see three of the zombies cocking their heads in our direction. I pick up two rocks lying at my feet and throw them at the mouth of the cave. The zombies hone in on the noise, all five of them turning toward the cave and loping toward it. Frederico and I duck around a tree and lose sight of them.

"We have to find a way around this mountain to the railroad tracks on the other side of the cave-in," Frederico says, voice low. He jerks a thumb in the direction of the tunnel. "I think it's too steep to climb."

I glance back toward the steep slope that rises over the tunnel. It's nearly vertical and covered with loose humus.

"It would be a good way to lose the zombies," I suggest.

Frederico shakes his head. "We'd make too much noise. And if either of us takes a fall, the zombies will be the least of our problems. We have to go around."

I nod in agreement. We take off at a lope. The forest continues at a gentle downward slope. Half a mile later it levels out, softening into sand. Frederico pushes aside a thick patch of shrubs, revealing a gray-green river. I peer over his shoulder. It's a good twenty feet to the other side of the water.

"We're going in." Frederico shoulders through the shrubs and steps into the water.

"Are you crazy?" I hiss. "What if there are zombies in the water?"

"There might be zombies behind us," he replies. "This gives us a chance to lose them for good. Besides, it's the quickest way around the mountain."

Without giving me a chance to argue, he plunges forward. Water swirls around his ankles, quickly rising as he wades upstream. I hurry after him, wrinkling my nose as my shoes and socks are submerged. God, how I hate running in wet shoes.

The water is cool, but not frigid. It rises past my knees, hips, and navel. I remove my pack, pausing to pull out my water bladder.

"I'm filling up," I call softly to Frederico. "You should, too."

Frederico considers the situation, then shrugs and unfastens his pack.

It's a measure of how much our perspective has changed since the beginning of our journey. Less than ten hours ago we poo-pooed river water in favor of a zombie-infested hardware store.

I like to think we've wised up since then. Besides, it usually takes two to three days for water-borne viruses to kick in. If I'm still alive in two or three days, giardia or dysentery will be a small price to pay.

The river cuts east, leading us around the mountain. Still no sign of our zombie pursuers. As we follow the curve of the land, something in my chest relaxes. The tension of the last few hours ebbs, and I begin to think that we just might make it out of Mr. Rosario's trap.

"Do you think we've lost them?" Frederico asks.

"I hope so." I glance down at my watch. "Hey, we've run ninety-two miles. And we're still alive."

"Hungry, filthy, beat to shit, but alive," he says. "What time is it?"

"Eight thirty."

"Not bad." He flashes me a quick smile. "We're on track to a do a sub-twenty-four-hour one hundred."

I return his smile. "Do the ten miles in the ATV count?"

"Yes," he replies firmly. "Because we've run the last ten with bell collars on our necks and zombies on our heels. The two cancel each other out."

I can't argue with his logic. We continue on in silence, following the river for another two hundred yards. I scan the land around us, trying to locate the railroad tracks.

"Do you see them?" I ask.

"Zombies?" He stiffens, looking over his shoulder.

"No, the railroad tracks."

"Oh." Frederico sags, visibly relieved. "I don't see the tracks." He glances around. "Maybe they're up that way?"

I peer in the direction he points. Up a hillside is what looks like an open patch of earth running beside a line of trees. Unfortunately, from our angle, there's no way to know if that flat stretch of land is the road, the tracks, or something else.

"Let's look." I wade to the shore, sloshing onto the sand. I tug unconsciously at the cloth-wrapped bells around my neck. "I don't know what I want more right now. Food or bolt cutters."

Frederico grunts, splashing up beside me. He looks like hell. But then, so do I.

We climb the short hill leading away from the beach. At the top of the rise, we find a narrow dirt road, the sort used for hiking. No railroad.

"Too bad we don't have our map," Frederico says. "I only have a vague idea of where we are."

"Should we follow this road, see where it goes?" I ask.

"I'd feel better if we could find the railroad." Frederico considers the battered footpath in front of us. "Okay, let's follow this. Maybe it will lead to the road. The tracks won't take us much farther anyway."

That's right. I'd forgotten they veer east, away from the 101, a few miles outside Willits. Turning our efforts to locating the highway makes more sense.

We set off at a jog. Puffs of dirt rise around our shoes. The grit sticks to our shoes, ankles, and shins. The bell collars rattle as we go.

After nearly ninety miles of running on the uneven tracks, the dirt road is a welcome change. It doesn't require the focus and attention of the tracks.

My body feels the wear of the miles. My injured knee throbs. The hydration pack is starting to chafe the inside of my arms. Both arms ache from the constant swinging.

There's a burning along the bottom of my breastbone—chafing from my sports bra. More chafing in my crotch from my underwear. God, what I wouldn't do for a stick of Body Glide. I can't believe I have to run another 110 miles without lube.

And my feet—my feet are bricks of pain. The constant pounding. The burn of the blisters. I feel new ones on the bottom of my feet and on the tips of my toes. Too bad our blister kit is miles behind us in the drug camp. What I wouldn't give for a thirty-minute stop to elevate my feet against a tree.

The road slopes up and disappears around a corner. Frederico puts his hand out to slow me down. He points to his ear, then points to the corner.

I stop and listen. At first, all I hear is the soft whistle of the wind as it stirs the trees and underbrush. A few seconds later comes the distinct scuff of a shoe on gravel, followed by a moan.

I recoil, taking several steps back. Frederico latches onto my forearm, backing up with me.

Three zombies come around the corner. It's a father and two kids. They look like they're dressed for camping: hiking boots, dirty jeans, and T-shirts.

I nearly trip over Frederico in my haste to get away. Instead of falling back with me, he breaks away. Eyes wild, he snatches up a rock from the side of the road and launches himself at the biggest zombie.

Well, shit. So much for running.

As he slams into the father zombie, I snatch up a rock, too. The littlest of the zombies—a boy maybe four years old—bares his teeth and darts toward me.

I bite back a squeal as I swing my makeshift weapon. My stomach lurches as the rock crunches into the little boy's head. He drops without a word—just in time for the other child to rush me. It's a little girl about eight. She trips over her brother's body, sprawling in the dirt at my feet.

Frederico lunges forward, delivering a succinct blow to her head.

Blood bubbles out of her crushed skull. I stare down at the kids in horror.

They were already dead when we got here, I tell myself. *We weren't the ones who killed them.*

Frederico raises his eyes from the dead child. I see my own anguish reflected in his expression. After a moment, he turns the child over and pulls off her Disney Princess backpack.

"We need food," Frederico says quietly. He opens the princess backpack and pulls out some dried fruit and two energy bars. Apparently, this little family was going out on a hike when they were turned. Frederico stashes the food in his pack. He gives me a look of self-loathing, then moves on to the body of the father.

This is what we've been reduced to. Scavengers who feed off the bodies of dead children. As much as I'd like to stand here and let Frederico search the bodies, it isn't right to let him embrace this new reality alone.

Swallowing, I turn over the little boy and pull off his SpongeBob backpack. Inside are two energy bars, a bag of trail mix, a water bottle, and prepackaged cookies.

I know I should eat, but my stomach is in danger of revolt. I shove the food into my pack.

Glancing up, I see Frederico rummaging through the pack of the father zombie. As he shoves scavenged food into his pack, something else draws my attention. Rising above the body is a small wooden sign painted with yellow letters. It says *Campground This Way.*

Shit.

"Kate," Frederico says, holding out two more energy bars, "do you have room in your pack—"

I spring forward and clap a hand over his mouth. His eyes widen. I turn him around and point to the sign.

Wordlessly, the two of us begin to back away.

That's when another two dozen zombies descend on us.

36

HAPPY CAMPERS

"Fuck me," I whisper. We've just roused an entire campground of zombies.

"Back! Back to the river!" Frederico cries.

In my haste, I trip over my own feet and land heavily on my ass. I slide backward down the slope. Letting the downward momentum pull me, I flip sideways onto my knees and scramble up.

Frederico sprints up beside me and delivers a vicious blow to a zombie right on my heels. "Run!" he hollers.

I obey, sprinting back to the water's edge. Frederico's pounding footsteps follow me. Our bells rattle around our necks. The collective howl of the zombies follow us.

I splash into the water. As I scan the surrounding landscape, looking for an escape, I see *them*—the goddamn railroad tracks. On the opposite side of the river, just up a steep hillside. How the fuck did we miss them?

"That way," I huff, pointing as we run. Frederico grunts in acknowledgment.

It's pretty hard to run through water, but we give it our all. I track the rocks and gravel underfoot, holding my arms out for balance as I go.

This part of the river is wide and shallow, the water never rising above our shins. It soaks my pants and flicks against the bare skin of my stomach.

The first of the undead plow into the water after us. One of them catches his foot on a rock, doing a face plant. He's crushed as the other zombies sweep forward, mowing over him like he's nothing more than a part of the scenery. Which I guess he is, in a way.

I scan the river, hoping to see the water deepen. No luck. It remains wide and shallow. Between our splashing and the rattling bells, we're sending up huge smoke signals for the undead.

"We have to outrun them," Frederico says. "There's nothing out here to slow them down and there's no place for us to hide."

It's like we're in a slow motion safari video, only with zombies instead of cheetahs. Frederico and I are the hapless gazelles bounding through a prairie with a beast on our heels. The camera tracks the chase, where ultimately the predator leaps gracefully onto the prey and rips its throat out.

We reach the opposite bank and begin a mad scramble up the slope. It's steep and covered with a thick layer of dried leaves. My foot sinks a good inch into the loose debris.

I drop forward, using my hands and feet to claw my way up. Frederico also drops on all fours. For every foot we climb, we slide back several inches.

Glancing over my shoulder, I spot the first of the zombies climbing out of the water and fumbling their way to the slope. There's no way to disguise our route, not with the amount of noise we're making. The zombies zero in on us, moving inexorably in our direction.

"Fuck," Frederico growls.

Turning my attention back to the hillside, I see the source of his ire: a huge patch of poison oak. Nothing for it. We plunge through the vibrant green leaves. I do my best to keep my head and neck above it.

As soon as we burst through the plants, my foot catches in a sinkhole. My right leg is buried up to my knee. I wrench it out, nearly losing the shoe.

Another ten feet, and we hit the railroad. Frederico and I land on the rotting ties at the same moment. We charge forward, plowing through the weeds and thistles that choke the tracks. The plants cut my hands and arms. More of them get stuck in my pants and worm their way in, chafing against the skin.

We've run just over half a mile when the first of the zombies scramble free of the hillside and reach the tracks behind us.

"We need to fuel." I reach into my pack, pull out a precious energy bar, and hand half to Frederico. Scavenging from the bodies of those poor kids may have been a low point, but it might also have saved our lives.

"More." Frederico pulls out the packet of dried fruit and passes a handful to me.

I pop the pieces into my mouth one by one, letting them soften on my tongue before chewing. It can be tricky to run and eat at the same time, especially when breathing hard through the mouth. I've bitten my tongue more times than I can count.

Mile ninety-three.

With the chest-high weeds and the twisting turns of the tracks, it's hard to see the zombies behind us. Besides that, rail running requires me to keep my focus on the tracks beneath my feet, lest I take another fall.

I may not be able to see the zombies, but I can hear them: the grunts, the howls, the moans, and the occasional keen. There are times when I can even hear the pounding of their feet and the swish of the weeds.

Along the way, we come across loose railroad spikes. We bend down, scooping them up as we go. By mile ninety-four, we're both reloaded with weapons. I feel much safer having them secured in the straps of my hydration pack.

Mile ninety-five.

The scenery begins to change. Oak trees give way to mountain pine. The tracks slant ever-so-slightly upward, indicating a rise in elevation. The smell of damp earth deepens. Mushrooms pop up in the soil.

"Do you see that?" Frederico asks.

For a brief instant, I raise my eyes from the tracks. A quarter mile up the road, suspended above the railroad, is a concrete overpass.

"Think we can lose them?" I ask. "Like we did back in the tunnel?"

"Maybe." The word is barely a grunt. Frederico passes me another half of an energy bar.

"Do you think that's Highway one-oh-one?"

"I hope so. I'm not in the mood for some desolate road in the middle of fucking nowhere. Fuck, I'm hungry. And tired. And pissed off."

I fall silent and give him some space, knowing that's what he needs. He's bonking again.

We reach the overpass. Vibrant graffiti art spans the concrete foundation. A pink octopus grins down at us, a wine bottle in one tentacle, a shotgun in another.

I gently touch Frederico's wrist as I step off the track. From the furrow on his brow, I can tell his mood hasn't much improved.

He wordlessly falls in behind me. We move at a brisk hike, churning up the steep hillside. From the higher vantage point, I have a clear view of the zombies on our tail.

"We've dropped a few of them," I whisper.

"There's still over a dozen back there," he replies.

Scrambling the last ten feet up a steep incline, we reach road.

It's silent. Deserted. Tall pine trees line either side of the road, scenting the air with their boughs. I don't know if this is Highway 101, or some other random road in the middle of bum-fucked Egypt.

I pull out the package of cookies I'd taken from the boy zombie, ripping it open and passing it to my friend. He stares numbly at the package. Then he takes two cookies from the package and pops them into his mouth. Relief spreads through me.

"How much food do we have left?" he asks.

I shrug. "I have one energy bar and one bag of trail mix. You?"

"Nothing. There was food in that father's backpack, but I dropped it when those undead fuckers found us."

"I have an idea. Come with me."

I lead him down the overpass, picking up a few large rocks from the side of the road. With our pace at a sedate walk, the bells barely rattle.

I take a position directly over the tracks. Frederico, eyeing me, picks up a few rocks of his own.

"This worked last time," I whisper.

Looking down, I spot the first of the zombies as they jog clear of the overpass. This is my first clear look of them. The three in the lead are young, perhaps in their twenties. They're decked out in expensive REI hiking gear and daypacks.

The leader—a girl with a long brown ponytail—has blood all over her face. A long trail of gooey white intestines is caught in the waist-band of her pants. Her companions are both twenty-something college boys.

They slow, turning their heads left and right to listen. I grip my rock, crank my arm back, and fling it as far as I can. Which isn't all that far. It flies perhaps twenty feet before plummeting to the ground. But it makes a sufficient racket as it rattles down through the trees branches and thunks to the ground. The zombies growl and set off in the direction of the noise.

Frederico nods at me in approval, then plucks the second rock out of my hand. He chucks it into the distance. It travels nearly twice as far before rustling through the trees and hitting the ground.

The three lead zombies let out a keen and pick up their pace, heading toward the second rock. The girl trips on a root and crashes into a tree. It only takes her seconds to regain her footing. She moves swiftly with no apparent injury from the fall.

Another half dozen zombies appear beneath us, following those in the lead. They're all dressed in casual camping clothes—shorts, jeans, T-shirts, and hiking shoes. They follow the keening of the three lead zombies, the pack of them disappearing into the trees.

I turn, sliding down against the concrete balustrade. Frederico slumps down next to me. Fatigue pinches the corners of his eyes and mouth.

After a few minutes, I pull out the last bag of trail mix and pass it to him. He scowls and refuses to take it. I push it against his hand. He ignores me for a few more minutes, then grunts and reluctantly takes it from me.

"We should conserve our fuel," he grumbles.

"Fuel won't do us any good if we're dead. You're bonking. You need to eat." I give him a severe look. Not because I'm feeling cross, but because I know he needs a little severity from me. "I have to have you sharp, Frederico. I need you. I can't do this on my own."

It's a semi-shitty card to play, but it works. He grumbles but obedi-ently tears into the package of trail mix. Opening his mouth, he dumps two-thirds of the package into his mouth, then shoves the rest of the package into my hands.

"I've told you that I despise road running, haven't I?" he asks around his mouthful of food.

"Yeah," I reply. "Yeah."

37

SILVER BUCKLE

THERE ARE MANY DIFFERENCES BETWEEN ROAD RUNNING AND TRAIL running, but the main difference is this: the road beats the shit out of you in ways a trail never will. Pounding on hard concrete for miles and miles does nasty things to joints and feet.

Frederico's loathing of the road is the only reason he never tackled Badwater, the iconic 135-mile race through Death Valley.

I did tackle that race. Only once, and I was beat to shit afterward, physically and mentally. The 120-degree heat didn't help things, either. But I'd take the pounding heat of a Death Valley summer over zombies any day of the week.

IT WAS at the Death Valley ultramarathon that I got my nickname, Jackalope. Kyle, Frederico, and Carter had all been there to crew for that insane adventure. They rode in an air-conditioned van while I ran.

The race started at ten in the morning on the last weekend in July. It began in Badwater Basin, the lowest point in the United States, and ended at the portal to Mount Whitney. Temperatures were already over a hundred when I—along with ninety-three other nut jobs— crossed the starting line.

I ran covered head-to-toe in white SPF clothing. A white visor with a long strip of fabric protected my neck. An ice-filled bandana around my neck was my constant companion. I carried a water bottle, which I alternated between drinking and squirting on my head.

Temps pushed close to 120 degrees that day. I spent a great deal of my rest time inside a man-sized ice chest, soaking in ice water. There were a few times I actually thought I was going to keel over and die. Is it any wonder that ten hours into that race from hell I started hallucinating?

"Hey, Kyle!" I shouted, jogging along in the dark. "Sweetheart!"

"Yeah?" He stuck his head out the window of the van, which rolled along beside me.

"Check it out!" I pointed out toward the scrub brush bordering the left side of the road. "It's a jackalope! They're real!"

"What?"

"It's a jackalope! Look how cute it is!" I pointed to the odd little creature that hopped through the brush only ten feet away from me.

Kyle's forehead wrinkled as he stared at me. A minute later, he pulled the van over. He, Frederico, and Carter piled out.

"Get the camera!" I said, waving excitedly to the jackalope. "Can you believe this? Hurry, get the camera!"

The three of them stared at me like I had lost my mind. In all honesty, I was pretty sure I had lost my mind back at the starting line. Who in their right mind paid money to run this hellhole of a race?

"Mom?" Carter, fourteen, gave a slight shake of his head. "There's no such thing as a jackalope."

"That's what I always thought, but look. There it is!" I laughed gleefully as the jackalope rose up onto its hind legs, sniffing at the air. The full moon illuminated his gorgeous antler rack.

"Mom, there's nothing there." Carter wore the appalled expression that only a teenager can muster for an embarrassing parent.

"You can't see it?" I demanded. "Look, it's right—"

Frederico, who had been silent all this time, burst out laughing. He laughed so hard he doubled over, leaning on his knees for support. Carter joined in, the two of them guffawing. Kyle, bless him, wiped a hand over his face, struggling not to smile.

I stopped dead, reality hitting me like a sack of rocks.

"Oh." I looked from the jackalope, to my family, and back to the jackalope. Dammit, but it *looked* real. I could even see its black nose twitching as it sniffed the air.

"I'm hallucinating," I said flatly.

Frederico and Carter laughed even harder, clapping one another on the back and wiping at tears. Kyle finally gave in to the hilarity of the situation, breaking into laughter.

"I'm hallucinating," I grumbled.

"Babe," Kyle said, "I told you this ultrarunning stuff was batshit crazy. You just proved my point."

The three of them dissolved into more guffawing.

A few days later, I was able to look back at the situation and laugh. But at that moment, blistered and baked to a fucking crisp, it was *not* funny. At all. Scowling at my crew, I jogged off into the night.

The jackalope continued to hop along beside me. That furry fucker had the audacity to talk to me. About management.

"They need to put capitalists in charge of this race," he said. "Then there wouldn't be any of this pansy-ass bullshit happening."

Even though I knew he was a figment of my imagination, I fired back at him anyway.

"What are you talking about?" I snapped. "There isn't a single pansy ass out here on this course."

"Look at you," the jackalope replied. "You can barely stand up. Efficiency has gone out the window."

"I'm efficient," I growled, even as I wondered why I was arguing with my imaginary friend. "It takes physical efficiency to run one hundred thirty-five miles."

"No, it takes stupidity to run one hundred thirty-five miles," the jackalope replied. "Capitalists would consolidate this madness. What will the big bosses say when they see your low performance rates? What are you doing right now, fifteen-minute miles?"

"What the hell do you know?" I asked him. "You're nothing but an imaginary animal."

The jackalope cackled madly. "You just keep telling yourself that."

He continued hopping along beside me for the next five miles, yammering in my ear. That little imaginary asshole knew how to push my buttons. I put my head down, focused on putting one foot in front of the other, and quit talking to him.

That was the last road race I ever ran.

FREDERICO and I walk delicately away from the overpass, doing our best not to make any noise. With luck, the zombies won't be smart enough to find us.

With any luck, we won't be stupid enough to tip them off.

We walk about a half mile up the road before we see the white-and-black sign proclaiming our location: Highway 101.

I sag in relief. "Thank god." I wasn't sure what we would have done if we hadn't found the highway, especially since Mr. Rosario took all our maps.

"One-oh-one isn't safe," Frederico replies dourly. By the dark expression on his face, I can tell he's still working through his bonk. "We're too exposed and there's too much chance of us running into zombies."

"Agreed," I say slowly. "But there's no other road to take us north." I glance toward the trees on either side of us. "We could go into the forest and run parallel to the road. It would give us some cover."

"We need to get these fucking collars off." He tugs at the cloth-bound chain around his neck. "I can't even think straight with this thing choking me. I wish we had our goddamn map. Fuck. This is a rotten fucking day." He glares at nothing in particular. "God, I wish I knew Aleisha was all right. I wish I had tried harder to get her to break up with Dumbo Dan."

"She's a grown-up," I begin. "You—"

His scowl cuts me off. The expression is directed at me, but his eyes are distant and unfocused.

"I didn't want to fight with her. That's why I dropped the conversation. It was the first time in months she answered one of my calls. God, I'm such a fuckup."

He leans forward, resting his hands on his knees. A second later, he throws up.

"I feel like shit." He's talking as much about his stomach as his heart. "I've always been a fuckup. If we find Aleisha—*when* we find her—I'm getting her out of Laytonville. I don't care what I have to do. I don't care if she hates me for it."

He heaves again, throwing up stomach bile and bits of energy bar.

"Walk it off," I say, tugging on his arm. "Come on, you have to walk this off."

Stomach trouble is common on long runs. The body, busy pumping blood to the arms and legs, leaves the stomach to fend for itself. As much as the body needs fuel, it often has trouble digesting it.

"We've been running for" —I glance at my watch— "ninety-six miles. We've barely taken any breaks. We just need to slow down for a while and give our bodies a rest."

He nods numbly, taking a sip of water. He swishes the water in his mouth, then spits to the side.

I blink, peering down at my watch. My eyes are dry and a bit bleary. I rub them twice to make sure I'm seeing clearly.

"Shit, it's only nine-fifteen in the morning. We just might make one hundred miles in twenty-four hours."

The beginning of a smile tugs at the corners of Frederico's mouth. Then he throws up a third time. He laughs while he dry-heaves. I find myself smiling.

"Those undead fuckers gave us the kick we needed," Frederico says between heaves. "Damn. What a fucking day." He straightens, wipes his mouth on the sleeve of his shirt, and takes another drink of water.

We plod on, moving at a tired walk. Frederico throws up two more times before his stomach settles.

Finally, at mile ninety-eight, he says, "I'm feeling better. I'm ready to jog."

"You sure?"

"Yeah."

"Okay." I nod. "I've been thinking about this. We need to stick to the road as much as we can. It's the fastest—and the only direct route —to Laytonville and Arcata. If we hear or see something we want to avoid, we go into the woods and pick our way around. Sound okay?"

"It sounds okay so long as we're lucky enough to spot trouble before it spots us."

I glance up at the tree-and-shrub-choked land on either side of us. "Bushwhacking through the woods will take too long. The quickest way to get our kids is to run on the road."

He doesn't say anything for a long time. When he does finally speak, resignation is thick in his voice. "I don't like it. The odds aren't good."

I make a face. "The odds went downhill with the start of the apocalypse."

Frederico grunts. "All right. Let's take the road."

We break into a jog, setting an easy ten-minute-mile pace. The road is eerily empty—no cars, no people. There isn't even a sign of wildlife—no whir of insects, no chirp of birds, no rustle of squirrels. It's just us and the trees out here. For now, anyway.

A short distance later, I glance down at my watch. It reads: 100.06.

"Frederico!" I turn and grin at my old friend. "We've officially hit one hundred miles!" Even though this is only the halfway point, it gives my spirit a boost. My aches and exhaustion don't seem nearly as bad as they did a few minutes ago.

Frederico is shading his eyes and staring up the road. He's so intent that he doesn't hear me.

"Frederico!"

"Hmmm?" He turns to me, a dent between his eyebrows.

"Did you hear what I said?" I demand.

"What?"

"We just hit one hundred miles!"

He blinks in surprise. Then a smile creases his face. He turns my wrist, taking a hard look at the watch.

"Damn, Kate. It's nine fifty-eight. We did that shit in a sub-twenty-four."

We slap high fives. In the world of ultrarunning, sub-twenty-four hours is every runner's dream for a one-hundred-miler. In most races, it gets you a silver belt buckle. Not that Frederico or I have ever worn any of our buckles, but it feels damn good to win one.

"If we survive, I'm going to have belt buckles made for us," I say, still grinning.

He returns the smile, then shifts his attention back to the road. "Do you see that?" he asks.

"See what?" I squint, peering up the tree-lined road.

"That white smudge. Do you think it's a car?"

"I can't tell. It's too far away."

"I think it's a car," Frederico says. "Let's go into the trees. We need to approach with caution."

I sigh, following him into the forest bordering the road. We're forced to a vigorous walk as we pick our way through the foliage. If there are zombies up the road—or something worse—at least we'll have some trees between us and them.

38

ATTACK AND STACK

"It's an RV," I whisper.

We crouch in the trees, staring at the road below us. A Cruise America RV lies on its side in the middle of the road. No other vehicles are in sight.

"I don't see any zombies," Frederico whispers.

"They could be on the other side of the RV," I reply. "Or inside."

We continue to watch the motionless scene in front of us, as if something miraculous will happen by the sheer force of our stares.

"We need to get inside that thing," I say at last.

"I know."

"There's probably food in there."

"I know."

I look at him. He ignores me, then finally turns and meets my eye.

"There's probably a kid or two in there," he says at last.

I swallow, understanding the self-loathing in his expression.

"We could move on," I say. "But it might be a while before we get another opportunity as good as this. The next wreck might be a ten-car pileup with thirty zombies to contend with."

"I know." He grunts. "I'm just being a pussy. Come on. Let's do this."

We creep toward the road, both of us armed with our railroad spikes. A quick circle around the RV turns up no zombies. Which means . . .

"They're all inside," Frederico says grimly.

"That's a good thing," I say.

He frowns. "How so?"

"Remember when we met Fallon O'Keefe at her book signing?"

Fallon O'Keefe is a sixty-something ultrarunner who's been running and racing ultras for over thirty years. She set a lot of records at a lot of tough races during her prime. Her memoir is a fascinating account of many of those races.

"Yeah, I remember."

"Do you remember Attack and Stack?"

Attack and Stack was one of O'Keefe's race tactics. The theory required her to "attack" the course right at the start of the race. She pushed hard to get out in front of her competitors when the trail was wide. Then, when the trail narrowed to a single-track—as it often does in ultra races—she forced all the other runners to "stack" up behind her. Passing on a single-track can be challenging, especially if there's a long line of runners. To a large degree, this allowed her to dictate the pace for large portions of the race.

"You want to Attack and Stack the zombies?" Frederico raises one eyebrow.

"Yeah. We make a narrow opening and force them to come at us one at a time."

He mulls this over. "That's not a bad idea."

We circle the RV once more, looking it over with critical eyes. Inside, we hear several zombies scratching at the walls and moaning softly. The door faces skyward.

"Front windshield," Frederico says. "We smash it."

"Force them to come at us in a single file," I agree.

"Attack and Stack." Frederico grins at me. "Good thinking, Jackalope."

We go back into the trees and forage around until we find a solid tree branch.

"This should make enough racket to draw the attention of every undead fucker in that RV," Frederico says, hefting the branch and smacking it against his palm.

"You do the smashing," I say as we return to the road. "You've got a stronger arm."

"Windshield glass is a bitch to get through." He makes a face. "I've smashed more than one or two."

"In your drinking days?" I ask.

"Yeah."

"You'll have to tell me more about them someday."

He shrugs. "I was a stoned, drunk, lonely asshole who did shitty things. They're not stories worth retelling."

With that, he swings the branch. It connects with a dull thud, tiny crackles appearing in the glass. He swings a second, then a third time —and then a zombie smashes into the window from the inside. It hits so hard the crackling glass bows outward.

"Oh, fuck." Frederico takes an involuntary step backward, raising the tree branch defensively.

The zombie snarls, smashing several more times against the windshield with frenetic desperation. Nails claw and teeth snap. Blood smears the glass.

It's a big, burly man in a tight T-shirt with shaggy dirty blond hair. I experience a terrifying moment where I imagine an RV full of WWF-sized zombies rushing me and Frederico en masse.

Holy fuck. What are we getting ourselves into?

There's an explosion of glass and blood. The burly zombie careens through the opening and skids across the asphalt.

Even though I'm supposed to be the one picking off the zombies as they crawl (or, apparently, *rocket*) out of the RV, Frederico closes in and starts hammering on the head of the monster, hitting him before he can even get to his feet.

Two more zombies follow right behind the first one. Fuck. The plan was to deal with these fuckers one at a time. But the hole in the windshield is larger than expected, thanks to the rabid, dinosaur-sized zombie. And the two undead crawling out are children.

Fuck me. More kids. Honestly, I would have preferred another dinosaur zombie.

I summon an image of my son: tall, broad-shouldered, lanky Carter with his lumberjack's beard.

"This is for *my* kid," I say to myself. With that, I angle my railroad spike and dart forward.

The closest zombie kid is a towheaded little boy. Hearing my approach, he bares his teeth and snarls up at me. One grubby hand swipes at my ankle. I let him grab me, getting in close enough to bring the spike down with brutal finality on the small skull.

I experience that familiar sensation of rusted metal punching through the skull, then sliding through the soft, yielding brains. The small towhead collapses, unmoving.

But the hand around my ankle is still moving, clawing me through my compression pants.

"What the fuck?" I try to step away, but the little hand is like a shackle. I stumble, falling backward onto my ass. I frantically jerk my leg, trying to free it from the little boy's grasp.

At first, I think it's some weird zombie rigor mortis. Then I realize the hand belongs to the second kid zombie—a little girl with the same intense white-blond hair. Her hand is lodged beneath her brother's body. Saliva drips from her mouth as she snaps her teeth at me.

Using my ankle as an anchor, she hauls herself forward. Glass shakes free and tinkles around her body. I deliver a brutal kick to her face. It's hard enough to slow her down but not enough to kill her. Or dislodge her grip from my foot, either.

I kick again, bashing the sole of my shoe against her nose and forehead. The delicate nose bones crack under the blow, but still the girl continues to drag herself closer to me.

Frederico leaps in my direction, swinging his branch. One brutal *thwack* breaks her skull like an egg. Her grip on my ankle instantly slackens.

"Another kid!" I yell, seeing a towheaded form rise up behind Frederico.

He spins around, whipping the branch with him. It hits a young teenage boy in the chest. The boy falls backward, landing hard on the steering wheel. Behind him is yet another zombie clawing at part of the glass that hasn't yet broken.

As the teen zombie struggles to regain his footing, I rush forward and ram my spike through his eye socket. He dies, head lolling on the steering wheel.

The zombie beating at the glass crawls over the body, snarling as he emerges. It's another kid, this one eight or nine.

"How many fucking kids are in there?" I squeal.

Frederico swings his branch like a golf club, denting the side of the zombie's skull. The undead kid collapses, blocking the opening. Behind him comes growls and howls.

"There're more inside," I say, staring dismally at the blocked opening.

"We have to pull the body out of the way," Frederico says. "Give the others a way out."

"Honestly, I was hoping there were only four people inside. We've already killed five." I grimace. "Maybe we should move on."

"Are you kidding?" Frederico gives me an incredulous look. "Your Attack and Stack idea is brilliant. It's working. We can't stop now. Just think of all the food waiting for us inside."

He's got a point. "Okay." I heft my spike and get myself into a balanced position. "Pull the body out."

Frederico grabs the arm of the dead zombie and yanks it out of the opening. As soon as he does, a sixth zombie scrambles free.

It's the mother. Her pale hair is streaked with gray and she looks pregnant—very pregnant. She rushes me, but I'm ready for her.

I sidestep, letting her tear past me. As she does, I stick out a foot and trip her. She sprawls, growling and gnashing her teeth all the while.

Like all the undead, she is unfazed by the pain of her fall. She barely hits the pavement before she rebounds onto her hands and knees. I pounce, stabbing her through the back of the skull with my spike.

"What the hell?" Frederico hollers behind me. "Didn't these people ever learn about birth control?"

I turn around to see two more children streak out of the RV—straight toward Frederico. They're small, maybe four or five. Two girls. I'd say they're twins, based on their matching skirts and shoes.

They reach Frederico at the same time. He rams the base of his tree branch through the skull of the one on his right. The second one grabs his arm, snapping her teeth as she tries to get a bite.

With a wild yell, Frederico drops his branch and swings his arm, trying to dislodge the child zombie. I'm about to rush to his rescue when movement near the RV windshield draws my attention.

A woman with gray hair and a wizened face climbs out, moaning. Drawn to the commotion Frederico and the undead child are making, she moves toward them.

"There's a grandma!" I cry. "Watch out for the grandma!"

I dash to intercept the old woman, putting myself between her and Frederico. I don't have time to get my spike into position. Instead, I ram both my hands into her chest. Her wrinkled, light form flies backward and strikes the hood of the RV.

Not giving her a chance to recover, I leap forward and jam my spike into her eye socket. I barely notice when blood sprays me in the face.

Spinning back around, I find Frederico picking himself off the ground. One of his spikes sticks out of the sixth zombie's skull. Pursing his lips, he pulls it free, wiping the blood off on the girl's shirt.

Our harsh breathing fills the air. We stand there, both of us poised and intent on the RV. Nothing else stirs inside. The vehicle is silent and still. And yet . . .

"Do you hear that?" I ask.

"Yeah." Frederico's mouth is pressed into a tight line. "There's another one."

It's a small, faint growl. At first, I think there's a zombie somewhere out in the woods, making its way toward us and all the racket we've just made. Then I realize the sound isn't coming from the woods.

Moving back to the mother, I roll over her body.

"Ah, shit." I stare down at her. What I had mistaken for a pregnant belly is in fact a very small infant secured tightly to her torso with a blue cloth that matches her dress.

The little thing turns its head sideways, baring bloody teeth at me. Now that I'm looking closely, I can see where it tore huge chunks out of its mother's breast and chest.

My hands go clammy. Tightening the grip on my spike, I take a few steps back.

"Should we . . . should we put it down?" Frederico says.

I shake my head. "We just took out the fucking undead Brady Bunch. I'm done."

Turning away, I step toward the RV. "I'll go in and forage," I say. "You keep watch."

Not giving him a chance to argue, I slip through the shattered glass and into the cab.

39
PAPERCLIP

A FEW YEARS AGO, A NEIGHBORHOOD RACCOON WAS HIT BY A CAR outside our house. The poor animal had the grace to drag itself off the road and onto our front lawn, where it died. Animal Control won't remove any animal on personal property, so the disposal of the raccoon corpse fell to Kyle.

Being an efficient man not overly burdened by details, Kyle scooped up the raccoon with a shovel and dumped the body into our garbage can.

We then went camping for two weeks, during which time the raccoon body commenced the decomposition process.

Inside the RV is an aroma similar to the one that plagued our trashcan after the raccoon incident—only multiplied by ten. If we hadn't gone to such efforts to empty the RV of zombies, I would have moved on.

I partially unwrap my shirt from around the collar, pulling it up over my nose and mouth. Breathing through an open mouth, I will myself not to gag. After hauling the dead teen off the steering wheel, I steel myself and venture into the RV.

The next thirty minutes are spent ran-sacking the interior. I get two pillowcases from the sleeping loft and fill them with everything edible I can find. And with nine people living in this tiny RV, there's a shitpile of food.

Canned chili, canned peaches, canned corn, and SpaghettiOs

make up the bulk of the foodstuffs. There are enough cracker-type foods to stock an aisle at Walmart: Wheat Thins, Goldfish, Cheez-Its, pretzels, Triscuits, Cheetos, and Ritz peanut butter sandwiches. Dessert for this family consisted of Hostess Twinkies and CupCakes. There isn't a bottle of water in sight, but there are several cases of juice packs for kids. I rip open a case of apple juice and dump the boxes into a pillowcase.

I leave behind the stuff that requires preparation: Top Ramen, mac-n-cheese, and Rice-A-Roni. I rummage through the kitchen and find two forks, two spoons, a can opener, and—miracle of miracles—a tube of super glue. Super glue can be an ultrarunner's best friend. I stash it in the pocket of my running pack.

In the tiny bathroom, I score a portable first aid kit, complete with Band-Aids, scissors, and Neosporin.

Pretending not to see the blood smeared all over the RV interior and pooled on the floor near the sofa, I grab my pillowcases and haul them up to the cab.

"I don't suppose you found any bolt cutters inside?" Frederico asks as he takes the pillowcases from me.

"No, but I found a first aid kit. We can take care of our blisters."

"How about a paperclip?" He fingers the fabric-wrapped collar around his neck. "There's got to be something in there to help us get these fuckers off our necks."

I duck back inside and continue my rummaging. After pawing through two drawers in the galley kitchen, I let out a garbled exclamation of triumph.

"There's a whole box of paperclips in here," I call out. "The jumbo ones!"

"Thank god. Bring them up!"

I scramble back outside and present the tiny box of paperclips to Frederico as if it's a bar of gold from Fort Knox. I eagerly unroll the shirt from around the collar. Wet dirt showers down as I do. The bells ring softly, making me wince.

Frederico bends open a paperclip and leans forward to inspect the chain. I feel him blow against the lock at the back of my neck, clearing away the dirt. Then the metal of the paperclip scrapes the inside of mechanism. A few seconds later, the lock pops open.

I let out a sigh of relief as the collar falls into my hands. I momentarily close my eyes, reveling in the weightlessness around my neck. There are chafe marks under my chin, but nothing worse than that.

"My turn." Frederico pushes the paperclip at me. "It's a cheap lock. Just poke around and it'll come free."

Careful not to make too much noise, I set my collar on the ground, then get to work on Frederico's. I've never picked a lock in my life, but he was right about the locks being cheap. After twisting and prodding for a minute, it pops open.

Frederico wads the collar into a ball and hurtles it through the broken window of the RV. There's a loud racket when it lands, making me wince.

"Did you have to do that?" I scowl at him.

"Yeah," he replies tersely. "I did. Come on, let's eat."

We haul the pillowcases a quarter mile into the woods. Finding a small clearing covered with damp pine needles, we settle down.

It's been about sixty-five miles since our last food binge. Time to fuel up.

We spend the next forty-five minutes in graceless consumption of food, passing the can opener back and forth. A pile of discarded packaging grows next to us. I barely taste the SpaghettiOs as I shovel them into my mouth. Frederico sucks down the syrup after polishing off a can of peaches. I use a few squirts of apple juice to clean a smear of blood off my arm.

In a perfect world, we wouldn't binge like this. There's a good chance one of us will get an upset stomach. But there's no way to carry the food we need for a run of this magnitude, and it's not like we can count on a well-stocked aid station every ten miles. No, we have to eat when we can.

"I used to buy these for Aleisha when she was a kid." Frederico holds up a box of Hostess CupCakes. "I always brought them home after a drinking binge, hoping she'd forget the fact that I'd been gone for two or three days. It really pissed off her mother."

"Can't blame her for that," I reply. "They don't exactly qualify as food." Despite this statement, I help myself to two of them. "Did it work?"

"Dif whaf wurf?" Frederico looks up around his own mouthful of Hostess.

"The bribe. Did Aleisha forgive you for being gone when you gave her the junk food?"

He shrugs, swallowing the last of his cupcake. "When she was little. By the time she was a teenager, she'd wised up to my game. I remember the day I brought them home wrapped with a red bow. She was twelve. She said, 'Dad, those will make me fat and rot my teeth. If you really loved me, you'd buy me an iPhone.'"

I snort with laughter. "Smart kid. Did you get her one?"

His shoulders sag. "Couldn't afford one. Wasted all my money on liquor and pot."

We eat the rest of our meal in silence.

By the time we're finished, there are only two boxes of Triscuits left. A huge mound of trash sits next to us. Frederico's brow is still furrowed in self-revulsion.

Knowing there's nothing I can say to make him feel better, I find a semi-comfortable spot against a tree and remove my shoes. The tread is two-thirds gone, worn down over the nasty miles behind me. Gingerly, I tug off my socks. The blisters I find underneath are to be expected after one hundred miles.

I get to work lancing blisters and applying Neosporin. The second toenail on my left foot comes off. I toss it to the forest floor without a second thought, barely noticing the pain.

Pulling out the super glue, I apply small drops between the wounds and the loose, lanced skin on top. It stings like hell, but it'll wear off in the a few minutes. When it dries, I'll have a nice, hard shell over the raw skin. The loose skin on top will stick to it, creating an extra barrier of protection. Way better than Band-Aids in a situation like this.

After a moment's thought, I even decide to apply super glue to the top of the toes with missing nails. The skin is tender and sore. A little extra protection will be a good thing.

When I'm finished, I toss the blister kit in Frederico's direction. I lie on my back and elevate my feet against the tree trunk. They hurt like hell.

Just fifteen minutes, I tell myself. Fifteen minutes to let blood drain from my feet while Frederico takes care of his blisters. I stare up at the blue sky, determined to keep my eyes open . . .

"Kate. Wake up. It's time to go." A gentle hand squeezes my shoulder.

My eyes snap open. I'm on my back, feet still propped against the tree. A bit of drool warms the right side of my jaw.

I roll sideways, getting guiltily to my feet. "Sorry." I rub at my eyes. "How long was I out?"

"Thirty minutes or so." Frederico's easy smile is back.

"You want to take a quick nap?"

He shakes his head. "I'm feeling okay. We're not too far from Laytonville. I'm anxious to get to Aleisha."

I nod in understanding, wondering where Carter is and if he's safe. A knot of anxiety immediately forms in my stomach, and I force myself to focus on the task at hand.

I take the two remaining boxes of Triscuits and open them, then tear a corner of the bags to let the air out. I pass one bag to Frederico. He has a zippered compartment on the outside of his pack where the crackers fit. I shove mine into the hydration compartment, on top of the water bladder.

"Ready?" I ask, surveying the mess we're leaving behind in the clearing. It's hard to care about litter when the world has ended.

"Ready," Frederico replies.

40

STRONG ENOUGH

MILE ONE HUNDRED FIVE.

With a freshly refueled body, I feel oddly energized. My body hurts from one hundred miles of pounding, but that's to be expected. I lock the discomfort into a small corner of my mind, focusing on the task at hand.

The landscape subtly changes as we run. Pine trees infiltrate the oaks, slowly and steadily taking over the terrain. The grassland disappears, succumbing to the forest. The miles are blessedly shady, the trees growing right up to the roadside and providing protection from the sun.

Human dwellings are few and far between. We pass the occasional rundown home or mobile trailer. These sparse pockets of humanity have yards filled with various debris: broken-down cars, piles of half-used building supplies, and plastic bags filled with trash and recyclables.

A few homes have a zombie or two in the front yard. So far, all of them are contained by a chain-link or wooden fence at the perimeter of the property. Even so, Frederico and I slow to a walk, making as little noise as possible until we pass the danger.

Mile one hundred nine.

There's something that happens during long runs. The miles blur together and pass in the blink of an eye.

The running feels good. Life feels good. Some people call it the runner's high. Some call it trail surfing.

It happens to me there on the road in the shade of the pine trees. Even with all the death and mayhem behind me—and likely in front of me—I find joy in running. It's fucked up, but it's the truth.

Mile one hundred thirteen.

We pass a rest area on a downhill climb. Other than a semi-truck, the parking lot is deserted.

"Do you see the drinking fountain down there?" I ask, pointing.

"Yeah." Frederico peers down into the rest area. "My water bladder is still half full. Yours?"

"Yeah, mine is fine."

"God, it'd be nice to take a shit in one of those toilets," he says. "Wipe my ass with real toilet paper. I'm sick of leaves."

"Yeah. It'd be nice to break into that vending machine, too. Get some snacks for the road."

Despite this conversation, neither of us suggests stopping. For my part, I'm loathe to go where I might have to fight zombies. I'd rather scrounge by with our meager supplies for as long as possible before facing the undead again.

I don't know what Frederico's excuse is.

Mile one hundred seventeen.

The green-and-white road sign informs us that Laytonville is ten miles away.

I glance at Frederico, gauging his reaction. His expression is tense, his eyes locked on the sign. He says nothing, so I stay silent.

We encounter a vehicular pileup. We skirt around it, scrambling up a steep embankment and picking our way through ferns and underbrush. By the time we make our way back to the road, the wreck is far behind us and out of sight.

God, please let Aleisha be alive, I think. I have no idea how we're going to get her out of Laytonville if and when we find her, but we'll figure something out.

Mile one hundred twenty.

My runner's high is gone. In its place is a growing queasiness in my belly, a feeling I am all too familiar with. I know I should slow down, let my body restore some of its equilibrium, but fuck that. The road is clear and I don't want to waste daylight catering to my pansy-ass stomach. I don't want to give into the nausea and barf up all the food we fought so hard to get.

I'm going to power through this. A small part of my brain tells me not to be an idiot, but I ignore it. I boarded the idiot train a hundred miles ago.

"Remember what Carter used to say at aid stations?" I ask in an attempt to distract myself from the physical discomfort in my belly.

Frederico doesn't bother to look up, but I see the corners of his mouth twitch. "You've never been any closer to the finish line."

I laugh at the memory. It didn't matter if Carter met us at mile eleven or mile ninety-six; he always said the same thing. Thinking of my son brings a mix of achy despair and desperate love.

"Sometimes it really pissed me off when he said that," Frederico says.

"Yeah, me, too. Especially when I was really hurting." I tilt my head, taking a moment to soak in the view of the trees towering above me. "But sometimes it gave me a much-needed dose of optimism."

"Me, too. Carter got his optimism from Kyle."

"Yeah. He did."

The temporary mirth fades from Frederico's face, replaced by the same tension I saw earlier by the Laytonville sign. He's thinking about Aleisha.

"When we find her, we're going to have to figure out another way to travel," Frederico says. "She can't run."

"Maybe we can find bicycles," I offer.

"Yeah, maybe." He falls silent, and I know he's doubting his ability to convince her to come with us.

I mentally calculate our odds of avoiding detection by zombies and military personnel while on bikes. I like our odds better on foot, but we can't expect Aleisha to run. For that matter, I haven't even considered how I'm going to get Carter out of Arcata when I find him. He can't run, either. At least, not like Frederico and me.

You don't finish a race by obsessing about the finish line; you finish a race by taking one step at a time. You focus on every turn in the trail, every climb, every decline, always putting one foot in front of the other.

First, we find our kids, I think. *Then, we figure out how to get them to safety.*

Mile one hundred twenty-four.

Fucking shitballs. Why was I such an idiot?

I stand on the side of the road, sides heaving. The SpaghettiOs I ingested twenty miles ago lay in a nasty pile by my feet.

"You need to walk it off," Frederico says. "Come on."

"No," I snap. "We need to keep moving."

Frederico gives me a firm look. "We're not stopping. Just moving at a slower pace. Come on."

I open my mouth to argue. As I do, my stomach gives another heave. This time canned chili comes up.

"What a waste," I grumble.

"Power walk," Frederico says. "Just keep moving."

I nod, knowing he's right. Slowing down will help my body right itself.

Taking a drink, I rinse out my mouth. Beside me, Frederico tenses. I freeze in response, eyes flicking back and forth.

A long moan reaches my ears. My head snaps around. A single zombie ambles around a curve in the road ahead.

Frederico clamps down on my wrist, pressing one finger against his lips. I nod in understanding. Maybe, just maybe, if we remain silent, the zombie won't notice us.

It's a teenage girl in a long yellow sundress. Even from a distance, I can see the blood matted in her short blond hair. More blood smears her face, giving the illusion of a lipstick application gone bad.

My stomach gives a violent roil. Bile rises in my throat.

No, no, no.

I hunch over, pressing both hands against my abdomen, and swallow. *Not now.* I shut my eyes, willing my stomach to settle.

The zombie lets out another long, low moan. In response to her call, two more teenage zombies appear around the bend, a girl and a boy.

Frederico's grip on my wrist tightens. I latch onto him with my free hand, digging my nails into his shoulder. More bile rises in my throat.

Stay down, I tell my food. *Stay—*

Round two of chili surges up my throat. My stomach heaves as another pile of vomit hits the pavement at my feet.

41

NAUSEA

THE ZOMBIES IMMEDIATELY BREAK INTO A RUN, COMING STRAIGHT FOR us. And it's not just three. Five more teenage undead round the corner —making it eight in total. I have only an instant to wonder what eight teenage kids are doing out in the middle of the woods before Frederico hauls me away.

"Too many," he whispers.

I nod in agreement. Even if my legs weren't shaky and my stomach was in better shape, going up against eight zombies on the open road would be suicide.

Frederico picks up a stick and flings it across the road. It thumps into the underbrush. The zombies veer toward the sound. Frederico throws two more in the same direction, herding the zombies away from us.

He gestures for me to move. I follow him, tiptoeing up the road. Frederico keeps bending down to scoop up rocks and sticks, keeping up a constant barrage of sound to keep the zombies occupied on the other side of the road.

We can only hope it will be enough.

We draw abreast of the zombies; they're a mere fifteen feet away, grunting and growling as they rifle through the underbrush. They were probably out here smoking pot before all hell broke loose and they turned.

The scent of rot wafts in the breeze. My stomach clenches in response. I swallow back rising bile and keep moving.

Frederico throws another rock. A zombie boy shifts, and the stone that should have flown into the trees hits the undead in the shoulder instead. The creature grunts and spins in our direction. A long, low growl issues from his throat.

We freeze. The other zombies turn, heads cocked as they listen. The girl in the yellow dress flares her nostrils, sniffing. She takes one step toward us, then another.

Wild fear rises within me. I imagine this is how deer feel when being stalked by a mountain lion.

I look at Frederico, running one finger along the rusted spike that rests in my pack strap. A silent question: do we fight? I lick my lips nervously, eyes moving between my friend and the zombies.

He hesitates, my fear reflected in his eyes. He gives the barest shake of his head: no.

No, we don't fight. I nod in agreement. Eight against two are impossible odds. We'd be overrun in minutes, if not seconds. Frederico and I are many things, but we are not ninjas.

The sundress zombie takes another step in our direction. Her lips pull back from her teeth in a snarl.

My mouth goes dry. My palms grow sweaty. My stomach clenches painfully, violently.

This time it's the Cheetos that choose this instant to develop an exit strategy. They surge up my throat and eject out of my mouth in a gooey, orange stream.

The zombies rush us en masse.

Even as I wipe a ribbon of vomit from my chin, I break into a sprint. Frederico follows suit, the two of us plowing up the road. Now that we're running, the zombies lock onto the soft tap of our feet.

I pump my arms and legs, propelling myself forward as fast as I can. I don't consider myself a sprinter, but I can haul ass for short distances. So can Frederico. He streams along beside me, curly gray ponytail bouncing between his shoulder blades.

"Think we can outrun them on the road?" I huff.

"We have to. I'm too tired for another forest run."

I understand how he feels. At almost one hundred thirty miles, our senses are dulled and exhausted. Neither of us has the focus or the strength for a good forest bushwhack right now. Not to mention my upset stomach.

The zombies move at a decent pace, though it soon becomes apparent that Frederico and I are outstripping them. Even exhausted, we're stronger runners than the undead.

A mile in front of us, Laytonville comes into view. The tiny town bisects Highway 101. Even from afar, I can see why Frederico wasn't thrilled to have his daughter living here. There's a scattering of homes, a biodiesel gas station, a beat-up motel, and a quilt shop. It's the sort of town that offers little to no opportunity to its residents.

"Do you see what I see?" Frederico asks.

"The jeeps."

"Yeah."

At the edge of town are three abandoned military-issue jeeps. One of them is crumpled against a light pole. Another sits in the middle of the road, doors flung wide open. A third one lies upside down in a pile of broken glass. Bright-orange road cones are scattered on the pavement.

There are only two zombies in the road with the cars. Or at least, only two zombies we can see. They're civilian zombies though, not military. Where are the soldiers?

Glancing over my shoulder, I see the sundress zombie and her posse two hundred yards behind us. We're ahead of them for now, but how long will that last?

"Let's take the car." I can't believe I make the suggestion, but I don't see a better option at the moment.

"Agreed," Frederico huffs.

"I'll take the zombie on the left," I say. "You take the other one."

In silent response, my friend draws his railroad spike. The zombies at the car wreck hear our approach. They straighten, heads turning in our direction, and growl.

If I weren't on the verge of puking up more Cheetos, I'd probably have paused to admire the swift efficiency with which Frederico and I dispatch the two undead. As it stands, we don't even pause to wipe the blood off our faces before jumping into the jeep.

I land in the passenger's seat, slamming the door as Frederico dives into the driver's seat. He lets out of bark of satisfaction.

"Keys!" he crows, jingling the ring that still hangs in the ignition. He fires up the vehicle and throws it into reverse. Sundress zombie and company are a hundred yards away as Frederico completes a three-point-turn.

"Do you know how to get to Aleisha's house?"

Frederico grunts, then floors it. "No, but I googled the bar where she works. We'll start there."

A half-full bottle of water bumps against my foot. I take a long drink, then pass it to Frederico. He downs the rest before tossing the bottle into the backseat.

Ahead of us, several zombies stagger down a long gravel driveway. Behind them is a faded, beat-up mobile home. Their heads turn in our direction, teeth pulled back in a snarl.

"The jeep is drawing attention," I say.

"I noticed," he replies tersely. "We've got company on this side, too."

Looking past him, I see several zombies stalk out from a gas station. A chill creeps down my spine.

"Holy fuck, what's happened to this place?" I whisper. "We haven't seen a living person anywhere."

He gives me a tight look. "I know." Uncertainty and worry flicker across his face, and I know he's thinking about Aleisha.

Why isn't there a heavier military and CDC presence in Northern California? How far south has the zombie outbreak spread? Why are the authorities concentrating their efforts on Portland, when it's so clear other parts of the country are in deep shit?

Another cluster of zombies, all emerging from a gas station, race out into the road in front of us.

"Seat belt," Frederico barks, pulling on his own.

My stomach roils. I snap on the belt, bracing myself. The car whips hard to the left, then to the right as Frederico tries to avoid the zombies. We clip one with our right bumper; the undead rolls onto our hood and smashes into the windshield. The glass spiders into dozens of cracks under his weight.

Instead of flying off like a decent piece of roadkill, the zombie latches onto the top of the hood.

"What is it with these fuckers?" I snarl. Did they come embedded with How-To-Cling-To-A-Moving-Vehicle handbook?

The zombie is a middle-aged, skinny man in black jeans. Wet blood is smeared over his mouth, chin, and neck. He keens and claws at the broken glass. The windshield begins to cave beneath his weight.

Frederico jerks the steering wheel left and right, trying to toss the zombie. The monster refuses to be dislodged. It's like he has superhero suction cups on his body. The glass begins the crumple, the first few shards raining down beneath his fist.

"The windshield's gonna give!" Frederico yells.

Dammit. I unbuckle my seat belt and roll the window down. Sticking my torso out the opening, I shout, "Hey! Hey zombie!"

The beast snarls, clawing his way toward me. I aim my spike for his head. Closer . . . just a bit closer . . . one more inch . . .

"Come and get me, you dead fuck!"

I jab the spike downward. At the same moment, Frederico swerves. I flail, scrabbling the keep from flying out of the car. My stake falls out of my hand, hits the hood, and bounces away.

The zombie snatches my wrist, which only seconds before had been armed with a spike. With a wild cry, I grab his hair with my free hand. His teeth gnash as he strains against me, trying to crawl closer. I tighten my grip in his unkempt, greasy locks, pushing as hard as I can against his skull.

He might be dead, and he might be skinny, but goddammit, he's stronger than me. Millimeter by millimeter, he draws closer to my flesh.

"Fuuuuuck!" I shrill.

"Incoming!" Frederico cries. "Hold on, Kate!"

I have just enough time to brace my feet against the floor and push my butt into the door before Frederico swerves wildly to the left. He misses three zombies, but hits a fourth. The car bucks as it rolls over the body. Bile rises in my throat.

Teeth brush my skin. I scream, pushing on biker zombie's head with all my might. His teeth continue to gnash, the tips brushing my skin.

And then the Cheetos make another grand exit, spraying out of my mouth. The vomit hits biker zombie in the face and sprays my captive wrist and hand.

My skin instantly becomes slippery. His grip loosens and he begins to slide away. Frederico whips the car around two more zombies and biker zombie at last goes flying.

42

NOTHING BUT THE DEAD

SAVED BY VOMIT.

That's a new one. Who would have thought ultramarathon digestive issues would save my life?

Shaking from the near miss, I drop back inside the car.

"You okay?" Frederico's voice is loud with panic. "Did it bite you?"

"I'm okay." I wipe bits of vomit from my hand onto the upholstery of the car. "Fucker couldn't hold on to me once I puked on him."

"Thank god." Frederico lets out a breath, sinking back into the seat. He opens his mouth to say more, then abruptly lets out a peal of hysterical laughter. "Way to go, Jackalope."

I give him a weak smile in return.

We exit the tiny town of Laytonville—population of 1,027, according to the sign at the city's northern perimeter—with several dozen zombies behind us.

"The car was a bad option," I say, staring back through the rear window. "It drew too much attention."

"There were no good options," Frederico replies. "We took the only one that made sense at the time."

"Where's the bar where Aleisha works?"

"A mile or so out of town."

I chew on my lower lip. "We have to lose the undead assholes before we get there. Any ideas?"

"Ditch the car and figure out a way to rig the horn?"

I roll this over in my mind, watching the zombies pursue us. There isn't a lot to slow them down. The road is uncluttered and mostly straight. Many of them run, managing a decent speed despite being blind. They still trip and fall, but the lucky bastards don't register pain and are always back on their feet in seconds.

"What if we just ditch the car and leave the motor running?" I ask. "Blare the radio like we did in Cloverdale?"

"Good idea." He glances in the rearview mirror. "We have to do it now, before we get closer to the bar."

"Okay." I tug on the straps of my running pack, mentally readying myself for another sprint, then flip on the radio. Country music fills the car. My hand hovers over the volume knob, ready to blast the twangy tune. "I'm ready."

"Let's do this," Frederico says through gritted teeth.

Adrenaline surges through me as Frederico jerks the car to the side of the road. I turn the volume to max, then throw open the door and rocket out of the seat.

I pump my arms, shoes grinding in the grit of the road margin as I break into a sprint. Though I'm tired and my muscles are fatigued from the long run, fear pushes all that to the periphery. I drive myself forward. I veer onto the asphalt, feet finding better traction for my shoes.

Frederico bails out on the other side and streaks up the road. We fall into step beside one another as soon as we clear the car. Pine trees rise on either side of us, lining the road like sentinels.

Two hundred fifty yards down the road, I risk a glance over my shoulder. The first of the zombies have reached the car. They claw at the glass windows, snarling and baring their teeth.

"It's working," I gasp. "The music is drawing them—"

"Oh, *fuck*."

I whip my head around. A handful of zombies is lumbering down the road. There are three soldiers and four rough-looking men in black leather that make me think they were bikers when they were alive.

Dammit. We'd been so worried about the zombies *behind* us that we hadn't considered zombies in *front* of us.

"We drew them out," Frederico hisses. "They must have come from Aleisha's bar."

"We need to hide." I snag his sleeve and haul him sideways into the trees.

Our feet sink into the thick hummus of the soil as we run. We jog one hundred yards into the forest and drop down behind a copse of trees and ferns.

We peer toward the road. The biker and soldier zombies run past us, never turning in our direction. I let out a sigh of relief.

"We dodged that bullet," I whisper. "We—"

The soft snap of a branch is the only warning we have. Something big and smelly barrels into me as I jerk toward the sound.

I scream before I can stop myself as a man smacks into Frederico and me. He's dressed from head-to-toe in military fatigues and hits us from the side. I twist, desperately trying to find purchase for my hands. I slam into the dirt, a fallen branch digging painfully into my arm and ribcage.

At first I think it's a zombie, but my eyes meet those of my attacker's. They're black and bore into me with frenetic intensity that tell me he's very much alive. A dirty hand covers my mouth.

"What the hell are you guys doing out here?" he hisses. "Do you idiots have a death wish?"

Frederico takes a wild swing, connecting with the man's jaw.

"Son of a bitch." The soldier lashes back with his own punch, stunning Frederico. A gun materializes in his hand. He cocks the safety and presses the barrel against my forehead.

The inside of my mouth turns to cotton. There's a slight tremor in his hand that's more unnerving than the cold metal against my skin. Frederico freezes.

"Up," says the soldier, the word falling from his mouth like a tremulous stone. He shifts his body weight and Frederico slowly—cautiously—gets to his feet.

"Back the fuck up."

Frederico obeys, expression wild as his eyes ping-pong between me and the soldier.

"Over there." The soldier uses the gun to motion to a tree ten feet away. His words never go above a whisper. He keeps me pinned to the ground.

Frederico hesitates. The soldier's mouth thins. The barrel of the gun presses harder against my forehead. His tremble travels along its length.

"Do as he says," I rasp.

Frederico retreats, never taking his eyes from me.

"That's better." The pressure of the gun eases against my forehead. "What are you doing out here?"

I swallow. "I don't think you'd believe me if we told you."

"Try me. I've seen some weird shit."

"The last person we told tried to kill us."

The soldier considers us, then abruptly releases me. He stands, keeping the gun in hand. I sit up, rubbing at my forehead where the gun's muzzle had been.

"I was only trying to help," the soldier says. "It's a deathtrap out here."

I resist the urge to tell him that body slamming two people to the ground isn't a way to instill trust. He's young, I realize. Couldn't be much older than twenty-two or twenty-three.

"We're looking for our kids," I tell him, carefully inching closer to Frederico.

The soldier shakes his head, sympathy flashing in his eyes. "Laytonville is overrun by those—those *things*."

"Zombies?" I supply.

He hesitates, then nods.

"My friend's daughter lives in Laytonville," I say. "We're trying to find her."

"You two should find some place to hide until all *this*," he gestures broadly with the gun, "blows over. My platoon was sent here to erect a road barricade, to keep infected people from spreading south. We were overrun at the far end of town. A few of us got away . . . I'm the only survivor now."

In his black eyes, I see a young man not much older than Carter. He wants to show us that he's in charge, when in fact the world is in a tailspin. Slamming us to the ground was his way of trying to make order in a shit storm.

"My daughter works at Rod's Roadhouse," Frederico says. "Any . . ." He trails off as the soldier pales.

"Nothing but the dead at Rod's Roadhouse," he says, voice catching. "I just left . . . I'm just heading south to Ukiah. Their blockade is holding. You should come with me."

I shake my head. "My son is in Arcata. I have to go north."

If possible, the young man pales even more. He opens his mouth, then closes it again.

"What do you know?" The mom in me surfaces, my voice taking on a no-nonsense, answer-me-now tone.

"Just—just snatches." He fingers the black radio on his belt. "I had to turn it off so it wouldn't attract *them*. But Eureka, Arcata . . . it's bad."

"Bad?" Tension shoots up my spine. "What do you mean by *bad*?"

Frederico squeezes my arm. "Keep your voice down."

I force a lower whisper. "What do you mean by bad?"

The soldier licks his lips. "Both towns are overrun by *them*. Military survivors have been told to retreat to the south and reinforce the Ukiah blockade."

Carter. I thump back against the nearest tree, feeling bleak.

"You're too late," Frederico says to the soldier. "We saw zombies in Healdsburg this morning. There's no place safe."

The soldier's lips part. No words come out. Our harsh breathing fills the silence. In the distance, the country music blares through the trees.

Then I hear other sounds: a moan and a snarl, both of them much closer than I'd like. I peek around the copse of trees.

Despite our attempts to be quiet, we've managed to draw the attention of two military zombies. They're moving through the forest in our direction.

"John and Zach," the soldier says, voice leaden as he stares at the approaching zombies.

"We have to move." I hesitate, then say to the soldier, "Come with us."

I don't relish the idea of bringing him with us, but I'm afraid if he leaves us he'll do something stupid and get himself eaten, or worse.

"I have to go to Ukiah." His black eyes fix on the approaching zombies.

"You need to keep yourself alive." Frederico clasps his shoulder, giving him a gentle shove in a northward direction. "Kate's right. You should come with us."

He breaks into a lope. I fall into step beside him. I don't like the idea of thrashing through the trees, but the zombies are between us and the road. What choice do we have?

The soldier follows us. His eyes are wide and wild, but he manages to put one foot in front of the other. I wish he'd put the gun away, but now isn't the time to argue about it.

We stumble across what looks like a deer path. I jump onto it, figuring it to be better for speed and silence.

I'm right. The noise of our passage nearly disappears with the firm path beneath our feet. The zombies slow in their pursuit, turning their heads as they attempt to track us.

We run another fifty yards. I put a hand on Frederico's arm and signal him to stop. The car music continues to blare in the distance.

Thirty seconds tick by. Sixty.

The soldier zombies turn, attention tracking back toward the road and the car. I exhale with relief as they lumber away.

"The deer path goes north," Frederico says. "Let's follow it as far as we can toward the bar."

I nod, then glance at the soldier. His breathing is ragged. He clutches the gun to his chest like it's a lifeline. Thank god the safety is on.

"What's your name?" I ask.

"Alvarez."

I figure this must be his last name, but it'll work for now. "Nice to meet you. I'm Kate. This is Frederico."

"We're two crazy fucks who want to find our kids," Frederico says. "Don't get in our way and you can stay with us."

His curtness tells me just how on edge he is. He breaks into a lope, leading us onward. The deer path zigzags through the woods, meandering in a northward direction. Twenty minutes later, the trees begin to thin.

"Do you see that?" I ask. "Is that a building up ahead?"

"Yeah." His jaw tightens. "That's Rod's Roadhouse. Where Aleisha works. I recognize it from Google Earth."

"You don't want to go there," Alvarez says. "They're all dead. I was—"

"Shut the fuck up." Each word falls from Frederico like a stone. The ferocious gleam in his eyes makes Alvarez clutch his gun a bit more tightly.

I squeeze the young man's shoulder and give him what I hope is a reassuring smile. His upper lip is beaded with sweat, and he won't meet my eye. Bringing him along may have been a mistake, but what choice did we have? He's just a scared kid.

We slow to a walk. Details of Rod's Roadhouse materialize as we draw near.

There are bodies in the gravel parking lot. Some in biker leathers, some in regular clothes, and a few in military fatigues. I see two military jeeps, at least a dozen motorcycles, and a few cars. Alvarez licks his lips, eyes glued to the scene.

The wood siding of the bar has faded over the years to a washed out brown. Patches of graffiti have been painted over with different colored paint, making the outside look like a schizophrenic patchwork. *Rod's Roadhouse*, once a big white sign with red lettering, is now faded and pitted with holes and cracks. The "d" is missing completely, making it look like *Ro's Roadhouse*. There are no windows, just double wooden doors that look like they were hijacked from a bad seventies movie.

I count seven bodies. All of them looked to have been shot in the head or bludgeoned with a heavy object. Blood is everywhere.

Dread fills me. God, why couldn't Aleisha have moved to some other little town in the middle of nowhere?

We creep toward the edge of the gravel parking lot, none of us saying a word. We crouch behind a copse of trees, watching. Nothing moves. Nothing stirs.

"That—that's Aleisha's car." There's a hitch in Frederico's voice. He raises a hand and points to a silver Mustang convertible that looks like it got in a fight with a semi and lost. The faded bumper sticker reads *I sell pot to your honor student.*

I don't respond. I don't know what to say. If this was the outside of Carter's dorm room, I'd be out of my mind. Frederico is pale, his hands clenching and unclenching on the straps of his hydration pack.

"What happened here?" he asks Alvarez.

"We—" He stops, swallowing. "My platoon ran into trouble. Those guys . . ." He gestures to the downed soldiers. "My friends." His mouth works, as if he has more to say, but no words come out. A glazed look fills his eyes. I get the feeling he's reliving whatever horror unfolded here.

"Hey." I squeeze his shoulder. "It's okay. You're okay."

Alvarez blinks, coming back to the present.

"I have to find her." Frederico stands up, eyes fixed on the heavy wooden double doors. "I have to go in."

I rise with him. The last thing I want to do is go into this shithole of a bar that probably has zombies inside, but I don't have a choice. If Frederico wants to go in, I have to go with him. I know without a doubt he'd do it for me. Hell, our roles might be reversed in another twenty-four hours when we get to Arcata.

My hand itches for the phone I no longer have. I want to text Carter and tell him what's going on. Part of me knows I might not make it out of Rod's Roadhouse. If I'm going to bite the big one, I want Carter to know about it.

"You can't go in," Alvarez croaks. "The things—they're inside —they're—"

Frederico's face darkens. I hold up a hand to silence Alvarez before he can further agitate my friend. It's clear we should move on, but Frederico won't go anywhere until he lays eyes on his daughter.

"Let's be smart about this," I say after a moment. "Let's see what we can find in the way of weapons on the bodies, then figure out a way to get inside without getting ourselves eaten."

I give Alvarez a *look*, a silent warning not to try and talk us out of this. He shrinks in on himself, eyes locked on his dead friends.

Frederico approaches the first of the bodies. Using the dirt-encrusted sole of his running shoe, he flips it over.

Alvarez stays crouched on the edge of the woods. I make my way to one of the dead bikers. It's a heavyset woman in chaps and a leather jacket with six-inch fringe. She's covered with bite marks. Several of her fingers have been chewed off. There's a bullet hole through the center of her forehead.

Swallowing against the nausea in my gut, I force myself to go through her pockets. I don't find any weapons, but I do find the next best thing: a cell phone.

I yank it up, swiping the screen. A text to Carter is already half-drafted in my head.

A prompt for a passcode comes up.

Shit. God dammit. I hurl the phone to the ground with a surge of frustration. Alvarez startles, fumbling his gun but managing not to drop it.

"What's wrong?" Frederico, poised over another body, looks up at me. There's a haunted look to his eyes that does not bode well.

I shake my head. "Nothing." What's a locked cell phone compared to what he's going through?

After a thorough search of the bodies, we have two handguns and six knives between us. I hesitate when Frederico holds one of the guns out to me. I've never handled a gun before, let alone aimed and fired one. What if I shoot myself in the foot, or something equally stupid?

"You can have them," I say. "I'll stick with the knives." They're scary looking things, the smallest of them at least six inches long.

"You should take one." He presses the cold metal into my hands. "Just in case."

I open my mouth to argue. Frederico gives me a look so fierce that all protest dies on my tongue. I silently take the gun. Not knowing what else to do with it, I slip it into the waistband of my compression pants.

"There's a bathroom window in the back," Alvarez says, taking a few tentative steps into the parking lot. "You can get in that way. The back door—it's, ah, barricaded."

We don't ask for details. My gut tells me we really, really do *not* want to go inside this place. I look at Frederico. In his face I see my own anxiety for Carter reflected back at me. If this were where Carter worked, nothing would stop me from going inside.

There's got to be a way to get in without attracting attention. I scan the parking lot, searching for inspiration. My eyes land on one of the military jeeps.

"Kate, you don't have to come with me." Frederico levels a grim expression at me. "I know I'm walking into a shit storm. But I have to know if she's in there. I—"

I cut him off. "We're in this together. We came to find our kids. Besides." I glance at the jeep. What worked once can work twice, right? "I have an idea."

"You two are crazy," Alvarez whispers.

I give him a faint grin. "You have no idea."

43

ALEISHA

I LAY OUT MY HASTILY ASSEMBLED PLAN TO FREDERICO AND ALVAREZ. The men nod as I explain, even though Alvarez looks like he wants to vomit.

"Just wait here," I tell him when I finish. "We'll come back for you afterwards."

"No." He shakes his head resolutely, sliding his gun back into its holster. "I want to help."

"How many zombies are inside there?" I ask.

He hesitates. "Four. Maybe five? I'm not really sure. My unit . . . We got out of there just as everyone started to go nuts. I couldn't really count, you know?"

I nod sympathetically, gathering an idea of what happened before Alvarez found us in the woods.

Frederic's eyes are dangerously flat as we advance on the military jeep. The windows are rolled down and the keys are still in the ignition. We throw the car into neutral and roll it against the double front doors of Rod's Roadhouse.

Frederico then sets the parking brake and fires up the engine. It hums to life.

We stand there, listening. After a moment, we hear a soft bump against the doors of the bar, followed by a few muffled moans.

Frederico nods grimly. "Nice and distracted," he says softly, running one hand along the side of the jeep. Without another word, he marches off toward the back of the building. Alvarez and I hurry after him.

The bathroom window is a good seven feet up, just to the left of a dumpster. Frederico locates a fist-sized rock and wraps his shirt around it. He then clambers onto the dumpster and breaks the window with the shirt-wrapped rock. He takes care to clear away the bits of glass stuck in the sill.

Between the distraction we created at the front of the bar and the dampening of the window break, we're hoping to get inside without attracting attention.

Alvarez paces back and forth, the gun still out. He scans the landscape around us, that slight tremor still in his hands. God, I hope he doesn't shoot off his own foot. Or worse, shoot me or Frederico.

It takes a few awkward moments for Frederico to get his legs hooked into the window. Twice he almost topples backward but at last manages to disappear inside. He's silent during the ordeal, not even swearing.

His quiet tightens my chest with worry. I scramble onto the dumpster after him, looking inside the window. I see his curly gray hair over the bathroom stall. He's cracked open the bathroom door and is peering out into the bar.

"You coming?" I call back to Alvarez, who's still pacing.

He pauses to look up at me. His eyes have regained some clarity. There's reluctance in his expression.

"On second thought, why don't you keep watch out here," I say, trying to give him an easy out. In all honesty, I'd rather his shaky trigger hand be a safe distance away. "We'll be back."

An inarticulate cry cuts me off, followed by a gunshot. I turn back to the tiny bathroom window just in time to see Frederico charge through the door. Another gunshot goes off.

"Motherfuckers!" he bellows. "You cocksucking motherfuckers!"

"Fuck!" I dive head first through the window, grappling with the wall of the stall as I haul myself in. *Frederico!* I scream silently, not daring to shriek out loud.

Two more gunshots sound, followed by a loud racket, like someone knocking over furniture.

"Goddammit!" I hiss. My shin drags painfully against the windowsill as I pull myself the rest of the way inside. I break my fall by hanging onto the stall. My legs dangle for a second before I drop to the floor.

"Kate? Kate!"

I hear Alvarez's frantic voice, but I can't spare the time—or the noise—to answer him. I draw one of the obscene knives scavenged from the parking lot and burst out of the bathroom.

It's like walking onto the set of a Jason Stathom movie—one where he single-handedly takes on fifteen bad guys, kills them all, and leaves behind a room covered in blood and bodies. That's what the inside of Rod's Roadhouse looks like.

The slaughter is contained in a dark-paneled bar room. Faded Grateful Dead posters in fake gold frames fill every inch of wall space, many of them splattered with blood.

I'm just in time to see Frederico take aim at a zombie in a too-tight tank top and jean skirt. He fires the gun. Instead of hitting her in the forehead, he grazes her clavicle.

Fuck it all, my friend is a terrible shot. And now the zombie is pissed. She leans back into a crouch, snarling as she prepares to spring forward.

I sprint past Frederico, lunging at the she-zombie. My aim is true —the knife slides right into the zombie's ear.

Just as the sharp metal pierces the soft flesh of the brain, the gun goes off again. A searing pain rips through my shoulder. I scream, reeling. Blood oozes from the zombie woman's ear as she sways, then drops.

I drop beside her, clutching at my shoulder as hot blood drenches my arm. I'm too dazed from the pain to do anything more than stare stupidly at the wound.

"Kate!" Frederico turns horrified eyes on me. "Kate, I—"

He breaks off and aims the gun over my head. It doesn't take a genius to know he's spotted another zombie. I wince as he pulls the trigger, but the chamber clicks empty.

"*Fuck!*" He hurls the useless gun over my head.

I turn in time to see it hit a bearded zombie in the face. Frederico races past me, brandishing one of his own wicked military-issue knives. Instead of stabbing the zombie through an eye, he delivers a vicious kick to the creature's gut.

It stumbles several steps back from the force of the kick. His lips peel back in a feral snarl, revealing blood and bits of skin stuck between his teeth.

Frederico lashes out a second time, planting one dirty running shoe in the zombie's sternum and shoving with all his might. This time the monster trips on a chair and goes down.

"Motherfucker." Frederico pounces, driving the knife downward. He doesn't stab the zombie in the eye or head, but rather in the chest. "Fucking motherfucker!" The knife falls in rapid succession into the zombie's sternum.

"Stop it!" I scream. "Stop fucking around—"

A moan brings my head whipping about. A female zombie fights her way free of several barstools, which have been thrown on top of her. She's about five-foot-eight with brown hair that's been bleached five too many times. She's dressed in a slinky black dress that shows off generous cleavage and a trim waist. She's not unattractive, though hard living has stripped away the beauty of her youth.

I've only met her a handful of times over the years that I've been friends with Frederico, but I recognize Aleisha immediately.

Vicious bite marks cover both her arms and the shin of her bare right leg. Both shoes are gone. Blood is smeared on her mouth and neck.

As she stumbles free of the barstools, I register two other zombies. Both have been shot through the head and lay on the dark, worn wooden floor in growing pools of viscous blood.

Aleisha growls, a low sound that rumbles out from deep in her throat. She takes a step in my direction.

Shit. My shoulder is on fire, not to mention saturated with blood. I am in no shape to grapple with a zombie.

She takes another step toward me, reaching out with both hands. Her lifeless white eyes roll in their sockets.

I fumble the dreaded gun out of my waistband. The feel of it in my hand turns my stomach to lead. Licking my lips, I thumb back the safety.

"Don't shoot her!" Frederico screams. "Don't you dare fucking shoot her!" He barrels past me, face and clothes spattered with gore.

Grabbing another barstool, he drives it into Aleisha's chest. She snarls, slashing at him with her nails. Frederico bears her to the ground, pinning her beneath the stool. He breathes raggedly as he struggles to hold her down.

"Frederico, what the hell?" I stagger toward him, still clutching the wound in my shoulder.

The crunch of boots on glass alerts me to Alvarez. The young soldier steps out of the bathroom, eyes wide as he takes in the scene. I barely notice him.

"You shot me," I snap at Frederico. "What the fuck? What happened to waiting for me so we could check out the scene before rushing in like kamikazes?" I'm too exhausted and in too much pain to properly filter myself. I regret the words as soon as they leave my mouth.

"Sorry." Frederico doesn't even look my way when he delivers the apology. His eyes are pinned on his daughter as she thrashes beneath him. His fists are clenched into two white-knuckled fists atop the barstool.

"Help Kate," he barks, jerking his chin in my direction.

Alvarez licks his lips, then nods. He approaches the bar where we stand, picking his way through the bodies, most of which were already dead before we got here.

I sway, the pain getting the better of me. I'm sure in the realm of bullet wounds, mine is pretty minor. But fucking hell, this is the first time I've ever been shot, and it hurts like a motherfucker.

I thump onto a tabletop, gripping my shoulder as blood boils past my fingers. Alvarez rummages behind the bar, tossing bottles onto the counter. Behind him is a giant chalkboard scrawled with a list of munchies sold by the bar. *French Fries* and *Burger* are nearly obliterated by gloppy spatters of blood.

Alvarez finds a tiny first aid kit, the sort stocked at grocery stores. Gripping the kit in one hand and a bottle of vodka in the other, he grimly marches toward me.

"Let me see," he says.

I pry my hands off the wound. Using what looks like a paring knife, Alvarez cuts away my shirt sleeve. Next, he opens the vodka bottle and gingerly dumps the liquid down my arm.

I yelp at the searing pain, then grit my teeth to keep from making more noise.

Through my haze, I see Frederico reach for a bottle of tequila sitting on the bar. Never taking his eyes from Aleisha, he pulls out the stopper with his teeth and raises the bottle to his lips.

Understanding what's about the happen, I leap to my feet. "No!" The shout rips from my throat. "Put that down, you idiot!"

He ignores me and takes a long swig, one foot resting on the bottom rung of the barstool to keep it in place over Aleisha.

"Frederico!" I don't care how much noise I'm making. "Don't do this, please!"

He throws his head back, chugging the golden liquid. I rush toward him, trying to wrestle the bottle away with my good hand. He shoves me away, his face twisted into a mask of fury.

"Stop it!" I lunge back toward him.

He lifts the bottle into the air, out of my reach. With his free hand, he snags the gun out of my waistband.

I freeze. My friend—my best friend—gives me a wrathful look. With the tequila bottle in one hand and the gun in the other, he says, "Get away from me, Kate."

"Frederico," I whisper, unable to staunch the sudden flow of tears. All his years of sobriety have just gone down the drain. My mind flashes back to that day so long ago when Kyle talked him off the ledge and kept him sober. God, I wish I knew what my husband had said to him that night.

"Get away from me," he repeats.

"She wouldn't want you to do this to yourself," I whisper, gesturing at his zombified daughter.

Frederico turns away from me. "Neither of us knows what she'd want."

"Kate." Alvarez rests a tentative arm on my good shoulder. His eyes are wild as they dart between me and Frederico, though his voice has a semblance of calm when he speaks. "Come on. Let me take care of your arm."

"Listen to the boy." Frederico takes another long swig from the tequila bottle.

I stare at the scene, at Frederico. At my friend, who's falling apart before my very eyes as he clutches a gun and a tequila bottle. At his zombified daughter, still snarling and pinned beneath a barstool. God, why did I agree to help him get inside this place? I should have dragged him away when I had the chance. Alvarez tried to warn us, but we wouldn't listen.

"Give me the gun back," I say.

"Leave it alone, Kate."

"Frederico—"

"Shut up!" he bellows. "Just shut up and leave me alone!"

I retreat, cowed by his display of emotion. I thump back onto the table and let Alvarez dump more vodka on my wound. The stinging pain is nothing to me now, not as I watch Frederico annihilate the tequila.

"It's just a flesh wound," Alvarez says. "You got lucky. I'm going to stitch it up."

My throat is tight with tears that threaten to overwhelm me. "Have you ever given anyone stitches before?" I ask hoarsely.

He grimaces. "No. But I used to watch my grandma sew patches onto my jeans when I was a kid."

The same basic concept?

"Woah." I hold up my good hand to ward him off. "You mean to tell me you went through boot camp and didn't learn how to stitch someone up?"

"They save that stuff for the medics. Grunts like me learn basic stuff, like applying tourniquets and a treating heatstroke." He shrugs. "I'm telling you, I watched my grandma sew all the time. I can do this. Besides, I have twenty-twenty vision and she had cataracts."

Cataracts. Fuck me. I close my eyes.

"All right, Twenty-Twenty," I say. "Do your best."

He lifts the vodka bottle and holds it in my direction, head tilted in a silent offer.

Frederico thumps down the empty bottle of tequila. He reaches over the bar and snags a bottle of gin and takes a drink. I look away, sickened.

"No thanks," I tell Alvarez. Someone has to be sober.

What am I going to do with Frederico? How am I going to get him back on the road when he's shit-faced drunk? What are we going to do with Aleisha? And what the hell does he plan to do with that gun? I need to get it back from him. But how?

"Ouch." I make a face as Alvarez starts sewing my arm with a needle and thread from the tiny first aid kit.

"Sorry."

"Sometimes when I get really bad blisters, I put super glue on them." I only half hear myself as I watch Frederico systematically obliterate the bottle of gin. "After I lance them, I mean. Could I just slather some super glue on the bullet wound?"

Alvarez drops his hand and stares at me as if I've completely lost it. Maybe I have. After all, I'm watching my best friend shatter twenty-five years of sobriety as he pins his zombie daughter to the floor in a dive bar.

"What are you talking about?" Alvarez asks.

I shake my head dully. "Nothing. Just running stuff."

For the first time, he takes in the details of my appearance: the running shoes, the hydration pack, the compression pants. Probably my smell and the vomit splatters on my shirt as well, or maybe he just chalks those up to the apocalypse at large.

"Are you guys out . . . *running*?" he asks.

"Yeah."

His lips part in surprise. "That's why you're still alive," he breathes. "You're not drawing attention when you move on foot. When my platoon moved in at the south end of town . . ." He shakes his head. "I think the jeeps drew them out. Wait." His gaze sharpens on me. "You guys are planning to . . . *run* to Arcata?"

I nod.

"That's insane," he breathes. "How far have you come so far?"

I shrug, then glance at my watch. "One hundred twenty-eight point three miles."

His eyes bug. "Holy shit. You guys are those crazy ultramarathon runners. I saw a documentary on people like you once. How long have you been running?"

"We left Healdsburg around ten yesterday morning."

Alvarez levels a look at me. "You guys are fucking crazy," he declares.

"No more crazy than what's going on in the world around us."

Alvarez purses his lips in response and continues sewing. I do my best to ignore the sting every time the needle pierces my skin.

Frederico continues to chug away on the bottle of gin. My heart breaks with every swallow he takes. For the first time since I lost Kyle,

I'm glad my husband isn't with me. It would kill him to see what I'm witnessing.

"I'm sorry, baby. I'm so sorry."

Frederico's broken voice is slurred. He leans over the barstool to look brokenly down at his daughter, the gun gripped in his hand. He's finished off the bottle of gin. His curly gray hair, in complete disarray, shields his face. Aleisha growls, sightless white eyes rolling up toward her father.

The gun. My eyes are locked on it. I have to get it away from him.

Licking dry lips, I rise from my seat on the table. Alvarez shifts, clearly planning to join me, but I shake my head. No reason to risk both of us.

"Frederico." I take two steps toward my friend. "You need to put the gun down."

His head whips in my direction. His expression is wild and lost.

He looks again at Aleisha. He lifts the gun. Panic seizes me. I have a flash vision of him blowing his brains out.

"No!" I lunge, but I'm not fast enough.

Frederico fires the gun twice.

44

SEPARATE WAYS

THE BULLETS SLAM INTO ALEISHA'S FOREHEAD.

The silence that descends is thunderous.

Frederico drops the gun to the floor and staggers into the kitchen. I hear the sound of plates breaking and pots being hurled against the wall. He's going to draw every zombie within a ten-mile radius. If we haven't already with all the gunshots and shouting.

I force myself to look at Aleisha's body. Her face is a bloody mess. I cover it with a bar towel, then hurry into the kitchen with Alvarez on my heels.

I find Frederico winding up to hurl a serving platter against the wall.

"Stop it!" I keep my voice soft and seize him by the wrists. "Dammit, I know you're hurting, but you're going to get us killed!"

"Let them come," he slurs, wrenching away from me. "I don't give a flying fuck."

He flings the platter like a Frisbee. It connects with the stainless steel dishwasher, denting the machine before falling to the floor and breaking into half a dozen pieces.

Frustration rises in me. "You may not give a fuck, but I do. Carter is still out there!"

"Carter's dead. Just like my girl. This was a hopeless quest, Kate. We both knew it. We're both just too fucking stubborn to admit it."

He kicks at the remnants of the platter, sending them flying through the air like shrapnel.

"I'm sorry you lost Aleisha," I say desperately. "This isn't the way to cope. Please. Please stop before you get us killed."

In response, he seizes a large stockpot and flings it. It hits a rack of cooking supplies. Four other pans are dislodged in the wake of the stockpot, all of them clanging to the floor with a racket that is nothing short of cataclysmic.

Frustration gives way to a heated rush of anger. I'm never going to find Carter if he keeps this up.

"You selfish jerk," I snap, my voice rising. "Is this what you were like when you were a drunk? No wonder Aleisha's been pissed at you for the last thirty years!"

It's a low blow. I know it as soon as the words are out of my mouth. Frederico rounds on me, eyes blazing.

For a second, I think he's going to hit me. Alvarez steps closer, as though he plans to insert himself between us.

Then all the air goes out of Frederico in a rush. He sags, tears welling in his eyes. He turns his back on us.

"Get away from me," he says, voice half slur, half sob. "Just leave me here." He retreats farther into the kitchen, shoulders shaking with grief.

I start toward him, but Alvarez lays a hand on my arm and shakes his head. I hesitate, then nod reluctantly. We retreat back to the main room.

"He needs a few minutes," Alvarez says, as though he's the authority on grief.

Hell, for all I know, maybe he is. I trudge into the main room and thump onto a pool table. My eyes bleakly roam the room, so much of it covered with blood and bodies. Then I spot something smooth and red behind the bar.

My spine straightens.

"What?" Alvarez asks.

"That's a phone." I hurry behind the bar, seizing the old-fashioned, bright-red plastic phone with white buttons. It must be at least thirty years old. "It's a phone," I repeat, hope rising inside me. "A phone with no password protection!"

I snatch the receiver off the cradle, daring to lift it to my ear. The low buzz of an active phone line greets me.

"It's working," I breathe.

I dial Carter's number, grateful I'd memorized it when I purchased his cell phone instead of just relying on my contacts list.

It rings, and rings, and rings, and then—

"Hello?"

"Carter?" My voice is half sob, half breathless.

"Mom?"

"Yeah, baby, it's me."

"Where are you? The caller ID says Rod's Roadhouse."

"We're in Laytonville. Me and Frederico." I lean against the wall, resting my forehead against the worn wood paneling. I can't stop the tears of relief that drip down my cheeks.

"Did you find Aleisha?"

I exhale sharply.

"Mom?"

"Yeah, sweetie. Yeah, we found her." I lapse into silence.

I don't need to say anything else. Carter is a smart kid.

"How is Uncle Rico?"

How is Uncle Rico? The question is like a one-hundred-pound weight on my shoulders.

"He's . . . struggling," I say. "I'm giving him a little space. How are you doing? Are you safe?"

Silence.

"Carter?"

"I'm as safe as I can be, Mom."

What the hell is that supposed to mean? "What—"

"Arcata is overrun, Mom." His words are clipped and bleak. "Turn around and go back to Healdsburg."

"No fucking way." The words come out harsher than I'd intended. "No way I'm going back."

Another long silence.

"Mom, you need to listen. The school is overrun. My friends and I are holed up in the Creekside Lounge with a few other students. We've barricaded the doors, but the zombies are everywhere. The soldiers . . . they rolled in here with the Hummers and guns and other weapons . . . there's been a lot of panic. The Internet is still working and Johnny's laptop still has some battery. We've been tracking the news . . . it's bad, Mom."

"I know," I reply, looking at Alvarez. "I know Eureka has fallen, too. So has Laytonville." *And Aleisha, too,* I think with an ache. "There's no place safe out here, baby. I'm coming to find you."

A pause. "I'll wait here as long as I can. I don't know how much longer we'll be safe here. Did your cell phone run out of battery?"

"Something like that. I'm using a landline in the bar right now." I take in a few breaths to steady myself. "I don't know when I'll be able to contact you again."

We're both quiet for a long moment.

"What shoes are you wearing?" he suddenly asks.

"My Altras. The Olympus." Carter has endured countless shoe talks with me over the years, so he'll know which ones I'm talking about.

"Your favorites." I hear the smile in his voice.

"Yeah, my favorites. They're covered with mud and burrs." And a little bit of blood from the bullet wound in my shoulder, but I don't say the last part out loud.

"What are you using for fuel?" he says.

"Whatever we can scavenge," I reply. God, it's so good to hear his voice. I'm so lucky he's alive and safe, at least for the moment. Why couldn't Aleisha have been safe, too? "We raided an RV twenty miles back and ate everything we could get our hands on."

"An RV, huh? No zombies inside, huh?"

"No, there were zombies inside. Seven of them. A whole family."

Pause. "You guys killed seven zombies?"

"Yeah. Remember the Stack and Attack racing theory?"

"Yeah."

"Well, we applied that to zombie killing. Created a narrow opening and made them come out at us one at a time. Sort of."

"Wow. My mom the zombie killer. That's . . . pretty cool."

I'm tongue-tied by the compliment. Unsure how to respond, I say, "Are you getting enough to eat?"

"We've been eating out of the vending machines." He pauses. "We had to break into it."

Poor Carter. Vandalism isn't in his nature.

"How long will the food there last you?" I ask.

"A while, I guess . . . Mom?"

"I'm here, sweetie."

"Do you remember that time we went spelunking for Dad's birthday?"

How could I forget? That trip took place less than a year before Kyle's accident. It was our last family trip together.

"Yeah, I remember."

"Remember how he made you crawl first through the tunnels so he could, you know, frisk you?"

Now it's my turn to smile. More tears come to my eyes, but they're happy tears. Kyle had tweaked my ass in those narrow tunnels, finding my squawks of protest hilarious. Carter had been thoroughly disgusted, as only a teenager can be in purview of his parents' physical affections. It didn't matter that he couldn't actually see what was going on, but he'd been smart enough to figure it out.

"Yeah, I remember."

"I'm glad you guys were happy together. When Dad was alive, I mean. I'm glad."

This feels too much like a good-bye. "Carter, you stay strong. You hold out. I have less than seventy-five miles to go. With any luck I'll be there in less than twenty-four hours. I'll see you soon, okay?"

"What are we going to do when you get here?"

His question stuns me. To be honest, I haven't thought beyond getting to Arcata and finding him.

"We'll find a way to survive," I say. "Somehow. Together. You, me, Frederico, and whoever else you're with. Okay?"

"Okay, Mom."

"I love you, Carter."

"Love you, too, Mom."

Hanging up is one of the hardest things I've ever done. I gently place the red phone back in its cradle, wiping at my eyes. I look up to see Alvarez watching me.

"I'm glad your son is alive."

I hear the unspoken *for now* in his words. Some dim part of my mind tells me I might be in Frederico's shoes in less than twenty-four hours. What will I do if I find Carter dead and zombified?

The thought is too horrible to contemplate. No, I can't think that way. I need to believe my son is alive. It's the only thing that will keep me going.

"Carter is strong. And smart. He'll be okay," I say. "Frederico and I are going north. Will you come with us? We're safer in a group. We can look out for each other."

He hesitates, then shakes him head. "No."

I study him. He avoids meeting my eyes.

"You're going on to Ukiah, aren't you? To join the soldiers there?"

He flinches, like I've caught him in a lie. "I could never keep up with you guys anyway. I ran a half marathon once, but that's as far as I've ever gone."

"What if they've already been overrun?" I say quietly. "What if—"

"I ran," he blurts out. "When shit got thick in the bar, I ran."

He stares at his shoes, shameful red creeping up his neck. I am very careful not to stare around at the slaughter that surrounds us.

"I should have died here with the rest of my platoon," he says quietly.

"So you're going to Ukiah to make up for not dying here?" I can't keep the sadness from my voice.

Alvarez meets my eyes. He doesn't say anything.

I resist the urge to sag. God, I'm so damn tired. I like Alvarez. I hate to see him rushing off to a hopeless case.

"We're not so different," Alvarez says, a touch defensive. "Neither of us has much chance of surviving."

He's got a point there. I sigh, resigned. "How will you travel?" I ask.

"On foot, like you guys. Walking, though, not running."

"Will you help me bury Aleisha? Before we go our separate ways?" It needs to be done and Frederico is in no shape to help me.

Alvarez stares at Aleisha's body. I see reluctance in his face, but all he says is, "Yeah, I'll help you. Come on."

It takes us a solid hour to dig the hole for Aleisha.

In the movies, characters always dig perfect rectangles in the earth. Alvarez and I managed a crooked oval using a shovel with a broken handle we found by the dumpster. It isn't very deep, but it'll have to do.

"Bye, Aleisha," I whisper. I jam the shovel into the earth, wiping away the sweat beading my forehead. "I'm sorry we didn't get here in time." Sorrow makes my throat tight. Even though she caused Frederico nothing but heartache, I'd have given anything to save her.

Frederico never comes out. I consider going in to get him, but the truth is that I'm a big chicken. I've never seen him drunk before. I'm in new territory with my oldest friend, and I have no idea what to do.

"How's your shoulder?" Alvarez asks.

"It's okay, thanks. You did a good job stitching me up."

In truth, the wound hurts like a motherfucker and the stitches look like they were put in by a dyslexic kindergartener, but I'm not going to complain.

"You should take the vodka with you," he says. "Use it to keep the wound clean."

I shake my head. "Even if I can carry the bottle, I can't have alcohol around my friend."

Alvarez gazes at me, saying nothing for a long minute. "You know why he drank, don't you?"

I look away. I do know. Deep down, I know. I'm too upset about his lost sobriety to put it into words.

"She had to be put down," Alvarez says. "He loves her and wanted to be the one to do it. It had to be him. That's why he turned to the bottle."

I focus on my dirty, bloody shoes. Alvarez is right. It was Frederico's last act of love for Aleisha, but he may have paid for it with his soul.

"I wish he'd let me do it," I whisper. "I would have done it for him."

Alvarez, though young, wears an expression of understanding that makes me think he's older than his years.

"My dad fell off the wagon when I was ten," he says.

"What happened?" I swallow, mouth dry, not sure I want to hear the answer.

"Lost his job. Couldn't afford our rent. We had to downsize into a two-bedroom apartment in a shitty part of town. Beat himself up over it every night, until he couldn't take it anymore. That's when turned to the bottle."

"What happened then? I mean, after he lost his sobriety?"

"Got caught pissing in public in a grocery store parking lot. Had to register as a sex offender for it." Alvarez sighs. It's a sad sound. "He got sober again after that, but he's carried around that label ever since."

Our eyes meet. I want to say something wise, something comforting, but I've got nothing.

After that, Alvarez and I return inside. On the way in, we step over the bodies of three zombies we had to kill before digging Aleisha's grave. They'd been drawn by with the racket made during Frederico's breakdown.

We find my friend in the far corner by the walk-in freezer, knees pulled up to his chest. A bottle of cooking sherry is in his hand. He is in the process of sucking it down like it's the elixir of life.

Something in me snaps. I stride over to him and yank the bottle out of his hand. "This stops now!" I overturn the bottle, letting the sherry sluice onto the floor.

I expect him to rage. Or maybe cry. Maybe both.

What I don't expect is for him to turn glassy eyes up at me. Those eyes, cradling infinite pain, roll up into his head. He collapses at my feet.

"Frederico?" I drop to my knees and give him a rough shake. "Frederico!"

Alvarez, surprisingly calm, checks his pulse. "Unconscious," he pronounces.

"Fuuuuck." I draw the word out in frustration.

Stalking to the sink, I turn the cold handle. To my surprise, water sputters out. I grab a frying pan out of the sink—probably one of those Frederico threw in his fit—and fill it with water. I dump it unceremoniously on his head.

Nothing happens.

"Shit-shit-*shit*." I stare down at his unconscious form. What am I supposed to do? Just sit here until he wakes up? While Carter is stuck in the dorm cafeteria, waiting for me?

"You could put him in the jeep outside," Alvarez says. "There's a long stretch of open road through the forest. You can probably drive a little way without worry of attracting a horde of zombies."

I consider this. "Where's the next military checkpoint?"

"The town of Scotia. Or at least, that's where it was." He shakes his head. "I don't think it's there anymore." That haunted look comes back into his eyes.

"I'll take the car." It's my best option, considering the circumstances, even though cars have been nothing but trouble. I glare sadly at Frederico's still form. "Will you help me move him?"

ALVAREZ and I spend twenty minutes scavenging supplies before setting ourselves to the task of moving Frederico. It takes us another fifteen minutes to haul him outside and get him strapped into the jeep. It's been humming away quietly all this time. Two zombies have wandered into the parking lot, which I dispatch with the shovel we used to bury Aleisha. Alvarez watches me in silence.

"You're going to make it," he says after I've bludgeoned the second zombie to death. "You're insane and tough."

I hold the shovel out to him. It's soiled with sticky blood and bits of hair and dirt. "Take it," I say. "It's quieter than a gun."

He takes it solemnly. "Bye, Kate. Good luck."

"Good luck, Alvarez." I take a moment to memorize his face, knowing it's unlikely I'll ever see him again. "Nice knowing you." I give him a quick hug.

With that, we go our separate ways. Alvarez disappears back into the forest, a duffel bag slung over one shoulder. He holds the shovel in the opposite hand, using it as a walking stick.

I get into the driver's seat of the jeep and pull out onto the deserted road, heading north with my drunk, unconscious friend.

45

OUT OF GAS

As Alvarez predicted, the road north of Laytonville is a lonely one. It narrows to two lanes. Oak trees have completely disappeared, replaced by tall pine trees. I drive with the windows down, using the cold air to keep me awake.

We're barely a mile gone from Rod's Roadhouse when the jeep gives a wicked cough. Alarmed, I look down at the dashboard—and find the gas light on.

"Fuck!" I slam one hand against the steering wheel. "Fuck it all, can't we catch a break?" I'd been so busy fretting over my unconscious friend that I hadn't thought to check the fuel gage.

The car makes it another half mile, coughs two more times, lurches, and then dies. I sit there in silence, listening to the soft click and hiss of the dead engine. What am I going to do?

I will not cry, I tell myself resolutely. I've cried enough already. Feeling sorry for myself isn't going to help anything.

I mull over my options, realizing there isn't much I can do. I can't carry Frederico, and I can't leave him here. The only thing I can do is wait for him to wake up.

Afraid to stay inside the car and be exposed, I retreat a short distance into the woods and deposit a trash bag of food I'd scavenged from Rod's Roadhouse. Then I get Frederico's limp form out of the car. Looping my hands under his armpits and around his chest, I drag him into the woods. It's slowgoing, but I manage. I drop him onto the ground and roll him onto his side. He emits a soft snore.

Exhaustion swells within me. Every ache in my body makes itself known. My tired, blistered feet. The bullet wound in my shoulder. The achy knee from my early fall. Exhausted, sore arms. Stiff back. Even just the short ride in the car was enough to make my leg muscles tighten up. Patches of rash from the poison oak have started to pop up on my arms.

It's 6:30. We've been on the move and awake for almost thirty-three hours. And we still have a long way to go.

I decide to sleep for thirty minutes. It will give me a much-needed boost and hopefully be long enough for Frederico to wake up from his stupor.

I set the alarm on my watch. Then I curl up on my side, pressing my back against Frederico's, and close my eyes.

I'm yanked from the depths of a dreamless slumber by the sound of someone throwing up. I bolt upright, breathing hard, unaware of where I am or what's going on. Drool and pine needles stick to my cheek.

It all comes crashing back: Aleisha, Alvarez, the stupid out-of-gas jeep, Frederico . . .

Frederico.

I turn to find my friend sitting up on his knees. His back is hunched as bits of vomit stream from his mouth. He heaves two more times, then wipes his mouth with the back of his hand.

"You should have left me behind," he says, not looking at me. "I'm not worth your effort."

"Bullshit," I reply. "You're my best friend. I'd never leave you behind."

"What happened to the soldier?"

"Went south. To Ukiah."

Silence. I don't want to fill it with useless epithets. Instead I stay quiet, waiting for to him to speak.

He sips on his hydration straw, rinses his mouth out with water, then takes several long drinks. Finally, he lifts his head and turns haunted eyes on me. "What did you do with her body?"

His anguish pierces me. "Alvarez and I buried her behind the bar."

"Thank you." He closes his eyes, a few tears leaking down his cheeks. "I . . ." He stops, swallows. "I couldn't bear to look at her. To see what I'd done to her—"

"You did right by her," I interrupt. "I know it was awful, but you did right."

He says nothing. I try to think of something comforting to say, but come up empty. What words of comfort are there for a parent who's lost a child?

"I hope Brandon is safe," he says, speaking of his son on military deployment. "I hope I die so I never have to look him in the eye and tell him how I failed his sister." He makes eye contact again. "I feel dead. I lost Aleisha and lost my sobriety."

At a loss for words, I reach out and take his hand. There's nothing I can say to patch up the hole in his heart.

That's when I noticed the long shadows and the chill rising from the ground. I lift my wrist, thinking the alarm must be about ready to go off—and see that it's 7:45.

"Oh, shit!" I jump to my feet, wondering why it didn't go off. Another look shows me the alarm *did* go off—almost forty minutes ago. I slept right through the beeping.

"What's wrong?" Frederico asks.

"It's almost eight," I say. "We need to get back on the road and get in more miles before dark. Without our headlamps, we won't be able to go very fast once the sun goes down."

I see the skepticism in his face and raise my hand to forestall him. "I got ahold of Carter. He's alive with a few friends. They're holed up in the dorm lounge."

Emotions churn over his countenance. I see surprise, relief, resentment, and then sadness. I understand it all.

"Help me find him," I say. "Please? I can't make this run without you."

He nods and awkwardly gets to his feet. There is soreness and stiffness in every movement.

"Inventory?" I say to him.

"My IT band is being an asshole. Always is on anything over fifty miles. And I'm hungover. You?"

"Knee hurts like a son of a bitch. I could use a clean pair of socks." Though I don't say it, my arms feel like lead, my shoulders ache from the pack straps, and my legs feel like jelly. The chafing from my sports bra is a bright throb. The poison oak patches have spread in the past hour. And of course the gunshot wound hurts like a son-of-bitch.

I don't bother listing the complaints, just as I know he's holding back from me. You can't run as far as we have without hurting like hell. Part of ultras is running through pain and running despite pain.

"I got a little food." I gesture to the garbage bag I brought from Rod's Roadhouse.

"No time," Frederico replies. "We can't burn daylight eating. Besides, I don't feel like eating."

I nod in understanding, relieved he's agreed to get moving again. We've already lost enough time.

I hurry to the car, grimacing at the stiffness of my body from the short rest. I swing my good arm and rotate my torso as I walk, trying to loosen things up.

For all that I was too afraid to sleep exposed in the jeep, we're alone on the road. I spot a stream of iridescent liquid running out from beneath the car. It's made a small pool next to the front passenger tire.

A lightbulb goes off in my head. I didn't take a car with an empty gas tank. I took a car with a leaky gas tank. We're lucky the damn thing didn't explode.

I step up to the car and rummage through the glove compartment, hoping to find a flashlight. Some good rifling doesn't produce a much-needed flashlight, but I do find a handful of condoms, a wad of McDonald's napkins, and a melted Snickers bar.

"Carter loves Snickers," I say as Frederico comes out of the forest to stand beside me. "I used to buy him a Snickers bar for every A he got on his report cards. He insisted I keep up the tradition through his senior year."

"You should save that for Carter," Frederico says.

"Save what?"

"The Snickers bar."

"It's so . . ." I turn the bar over in my hands. "Melted."

He shrugs. "It's still a Snickers bar."

He has a point. I tuck the lumpy chocolate bar into my pack, imagining Carter's face when I deliver it to him in Arcata.

"I gotta take a leak." Frederico moves stiffly to the far side of the car.

I resist the urge to ask him if he's okay. It's a stupid question, and besides, it doesn't matter how he feels. It doesn't matter how either of us feels. We have to move. Staying stationary is not an option.

I decide I'd better go, too. I squat on the side of the road. I try to gauge the color of my urine; the darker it is, the more dehydrated I am. Though it's hard to discern the exact color in the shadows, it's darker than I'd like.

"I could use a few electrolyte tablets," Frederico calls to me from the other side of the car. "They'd help with the hangover. My head feels like it's splitting in half."

"I think I could eat electrolyte powder straight out of the bottle," I call back. "Though not for a hangover."

I straighten gingerly, every muscle in my body screaming.

"What would you rather have right now?" I ask Frederico, pulling my pants up. "A hot tub or electrolytes?"

"Ibuprofen," he replies. "A whole fucking bottle."

"Yeah. I hear you there."

I move toward the front of the car. There's a slight dip between the asphalt and the dirt. As I scan the highway, my foot hits it at an awkward angle.

I stumble. My ankle rolls, and I go down.

46

SUFFER BETTER

As I fall, something pops in my ankle.

"Kate!" Frederico darts around the car to me.

Pain shoots up my ankle. I stagger, catching myself. I take long, gulping breaths, nostrils flaring as I fight back the pain.

Frederico grasps my shoulder, the two of us looking down at the ankle. No doubt it will begin to swell in the next few minutes.

"I think I twisted it." God, please don't let it be a sprain. I lean over my good knee. "Goddamn rookie mistake. I know better than to take my eyes off the road. Dammit."

Frederico touches the side of my face, forcing me to look up at him. "This isn't the end. Your ankle will swell up. That will act as a natural splint. You can run through this."

This time I do laugh, though it's a pained noise. As crazy as it sounds, what he says is true. There are ultrarunners who *have* finished races with fucked-up ankles. Just not very many of them.

"That's the sort of thing badass elites do," I say. "Not normal, middle-of-the-pack runners like me." This wouldn't have happened if I wasn't so tired. It's too easy to make mistakes when exhaustion sets in. "Carter doesn't even need me. Not really." I rub tiredly at my face. God, my ankle is on fire. "He's a grown man. I need *him*, Frederico." This is the naked, humiliating truth. "I lost Kyle and he's all I have left. I'm out here running to Arcata because my son is the only reason I have to live." Tears well in my eyes.

"Fuck your twisted ankle," Frederico says ruthlessly. "I lost my daughter. My baby. All I want to do is lie down on the side of the road and die. But I'm going to keep running. You're going to do the same. Now, move. We're finishing this run if it kills us."

I nod, pushing myself upright. He's right. Despair and self-pity are demons that nearly devoured me when Kyle died. I can't let that happen again.

"Remember what Kyle used to say when he crewed races for us?" I ask.

"What? The bit about suffering better?"

"Yeah." I swing my arms, pushing the agony of my ankle into a small part of my brain. "*Suffer better, babe.*"

Ultrarunners suffer better than most people. That's what Kyle meant. You can't take up a sport like ultrarunning if you aren't good at suffering. It doesn't matter how much you train; racing long distances hurts. Sometimes, it hurts a little. Usually, it hurts a lot. That's what happens when you pound the hell out of your body.

Which raises the question: why do something that hurts? On purpose?

It's a question all long-distance runners get asked. The answers are as varied as the people.

"Hey, Mom." Carter greeted me with a chipper smile at the forty-mile aid station on the Cactus Rose one-hundred-miler. He passed me a baggie of electrolyte tablets. "Guess what?"

"What?" I dug around in my gear bag, looking for some disinfectant wipes. The desert plants had sliced the shit out of my arms and legs, and I wanted to clean the wounds before heading back out.

"You've never been any closer to the finish line."

I pause, raising one eyebrow at my son. "I've got another sixty miles to go."

"Yes, but you've still never been closer to the finish line." He made a goofy face, crossing his eyes and touching his tongue to his nose.

It was impossible for me not to laugh. I leaned back in the collapsible chair he'd set up for me, letting the humor ripple through me.

"Is this what you're looking for?" He passed me a Ziploc filled with single-wrapped disinfectant wipes.

"Yeah, thanks." I rip open one of the packages, wiping the disposable cloth up and down my arm. My skin stung in response.

The director of the Cactus Rose was famous for saying that everything on the course stung, scratched, or bit. There was no way to run this course without getting bloody. In fact, there was a demented pride that went along with getting beat up by the trail.

"Where's your dad?" I ask as I finished cleaning my arms. I leaned down to start working on my legs, which had twice as many cuts as my arms.

"Napping in the car," Carter replied. He watched in silence as I wiped up a long streak of dried blood. "Hey, Mom?"

"Yeah, honey?"

"Why do you do this?"

"Do what?"

"*This.*" Carter gestured emphatically to the surrounding desert. "Ultrarunning. I mean, you could run half marathons or things like that. Easier races. Why do you always pick the hard ones?"

I took a long drink of water, considering my answer. Carter's question was one I'd asked myself periodically over the years. Sometimes I ran to burn off stress; sometimes I ran to work off a particularly large bowl of ice cream; other times I ran for the sheer joy of the sport. But underneath all that was another, more profound reason.

"There are a lot of reasons," I said at last. "If I had to boil it down, I'd say I run ultramarathons to learn about myself. To find myself. You can't run one hundred miles without learning something. Crossing the finish line of an ultra . . ." I shrugged, struggling to find the right words. "There's nothing like it. I find new places inside myself on every race."

Carter took that in introspective silence, passing me a clean pair of socks. "You should put these on. Dad says you don't blister as badly if you change your socks halfway through."

I passed the socks back. "I'll get them at the next aid station."

TODAY, right now, I am running with a new reason. I run to find my son. I'm running toward Carter, toward my family. If ever I had a reason to suffer better, today is it.

Perhaps the last twenty years have been nothing but a series of training runs for this, the ultimate run—the run to find my son.

"I don't think I really understood the meaning of suffering until today," Frederico says. His voice is brittle, his face lined with grief and sorrow.

I fumble with a front pocket in my pack and pull out a small paper towel filled with espresso beans. "Here," I say, holding a few out to him. "I took them from the espresso machine in Rod's Roadhouse. They'll help us stay awake."

The corners of his mouth turn up, but the smile doesn't touch his eyes. He plucks a few out of my hand and tosses them back like they're pills. Then he starts to run.

I fall in beside him. My body shrieks in protest. It's a good ten minutes before things loosen up and I find myself slipping into a rhythm. The ankle, already swelling, tells me to sit the fuck down, but I ignore it. I push the pain to my periphery, focusing instead on putting one foot in front of the other. I hear Kyle's voice in my head saying, *Suffer better, babe. Suffer better.*

The road climbs away from Laytonville. Though it undulates, there's a steady rise in elevation. We lean into the hills, pumping our arms to help propel us upward. The downhills bring some relief as we let gravity pull us forward.

My calves burn. My lungs rasp. My arms ache.

My ankle tells me I'm the biggest fucking idiot on the planet. I tell my ankle to shut the hell up.

The sun sinks lower and lower. It becomes harder and harder to see. I lament the loss of our headlamps.

"I think we've crossed into the part of the race where we can't be wimps," I say.

"Are you kidding? I hit that point fifty miles ago. I'm just faking it till we make it to Arcata.'"

Mile one hundred thirty-two.

Pain is a state of mind. Running is a state of mind. I am the runner, not the pain.

The road is dotted with big yellow and red signs advertising Confusion Hill. It's one of the many tourist traps dotting the 101.

Carter and I didn't stop at Confusion Hill when I helped move him north to college. I'd battled a storm of emotions that day. Pride because I was sending a kind, responsible, hard-working young man out in the world. Joy because Carter was getting an opportunity I never had. Fear because I was afraid of how I would cope with being alone. Sadness because experiencing this day without Kyle felt fundamentally wrong.

I dragged out the drive as much as I could. I forced him to stop at several goofy tourist traps, like the Drive-Thru Tree and the Chimney Tree. We hadn't stopped at Confusion Hill, though.

Tears well in my eyes. Why didn't we stop? Why didn't I insist on one more goofy memory before sending him off into the world? Why am I crying over some stupid tourist trap I've never been to? I don't even know what Confusion Hill is.

Mile one hundred thirty-four.

It's dusk. Another red-and-yellow sign looms in front of us. It says, *Approaching Confusion Hill*.

The road curves. The left side of the road drops off in a near-vertical slope; the right side, equally steep, is terraced with a tall stone retaining wall. Between the darkness and the curve in the road, our vision is limited.

As we round the corner, my eyes are dazzled by a sudden brightness. Before us is a jumble of neon lights, eye-tingling red-and-yellow signs, and brightly colored flags strung through the redwoods.

Confusion Hill. We have arrived.

The tourist trap is nestled next to a bridge that spans the Eel River. The river lies just past the parking lot, down a cliff tangled with redwoods and ferns. Anyone driving over the bridge can't help but get an eyeful of Confusion Hill. It's a prime location for snagging tourists.

There are a few cars in the parking lot. Bordering the asphalt lot is a chain-link fence, presumably protecting the secrets of Confusion Hill from the unpaying populace. Behind the fence are a few zombies. Lucky for us, it appears traffic was light when the zombie apocalypse came through.

The tapping of our feet has alerted the zombies to our presence. Trapped behind the chain-link fence, none are in a position to come after us. They rattle the fence at our approach, moaning and snapping their teeth. One lets out an awful keen that raises the hairs along the back of my neck.

An answering keen fills the night. But it's not from an undead in Confusion Hill; it's from somewhere off to our left, in the woods.

Something large and black blots out the forest to our left. I'd been so focused on Confusion Hill I hadn't paid attention to the other side of the road.

"What is that?" Frederico whispers.

The big black shape solidifies in my vision. It's a big tourist bus. The reason we can't see it very well is because its laying on its side, its dark undercarriage barely visible in the night.

Several more keens rise up from the other side of the bus. Then a rush of bodies swarm around the vehicle toward the road—coming straight for me and Frederico.

47

TOURIST TRAP

THE ZOMBIE TOURISTS ARE ASIAN, EVERY LAST ONE OF THEM SPORTING A camera around the neck. They rush en masse, cameras bouncing on their chests as they run.

"Shiiit!" I squeal. "Run, Frederico!"

I break into an all-out sprint, tearing toward the bridge. My fear numbs the pain in my ankle. Frederico hauls ass next to me.

The foremost of the zombies—five of them altogether—come around the front of the bus and angle toward us at a run. Their blind trajectory will cut us off from the bridge if we don't move faster. Another three dozen Chinese tourists pour around the back of the bus.

Fuck. We can't stop to fight the zombies in front of us to clear the path. If we don't beat them to the bridge, we're going to be trapped.

"Faster!" Frederico yells.

I pour every last ounce of speed I have into my tired legs. My arms pump. My breath rasps. My legs churn as I lean forward, straining toward the bridge.

The first of the zombies reaches us, arms outstretched. With a feral shout, Frederico angles his left shoulder and plows straight into the beast. The monster flies backward, skidding across the pavement on his back.

Frederico never slows. I maintain my course, sprinting beside my friend. We outpace the other four zombies, our feet hitting the bridge before they catch us.

Behind us, an eerie keen fills the dusk. We have an entire undead tour bus on our asses. There's no hiding from them. A few well-thrown rocks won't save us this time.

"Push hard," Frederico says. "Push hard and lose them. It's the only way."

Mile one hundred thirty-five.

Despite the hangover I know he has, Frederico sets a grizzly pace. We manage to put a solid one hundred yards between us and the undead. We're not sprinting, but we are running hard.

I'm not sure how long we can maintain the lead. Their awful keening follows us through the night. They are hunters, and we are the prey.

No pain no pain no pain.

This mantra rolls through my mind as I run. Mantras are an ultra trick I picked up somewhere, though now I can't recall who gave the advice.

No pain no pain no pain.

If you lie to yourself long enough, you actually start to believe it.

Mile one hundred thirty-seven.

My mantra changes.

Don't be a wimp. Don't be a wimp. Don't be a wimp.

Hunger gnaws at me from the inside out. It battles with my physical pain. I battle both of them. I can't remember when my hydration pack ran dry, or when I had my last drink.

I'm bonking—again. The last two days has been an unending series of bonks.

Don't be a wimp.

The zombies are still behind us. They aren't gaining on us, but we aren't widening the gap, either. Frederico keeps a close eye on the zombies. He pushes us hard, so hard.

Mile one hundred thirty-nine.

The zombies have narrowed the gap to seventy-five yards. They're gaining on us.

We're high in the mountains, the darkness a deep umbrella around us. I miss our headlamps. If we had lights, we could take to the forest and try to lose the zombies. With only the stars and a sliver of moon in the sky, there isn't nearly enough light for us to risk the woods.

They've only been chasing us for five miles, which isn't all that far. If Frederico and I were at the start of this insane junket, we could lose them. I'm sure of it. But we've been on the move for almost two days straight. We're beat to shit and exhausted.

One foot in front of the other. That's our only option.

Are we just delaying the inevitable?

Mile one hundred forty-one.

Fifty yards and closing. My whole body hurts, from the top of my head to the bottom of my toes, and everything in between. My head screams for me to move, to pick up the pace, but my body can't comply.

I begin to think death wouldn't be a bad option. Yeah, it would suck to get eaten to death, but with the throng of zombies behind us, it would probably be quick. Running another fifty miles at this pace seems like slow torture.

What if we just ran off into the woods? How far could we go before one of us fell and broke something? Maybe, if we were lucky, we'd both run straight over a cliff and break our necks. Death would be swift. That wouldn't be such a bad way to go. At least we'd die running.

If only we could find a cliff.

Mile one hundred forty-two.

I try to focus on the road, on my form, on mentally managing my hunger and pain. I feel like the unraveling hem on an old pair of jeans.

My eyes flick out to the forest. Should we try it? Brave the woods in the dark? I imagine tripping on a log and breaking my other ankle or knocking myself out on an errant, low-hanging branch.

In the daylight, we'd stand a chance. In the dark, we'll be dead meat.

"I hurt," I gasp. "Everything hurts."

Frederico, eyes glued to the road, doesn't look up when I speak. "Yeah," he agrees.

I recognize the set lines in the profile of his face. He's bonking, too. He might not have a fucked-up ankle, but he's got his own physical pain.

Mile one hundred forty-four.

Twenty-five yards and closing.

The zombies are running us into the ground. Frederico and I are barely holding on. We're hungry, tired, and hurting. We're two steps short of roadkill. How much farther can we get before the undead catch us?

We're nearing another bridge. Maybe we should jump off. Throw in the towel and just end it.

"Kate." When Frederico says my name, I sense the depth of our friendship in the word. "You're a finisher, Kate. Don't let yourself forget that. You might not look pretty when you arrive at the finish line, but you always arrive." He pushes a small bundle into my hands. In my exhausted, pain-riddled state, I take the objects automatically, barely noticing them.

Frederico smiles at me. The moon and stars cast the lean angles of his face into planes of shadow and light. Strands of his curly gray hair, escaping from his ponytail, create a fuzzy halo around his face.

"Tell Carter Uncle Rico says hi."

Then he does something strange. He lets out a long, loud, word-less holler. Then he turns and sprints away from me.

His yell lashes the night with sound. The zombies, zeroing in on the sudden noise, let out a collective keen.

48

RUN, JACKALOPE

I SWAY ON MY FEET, STARING STUPIDLY AFTER FREDERICO IN incomprehension.

To the right of the bridge is a small, single-lane road. I hadn't seen it until now. It's onto this road that Frederico runs. The tourist zombies stream after my friend in an undead rush.

Frederico bellows into the night. "Run, Jackalope! Goddamn you, run!"

His words are like a pair of jumper cables to my brain. Understanding fills me with horror.

"Run, Jackalope!"

I turn and run.

Gone is the pain of my swollen ankle, of all the little aches and pains that have accumulated over the last one hundred forty-four miles. Gone are the fatigue and the hunger and the thirst.

Crowding all of it away is frantic grief.

"Run, Jackalope!"

His words, faint in the night, drive me forward. My legs churn over the black asphalt. I sprint over the bridge and away from my friend, tears running down my cheeks.

The bridge spans a wide gorge, crossing yet another section of the Eel River. Free of the trees, the landscape around me brightens under the light of the moon and stars. Something moves to my right, off in the distance.

Without slowing, I turn my head. Half a mile away is the narrow, single-lane road. It leads away from the 101 and winds down to the river below the bridge.

Frederico sprints down that road, the horde of zombies on his heels. His wordless yells and whoops echo into the night, a beacon that draws the zombies the way flowers draw bees. The intensity of the noise sets them into a frenzy. They keen, voices filling the air like a discordant church organ. Frederico, pouring on one last burst of desperate speed, has perhaps fifty yards on them.

But the zombies are gaining. Even when they trip or veer off the road and run into a tree or trip over a bush, they gain on him.

I grind to a halt in the middle of the bridge, breath catching in my throat. I stretch out a hand, as if I can somehow reach my friend from here.

"*Frederico!*" My throat, parched with thirst, turns the word into an anguished croak.

He doesn't hear me. He's focused on the road—on keeping as much road as possible between him and the monsters. The gap has narrowed to twenty-five feet. His body is giving out on him. The miles and miles of running have taken their toll.

The tiny road disappears from sight, winding beneath the bridge. I race to the opposite railing, following Frederic's progress with my eyes. His road snakes away into the trees, disappearing from sight. As he nears the trees, still shouting, there's only ten feet between him and the undead.

Maybe he senses my anguished gaze. Maybe he just wants one last look at the world. Or maybe he's looking back at the zombie horde bearing down on him.

Whatever the reason, Frederico pauses to look back, and up. Even in the dark—even with the distance separating us—I feel it when our eyes meet. A silent good-bye hangs in the night between us. That single word is a giant, imploding echo of nothingness.

And then he's gone, disappearing into the trees. Disappearing from my life.

Tears pour down my cheeks. I turn, sprinting away.

A single, solitary scream breaks over me like a crashing wave. I feel myself drowning in it. The screaming stops, abruptly cut off. I choke on a sob.

I pump my arms, running away. Away from the death of my friend. Away from the sorrow that wraps around me like a constrictor. Away from every heartbreaking pain life has delivered me.

Frederico dies so I can run.

His nonexistent voice rings in my head: *Run, Jackalope.*

49

BFF

MY EYES SNAP OPEN.

The first thing I see is a spider web. The multifaceted silk hangs delicately from small shrub, the strands bedecked with pearls of dew.

Frederico.

His name hangs in my mind like that spider web—shining and impermanent. There's a Frederico-sized hole in my heart. Right next to the Kyle-shaped hole.

Where am I? I push myself up into a sitting position. My body screams from the movement, demanding I lie back down.

I ignore it.

I'm somewhere in the forest, a canopy of redwoods towering above me. Damp earth and pine needles stick to my cheek, torso, and arms.

Frederico.

It doesn't matter how far or how hard I run. I'll never escape the grief and emptiness.

Kyle.

Gritting my teeth, I push myself into a standing position. My swollen ankle throbs. I consider pulling off the shoe and sock to inspect it, but quickly dismiss the idea. If I take the shoe off, I'll never get it back on. I make up my mind right then that the damn shoe isn't coming off until I get to Arcata.

It's seven in the morning. I've been on the move for forty-five hours. My watch shows me at mile one hundred forty-seven. How long did I sleep? I don't even remember how I got here.

My eyes are swollen from crying. My nose is clogged with snot. Hunger scrapes at my insides. My tongue is parched. My body feels like it's been pounded with a hammer—which in fact, it has.

Pain is irrelevant.

Hunger, too, is manageable. At least for now.

Hydration, however, is neither irrelevant or manageable. I need to get some liquid into my body. Soon. I won't make it far if I'm too badly dehydrated. Lack of water can lead to kidney malfunction, which has forced many a runner into a DNF.

That is not going to be me. Not today, at least.

My mind flashes briefly to a documentary I saw on Genghis Khan. His warriors drank blood from their horses to stave off dehydration in the desert.

Any horses around? I wonder.

I have a brief vision of me catching a horse, slicing its flank open with a knife I don't have, then draining some of its blood into my hydration pack. I bark a mad, desperate laugh.

Something crinkles under my hand.

I look down and see a small pile of stuff on the forest floor. There's half a candy bar and a small Ziploc with needles, sterile wipes, Super Glue—a blister kit, I realize. Like the one Frederico and I put together after we raided that abandoned RV.

Thoughts of last night flood back. I have a vague recollection of Frederico shoving things into my hands before he led the zombies away from me.

My eyes swell with tears. Did he give me these things? Did I carry them all this way?

Frederico lost everything yesterday. His daughter, his sobriety, and his life. He sacrificed his sobriety for Aleisha and his life for me.

Tears spill down my face. I blink them away; now is not the time to cry, not when I'm already dehydrated.

I tuck the blister kit and half-eaten candy bar into my pack. Logic tells me I should tend to my feet—or at least, my good foot—but I'm too tired and honestly, I just don't give a fuck about blisters right now. Even so, having the little kit makes me feel like I have a tiny piece of my friend still with me.

"He's dead, you idiot," says a nasally voice. "There ain't no piece of Frederico left anywhere."

My head whips round. Standing beneath a tree, only five feet away, is a dun-colored rabbit with tall ears. Rising above his ears are a pair of antlers.

My stomach drops at the sight of the jackalope. I quickly turn away, pretending not to have seen or heard him. Now is not the time for a hallucination. Especially an antagonistic one.

"I know you saw me, you weakling," the jackalope sneers. "What, don't have the stomach for the truth? You had the stomach to run away from your friend when he needed you."

I climb to my feet, gritting my teeth at the pain. I glance around—meticulously avoiding the jackalope—looking for the road. There. It's off to my left, about twenty paces.

"So that's how you're going to play it? Pretend you can't see or hear me? This is your fault, you know. You voted for those fucking Democratic pansy-ass do-gooders. If the elephants were in charge, they'd have dropped a few bombs and nipped this zombie bullshit in the bud. None of this apocalypse mumbo-jumbo would have happened. Then you wouldn't be here, and Frederico would still be alive."

My hands tremble. From fatigue, from stress, from grief, from the appearance of the jackalope—who can say?

I pick my way through the forest, paying close attention to the placement of my bad, swollen foot. My leg brushes a bush and comes away wet, soaked with dew. I pause, staring down at the bush.

A minute passes. I unbuckle my hydration pack and drop it to the forest floor. Next, I pull off my stinky, sweat-stained, grimy T-shirt. I drag the shirt across the bush, trying to soak up the dew. Twigs and leaves snag on the material. Three days ago, that would have annoyed me. Today, I barely notice it.

I repeat this process with the shirt on three more bushes, by which time the fabric is nice and wet in my hands. I shove the material into my mouth and suck, pulling the dew onto my tongue and down my throat. The nasty, salty tang of my sweat accompanies the dew, but I'm too exhausted and too thirsty to care.

"Way to go, survivor," says the jackalope. He applauds my efforts with his front paws, which somehow sound like human hands as they clap. "Guess you've got some grit in you after all. Who would've thought?"

Once I suck my shirt dry, I move farther into the forest in search of more shrubs. I spend the next forty-five minutes soaking my shirt with dew and drinking. The jackalope keeps up a running commentary, alternating between insults and political tirades.

"Seriously, Kate, I want you to take a good look at our country. Ask yourself this: wouldn't things be better if automatic assault rifles were legal? Wouldn't you like to have one of those suckers slung across your back right now? I'd bet my left nut you'd trade that stupid water pack for an automatic."

Does my imaginary jackalope have nuts? I blink rapidly against the grit in my eyes, willing myself not to look at him. His reproductive organs are none of my business.

Being able to function with little to no sleep is an art. It's a skill I've practiced and honed over the years. Every six weeks or so, I make it a point to stay awake for a twenty-four-hour period. This keeps me primed for races that require me to be on my feet for twenty-four hours or more. It's a practice I put into place after the Badwater race through Death Valley, when I first encountered this fuzzy little asshole.

I've never hallucinated since then.

Until now.

Maybe I should have been staying up for forty-eight-hour increments. Maybe that would have helped stave off this hallucination.

"What's your big plan now, champ?" the jackalope asks. "No way you'll make it to Arcata with nothing but dew in your stomach."

Something in me snaps. My careful wall of self-control crumbles around me.

"Shut the fuck up," I growl, turning my back on him. "Shut up and leave."

I stalk away—or at least, I try to stalk. I manage a huffy limp with my gimpy ankle.

"Hey, is that any way to treat an old friend?" The jackalope hops after me. "We're BFFs. Badwater Friends Forever."

"*We* are not friends." I pause, scanning my surroundings. I spot a solid branch and limp over to it. "*You* are a figment of my batshit crazy mind. I'd like you to go away now."

"You gotta stop with this patchouli hippie bullshit," the jackalope replies. "The human mind is not nearly as powerful as your kind thinks it is, with your yoga mats and organic food. You think you can just will me away with a Jedi mind trick? Think again, sister."

I yank the branch out of the undergrowth, then set about stripping off the smaller twigs. I rip with more vigor than necessary, struggling against the urge to tell the jackalope that I've never set foot in a yoga studio.

When I'm done stripping the branch, I'm left with a decent walking stick. Not quite as nice as a trekking pole, which I use on steeper races, but it'll do.

I pick my way to the road, brushing off the last of the dirt and pine needles. I emerge onto the asphalt. Above me is a big sign that says, *1 Mile: World-Famous One-Log House!*

To my dismay, the jackalope hops out of the forest and lands beside me. "God, you're rank," he tells me. "I may need to find a new BFF if you don't do something about that smell."

I pause, closing my eyes and taking a deep breath.

The next fifty miles are going to be long.

50

FATIGUE FACTOR

THERE'S AN ULTRA RACE PHENOMENON CALLED FATIGUE FACTOR. AS I stand there on the deserted mountain road, feeling pain in every part of my body, I know I'm coming face to face with it.

Fatigue Factor can easily double a standard mile time. On fresh legs, I can knock out fifty miles in ten to twelve hours, depending on the weather and the terrain, putting me in a range of twelve-to-fourteen-minute miles. A decent pace for a middle-of-the-pack runner.

But I don't have fresh legs. I'm exhausted, hungry, thirsty, and injured. Feeling as shitty as I do, I estimate I'll be lucky to log three miles an hour. I'm also going to have to stop to forage for water and food, which will take even more time. If I get to Arcata in the next twenty-four hours, it'll be a miracle. More likely, it'll take longer.

The idea of being on my feet another day or more almost brings me to tears. I dig deep, hunting within myself for every last scrap of resolve.

"What are you waiting for?" the jackalope asks. "Frederico didn't sacrifice himself so you could loaf around feeling sorry for yourself. Get your ass moving, chica."

I set out at a brisk walk, pushing forward with my injured ankle. Honestly, the ankle is just one of many aches and pains. The walking stick helps a little, but not much.

"Suffer better," I mutter to myself. "Suck it up and suffer better."

"Talking to yourself is the first sign of insanity," says the jackalope.

The two-lane road is bordered by towering pine trees and redwoods. The air smells good—fresh and laden with the scent of pine. For this moment in time, surrounded by nothing except trees and empty road, I can pretend the world hasn't gone to complete shit.

I continue on at a fast walk, trying to work through my achy soreness. A mile later, I round a corner and find myself in Garberville, population 913.

To my right is the One-Log House. It's an ancient redwood tree that's been turned on its side, hollowed out, and made into a tiny house. It was one of the silly stops Carter and I made on our trip to Arcata. We'd taken a few goofy pictures in front of the One-Log House.

Clogging the highway is a jumble of deserted cars. Just past the House are a few gift shops catering to tourists. On the opposite side of the road is a gas station and a campground.

On the ground near the gas pumps is a pile of bodies. My heart stops at the sight of them. I scurry off the road and take cover in the trees.

Nothing happens.

I peer out cautiously from between the cover of two redwoods. The bodies, upon closer inspection, are zombies, each with its head smashed in.

Besides the pile of zombies, there are no other signs of the undead. There are none milling around the cars and stumbling out of the campground. There are none clawing at the windows of the tourist shops or bumping into the gas station pumps.

Someone has rounded up the zombies and made this neat stack of bodies. Someone has cleaned up this tiny little town in the mountains. Who?

"I bet whoever did this voted for the elephants," the jackalope says. "No way they cleaned up this many zombies without some heat. You should try to get your hands on a gun."

I consider my options, chewing my lip in thought. I really need food and water. It's a good bet I can get both in one of the shops. Then again, it's a good bet I will run into whoever made that pile of zombie bodies.

After a moment's thought, I decide food can wait. It's just not worth the risk. Water, on the other hand, is essential. My dew drops repast won't hold me much longer.

I'll avoid the shops and find a hose or faucet instead. The back of the stores seems like a good place to start. With any luck, I'll find a hose and get out before anyone notices me.

"You're not exactly at the top of your game," the jackalope says. "You sure you wanna risk this?"

Fuuuuuck. I close my eyes, wrestling with my temper. Screaming at my imaginary friend is a sure way to draw attention.

"Forget the water. Your ass needs a gun."

The furry asshole has a point, although if I did have a weapon I'd probably blow my own foot off.

I pick my way through the trees, circling behind the back of the One-Log House and gift shops. Finding a tree with some low-hanging branches for concealment, I spend fifteen minutes monitoring them. There are several cars parked behind the buildings, but no sign of people or zombies.

The cars conceal most of the building, but I figure I have a good chance of finding a hose or water spigot there. Find water, fill my pack, and get back on the road. That's my plan.

I will *not*, as my jackalope keeps insisting, go in search of a gun.

He's on his hind legs, shoving paws into my chest to emphasize each word as he speaks.

"Will you shut up?" I hiss at him. "I'm trying to concentrate. Besides, my railroad spikes and screwdrivers have gotten me this far."

The jackalope *tsks*. "The gun," he sneers, "is for *you*."

It takes a moment for his meaning to sink in.

My hallucination just told me to kill myself. I squeeze my eyes shut. I'm losing it.

"Seriously, why do you want to go on?" he asks. "What do you have to live for? You lost Kyle and Frederico. Carter is probably dead, too. Why put yourself through more hell just to have your heart broken one more time?"

I clap my hands over my ears, trying to block out the jackalope. My pulse ramps up. My heart pounds in my chest.

I feel the world unraveling around me. God, how I wish Frederico was here. How I wish Kyle was here.

"Seriously, just get it over with," the jackalope says. "Let us both get some much-deserved rest."

I dig nails into my scalp, knotting fingers in my hair. I can't quit. I can't. Carter is still out there, alive. Kyle and Frederico would want me to keep going.

"No," I whisper. I can't give up. I *won't* give up.

"Did you say something?" the jackalope asks. "Or were you just sniveling in self-pity?"

Fuck this little asshole.

I lash out with my good foot. The tiny, furred body flies through the trees and disappears.

I stand there, panting and tense, waiting for the jackalope to return. My heart continues to hammer in my chest.

Two minutes goes by. Five. Ten.

My heart rate slowly returns to normal. The forest around me is quiet. Nothing moves. The jackalope doesn't come back.

If I'd known it was that easy to get rid of him, I'd have dropkicked him sooner.

"Good riddance," I mutter.

I turn my attention back to the shops. Nothing has changed. Everything is quiet and still.

I creep forward, making my way toward the buildings. I pull out a screwdriver I pilfered from a toolbox behind the bar in Rod's Roadhouse. It helps fortify my nerves.

I reach the first of the cars—a beat-up Dodge Caravan—and crouch behind it. Lowering my head, I scan the ground under the car and beyond. Specifically, I'm looking for feet—for any sign of another human or zombie. At the sight of either, I'm out of here.

What's more terrifying—the living or the dead? The dead may have wanted to eat me alive, but they haven't thought of raping me. They didn't murder an innocent animal for shits and giggles, or put a bell collar on me and set a horde of zombies loose.

There's no sign of anyone, only the rough gravel road and bits of litter: a crumpled beer can, a black trash bag overrun with ants, and discarded cigarette butts.

I ease around the car, moving closer to the building. There—a spigot. Right next to a battered screen door.

I pull off my pack and open the water bladder inside. I quickly scan the area one more time, then dash forward.

I turn the spigot. Water hisses loudly in the pipes, then gushes forth in a cool stream. I'm so busy watching the door and scanning the parked cars that I end up drenching half my pack before getting the bladder in place.

Inside the building, something creaks. I stumble back from the water valve just as the screen door opens.

There's an instant when my eyes meet those of a thirty-something man with blond hair and a goatee. He's mostly clean, with only a little bit of blood splattered on his plain green T-shirt.

At the sight of him, I scramble away.

"Hey," he calls, stretching a hand out in my direction. He looks like a high school basketball coach.

He also looks twice my size and strength.

Panic rises in me. I turn and bolt.

51

BATSHIT CRAZY

I CRASH THROUGH THE TREES, SLOSHING WATER ALL OVER ME.

"Wait!" the man calls. "I won't hurt you!"

Fuck that.

Pausing only to seal my water bag, I sling my pack around my shoulders and haul ass. I make a ton of racket, but I'm more concerned with speed than stealth, betting on my ability to outrun the stranger. I use the walking stick to knock branches out of my path.

I may be beat to shit, and I may be dodging through the woods like a feral Ewok, but I've logged more time running through trees than most normal people. I can lose this bastard, even with my fucked up ankle.

"Come back!" The man's shout echoes through the trees, sending another spike of panic through me. "We won't hurt you! We can help."

We.

Fuck. He's got friends.

A waking nightmare blazes through my brain, and I briefly imagine the basketball coach and his buddies gang-raping me in the One-Log House.

Panic grips my throat, making it hard to breathe. Breath hisses in and out of my mouth.

"Lady! Please! We won't hurt you!"

The stranger's shouts are like the whip at my ankles; all it does is drive me harder. I trip on a root and catch myself on a tree. The impact jars my arm, but I push off and keep going. My ankle screams as I half slide, half run down a small hill. I mentally tell it to shut the hell up.

I scramble up a ravine, whip through the trees, and at last slide to a halt behind a large boulder. I crumple to the ground, breathing hard and pressing my back against a mossy stone.

I huddle there, hands and arms trembling. It occurs to me that I'm close to cracking. My sanity is held together by spider threads. One stiff breeze, and I'll unravel.

It also occurs to me that my fear is possibly unfounded and irrational. Basketball coach might be a nice person. The taint spoiling our world might not yet have touched him.

I could be misjudging the situation, but I don't care. No way I'll let that man or his friends get close to me. I don't care if they're the reincarnation of Mother Theresa.

I take a deep gulp of water, listening for signs of pursuit. The trees are quiet. There are voices in the distance—the basketball coach's "we," no doubt—but nothing immediate moves in the forest around me.

Until the jackalope hops out of the underbrush. His fur is rumpled. Leaves and twigs are lodged in his antlers. He gives me a narrow-eyed glare and hops closer.

"Just remember," he says. "What you do to me, you really do to yourself."

I look away from him, my delicate spider web of sanity shivering dangerously.

I summon a memory of Kyle. *You're batshit crazy, babe. But that's why I love you.* I hear his voice in my head and see his lopsided, loving smile.

"I love you, too, babe," I whisper.

"Talking to yourself now?" the jackalope asks.

"Yeah. I'm losing it. But I don't really give a shit." I push myself to my feet. "I'm going to finish what I set out to do, or die trying."

I owe that to Frederico. He gave his life so I could get to Arcata in one piece.

I expect the jackalope to sneer at me, but instead he says, "That a girl. Dig deep, sister."

I power hike south through the forest, angling in the direction of where I think the road is. Two miles later, I find it. Through the thinning trees, I see another tourist trap selling larger-than-life wood carvings. The sign above the shop reads, *The Legend of Bigfoot* in big, bold letters. Outside are carvings of Big Foot, forest animals, and cartoon characters.

There are two men wrestling a giant wood carving of a dwarf across the parking lot, hauling it toward the shop. Nearby is another pile of zombie bodies. I continue south in the trees, avoiding the shop.

"They could be nice," the jackalope says. "I bet they have food."

"No fucking way," I whisper, and continue on.

Half a mile later, I emerge onto the road. All the walking has helped combat some of the stiffness. My body still hurts like hell, but that's to be expected. I toss the walking stick aside and break into a jog.

Mile one hundred fifty-one.

I reach the small hamlet of Benbow. The highway runs on a ridge perched above the town. To the right is a KOA; to the left is a Tudor-like chalet perched on the edge of the freeway.

I see evidence of the outbreak. A large fire burns in the KOA, enveloping several of the burning buildings. A car is overturned on the off-ramp. Half of the Tudor-like hotel has also burned, the north side collapsed in its own smoldering ash.

A six-car pileup lies in the middle of the highway before me. Three zombies shuffle aimlessly on the asphalt. I slow to a walk, trying to make as little sound as possible. I pull out my screwdriver and a railroad spike, holding one in each hand.

Making a wide arc, I steer around the car wreck. One of the zombies—a teenage girl in jeans and a tank top—pauses in her shuffling, cocking her head in my direction. I freeze.

The zombie girl and I stand in suspension: me stock-still on the side of the road, her with her head tilted toward me as she listens.

Just when I think she's going to turn away, she moans and takes a step in my direction.

My stomach knots. I have to do something. I won't survive another run like last night.

The jackalope sits unconcerned at my feet, grooming his hind leg. Little fucker.

With a silent scream, I charge the zombie girl. She has only seconds to register my attack. Her lips peel back in a snarl, and she takes two more steps toward me, arms reaching. I sidestep her fumbling hands and ram a spike through her eye.

The two remaining zombies converge on me. One is a man in tight Wranglers and a cowboy hat, the other a teenage boy in an Abercrombie & Fitch T-shirt. I sprint away from them and scramble onto the hood of a Honda Civic, putting myself momentarily out of reach.

I crouch on the hood, calculating my next move. Both zombies flail at the front of the car, moaning and stretching their hands toward me.

I need to split them up. Divide and conquer.

Out of the corner of my eye, I spy the jackalope. He's holding a video camera.

A fucking old-school VHS recorder. The red light blinks at me, confirming my suspicion that he's filming my exploits.

He gives me a thumbs-up, which is odd, considering rabbits don't normally have thumbs. "You got this, sister!" he calls.

I clamber onto the roof of the car, purposely making noise. I hope they'll split up, each coming at me from a different side. Then I can fight them separately.

No such luck. They both circle to the left, bumping into each other and growling.

Dammit.

Plan B.

I swing my good foot and kick the cowboy in the face. He staggers back with a growl. I take the opening and dive across the roof of the car, grabbing the teenage zombie by the collar of the shirt. I haul him forward and stab him through the eye.

Cowboy zombie recovers and makes a swipe at me. I cry out involuntarily. He grabs my arm, jerking it toward his mouth.

Using his grip on me as leverage, I jerk my torso around and deliver another brutal kick—this time with my bad foot. Pain lances up my leg, but I ignore it. The zombie momentarily loosens his grip. I jerk free.

Then I leap off the car like I'm a James Bond stunt double, knocking into the cowboy zombie. I grunt at the impact, landing heavily atop the undead monster. His hat goes flying. My elbow scrapes against the asphalt.

He reaches for me, but I'm quicker. I bring the spike down. Hard.

The fucking zombie moves. I miss his eye, connecting with the concrete instead. A shock goes up my arm from the impact.

"Undead fucker," I snarl. I slam my other hand onto his forehead, holding him in place. He claws at my arms, drooling.

My spike comes down again—once, twice, three times. Then several more times for good measure, until red mush is all that's left of the cowboy zombie's face.

"That's for Frederico, you undead fuck." I get shakily to my feet. My hands are smeared with blood. I wipe them as best I can on the cowboy's Wranglers.

"Bravo!" The jackalope hops into view, still wielding his video camera. "You're going to be famous on YouTube!" he crows. "The title of your video will be Crazed Runner takes down Undead Cowboy."

Grimacing in disgust, I turn my back on him.

52

DEATH RUN

I MAKE A QUICK SCAN OF THE VEHICLES. THERE ARE ZOMBIES IN FOUR OF them, clawing and salivating on the windows. The other two are empty, one of them with the passenger door hanging open.

"Gonna try your luck with another car?" the jackalope asks.

"No. I'm done with cars." I'm also past caring about the fact I'm having a conversation with an imaginary nemesis.

I rifle through the first car and hit the jackpot. The trunk is full of camping supplies. Among the sleeping bags, cooking gear, and tarps is an ice chest full of food. Next to the ice chest are several grocery bags crammed full of dry goods.

Stomach rumbling, I reach greedily into the bag, grabbing the first thing I touch. It turns out to be a box of Hostess CupCakes.

I flash back to the last meal I shared with Frederico on the side of the road, after we cleared that RV of zombies. I see him shoving his face full of Hostess CupCakes as he talked about his failed attempts to connect with his daughter.

I was a shitty father, Kate, I hear him say. *Still am.*

I burst into tears. They come streaming out of my eyes, pouring down my cheeks and dripping off the tip of my chin. My chest heaves and my nose clogs up with snot.

I slump down to the ground, hugging the box of cupcakes to my chest.

Frederico should be here. He should be here to eat these with me.

God, I miss him. I miss him so much. I want to see his wild, curly gray hair and the gentle crow's-feet around his eyes when he smiles. I want to hear him call me Jackalope.

Frederico! I scream his name silently. Tears dampen the cupcake box.

"It's your fault," the jackalope says calmly, coming to sit beside me. The fucking video camera hangs around his neck. "You should have stayed home. You never should have left Healdsburg."

His words pierce me like venom. I push violently away from him and return to the car.

A bit more rifling reveals a plastic two-gallon water jug. With slightly trembling hands, I yank it free. I take a long drink, then fill my pack.

"You never should have left Healdsburg," the jackalope repeats. "Instead, you dragged Frederico out here on this death run."

Death run. That's a good name. I'm on a fucking death run.

I stare at the array of food before me, trying to figure out what to do. I've completely lost my appetite, but I know I need to eat.

Hell, does it even matter what I eat? No. No, it doesn't matter. I just need fuel in whatever form it comes in. I seize the closest bag of groceries and yank on the cloth handle, tucking the cupcakes in on top.

"You brought Frederico out here on this run because you're broken," says the jackalope. "You're broken, and you think running is the only thing that will put your insides back together."

His words fly into me like darts, wounding me in places I didn't know existed. I shrink from him, momentarily curling my body around the grocery bag.

As if that will protect me.

"No," I whisper. "That's not why I run."

"Liar."

The word cracks across me with the sting of a barbed whip.

I turn away and break into a run, fleeing from the jackalope. I hug the groceries close to me, clinging to them like they're my last lifeline.

"That's right," the jackalope calls after me. "Run, Kate! Run! That's all you know how to do."

Mile one hundred fifty-one.

I leave Benbow at a fast clip, trying to lose the jackalope. His words drive me forward.

Run, Kate! Run! That's all you know how to do.

My breath burns in my throat. The grocery bag jiggles and bounces in my arms. My body is a solid block of pain.

Mile one hundred fifty-two.

I've given up trying to lose the jackalope. I'm too tired, too beaten down.

I polished off the Hostess CupCakes and currently work my way through a bag of barbecue chips, shoveling the salty wafers into my mouth. I eat as I move, committed to a fast walk. It's the best I can manage while simultaneously eating and wrestling with a shopping bag.

The jackalope trails me, keeping ten feet between us.

"That's right, Kate," he jeers. "Keep running! Doesn't matter how fast you go. I'll always be here." He lets loose a creepy laugh that would do justice to any horror movie.

Mile one hundred fifty-five.

Even now, with all the pain and physical discomfort I'm shouldering, I can honestly say I still love running.

To be honest, pain is part of what I love. Why is that? It's a complicated facet of my obsession for this strange sport.

When I first started to run, it was to escape the maze of my relationship with Kyle. The maze was our own making, and the physical stress of running was a distraction to the larger pain I faced at home. To be honest, I had never truly forgiven myself for running way from Kyle all those years ago.

Mile one hundred fifty-eight.

I shovel uncooked pasta shells into my mouth, crunching them as I jog. Vaguely, I wonder what they'll feel like if I throw them up later. I've thrown up lots of things on ultra runs, but never uncooked pasta. Will they cook in my stomach? Soften in the stomach acid?

In front of me is a sign that reads *Avenue of the Giants*. The Avenue of the Giants is a 31-mile stretch of highway that winds through towering, ancient redwood trees. I veer right, unconsciously heading for the exit.

It's not until I'm a mile down the road that I realize I've left Highway 101.

I pause, glancing at the redwoods looming up on either side of me. It's hard to grasp the enormity of the giant trees without seeing them in person. They're living high rises, remnants of a world that no longer exists. It's hard not to feel insignificant and full of awe, even in the midst of a zombie apocalypse.

Carter and I drove this road together. Is this why I came this way?

In the quiet solitude of the ancient trees, I can almost imagine zombies don't exist. That Frederico and Kyle are still alive. That the world is still right side up.

"Keep dreaming, sister." The jackalope hops up and sits at my feet. "The world is fucked up, and so are you."

"Shut up." Upending the half-full box of pasta shells, I dump them on his head. "No one asked you."

The jackalope scowls at me, swatting irritably at the pasta. "Face it, Kate. Running is the only thing you're good at."

Mile one hundred sixty-one.

I haven't always run away from things. As Kyle and I worked through our issues, I found myself running toward him. Toward us.

Every time I finished a tough race and crossed a finish line, I found proof of inner grit and strength. I found a woman worthy of Kyle's love—a person who didn't quit when things got hard and painful.

I like that woman.

Mile one hundred sixty-three.

I'm down to the bottom of my grocery bag. All that's left is a six-pack of Sprite. Seeing it makes me think of Frederico. I've never been a fan of soda, but he always took some to ultra races, often downing a can at every aid station.

Slowing to a stop, I drop the grocery bag and pull out a can. I glance at the jackalope.

"For Frederico," I say softly, then crack open the can and take a long drink.

"For Frederico," the jackalope echoes. I'm grateful when he doesn't make a caustic remark.

The carbonation fills my throat with an uncomfortable pressure. I ignore it and continue to drink.

"Too bad you killed him."

Something in me snaps. The soda falls from my hand and splats on the ground.

I spin around and seize the jackalope by the horns. He lets loose with a very human-like yell. Face twisting in a violent rictus, I tear off his antlers and fling them into the woods. Blood oozes from the sockets.

His yell turns into a scream. I pick up his furry body and hurl him into the forest, a crazed hiss passing between my teeth. He collides with a tree and falls out of sight, rattling through the bushes as he thumps to the ground.

My chest heaves. I clench my fists and stare into the trees, waiting for him to return.

One minute ticks by. Two. Three. Five. Ten.

No sign of him. No movement from the trees. I'm alone on this desolate road. At least for now. I know the jackalope will be back. He always comes back.

I sag, an anguished sob wracking me.

Frederico! I scream his name silently in my mind.

It's my fault he's dead. He died because he cared about me more than he cared about himself. It doesn't matter if I didn't ask for the sacrifice. It doesn't matter that I don't feel worthy of the sacrifice. The simple fact is that he died so I could live.

This knowledge settles around my shoulders with an unwelcome weight.

I want Frederico's death to mean something. I want to make him proud. I want to make Kyle proud.

Hell, I want to make *myself* proud. Will I ever be able to do that?

Swallowing back my tears, I pull out another can of soda. I silently say good-bye to my friend with each gulp.

53

AVENUE OF THE GIANTS

I LEAVE THE EMPTY GROCERY BAG AND THE REST OF THE SODAS ON THE side of the road and start to run. It's impossible to suppress the mega burps that result after the pounding of the Sprite. Worried I might alert every zombie in a ten-mile radius, I muffle them against my arm.

The enormous redwood trees line the two-lane country road. On encountering a few abandoned cars, I head into the woods and creep past them.

Mile one hundred sixty-four.

My legs are numb. When did that happen?

This is another sign that I've been running for a really, really, *really* long time. The body, pushed past the brink of exhaustion, diverts energy to the core. Nonessential extremities, like arms and legs, go numb as a result.

Corporal therapy. That's what running is to me.

Some days, I may as well be flogging myself.

Mile one hundred sixty-five.

Miranda.

It's a hamlet with a population of 520. If you blink, you might just miss it.

There's a post office, a few restaurants, a motel, and a smattering of mobile homes. Carter and I stopped in a cute cafe here and had burgers.

I decide to avoid Miranda. I cut into the forest, slowing to a walk so I won't make too much noise. It takes a solid hour to make my way back to the road on the north side of town, but I get there without any confrontations. I spot a few zombies, but manage to creep past them without drawing attention.

Mile one hundred seventy-one.

It's not fair to boil running down into a form of corporal therapy. Yes, there's a twisted embracing of pain, but there have been countless times I ran for the simple love of the sport.

Escape, therapy, joy—running is all these things. How can one simple act have so many facets and such deep meaning in my life? The person I am is inextricably enmeshed with a verb.

Mile one hundred seventy-four.

Did Kyle die so I could save Carter? The question crashes into my head, reverberating with the force of a gong.

I come to a dead stop on the highway, rocked to my core by this thought.

Ever since Kyle died, I've run to manage my anguish. Before that, I logged fifty to seventy-five miles a week. After he died, my mileage crept up. Eighty-five miles a week. Ninety-five. One hundred five. Up and up, until I found myself logging a minimum of one hundred twenty miles every week. Never have I been in such incredible shape.

If Kyle hadn't died, I wouldn't be in a position to make this two hundred mile run to Arcata.

My husband believed things happened for a reason. Even shitty things. Sometimes it took years to understand the lesson behind shitty events, but he maintained there *was* a reason.

He was always more spiritual than I was. Have the last two years of hell on earth been in preparation for—for this?

The revelation breaks over me like a golden wave. It brings me a tiny bit of peace.

Mile one hundred seventy-six.

I run to myself. That's the simplest distillation of my obsession with long distance running. Somewhere, in all the countless miles, I find myself. Every time I lace up my shoes and roll out the front door, I connect with myself. Through pain and joy, I find me.

Mile one hundred seventy-nine.

The road is silent and beautiful, the redwood giants the only witnesses to my solitary passage.

I jog into Pioneer Grove, a stand of the beautiful giant trees on the northern end of the Avenue. Some of the trees are as much as eight to ten feet in diameter.

The Grove is deserted. No zombies. No death. Just beauty and life.

A tree stump about twenty feet wide stands before me. It was cut down in the heyday of the logging industry. Every inch of the stump is covered with carvings.

I run my fingers over the carvings, searching, searching, searching.

There. Facing away from the road, about five feet up: a carving.

Our carving.

"WHAT ARE YOU DOING, SWEETIE?" I held a long twig in my hand, snapping off little pieces as I wandered through the redwood grove toward Carter.

My son was dressed in loose jeans and a plain blue T-shirt. A ball cap sat atop his shaggy hair, the ends of which curled around his cheeks. He'd trimmed his beard recently, though it was still full and bushy.

In Carter's hand was a pocketknife, a high school graduation gift from Frederico.

He glanced up at me from a heart he'd carved on the tree trunk. His eyes were unfocused, distant. I could tell he heard me speak, but he hadn't heard my question.

"Hey, Mom," he said vaguely, returning his attention to his carving.

Coming to stand beside him, I gave his shoulder a squeeze as I watched him work in silence.

With infinite care, Carter carved the letters K, K, and C inside the heart. Kyle, Kate, and Carter. My chest tightened.

He leaned forward, blowing away the loose shavings, then spent a few more minutes smoothing out the letters. When he finished, he looked at me. His eyes were wet, but his cheeks were dry.

"We're together, Mom," Carter said. "Doesn't matter where we are. You, me, and Dad—we're always together."

It took all my willpower not to burst into tears. I dragged the trip out, doing everything I could to delay Carter's inevitable drop off at college. He knew it, but he never complained.

I sniffed and nodded, running my fingers over the letters my son had carved with such love.

This was my fate: to drop off my son and drive home to an empty house. I couldn't let him see how much it terrified me. He shouldn't have to take care of his mother.

"Thanks, sweetie." I gave him a hug, trying not to clutch him. "Dad loved the redwoods, you know."

"I know." Carter flashed me a quick smile. "He would like it, the three of us here together." His fingers caressed the carving.

"Yeah. He would." I turned away, willing away my tears. I forced my voice into a cheerful tone. "Come on. We should get going if we want to make it to campus before dark."

Now, two years later, I find Carter's carving in Pioneer Grove. I run my hand over the heart and letters. The carving has faded and blended in with the dozens of other initials in the wood beside it.

I pick up a small rock and press it against the stump. I chip away at the bark, carving a rough F next to my family heart. I take my time, wanting it to look nice.

When I finish, I stand back to admire my crude handiwork. Then I close my eyes and imagine they are all here with me: Kyle, Carter, and Frederico.

I can almost smell Kyle's soap and see Carter's bushy beard in the corner of my eye. I hear Frederico say, *Get moving, Jackalope.*

I let myself pretend, if only for ten seconds, that we're together. That I am with the three people who matter most to me.

It feels good to pretend. Here, in the avenue of ancient giants, a sense of peace washes over me.

Something rustles in the grove. I open my eyes and see the jackalope. He hops resolutely toward me, ears wilted.

The blood on his head has dried to dark lumps. A new set of antlers has already begun to sprout. They are two pale nubs on his forehead.

Five feet away from me, he draws to a halt. We stand there, staring at each other in silence.

The weight of my life hangs between us. Everything I am, everything I'm not—it's all there. It's so heavy it could crack open the earth.

But it doesn't. The earth remains solid beneath my feet.

I know what I have to do.

I swallow and take a step forward. The jackalope tenses, ears swiveling toward me in alarm. I pause, keeping my arms at my side so he can see I mean him no harm.

The jackalope's ears relax. His nose twitches. I take two more steps, closing the distance between us. Slowly, gingerly, I stoop down and lift him into my arms.

He tenses. I cuddle him, pressing my nose into his dirty, bloody fur. After a moment, he relaxes and nuzzles my chest.

We don't speak. We don't move. We just stand there, wrapped in the silence of the redwoods.

And then the jackalope disappears, vanishing from my arms and dissolving into a puff of mist.

54

ARCATA

THE JACKALOPE DOES NOT RETURN. I AM A LONE RUNNER ON THE ROAD, slowly and steadily making my way north. The highway climbs, steadily rising with the mountains.

I fall into a pattern. I stick to the asphalt as much as possible, only veering into the woods when I see zombies or wrecked cars on the road.

Mile two hundred one.

Where the fuck is Arcata? Where the hell is that fucking town?

Two hundred and one point three miles. That's how far Frederico said it was from Geyserville to Humboldt University.

Here I am, at mile two hundred one, and there is no fucking college campus anywhere in sight. For that matter, there isn't *anything* in sight. Just trees and mountains and the goddamn Eel River.

Fuck, fuck, fuck.

Who knows how many miles we added to our run on the various side trips we took? I could have another fifteen miles to go, or fifty. I don't even know where I am.

The thought makes me mad. Really mad.

I glare at the world at large, my stride never faltering.

"Fuck you, world," I say. "I'm finishing this. Just try to stop me."

Mile two hundred five.

Dammit. I need more water.

I veer off the road, jogging down a slope to the Eel River. Ignoring the fact that I'll likely manifest symptoms of dysentery, giardia, or schistosomiasis in the next day or two, I fill my pack up with river water.

As I fasten the pack back into place, I see it: a dull glint off to my right, on top of a small rise.

I squint, peering up the slope. Could that be . . . a railroad track?

I scramble up the hill. Sure enough, there in front of me are the crooked, rusty tracks of an abandoned railroad.

I stare at it dumbly. I recall bending over the map with Frederico and noting the point when the railroad gave up following Highway 101 and veered east to end in some faraway town. We never looked to see if there were other tracks. It makes sense that there would be, though. Logging was once the life blood of northern California. Trains would have been used to haul the lumber.

I weigh my options. Sticking with the road has a lot of risks, especially considering some of the larger towns in front of me: Scotia, Fortuna, and Eureka. There's a good chance they'll be overrun with zombies.

Following the tracks has its own set of risks. It will be much harder to forage for food. Water, too, if the tracks veer from the river for long batches of time. And the tracks are a bitch to navigate. But they are safer.

I deliberate for a long minute. Road or rails? Rails or road?

"Fuck it," I mutter. I'd rather face starvation, dehydration, and injury.

Setting my jaw, I step onto the tracks.

They're as brutal as I remember them. Uneven. Clogged with foxtails and stickers and weeds as tall as I am. And here, farther north, are vicious blackberry briars. It's too early in the season for there to be fruit, which make the bushes both annoying and useless.

Even without my injured ankle, it is a race from hell. I run when I can, but most times I am forced to move at a brisk hike.

The miles blur. I focus on the monumental task of putting one foot in front of the other.

The tracks roughly follow the Eel River, giving me plenty of water to drink. I pass the occasional house or trailer home on my trek. There are times when the tracks draw close to the road, bringing me near cars. I forage for food when I need to, killing zombies when I can't avoid it.

My feet are bricks of pain. The swollen ankle is just one of the many aches. My injured knee has also swelled up. An old injury has resurfaced on my right foot. It feels like someone is ramming an ice pick into the top of it, right at the base of my toes.

Blisters on the toes push against my socks and shoes. There are other blisters on the top and bottom of my feet. I wish I had the energy to stop and tend to them, but I don't. I'm pretty sure I'll have no toenails left by the end of this trip. Fuck it. They'll grow back eventually.

My arms are leaden weights at my sides. Achy soreness crawls along my back, neck, and abdominals. There's chafing along my inner thighs, under my sports bra, and along my shoulders and armpits.

The poison oak has spread up both arms. A few patches have also popped up on my neck and cheek, too. In an effort to combat the itchiness, I've slathered mud on the rashes. I look like a crazed golem.

My bullet wound throbs and aches. I embrace that particular pain. It's a reminder of a time when I still had Frederico by my side.

The sun sets and rises. Still, I run.

Sometimes I cry for long stretches of time. Occasionally I laugh madly at nothing in particular. Mostly, I keep my head down and slog forward.

Do I stop to sleep? I wish I knew.

Mile two hundred twenty-nine.

Arcata. Population 17,697.

After seventy-eight hours and forty-seven minutes, I have arrived. The railroad tracks have, at long last, delivered me to my destination.

I'm filthy, in pain, hungry, thirsty, bloody, and covered in mud, but I'm here. I'm here, and I'm alive.

A dark cloud of smoke sits on top of the town. Ash flicks fill the air. Somewhere, a fire burns. A big fire.

I half limp, half jog into this strange town of hippies, artists, druggies, anarchists, and college students. Most of the buildings and homes are colorful and ornate relics of the once-booming logging industry.

The tracks have taken me into the west side of town. The college is, of course, on the opposite side, but that seems like a small obstacle in light of everything.

I easily navigate the streets of Arcata, having run through most of them whenever I visited Carter. A hush has fallen over the college town. It's a hush of necessity—a hush adopted by prey.

I move at a walk, partially because running is too much of an effort, partially because I don't want to make noise.

The zombies moan and wander the streets in blind packs. Their numbers thicken toward the center of town. I steer clear of them, a few times hunkering down and hiding until they pass.

I find remnants of military presence. There are two Hummers near the town square. One of them is half buried in a storefront; the other lies on its side. I count eight zombie soldiers, all of them bloody and ghastly.

There are dead bodies—real dead bodies—in the street, all them partially or mostly eaten.

Some houses have clearly been vandalized: shattered windows, busted doors, driveways and streets strewn with discarded loot. Other homes and shops have been boarded up. In a second-story window of a blue house, a pair of eyes watch me as I pass. When I meet the person's gaze, the blinds immediately snap shut.

This is a cowed, dead town.

Mile two hundred thirty.

Finish Line.

Humboldt State University.

It's in ruins.

I stand at the entrance to the university, staring at the remains of the once-beautiful white-stucco student apartments. These had been new buildings, built to attract more students. Most have burned to the ground.

There isn't a living human in sight.

A giant football field nestles in the crux of the apartments. Dozens of zombies mill around the field, many in military uniforms. Students and faculty are among them. Wrecked and burned military jeeps dot the landscape.

My worst fears dance before my eyes. I crouch behind the broad stucco sign bearing the university's name, taking a moment to steady myself.

Keep it together, I tell myself. *You're almost to the finish line.*

Luckily, there are four lanes of traffic and a wrought iron fence between me and the zombies. I veer to the far margin and creep past the fence. I break into a run when there's a pile of rubble between me and the undead, following the road that runs along the perimeter of the campus. Strangely alert and awake, I scan the surroundings for signs of danger, my screwdriver and railroad spike in hand.

I head toward the dorms where my son lives, hoping the Creekside Lounge is still standing and not a pile of rubble. Hoping Carter is still safe and alive.

How long has it been since I spoke to him from the old phone in Rod's Roadhouse? One day, I think, though my sense of time has been completely blurred.

A scattering of bodies lies in the road ahead of me. Most look to have been students, but there are a few soldiers in their midst. There are chunks of torn flesh everywhere, strewn body parts, and way too much blood. They look like they were killed by some sort of explosion. God, what happened in this place?

I approach cautiously, wondering if any have turned into zombies. But in the growing morning light, none of them move. They're all dead. Really dead.

I continue on. The road is quiet. In the air is a mixed scent of rot, blood, smoke, and pine. I pass other dead bodies, as well as a dozen or so abandoned cars that show evidence of violence: smashed windows, smears of blood, and occasionally a living zombie trapped inside.

There are no signs of living humans anywhere.

The fire appears to have been focused in the front part of campus. Buildings farther north are untouched by flames, though they bear other scars of conflict. One looks like it was hit by a grenade or rocket launcher; half its roof and western wall are gone, reduced to piles of debris. Other buildings are riddled with bullet holes.

There are bodies and blood everywhere. So many dead kids it makes my heart ache.

I at last arrive at Granite Avenue, the road leading up to the Creekview dorms where Carter lives. I power hike as the road angles uphill. Tall redwoods crowd the side of the asphalt.

There are over a dozen different dorm buildings along Granite

Avenue. They're reddish-brown, three-story buildings with dark green window trim tucked into the trees and ferns.

My breath catches as I draw abreast of the first dorm.

Dozens of bodies are scattered in the parking lot and along the road, all of them riddled with bullet holes. Some of the bodies look like they've been crushed by something large and heavy, like a car. Flies mass above the bodies in thick swarms. Carrion birds have already begun their work, pecking at eyes and open wounds on the bodies. Besides the flies and the birds, nothing moves. If there are zombies out there, I don't see them.

The dorm buildings bear similar signs of abuse, pock marked with bullet holes and broken windows. There are dead kids on the steps.

I double over and gag, throwing up the little bit of food in my stomach. Tears blur my eyes.

These kids have been massacred. I have no doubt. There may have been zombies among them, but most look to have been alive when they were killed. What the hell happened here? Had they been mowed down by a military force?

I recall Carter saying something about the military showing up with Hummers, guns, and weapons. He'd mentioned a lot of "panic." Is this what he'd meant by *panic*? Had that panic been this massacre?

God, Carter is so much like his dad sometimes. Details are not their strong points.

I grit my teeth, put my head down, and keep moving. The road is littered with bodies. Kids, all of them in their late teens or early twenties. There are soldiers among the dead, but only a few.

Farther up Granite Avenue, I spot movement among the bodies. One is a girl with short red hair. Both her legs have been crushed, pulverized into mashed red stumps. She's dragged herself into a cluster of bodies, where she feeds on the arm of a boy with bloody dreadlocks. If she hears my approach, she's so busy eating that she ignores me.

The second is a boy with shaggy black hair. The right half of his body has been shredded by bullets, but both of his legs appear to be in working order. Lucky for me, he's feasting on the body of a chubby girl. He briefly raises white eyes in my direction, then returns his attention to his meal.

It's an all-you-can-eat zombie buffet out here. Apparently, if a zombie is feeding, it doesn't care about other, more alive game. I file away this bit of info for later.

I pick my way carefully through the bodies on the road, carefully watching for any stirring that would indicate a zombie instead of a normal corpse.

The body of a girl twitches as I approach. She peels her bloody head up from the pavement, a low growl issuing at my approach. Something large rolled over her torso, crushing her from the shoulders down.

I bury my screwdriver in her head, putting the poor girl out of her misery. My heart aches.

The Creekview dorms are at the very end of Granite Avenue. I'm forced to put down two more zombies—both with ruined bodies that have rendered them immobile—before at last reaching them.

Crouched among the redwoods are the three-story dorms where my son lives. Like all the others I've passed, these dorms have black pock marks from gunfire. A wide oval parking lot sits at the base of the dorms. Like the other parking lots I've seen, this one is strewn with bodies.

But there's something different here, a sight that makes my heart swell with hope.

Moving amongst the dead are four living kids. They're covered in grime, soot, and blood, but they are most definitely *alive*.

55

FINISHER

THE KIDS DON'T NOTICE ME AT FIRST. THEY'RE MOVING AMONGST THE bodies, dragging them one by one into a gazebo on the far side of the parking lot. So far they've managed to clean up two-thirds of it, which tells me they've been at it for quite a while.

I count three boys and one girl. They wear jeans, hiking boots, and have wooden chair legs slung through belt loops at their waists. The chair legs have been sharpened to points, and all are stained with brown-red blood smears.

My heart thumps erratically at the sight of the spears. Carter had said he and his friends were turning chair legs into spears. I want to call out to the kids but resist, not wanting to spook them or inadvertently draw the attention of a zombie

The boys have the shaggy Humboldt look about them. One has hair well past his shoulders and wears a shirt with the silhouette of Bob Marley on the front. Another dark-skinned boy in a tie-dyed shirt has a spectacular afro that sticks out a good eight inches from his head. The third boy sports a T-shirt with a big marijuana leaf on it and has sideburns to rival those on Wolverine.

The girl wears her light brown hair in two braids, which she's fastened into buns on either side of her head like Princess Leia. She wears a tight tank top covered with tiny skeleton heads.

It's the girl who spots me first as I move into the parking lot. She calls a warning to her friends and draws her chair leg spear, lifting it into a defensive position.

The boys respond immediately, all of them drawing their spears. They don't shout or call out—they've obviously learned not to make noise—but instead warily watch me approach. I hold up my hands to show I mean no harm, making my way toward them. The students exchange glances and whispers, watching me all the while.

I stop twenty feet away from them. Pitching my voice just loud enough to carry, I say, "My name is Kate. I'm looking for a student named Carter Stevenson. Do any of you know him?"

The girl's eyes widen in surprise. Her lips part as if to respond.

A scream cuts off whatever she's about to say. An Asian girl comes sprinting out of a nearby building.

"There were two in the janitor's closet!" she shrieks.

As if on cue, two zombies roll out of the building after her. They move at a good clip, their bodies barely decomposed.

"Shit," says one of the boys. "Can't she learn to keep her mouth shut?"

The four of them move toward the girl, wooden spears raised. I run into their midst, brandishing my screwdriver and railroad spike. They glance at me, then apparently decide to let me join their posse.

The scared girl dodges between two cars. The pursuing zombies smack into one car, hitting so hard they bounce off and sprawl onto their backs.

The five of us form a semi-circle around them. The first girl—the one not screaming like a sissy—lunges in, swinging her spear sharply toward the skull of the nearest zombie. The beast snarls, sensing her approach. Her spear arches down toward his head.

The zombie flips onto his stomach and grabs her ankle. His teeth come down on her thick leather boot. The spear connects harmlessly with the pavement.

I have to give the girl credit. She doesn't do more than gasp in fear, trying to jerk free while she raises her spear back into a defensive position.

I dart in and deliver a vicious kick to the beast's head, effectively dislodging him from the girl's boot. She skips back, leveling the spear for a killing blow.

I'm quicker. I sweep the screwdriver in a downward arc, burying it in the zombie's skull. He shudders once, then dies. Blood oozes from wound, spreading down the head like a red egg yolk.

Five feet away, the boys finish off the second zombie, each stabbing the head of the beast in rapid succession.

"Thanks," the girl says to me. She pauses to wipe sweat from her forehead. "That was a good kill. My name's Jenna. I'm C—"

"Dude, Lila," says the boy with Bob Marley on his shirt. "What the hell? You know better than to make so much noise."

Lila emerges from behind the cars, clearly still frightened but equally indignant. "*Dude*, Eric," she snaps. "I was all by myself trying to clean up the kitchen and those *things* practically fell out of the closet on me. I—"

"Mom?"

I spin around at the familiar voice. A bedraggled young man races across the parking lot. His beard has grown to massive proportions, the longest parts brushing the top of his chest. His jeans are ripped at both knees and blood stains the hem of his faded shirt. Wide blue eyes—so much like his father's—stare at me in shock.

"Carter!" His name bursts from my mouth.

"Mom!" he says again. "You really made it!"

"Carter!" I sprint toward my son.

The two of us close the distance, dodging around cars and over a few bodies. We practically crash into each other. Our shoes squelch in a squishy pool of dried blood, but we hardly notice.

I throw my arms around my son in a bruising hug. He wraps me in an equally ferocious embrace, saying my name over and over. Tears dampen his beard—his, mine, I'm not sure whose.

I'm half laughing, half sobbing. My son is *alive*. He's alive, alive.

I grip his face between my hands, studying him, assuring myself that it's really him, that it's really my Carter.

"*That's* your mom?" someone says.

Carter's face splits into a goofy smile, a few tears still shining on his cheeks. He glances past me at whoever's speaking, then back to me.

"This is my mom," he says, and I'm startled at the pride in his voice. "I told you she was tough."

"It's Carter's mom." The words ripple around me as the group of kids congregate, whispering loudly to each other.

"She made it," someone else says.

"She ran over two hundred miles!"

The students crowd closer to me. There are six altogether, including Carter.

"Why is she covered in mud?" Lila asks, wrinkling her nose.

"What happened to her arm?"

"Dude, look at her ankle," Eric says. "It looks really fucked up."

Everyone looks at my ankle, which has swollen to twice its normal size. An uneasy silence falls, as though they've just now realized I'm standing here and can hear everything they're saying.

"I fell a while back," I offer. God, that was nearly a hundred miles ago. No wonder it looks like hell. "The mud is for the poison oak." I lightly touch the crooked stitches in my arm, which has scabbed over. "I was grazed by a bullet here."

"You were *shot*?" Carter asks, agape.

"No, not shot." I make my voice casual, not wanting my son to fret. "Just grazed by a bullet."

Another beat of silence as the kids look me up and down, taking in my horrific appearance. And likely my smell. Hopefully, they won't notice the bits of vomit spattered on my shoes, pants, and shirt. Possibly they'll just mistake it for general grime.

The pretty girl with Princess Leia hair clears her throat. "We, ah, used your strategy to get rid of the zombies that massed outside the Creekside Lounge," Jenna says.

"My strategy?" I echo.

"Your Stack and Attack strategy," Carter says. "The one you used to empty the RV."

"We wedged open a door with some chairs and tables," Eric says, gesticulating wildly. "We made the opening just wide enough for one of them to get through at a time. Then we made a bunch of noise and drew them through, one by one."

"Carter told us about the time you ran that race in Utah and got caught in the snowstorm for ten hours," says the boy sporting the shirt with the marijuana leaf. "We figured if some old lady could do that, we could take care of a few zombies." He cracks up at this.

The eyes of the other kids widen as they look from marijuana boy to me.

Lila elbows him in the ribs. "*Johnny*," she hisses.

Johnny, abruptly realizing what he just said, throws me a look that's half panic, half horror.

"It's okay," I tell him. "I am old. I'm okay with that. It's better than being dead." I try to make my voice light, but for some reason the tension balloons.

"What Johnny is *trying* to say," says afro boy, "is that you inspired us to get off our asses and survive."

"Yeah, you really inspired us, Mrs. S," Eric says.

Then tension melts away from the group, leaving me speechless. I *inspired* them? I don't think I've ever *inspired* anyone in my life. Especially with running stories. I'm used to people telling me I'm crazy, not inspirational.

"Relentless progress forward, right, Mom?" Carter asks, quoting a famous saying by ultrarunner Bryon Powell.

I laugh, swaying on my feet. "I'm so proud of you all," I say.

A frown suddenly creases Carter's brow. He scans the parking lot, as if looking for something.

"Where's Frederico?" he asks.

The strain of the last two hundred thirty miles come crashing down on me. My legs buckle.

"Whoa." Carter catches me, easing me to the ground. "You okay?"

"Dude, that's a dumb question," Eric declares. "She's just ran two hundred miles and has a fucked up ankle, poison oak, and a bullet wound."

Carter glares at Eric before shifting his gaze to the afro boy. "Reed, can we borrow your water bottle?"

Reed nods, handing over the bottle that had been hanging from his belt by a carabiner. I take a long drink, steeling myself to answer Carter's question.

I force myself to look into his eyes. *Frederico is dead.* That's what I should say, but it's not enough. It's doesn't even begin to encompass all that his death meant, all that he suffered on our journey.

"He's gone, isn't he?" Carter says at last. "Uncle Rico?"

I nod, somehow finding my voice. "He died so I could get here."

Carter scrubs a hand over his eyes.

I pull out the melted Snickers bar I'd found inside the jeep we drove out of Laytonville. "Uncle Rico told me I should bring this to you." I press the crushed candy bar into his hands.

Carter sniffles, once again scrubbing a hand over his eyes. Jenna puts her arms around him.

Even in my exhausted state, I see the familiarity and—is that affection?—in the gesture. My eyes narrow as I study the girl.

Carter catches my look. He pockets the Snickers bar and grabs Jenna's hand. "This is my girlfriend, Mom," he says. "Jenna."

"Your *girlfriend*?" I say, stunned. And not in a good way. "Since when?"

Awkward silence descends. The boys scuff their feet behind us. Jenna chews on her bottom lip, eyes flicking between me and Carter. My son looks like I've just slapped him.

I take a deep breath, trying to get my emotions under control. "Sorry," I say to both of them. "It's just a bit of a surprise, that's all." I refrain from saying, *You never mentioned her to me. Not once.* Though the look I give him clearly communicates this.

Carter scrubs a hand through his shaggy hair. "I was going to introduce you the next time you came up to visit. I just didn't expect your visit to come in the middle of an apocalypse."

He's got me there.

I give Jenna a thorough appraisal. From the smell of things, she doesn't wear patchouli, thank god. A deodorant fan. Not that I'm really in a position to judge another human being by her smell.

A closer look reveals blondish tufts of hair poking out from beneath her armpits. I groan inwardly. God, all I wanted was for Carter to meet a nice girl who shaves her pits. Is that so much to ask? There *are* girls at Humboldt that shave. I've seen them.

Seeing apprehension seeping across Carter's features, I realize I've been staring a bit too long.

Don't get caught up in armpit hair, I scold myself. *Give yourself a chance to get to know the girl.*

I muster my best smile for Jenna. "My name is Kate," I say, extending my hand to her. "Nice to meet you."

Carter visibly relaxes, putting one arm around Jenna's shoulders. "All my friends call her Mrs. S."

"Hi, Mrs. S." Jenna extends a hand in my direction, offering me a tentative smile. "Nice to meet you. Carter's told me so much about you." She laughs nervously. "He talks about you all the time."

"He does?" My smile morphs from forced to genuine.

"Yeah." She relaxes a little. "I can't believe all the crazy running things you've done."

"Carter told us you run so far that you sometimes hallucinate," Eric says.

"Is that true?" Lila asks. "You've run so far you hallucinate?"

"Yeah. Sometimes," I say.

"He told us you got attacked by hornets four times at another race," Reed says. "He said they flew inside your shirt and bit you all over."

The Quad Dipsea. I hadn't thought about that race in a while. Runners ran same route four times—twice going west, twice going east—and each time I'd passed that hornet nest, the little fuckers had come after me. Just thinking about it makes me itch.

"Yeah," I say. "That sucked a lot."

The kids make wordless sounds of awe and approval. It's strange to have them all looking at me like I'm something odd and extraordinary.

"You should come inside," Carter says. He disengages himself from Jenna and helps me to my feet. "We're using the Creekside Lounge for a home base right now."

I want to ask him what's happened here. Why so many kids were murdered. How he and this small group managed to survive the last few days.

These questions and many others crash around in my head, but I hold back. The answers will be there later, and right now I'm tired. Really fucking tired.

I lean on Carter, letting him lead me to the Creekside Lounge. The rest of the students trail in our wake. I recall visiting the lounge on one of my earlier trips. It's a big room with comfy chairs and a plethora of vending machines. It sounds like a nice place to rest. And maybe take a nap. I could use a nap.

As I half walk, half limp toward the building, I let myself appreciate this moment in time. Me and Carter, together, as a family should be. I appreciate our companions, the other five remaining kids. And a decent shelter.

Hell, I'm even grateful my son has someone special in his life. I'm grateful ultrarunning has given me the strength to come all this way and share it with him.

You can't run an ultramarathon and not learn something about yourself. Throw in zombies, dehydration, crippling hunger, perverted thugs, a murdered dog, masochistic drug dealers, and a dead best friend . . . the learning doesn't stop, no matter how much I wish it would.

I'm a finisher. This is the singular most important thing running has taught me.

I am flawed. I am as imperfect as they come. But I have grit inside me. I have the capacity to slog through the deepest, nastiest shit, on the trail and in life.

This is what Frederico was trying to tell me right before he died. I might not be pretty when I arrive at the finish line, but I *do* arrive. Though it's rarely easy, I find a way out of hard times. This is my strength, my inner beauty.

I've finished what I set out to do. For Kyle, for Carter, and for Frederico, I have finished.

I don't know what the future holds for our small group. But for the first time in my life, I know I have the strength to face it head on.

THE END

Want to find out what happens to Alvarez after he leaves Kate and Frederico?
Sign up and get a FREE copy of *Foot Soldier*:
subscribepage.com/footsoldier

Kate's adventure continues in Book 2, *Dorm Life*. Get it on Amazon at mybook.to/dormlife

Thanks for reading!

Printed in Great Britain
by Amazon

79945884R00185